Praise for Erica

'Erica James' sensitive story . . . is as sparklingly fresh as dew on the village's surrounding meadows . . . thoroughly enjoyable and fully deserving of a place in the crowded market of women's fiction' *Sunday Express*

'This book draws you into the lives of these characters, and often makes you want to scream at them to try and make them see reason. Funny, sad and frustrating, but an excellent, compulsive read' *Woman's Realm*

'There is humour and warmth in this engaging story of love's triumphs and disappointments, with two well-realised and intriguing subplots' *Woman & Home*

'Joanna Trollope fans, dismayed by the high gloom factor and complete absence of Agas in her latest books, will turn with relief to James' . . . delightful novel about English village life . . . a blend of emotion and wry social observation'
Daily Mail

'. . . dal, fury, accusations and revenge are all included in E . . . mes' compelling novel . . . this story of village life in C . . . told with wit and humour' *Stirling Observer*

'A . . . ning read with some wickedly well-painted cameo ch . . . It's a perfect read if you're in the mood for ro . . . *Prima*

'An engaging and friendly novel . . . very readable'
Woman's Own

'A bubbling, delightful comedy which is laced with a bittersweet tang . . . a good story, always well observed, and full of wit' *Publishing News*

Erica James grew up in Hampshire and has since lived in Oxford, Yorkshire and Belgium. She now lives in Cheshire. She is the author of fourteen novels, including *Gardens of Delight*, which won the 2006 Romantic Novel of the Year Award.

By Erica James

A Breath of Fresh Air
Time for a Change
Airs & Graces
A Sense of Belonging
Act of Faith
The Holiday
Precious Time
Hidden Talents
Paradise House
Love and Devotion
Gardens of Delight
Tell it to the Skies
It's the Little Things
The Queen of New Beginnings

Love & Devotion

ERICA JAMES

An Orion paperback

First published in Great Britain in 2004
by Orion
This paperback edition published in 2005
by Orion Books Ltd,
Orion House, 5 Upper Saint Martin's Lane,
London WC2H 9EA

An Hachette UK company

Reissued 2008

15 17 19 20 18 16

A CIP catalogue record for this book is
available from the British Library.

ISBN 978-0-7528-8341-0

Typeset by Deltatype Limited, Birkenhead, Merseyside

Printed and bound in Great Britain by Clays Ltd, St Ives plc

The Orion Publishing Group's policy is to use papers that
are natural, renewable and recyclable products and
made from wood grown in sustainable forests. The logging
and manufacturing processes are expected to conform to
the environmental regulations of the country of origin.

www.orionbooks.co.uk

To Edward and Samuel,
with love and devotion

ACKNOWLEDGEMENTS

Special thanks must be given to all those who helped me put this book together.

To Paul Morris, for his endless patience while trying to help a numpty-head like me understand the first thing about computers.

To all those in the antique trade who were so generous with their time. And gossip!

To Mike and Allyson for a splendid night on board their boat. Never have I seen such gleaming brass-ware or tasted such heavenly chip butties.

To Celia Lea for her invaluable and personal understanding of ME.

And to those who would rather not be mentioned (for professional reasons), thank you.

A special thank you to my neighbours, Jenny and Alan, for letting me pinch their cute dog, Toby. I hope the fame doesn't go to his head.

And lastly, thank you to everyone at Orion for making the process as painless as possible.

Prologue

Christmas Eve. The night sky was patchy with clouds racing across the moon and stars, and the wind was gusting. Harriet and her sister were in the Wendy house. It was quite a squash; they were no longer the size they'd been when their father had made it for them more than twenty years ago. Felicity, six months pregnant with her second child, was having trouble getting comfortable on the small wooden chair.

It had been Felicity's idea for them to sneak out here in the freezing cold and the dark. But she was known for her impetuosity. It was what everyone loved about Felicity – her spontaneity and sense of fun. Harriet watched her sister light the candles they'd brought with them and once shadows were dancing across the panelled walls, they switched off their torches.

'So why are we here,' Harriet asked, 'when we could be in the warm, wrapping presents and bingeing on Mum's mince pies and marzipan dates?'

In the flickering candlelight, Felicity's face was suddenly solemn, her eyes large and luminous. 'I have something I want to ask you,' she said. 'I want you to make me a promise, Harriet. If anything happens to Jeff and me, I want you to look after our children.'

The wind gusted outside and the flimsy door rattled in its frame. A shiver went through Harriet. 'Nothing's going to happen to you, Felicity,' she said. 'I'm always going to be the eccentric aunt who makes it her business to turn up with embarrassingly inappropriate presents for your children.'

'I'm being serious, Harriet. You have to promise that if

anything happens to me, you'll take care of them. I wouldn't trust anyone but you. Please say you'd take my place. I need you to say yes for my peace of mind.'

Putting her sister's irrational insistence down to cranked-up hormone levels – that and Felicity's famously temperamental nature – Harriet said, 'Of course I will. Providing you don't have more than two. Two I think I could handle. Any more and I'd turn into the Child Catcher from *Chitty Chitty Bang Bang*.'

'You promise?'

'I promise.'

'Hand on heart?'

'That too.'

Smiling once more, Felicity said, 'Good. That's settled then. Now I have nothing to worry about.'

The promise was never referred to again. Not until four years later, when it dominated Harriet's every waking thought.

August

'Song'

When I am dead, my dearest,
Sing no sad songs for me;
Plant thou no roses at my head,
Nor shady cypress tree
Be the green grass above me
With showers and dewdrops wet;
And if thou wilt, remember,
And if thou wilt, forget.

I shall not see the shadows,
I shall not feel the rain;
I shall not hear the nightingale
Sing on, as if in pain:
And dreaming through the twilight
That doth not rise nor set,
Haply I may remember,
And haply may forget.

Christina Rossetti

Chapter One

Swift by name and swift by nature, Harriet shut the door after her and marched quickly down the drive, her arms swinging, her shoes tappety-tap-tapping in the still August air. Hand in hand, the children trailed silently behind her. She was often told that for someone so small, she walked remarkably fast. Those who knew her well knew that it was a side-effect of a restless mind, of a mind on the run.

For what felt like for ever, Harriet had been plagued with a sense of permanently running on the spot, of getting nowhere fast. There had been so much to do, and far too much to come to terms with. She doubted the latter was ever going to happen. But that was something she kept to herself. It was better to let people think that she had it all under control, that she believed them when they said time would heal, and as one door closed, another would open, and, oh, this was a good one, apparently we are never given more than we can handle. What was that supposed to mean? That this was deliberate? That she and her family had been picked out especially for this particular assignment, that of all the families around them, theirs was considered the safest bet. Oh, the Swifts – they'll handle this one; they'll cope just fine with the death of their eldest daughter and son-in-law.

Anyone observing them would think that Harriet and her parents were coping admirably, but Harriet knew all too well that Bob and Eileen Swift had their brave public faces for neighbours and friends. Once the front door was closed, the masks would drop. But only so far. There were the children, Carrie and Joel, to think of.

'Oh, those poor little ones!' had been the cry when news

of the accident had spread. 'To lose both their parents – what a heartbreakingly cruel thing.'

Tappety-tap-tap went Harriet's shoes as she walked faster, her head lowered, her gaze to the ground so there would be no risk of catching the eye of a neighbour who, given the chance, would seize the opportunity to console or advise and smother her with sympathy. She wanted none of it. All she wanted was for their lives to be the way they were four months ago, before a joyriding kid high on God knew what smashed into her brother-in-law's car killing him and Felicity instantly.

Harriet had been called many things in her life – aloof, pig-headed, obsessively independent, opinionated, analytical, quick to judge, reliable, insular, logical, quick-tempered, cynical, pragmatic, even too loyal for her own good – but not once had she been described as motherly. And yet here she was, at the age of thirty-two, the legal guardian to her sister's orphaned children. Some days she wanted to scream and kick against the unfairness of it all. Some days she woke up terrified she didn't have the strength to do what was expected of her. Other days she had to fight the urge to walk away.

'Auntie Harriet, please can we slow down?'

Harriet stopped abruptly. She turned. 'Carrie, I've told you before, it's Harriet. Just plain old Harriet.' She was convinced her niece was doing it deliberately. Carrie had never called her 'auntie' when her mother had been alive.

The nine-year-old girl stared back at her, a frown just forming around her blue-grey eyes. Harriet didn't find it easy looking at her niece; it was too much like looking in a mirror. They had the same pale complexion that tended to freckle across the bridge of the nose, the same cool, wide-set eyes and neat chin (the Swift Chin as it was called), and the same dark brown, almost black hair – the only difference being that Harriet's was shoulder-length and loose today, and Carrie's was plaited in a single rope that hung down her back to her waist. At nine years old, as if possessed of some kind of superior X-ray vision, Carrie had already perfected the art of being able to see right through a half-truth. Harriet knew she would have to play it straight with her niece; she was one smart cookie.

'You always walk too fast,' Carrie said. 'It's not fair to Joel. He can't keep up; he's only little.'

Joel, four years old, vulnerably sweet-natured and unbearably anxious, was as dark-eyed as his mother had been. Moreover he was the spitting image of Felicity, with the same mousy hair streaked through with sun-lightened gold. Sometimes, when Harriet's heart was heavy with the rawness of grief, she couldn't trust herself to look at him. 'If he can't keep up, then we're going to have to stretch his legs,' she said matter-of-factly.

The little boy bent his head and peered doubtfully at the crumpled material of his trousers, which were several inches too long. 'Will I be as tall as Carrie then?'

Harriet eyed him thoughtfully. 'Maybe.' She straightened his hair – she must have forgotten to brush it before leaving the house. At what age did they start doing it for themselves? Taking his hand and moving on, trying not to react to the soft warmth of his fingers wrapped in hers, she said, 'If you really want to be as tall as your sister you should eat more.' She hoped her voice held the merest hint of a reprimand.

Since their parents' death neither child had eaten properly and it was driving their grandmother to distraction. 'They need to eat more,' Eileen said after every meal, when yet again she was scraping their barely touched plates into the kitchen bin and the children had melted away to their bedrooms. 'It's not healthy for them to eat so little.' Harriet didn't argue with her. While Eileen was fussing over her grandchildren's eating habits, it meant she wasn't quizzing Harriet on hers. She could quite understand why her niece and nephew didn't want to eat. If they felt anything like she did they'd be scared nothing would stay down.

Harriet doubted there was anyone less suited or more ill-equipped to take care of her sister's children, but she'd loved Felicity and a promise was a promise. Even if that promise had been made in the sure knowledge that she would never have to keep it. After all, sisters didn't die, did they? Especially not when they were only thirty-three. Tragedy happened to other families, not to ordinary people like the Swifts.

When her father had telephoned Harriet to break the awful news to her, his voice had been so choked with tears it was scarcely recognisable. Harriet had heard his words all too clearly, but a part of her had refused to take them in. She and Felicity had been talking on the phone earlier that week; Harriet had been trying to encourage her to come and stay in Oxford but Felicity had cried off, saying she was too busy sorting out the house she and Jeff had recently moved into in Newcastle.

The days that followed were a blur of confusion and shock, and it was a while before the full extent of what lay ahead hit Harriet. Her brain was conveniently numbed; it fooled her into thinking that the upheaval they were facing was only temporary. That just as soon as they had all recovered from the worst of their grief, they would pick up the broken pieces of their lives and carry on. Carrie and Joel would now live with their grandparents, while Harriet would spend Monday to Friday working in Oxford and the weekends in Cheshire looking after the children so that her parents could have a break.

For more than three months this was the structure of their lives, but Harriet had known that it could only ever be a short-term measure. Every Friday night she would battle through the traffic on the M6 up to Cheshire and arrive in Kings Melford to find that her mother looked more tired than she had the week before. The strain of taking care of the children was clearly taking its toll, and not just because Bob and Eileen weren't young any more. Five years ago Eileen had been diagnosed as suffering from ME and while she never uttered a word of complaint, Harriet knew that as much as Eileen wanted to cope – she was one of life's serial copers – there was a limit to what she could do. And always in the back of Harriet's mind was the promise she had made: *You have to promise that if anything happens to me, you'll take care of them. I wouldn't trust anyone but you.* Another person might have conveniently forgotten those words, but not Harriet. They kept her awake night after night. In the end she knew she had only one realistic option. But it was such a costly sacrifice and she tried every which way to avoid it. For a while she managed to convince herself that the children should move down to Oxford and live with her. But it was out of the question; her one-bedroomed flat was far too small for them all. And even if she found a larger place and paid for childcare, the thought of being solely responsible for Carrie and Joel, without her parents on hand, panicked her. The truth, and she hated to admit it, was that she was completely out of her depth and needed Bob and Eileen there as a permanent safety net. The answer, then, was to resign from her job as a computer programmer, sell her flat and return to Cheshire.

This she had done and she'd been living back in Maple Drive, her childhood home, for a fortnight now. It was far from ideal, even nightmarish at times, and every morning she woke up with a sense of sick dread, reminding herself that it was only a stopgap. Just as soon as she'd found a new job and could afford to buy or maybe rent a house – near her parents so they could help with the children – she wouldn't feel as if her sacrifice had sucked the life out of her.

But it was proving harder than she'd imagined. She missed her old life, her job and of course her boyfriend, Spencer. Often the only thing that got her out of bed in the morning was the thought that the following day had to be easier. She almost believed it, too.

Chapter Two

At the end of Maple Drive they turned right at the postbox and, holding hands, one child either side of Harriet, they continued along the busy street that was the main road into Kings Melford. Rush-hour traffic had petered out, but the centre of town, less than a mile away, wasn't their destination.

Edna Gannet's corner shop was not for the faint-hearted. The caustic old woman who had run Gannet Stores for more than thirty years had terrorised generations of children with her meanness and breathtaking rudeness; grown men had been known to quake in her presence. Harriet searched the shelves for a product she wasn't sure still existed (but if it did, Edna Gannet would be sure to sell it) and listened to an elderly man lodging a complaint that the pot of single cream he'd bought the day before yesterday was off. He nudged it across the counter towards Edna. Slipping on her half-moon glasses, which she wore round her neck on a chain held together with sticky tape, Edna said, 'It's still within its sell-by date. Which means it must be all right.' She pushed it back towards the customer and removed her glasses: *case dismissed!*

The man used his thumbnail to lift a segment of the foil lid. 'Please, if you'd take the trouble to smell it, you'll see what—'

'And if you took the trouble to store it at the correct temperature you wouldn't be wasting my time. You have to be very careful during August, everyone knows that. Young man, kindly stop poking those Jelly Babies!'

Across the shop, over by the shelves of sweets, Harriet saw Joel nearly jump out of his skin. She went to him.

'Take no notice of the silly old dragon,' she murmured in his ear. 'She only breathes fire to attract attention.'

Back at the counter the disgruntled man was proving a stayer. 'A full return is what I'm entitled to,' he persisted. Harriet noticed his polished shoes were firmly together as he spoke, as if this was the only way he could stand firm.

Edna Gannet surveyed him through sharp, narrow eyes, her arms folded across her chest, her lips pursed.

The man swallowed. 'I'm only asking for what the law says I'm entitled to.'

Edna leaned forward, the palms of her hands flat on the counter. 'Here's what I'll do for you. I'll do you an exchange. How's that?'

The man looked unsure. 'I'd prefer a full refund.'

'And I'd prefer to be lying on a beach with Sean Connery at my beck and call. Take it or leave it.' By the time he'd made up his mind, Edna was already riffling through the cabinet of chilled dairy products. 'Here,' she said. 'And to show what a generous woman I am, this is a more expensive pot of cream and I won't even charge you the difference.'

He was almost out of the door when he turned round.

Edna glared at him. 'Now what?'

He hovered uncertainly. 'Um . . . the sell-by date on this, it . . . it says it's tomorrow.'

Edna stretched her lips into what Harriet knew passed for a smile. 'Well then, you'd best hurry home and use it up fast.'

The man quietly closed the door after him.

With a hand on Joel's shoulder, Harriet approached the counter. 'Mrs Gannet,' she said, 'I wonder if you have—'

Edna cut her dead. 'I'll be with you in a minute.' Harriet watched her tidy away the returned pot of cream and smiled to herself when, just before Edna disappeared into the back of the shop through a beaded curtain, she caught sight of her lifting the foil lid and grimacing.

'Why is she so rude?' asked Carrie in a foghorn whisper. 'She's like it every time we come in.'

'She's not rude, Carrie; she's honest and direct. She just says what she thinks, which is more than most of us do.'

'She frightens me,' Joel whispered.

'Rule Number One kiddo: don't let anyone scare you.' Harriet bent down so that she was face to face with her nephew. 'Do you want to know what I do if I think anyone might have the power to frighten me?'

He nodded solemnly.

'I imagine them with no clothes on. It works every time.'

He stared at her wide-eyed. But Carrie let out a loud, horrified cry. 'Yuck! That's disgusting.'

'What's disgusting?'

Edna was staring at them from behind the counter. Harriet had forgotten how quietly Edna moved about the shop. Her father had nicknamed her the Stealth Bomber, so adept was she at creeping up on would-be shoplifters.

Ignoring the question, Harriet said, 'Mrs Gannet, do you have any large blocks of salt like my mother used to buy when . . .' Her voice trailed off. She was about to say, 'when Felicity and I were little'.

Not missing a beat, Edna said, 'And what would you be wanting with blocks of salt?'

'Sculpture classes for the children. Michelangelo worked with marble, but I'm prepared to make do with salt. Do you have any?'

'I've not sold blocks of salt for many a year. Not much call for it these days.' Forever the consummate shopkeeper, Edna added, 'Why not use lard? I've plenty of that. Or margarine.'

'It wouldn't be quite the same thing.'

'Suit yourself.' The old woman shrugged and pulled a tatty yellow duster out of her overall pocket. She began flicking it over the glass jars of sweets on the shelves behind her.

Standing by the comics now, Carrie said, 'Could I have this, please?'

With the scent of a sale in her nostrils, Edna whipped round, the duster back in her pocket.

Harriet said, 'Whoa there, little miss. I bought you one the other day. Do you think I'm made of money?' She saw a determined expression settle on Carrie's face, and knew that the girl was too much like herself to beg. She just stood there silently staring Harriet out, her gaze unnervingly level for one so young. She was not a child who would willingly endure a moment's loss of dignity.

'Surely you wouldn't deprive the girl of a bit of reading matter?' chipped in Edna. 'They're educational these days. Not like the rubbish you used to read.'

Harriet shot her a sharp look. She wasn't going to be emotionally blackmailed by anyone. Especially not by Edna Gannet. 'If Carrie wants to read, she has plenty of educational books at home to enjoy.' She felt a tug at her sleeve. 'Yes, Joel, what is it?'

'Can I have one too? *Please?*'

Heaven help her, but Harriet gave in. She handed her money over to Edna, who was openly smirking, and the children thanked her. Then the wretched woman slid two small paper bags over the counter. Carrie and Joel looked inside the bags and, suddenly shy, they smiled awkwardly at the old woman. Edna brushed away their mumbled words of thanks and not quite meeting Harriet's gaze, said, 'Just something to keep them from dwelling on . . . well, you know, just to stop them brooding.'

With unspoken sympathy quivering in the air, Harriet hustled her niece and nephew outside. In all the years she had known Edna Gannet, she had never seen her act so out of character. Not a word about Felicity's death had passed her lips in Harriet's presence, even though everyone in the neighbourhood was talking about little else, but here she was giving sweets to two children she hardly knew. She took a deep, steadying breath to fight back a wave of tearful panic. With Joel on her hip and Carrie running to keep up, she headed for home. Only when they'd turned the corner into Maple Drive did she slow down.

Maple Drive was the archetypal suburban cul-de-sac, flanked either side with tidy gardens and rows of fascia-boarded houses. Harriet's parents had bought number twenty in 1969 when they had been expecting Felicity – Harriet had followed on only a year later. They'd paid three thousand pounds for it then and it was now, according to her father, who kept his eye on such things, worth two hundred and fifty thousand pounds. 'The best investment we ever made,' he used to joke. Harriet suspected he'd dispute this now. Compared to having Felicity, it was worthless.

The only people who had lived in the neighbourhood as long as the Swifts were the McKendricks: Dr Harvey McKendrick and his wife, Freda. They lived at number fourteen and Harriet knew their house as well as her parents'. She and her sister had been more or less the same age as the McKendrick boys, Dominic and Miles, and they had all grown up together. Passing the recently decorated house with its integral garage, where ten-year-old Harriet had slapped Dominic's face for trying to look at her knickers one rainy Sunday afternoon, she kept her gaze firmly on the pavement. Freda never went out but she was sure to be watching the world go by. Freda was agoraphobic, but everyone pretended she wasn't. It maddened Harriet that they all carried on as though it was the most natural thing in the world that Freda was too terrified to set foot outside her own front door. 'Why doesn't Harvey do something about it?' Harriet had often asked her mother. 'He's a doctor, after all.'

'These things aren't so cut and dried,' Eileen would say.

'Yes they are,' she'd argue. 'If there's something wrong with you, you get it sorted. It's as easy as that.'

Several years ago, at the McKendricks' New Year's Day drinks party, after one too many glasses of mulled wine, Harriet had said as much to Dominic and Miles. Dominic, who lived in Cambridge and rarely honoured his parents with his presence, had agreed with her. But Miles, who lived in nearby Maywood, had disagreed and suggested that maybe his brother should spend more time with their mother before he offered an opinion.

Both Miles and his father had attended Felicity and Jeff's funeral; Freda, not surprisingly, had made her apologies. Dominic hadn't even bothered to send flowers or a card. Harriet didn't think she would ever forgive him for that.

Walking up the drive of number twenty, Harriet could hear her father mowing the lawn in the back garden. It was a comforting sound. The sound of a normal family going about its normal everyday business.

If only.

Chapter Three

Bob Swift switched off the mower and, walking stiffly – his arthritic knee was playing up – he carried the grass box down to the compost heap behind the greenhouse. The garden had always been a place of refuge for him, somewhere he could be alone to work through whatever was troubling him. But he knew he could potter about here for the rest of his days and never work through the pain of losing Felicity.

For the first ten years of their marriage, he and Eileen had been desperate for a baby, but they'd had to endure a string of heartbreaking miscarriages before Felicity had finally arrived. He could still remember that moment when he'd first held her, when he'd cradled her tiny, perfect body in his large, clumsy hands and had been overwhelmed at the fragility of the life for which he was now responsible.

It had been love at first sight, for both him and Eileen. They had doted on their precious child and ignored anyone who said she would be the ruin of them. How could that possibly be? Felicity was the absolute making of them. Her presence in their lives made them feel complete. Maybe even more so for Bob.

After waiting so long for a baby, they doubted they could be so lucky again, but miraculously, a year later – sooner than they might have liked – he was standing in the same hospital cradling a second daughter: Harriet. 'Look, Felicity,' he'd said, 'what do you think of your little sister?'

She'd smiled and stroked one of Harriet's tiny hands, then reached out to hold her as though she were a doll. Friends had warned them that they would have terrible sibling rivalry to cope with, that because they'd given

Felicity so much love and attention, had made her the centre of their world, she would inevitably be jealous. How wrong those doom-mongers had been. Felicity, an easy-going, good-natured child, never showed any jealousy. She would play happily while her mother rested or nursed Harriet, and was quick to show off her sister to anyone who visited the house. She was protective, too, and got upset with the doctor when he gave Harriet her immunisation jabs. Eileen often told the story that when Harriet had cried, more with indignation than actual pain, Felicity had told the doctor off for hurting her sister. And if Felicity was always there to look out for Harriet, Harriet in turn worshipped her older sister and hated to be separated from her. They each had their own bedroom but preferred to sleep together in the same bed. They spent hours playing together, devising complicated games that no adult was allowed to participate in.

The years passed, and unlike so many of their friends who dipped in and out of phases of hating their siblings, their close relationship survived the strains of puberty and adolescence.

'We're such a lucky family,' Eileen used to say. She said it the last time they saw Felicity alive. They were driving home after spending a couple of days with her and Jeff and the grandchildren in their new home in Newcastle, where Jeff had just secured a post as a senior lecturer at the university. It was the third move in as many years for the young family and Bob suspected that Felicity longed for a time when Jeff would be happy to settle and put down roots, if only for the children's sake. That was something Bob had always been proud of – that he'd never uprooted his daughters while they were growing up. He'd always put their happiness before his own, always wanted to keep them safe.

But he hadn't, had he? He'd failed to keep Felicity safe. It used to amuse him that not so long ago Felicity started to end her phone calls by telling him to take care. 'Take care, Dad,' she'd say, the child now looking out for the parent.

Had that been the trouble? Had he been in dereliction of his duty? If he'd been a better father would Felicity still be alive? If he had never let her out of his sight, he'd always wake knowing there was still a chance of hearing her carefree laughter again, of basking in her happiness that life had been so good to her.

Suddenly fearful that his legs would give way, Bob dropped the grass box and reached out to one of the wooden sides of the compost heap. He put a hand to his face and felt wetness on his cheeks. He hunted through his trouser pockets for a tissue, scoured his eyes with it and blew his nose. The sun was high and sweat was pooling between his shoulderblades, yet he felt icy cold. It was always the same when he thought of his darling girl. Every time he thought of her and how much he missed her, thirty-three years' worth of memories gripped at his insides and made it hard to breathe.

On an irrational impulse, he glanced back up to the house and, making sure no one was watching him, he crossed the lawn to the Wendy house. He turned the handle on the door and slipped inside. It was stuffy from having the sun on it and was cast in a gloomy darkness – the faded curtains Eileen had made for it were drawn. There wasn't room for him to stand, so he pulled out one of the Early Learning Centre red plastic chairs – Eileen had bought them for Carrie and Joel, along with the table and all the other playthings a doting grandmother takes pleasure in providing – and sat down cautiously, checking the chair would take his weight.

Stuffing the tissue back into his pocket, he told himself there would be no more tears. Tears would help no one, least of all himself. He had to focus his thoughts on how they were going to get through this mess. He had to be strong, for Eileen and for the children. Whatever else, he mustn't let Carrie and Joel see him cry. Or Harriet. He didn't want her to think he couldn't cope.

But thank God for Harriet. Thank God she had accepted that he and Eileen couldn't do this alone. Eileen was concerned that Harriet had made such an enormous sacrifice in coming back home, that perhaps they should have stopped her, but as he'd told his wife, 'What choice do we have?'

There were no relatives on Jeff's side of the family who could take on the children – Jeff had been an only child; his mother had died when he was twelve and his father had passed away when he was nineteen – so it was down to them: there was no one else.

His memory of the night of the accident had already become blurred around the edges. He could remember some bits with painful clarity, but others, such as the journey up to Newcastle, were very hazy. He could remember thinking that before he broke the news to Eileen – she'd just popped across the road to see Dora when the telephone had rung with the news – he ought to call Harriet. He'd stupidly imagined that he'd be able to say the words without breaking down, but hearing the shocking truth out loud, his voice had cracked and the tears had flowed unbidden. Worse was to follow when he heard Harriet crying at the other end of the line. He'd felt so helpless. It was a while before either of them could speak, and when finally they could it was Harriet who took control. 'I'll drive up straight away,' she'd said. 'Who's looking after the children? And do they know? It would be best if they were kept in the dark until we can be with them.'

It was another of those moments when he'd felt that his role as a parent had been usurped, that he was the child and Harriet was the grown-up in charge. Perhaps that was how things had been ever since. In the following weeks it seemed as if Harriet was the one making all the decisions. But it couldn't go on. He had to pull himself together. He had days when he alternated between relief that Harriet was so capable and shame that he wasn't doing more. Other times it seemed his grief was like a volcano, that one day soon it would erupt and spew out molten anger that would destroy him and anyone around him. He felt this now as he reflected how, thirty-three years ago, Felicity's birth had wiped his slate clean. Had made a new man of him.

Chapter Four

A week later Bob was cutting the grass again.

Eileen stood at the open window in their bedroom and watched him. He'd almost finished; just one more meticulous stripe to add to the lawn.

Grief changes a person for ever, she thought. And no one knew this better than she did. With each baby she had lost and grieved for, a little bit of her had changed and slowly died. Without meaning to she had grown anxious and fearful of the future. Before Felicity's birth she had lived in constant dread that if she and Bob had to resign themselves to being a childless couple, then the darkness that had been edging in would eventually eclipse their love for each other. It stood to reason that Bob's love would only stretch so far. His need for a child was as great as her own, and always at the back of his mind must have been the thought that with a different woman his wish would be granted. They'd contemplated adoption, but because hope had always been around the corner – that this latest pregnancy would be the one – they'd never got as far as approaching an agency. Eileen always thought of that period in their lives as the Wilderness Years.

But then Felicity had been born, a miracle baby in all ways. At once the world was a brighter place. No more anxiety. No more worries that Bob would stop loving her and seek permanent solace in the arms of another. To this day Eileen had kept to herself her knowledge about his two affairs during the Wilderness Years. She had never wanted to confront Bob because as hurtful as it was, and as dark a shadow on their marriage as his behaviour had cast, she'd understood why he'd done it. It was nothing more than an antidote to the anguish they were going through. It was survival.

Still staring down at her husband – he'd put the mower away and was now calling to the children, who were playing in the Wendy house – Eileen tried to shake off the fear that the shadowy darkness might return. Retirement earlier in the year had been a big enough adjustment for Bob, but now there was this catastrophe to live with. Felicity had meant the world to him. He loved Harriet too, of course, but from the moment she was born, Felicity had been the centre of his universe; there was nothing he wouldn't have done for her.

Tears filled Eileen's eyes. She turned away from the window, blinking. She had work to do. She was supposed to be helping Harriet pack up the last of Felicity's clothes for the charity shop. It was only now, four months since the accident, that Bob had allowed them to do the job. The more practical side of things he'd gone along with, such as selling the house in Newcastle along with most of its furniture. He'd also been instrumental in putting the bulk of the money into a trust fund for the children, just as Jeff and Felicity would have wanted, while also leaving an amount to go towards their upbringing. However, he couldn't deal with the personal possessions that had marked out his daughter from all the other daughters in the world. It was no easy task for Eileen either. It was taking all her strength to resist the urge to hang on to everything in the hope that Felicity would seem closer.

When Bob had realised what she and Harriet would be doing today he had told them that he'd cut the grass and then take the children out. 'It's not right for them to see their mother's things being shoved into bin liners.'

He was right. But then neither did Eileen relish seeing the remains of her daughter's life bundled unceremoniously into plastic refuse sacks.

She could hear Bob in the kitchen washing his hands and asking the children if they needed to use the toilet before they went out. Minutes later, the back door shut and then the car engine started up. He hadn't even come upstairs to say goodbye.

Moving round the bed that was covered with neatly folded clothes, Eileen looked out onto the landing, where Harriet was sorting through her sister's shoe collection. Harriet and Felicity had been practically identical in size. As teenagers they had always been borrowing each other's shoes and clothes. Eileen wondered what was going through Harriet's mind as she matched up pairs of sandals – strappy high-heels, comfortable slip-ons – and an array of boots – ankle boots, knee-high boots and tasselled suede boots. Felicity had loved her boots. Of the two daughters, Harriet had always been the more conservative and guarded. Whereas Felicity had been a powder keg of enthusiasm, Harriet had played her cards much closer to her chest. To Eileen's knowledge Harriet had only ever confided in Felicity. Without her sister around, who would Harriet turn to now? It seemed unlikely that the boyfriend in Oxford – a young man they'd yet to meet and who, predictably, they had heard little about – would fill the space Felicity had left.

Neither Eileen nor Bob was surprised that Harriet still wasn't married. 'I'm never going to marry,' she'd announced when she was twelve years old. 'I'm going to live alone in a huge mansion and I'll be my own boss with my own company and make loads of money. I don't want anyone ever to tell me what to do.' She had spoken with a solemn intensity well beyond her years.

The mansion hadn't materialised, nor had her own business, but Eileen knew her daughter relished living alone. Whenever she and Bob had visited Harriet in Oxford they had always been taken aback by the simplicity of her life. Her small ground-floor flat in a house just off Banbury Road was simply furnished and, in Eileen's opinion, verging on the austere. She knew the minimalist look was all the rage, but this seemed such a barren existence. The sitting room, with its clinical white-painted walls held just two reclining leather chairs, a rug, and a double-width floor-to-ceiling bookcase that was sparsely filled with books and CDs. There was a small television and a hi-fi, but no ornaments or clutter. The bedroom was equally sparse: a double bed, a built-in wardrobe and in place of a dressing table, a desk with a laptop and printer. The only stamp of sentimentality was a collage of photographs Felicity had made for Harriet on her thirtieth birthday. The black-framed collage hung above the printer, and other than a mirror, this was the only object adorning the walls. How different it was for Harriet now, thought Eileen sadly, squeezed as she was with all her things into Felicity's old bedroom, where she couldn't move for bumping into something.

With enormous effort, Eileen tried once more to concentrate on what she was supposed to be doing. She picked up a pair of jeans, smoothed out the wrinkles in the legs and folded them carefully. Lovingly.

The Oxfam shop where she used to work two mornings a week – before ME sneaked its way into her life and sapped her energy – would not be receiving any of the bags of clothes. It would be too painful knowing that her old colleagues were picking over her daughter's belongings. Better for it all to go further afield, to one of the charity shops in Maywood, where there would be less risk of her one day catching sight of a young woman in town wearing something of Felicity's. That would be too much. It would add another bruise to all those ones she had deep inside, which nobody could see. Overcome by a sudden wave of sadness, she buried her face in a brightly coloured woollen sweater. It smelled so evocatively of her daughter, it caused a sob to catch in her throat. She let out a stifled cry. At once Harriet was by her side. 'Are you okay, Mum?'

'It's all right, I'm just being silly.' But despite her brave words, she couldn't fight the misery that had crept up on her as it so often did.

Clearing a space on the bed for her mother to sit down, Harriet reached for the tissue box on the dressing table. It was empty. She went back to the landing, to the airing cupboard where her mother kept a stock of toilet rolls and boxes of tissues. From downstairs came the sound of knocking, followed by a familiar 'Yoo-hoo!'

Without checking with her mother, Harriet leant over the banister. 'Come on up, Dora.' If anyone could lift her mother's spirits, it was Dora Gold. She lived across the road and was her mother's closest friend. She was two years younger than Eileen but managed to defy the aging process that affected everyone else. She put it down to drinking plenty of water and keeping out of the sun. That and the occasional trip to a private clinic in south Manchester. She'd been divorced and widowed, in that order, and was prepared to kiss as many aging frogs as it took to find husband number three. She was always telling them some tale or other about a date she'd just been on. Harriet hoped Dora had an interesting tale to share with them today. Something that would distract Eileen and take her mind off Felicity.

Dora did better than that. She took one look at Eileen and the piles of clothes on the bed and said, 'Here's how we're going to do this. I'm giving us exactly one hour to sort through everything and then we're going to load up the car, drop everything off where necessary and then the three of us are going for lunch. How does that sound?'

In the end it was only Dora and Eileen who went for lunch. Harriet excused herself by saying she had a phone call to make. She hadn't seen or spoken to Spencer in three weeks because he'd been away in South Africa visiting distant cousins. It was a trip he'd arranged just days before they'd started seeing each other. Today was his first day back in the office.

Spencer had asked her out three months before Felicity's death (everything was now measured in terms of pre or post Felicity's death) and initially they'd kept their relationship from everyone at work – an office romance was such a cliché. When they went public everyone laughed at them. 'Sorry to disappoint you, Harriet,' Adrian, her immediate boss had said, 'but it's hardly the breaking-news item you clearly thought it was.'

What's more, Ron, the graduate trainee programmer who was supposed to be nestling under her wing while she taught him all she knew, had opened a book on how soon it would be before they came clean. 'And who won the bet?' she'd asked, her hackles rising.

'I did,' he said proudly.

'Well, Ron, seeing as you're such a clever dick, you can put your cleverness to good use and get me my coffee. White, no sugar. And make sure the mug's clean.' She'd never pulled rank before, but now seemed as good a time as any to shake the dust from her epaulettes and bring them to his attention.

'Go easy on the poor lad,' Spencer had said during lunch, 'it's just an office thing. A bit of a lark.'

She knew he was right, but her privacy was important to her.

Spencer had only been at C.K. Support Services for five months, whereas Harriet had been there for five years. It was her second job since leaving university, but despite the lack of career opportunities within the small software house, she hadn't foreseen a time when she would want to quit. The work, and the level she was at – Senior Analyst – suited her perfectly. She was good at her job, could run rings round most of her colleagues, and so long as they left her to get on with what she was paid to do and didn't force her to get involved with management decisions or in-house politics, she derived enormous satisfaction from what she did. Some would say that she did nothing but sit with her feet up on the desk staring at a blank computer screen for most of the day. And they'd be right. But that was when she was at her most creative. Computer programming involved a lot of thinking. In fact, the bulk of what she did was in her head. Occasionally, though, she was dragged kicking and screaming away from her desk to help install the software she'd designed.

The first time she'd met Spencer, he'd been sitting with

his feet up on the desk, his eyes closed, his fingers drumming rhythmically on the arm of his chair. She'd recognised a kindred spirit and wondered if this would be the meeting of minds she'd always craved. It was no secret amongst her friends that she didn't suffer fools gladly. 'Your bog-standard lager-loving footie fanatic stands no chance with you, does he?' Erin had once remarked. Erin was the same age as Harriet and lived in the flat above hers; she had no qualms about who she came home with after a drunken night out.

As she got to know Spencer, Harriet realised he ticked a good number of boxes, but when he started dropping hints about them moving in together, she instinctively backed off. Living with someone scared her. All that sharing. All that tiptoeing round one another's feelings. All those arguments over hairs in plugholes and dishes left in sinks. The unmade bed. The wet towels on the bathroom floor. The rolled-up sock stuffed under a cushion. The shoes left just where she'd fall over them. All these things made her reluctant to throw in her lot with anyone on a more permanent basis.

The only person she came close to sharing her life with had been Felicity, and quite naturally it was her sister to whom she turned for advice about Spencer. 'Am I being stupid?' she'd asked Felicity.

Expecting her sister to urge her to throw caution to the wind, as she so often did, she had been surprised when Felicity had said, 'If you have to ask the question, then you're clearly not ready for such a step.'

Perversely, Harriet then tried to prove to herself that she *was* ready for such a step. She systematically listed everything that she liked about Spencer – his clear-cut way of thinking, his steadiness, his understanding and appreciation that she needed her own space – and gradually some of the fear crept to the furthest reaches of her mind.

But then Felicity died and everything changed.

Spencer was the first person she told about her decision to hand in her notice and move back to Cheshire. They were in his flat when she broached the subject. He was cooking one of his messy meals – every pot, pan and mixing bowl had been used. 'Aren't you surprised?' she'd said when he hardly reacted.

'Sorry, Harriet, but I saw it coming. It was obvious.'

Never afraid to confront an issue, she said, 'It's going to change things between us, isn't it?'

He'd stopped what he was doing and put a hand on her shoulder. 'Let's save the crystal ball-gazing for the end-of-the-pier crowd, shall we? For now, you've got more than enough on your plate without worrying about us. We'll find a way.'

But she did worry. And it annoyed her that she did. Being needy had never been on her personal agenda.

It was ages before Spencer answered his mobile. Time enough for paranoia to set in. Was he trying to avoid her?

'Hi there, Harriet. How's it going?' The sound of his voice, so easy, so assured, chased away the doubts.

'Not bad,' she said, 'all things considered.' She wanted to explain what she'd spent the morning doing, but couldn't be bothered. Would he be interested, anyway? Other people's problems were exactly that. Other people's. Given the choice, wouldn't she rather cross the road than risk being contaminated by grief? Keeping the conversation light, she asked him about work. 'Anything new to report?'

'I haven't been back long enough to know the full ins and outs, but there's a bit of flapping going on over some new contract or other.'

She felt the pinch of isolation, of not being a part of things. It was hard to accept they were all carrying on without her. Harder still to think of anyone new occupying her old office. 'What contract would that be?' she asked.

'Too boring to discuss. Tell me what you've been doing.'

'No,' she said, realising that she hadn't asked him about his holiday, 'tell me how South Africa was. Did you send me a postcard?'

They discussed his trip and then, because they seemed to be running out of things to say, she told him about packing up the remainder of Felicity's stuff. She mentioned that she'd kept some of her sister's clothes and things as keepsakes.

He groaned. 'Wouldn't it be easier just to ditch the lot? It sounds kind of macabre, wanting to keep anything your sister wore.'

Anger flared. And just what the hell would you know about it! she wanted to shout at him. But she kept her voice level. 'It's more complicated than that. There's stuff I've put aside for the children; they need to be able to remember their parents. When they're older, they can look through the selection I've made and perhaps piece together the memories.'

'Yeah, I can see that would be a good idea. Look, I can't chat for long, but are you still coming down tomorrow?'

'Of course. Why do you ask?'

She caught the sound of background noise, of someone calling to him. When he didn't answer her question, she said, 'It shouldn't take too long to pack up the last of my things at the flat. The agent says the buyer is all set to go.' She couldn't bring herself to ask if he was still on for lending a hand as he had promised. Instead she said, 'Spencer, if you've got something to say, just say it.'

'I don't know what you mean.'

'I'm sure you do.'

A pause. And then: 'This isn't the time, Harriet. Why don't we speak tomorrow? I'll meet you at your flat as we agreed. Around twelve.'

After a brisk goodbye she rang off. Without the aid of a crystal ball she knew exactly what the future held. It was adios time, inevitably. Why would Spencer want to stay involved with her now that she lived so far away and had two children to bring up? She'd been mad to think it could be otherwise.

Smarting with hurt pride and the sheer unfairness of it, she flipped open her mobile again and scrolled through for the number she always tapped in when she needed a good rant. She'd got as far as putting the phone to her ear when she realised what she was doing. Very slowly, she closed the mobile and held it tightly in her fist. It was one of the things she found almost impossible to come to terms with: accepting that Felicity was no longer around to talk to, that she wasn't there at the other end of the line to be told the latest office joke, or to fill Harriet in on a missed episode of *Footballers' Wives*, or just to gossip about nothing in particular.

She decided she needed some fresh air to clear her head and improve her mood. But when she stepped outside and locked the front door behind her, she found that fresh air was in short supply. August, with its unbreathable, muggy air that was thick with pollen, was her least favourite month of the year. It was when her asthma was at its worst and she always had to be sure she was never too far from her inhaler. But a short walk along the canal would be okay. The moment she started to feel a tightness in her chest, she'd turn round.

Pocketing her set of keys, she looked across the road and saw a large white van. Its tailgate was lowered and furniture, piled higgledy-piggledy, was clearly in the process of being removed and carried up the drive. A self-drive Rent-A-Van, noted Harriet. The people who usually moved in to the four-bedroomed house were never around for long. For the last twenty years it had been owned by a couple who worked abroad and rented it out in their absence. Dozens of young families and professional couples had come and gone; consequently it was the shabbiest house in the road. The general feeling in the neighbourhood was that a permanent resident would smarten the place up. But judging from the tatty-looking Rent-A-Van, yet another temporary occupant was moving in. She wondered who. It was strange that Dora hadn't been on the case and brought them news of who, what, when and how. Just then, a stockily built man in baggy shorts appeared in the open doorway. Annoyed she'd been caught gawping, Harriet pretended she hadn't noticed him and walked on down the road.

Chapter Five

'Where do you want this?'

Will bobbed up from behind the sofa, where he was plugging in the CD player, and checked out the large box Marty was holding. 'Bung it on top of the other box over there in the corner,' he said.

'I will, but on the condition that we stop for some lunch. If not, I'll have you in an industrial tribunal faster than you can say, "Put the kettle on."'

'Would that be before or after I've had you arrested for a breach of the Public Order Act? Who'd you borrow those shorts from? Johnny Vegas?'

'Ha, ha. And here's me doing the best-friend routine only to be on the receiving end of fattist jokes.'

'I could run through my extensive collection of follically challenged quips, if you'd prefer.'

Marty put the box down with a thump. 'What I'd prefer is for you to get your arse into gear and make me a sandwich. I'm starving.' He wiped the sweat from his forehead with the back of an arm. 'Don't suppose you know where I can lay my hands on a cold beer, do you? Trust you to move on the hottest and muggiest day of the year.'

'I can do damn-all about the weather, but the cold-beer situation is well under control. Help yourself to a can from the cool-box on the kitchen table.'

'And lunch?'

'If you stop whingeing long enough, that will be brought out to you in the garden in about quarter of an hour.'

'Now you're talking.'

Minutes later, with Marty taking a break outside, Will

retrieved a loaf of bread, a tub of Flora, and a packet of bacon from the cool-box. He cleared a space around the cooker and set to work on throwing some lunch together. Once he'd sussed how the gas hob worked, he loaded up the frying pan with rashers, then buttered half a loaf of sliced bread and squirted a generous amount of HP sauce onto Marty's bread. They'd been friends long enough to know each other's likes and dislikes perfectly. Not dissimilar from a marriage, really. Except Will's friendship with Marty had never turned sour, unlike his marriage.

It was eight years since he and Maxine had divorced but it still felt as if it were yesterday, probably because Maxine never let him forget what a bastard he'd been. Oh, and a loser, too. That was a constant favourite of hers. 'The trouble with you, Will,' she'd say, as if he'd ever asked for her opinion, 'is that you're never going to amount to anything for the simple reason that you refuse to grow up.'

'And there was me thinking it was my boyish charm that got me where I am,' he'd said only last week when she was in his office, once again raking over the coals of their burnt-out marriage, listing yet more of his failings.

She was interrogating him about his reasons for moving. 'What's wrong with where you are?' she'd asked.

'Well, honey,' he'd replied, all silky-smooth and knowing it would annoy the hell out of her, 'I'd tell you if it was any of your business. But seeing as it isn't, you'll have to reach your own conclusion.'

'You're moving in with someone? Is that it?'

'I might be.'

'Okay, so you're not. I can't say I'm surprised. And not just because you change your women more often than your boxer shorts. Or maybe it's them. Perhaps they see the light just in time and turn tail.'

'I'm sure you're right, dear. You usually are. Now, if you've had your fun, I have important things to do.'

She'd tipped back her head and laughed, her even, white teeth framed by glossy pink lips. 'William Hart doing something important. Now this I have to see.'

'Then pull up a chair and learn from the master.' Reaching for the phone, he'd added, 'While you're here, you could make yourself useful by putting the kettle on. If that isn't beneath you these days.'

Fortunately she hadn't stuck around and after she'd swept off in one of her up-yours-see-you-around-sucker flounces, and after he'd said, 'Be sure to give my best wishes to PC Plod, won't you?' he'd been able to get down to business. Putting the phone back in its cradle, he'd closed the door of his ramshackle office and, tuning to Radio Four, he'd rolled up his sleeves for his afternoon fix of *The Archers*. It didn't take much to please him these days.

Turning the rashers over and lowering the heat on the gas hob, he supposed that Maxine's opinion of him would never change. In her eyes he would always be the bad guy.

The big girl's blouse of a husband who dared to have an early mid-life crisis.

The lousy husband who played around.

The brute of a husband who broke her heart.

Although it was debatable she had one of those.

One way or another, he had a hard reputation to live up to. It wasn't easy playing the villain every day of his life. Or the village idiot. Just occasionally he'd like to think he was a cut above your average no-good ex husband. He'd never once raised his hand to a woman. He'd never drunk to excess. He'd never picked his nose in public. And surely, what counted for more than anything, he was perfectly toilet-trained and never splashed or left the seat up. In some quarters, he'd be considered quite a catch.

And if he'd been such a bad lot, why had she stuck around as long as she had? Thirteen years in all.

The answer to that, as she'd repeatedly flung at him, was the only good things to come out of their relationship: Gemma and Suzie. Apples and eyes didn't come close. His gorgeous daughters – Gemma, seventeen and Suzie, nineteen – were the crowning glory of his life. In many ways, marrying Maxine had been the best thing he'd ever done. But he'd withhold that fact from her to his dying day. She could burn him at the stake and he'd never utter those words in her presence. A man was entitled to his pride.

'Hey, you in there!' called Marty from the garden. 'Any chance of something to eat? My stomach's panicking; it thinks it's been stapled shut.'

They took their lunch down to the end of the garden, unlocked the rotting wooden gate and went and sat on the rickety bench that overlooked the canal. It was the most perfect spot, the main reason Will had bought the house. The house itself, as it was, left him cold. Modern but seriously dated, it was totally lacking in any character; it failed on all counts. But the location was superb and he could understand why the owners – clients of Marty's who in their retirement had now decided to settle in Geneva – had hung on to it for as long as they had. However, their loss was his gain and by the time he was finished with it, he'd have it transformed and ready to sell on for a tidy sum.

As if picking up on his thoughts, Marty said, 'Here's to you and your new home.' They tapped their cans of beer together. 'Cheers. So how do you think you'll like living here?'

'It'll do. Though it's tempting to nuke the house and start over.'

'I'll tell Marion and Joe you said that.'

'Tell them what you like. They should be rounded up and shot for having such appalling taste. Those hideous carpets and curtains can't have slipped your notice, surely? And as for that chocolate-brown bathroom suite . . . that can be first to go in the skip.'

Marty laughed. 'Not everyone is blessed with such high-minded style as you. Besides, I thought retro was all the rage.'

'In lesser circles, maybe. But I'm a purist. Give me a fine pair of Queen Anne legs any day.'

'You antique dealers are all the same; just a bunch of screaming snobs.'

'You say the sweetest things.'

'I caught sight of one of your neighbours earlier. As

35

natives go, she didn't look the sort to welcome you with open arms.'

'I expect she was in shock at the sight of you in those shorts.'

Marty looked down at his legs. 'What's wrong with them?'

'What's right with them? You look like that short fat guy from *It Ain't Half Hot Mum*. If you're not careful, you'll turn into your dad.'

'I'd rather turn into him than Peter Stringfellow.'

'So there's no middle ground? It's one or the other?'

'I didn't say that. But gravity and nasal hair come to us all. Even you, Will. It's time to give in. It's time to grow up.'

'Hey, this is not the talk I'd expect from a fine young blood. We're in our prime. The last time I checked, I had plenty of fuel left in the tank.'

'In our prime? We're forty-six, heading fast towards our pensions, arthritic joints and overactive bladders.'

'Speak for yourself. I'm only forty-five.'

'Bullshit! You're forty-six next month.'

'So what's brought this on? Why the mood? Some young whippersnapper overtake your Merc in a souped-up Corsa?'

Marty looked glum and drank some more of his beer. 'Perhaps it's my turn now for the mid-life crisis.'

'Ah well, there's your mistake. You should have got it over and done with in your thirties, as I did. With all that behind me, the world looks pretty rosy from where I'm sitting.'

'Smug bastard.'

Will laughed. 'But a happy one.'

'You've never regretted it, then? Never thought what it might have been like if you'd kept your nerve and played the game?'

'Not once. If I'd stayed, the stress would have had me going on the rampage with a machete and wiping out the entire firm, and anyone else who got in the way. I know I made the right decision. Life's been bloody good to me since I opted out.'

'That's what I hate about you, Will; you're perpetually upbeat. You've no idea how sickening it is.'

Will threw a handful of crusts into the water, where they were instantly seized upon by a family of ducks. 'Come on, eat up; we've got the rest of my earthly goods and chattels to unpack.'

Chapter Six

Marty left after he'd helped Will heave the last of the beds upstairs. There was a double in the main bedroom and two singles: one in the room that would be Gemma's and another in the room that would be Suzie's. These days the girls rarely stayed with him – Suzie was away at university and only home for the holidays – but it was important to Will that they knew they could stop over with him whenever they wanted to.

He liked to think that despite their differences, he and Maxine had done their best by the girls, that their divorce hadn't harmed them too much. It was possible, though, that he'd got it completely wrong and was fooling himself. Beneath the apparent acceptance, they might despise him as much as Maxine did. And as Maxine would have it, they had every reason to.

The affairs, none of which were of any real consequence, had been the final straw for Maxine. He wasn't proud of what he'd done and still cringed at the memory of the lies and skulking about he'd got up to; all those times he'd said, 'I'm just nipping out to clear my mind and stretch my legs.' Within minutes of leaving the house he'd be standing in a phone box that stank of urine – this was before the convenience of mobile phones – and arranging a meeting with the woman on the other end of the line. As red-hot phone sex went, it was pretty pathetic.

It was also madness.

How he'd ever thought Maxine wouldn't see through him, he'd never know. He'd been out of his tiny mind.

Which wasn't far off the literal truth.

Officially, he'd had some kind of nervous breakdown.

Unofficially, he'd just been a bloody idiot, had thrown away his promising career and when that was good and buried, he'd deliberately wrecked his marriage.

It was not the future he'd planned for himself, when, fresh out of law school with Marty, he had landed a plum of a training contract with Carlton Webb Davis, a top Manchester law firm. They'd both opted to work in Manchester rather than London, figuring that they'd soon become a pair of big fish in the small pond. But Will had another compelling reason to move back to the north-west where he'd grown up; he'd just met the most stunning girl. She lived in Cheshire and worked for her father, who ran an auction house in Maywood. They'd met during his last term at law school. He was home for the weekend, a few months after his dad had died and his mother was having a clear-out. She wanted to sell some of the furniture that had belonged to her mother-in-law, pieces she'd never much cared for. She hadn't been too keen on her mother-in-law, either. Will had arranged for a valuer to come to the house when he'd be around, just to ensure that his mother wouldn't be shafted by some smart-talking smoothie in a camel-coloured coat with rolls of cash stuffed into his pockets. In Will's opinion, antique dealers were right at the bottom of the food chain, along with politicians and second-hand car dealers. Coming from a lawyer, as was later pointed out to him, this was rich indeed.

Bang on ten o'clock, he'd opened the front door and got the surprise of his life. The attractive girl produced a business card: *Maxine Stone, of Christopher Stone, Auctioneers and Valuers of Fine Art, Antique and Contemporary Items, Maywood, Cheshire*. He stepped back to let her in, clocking at once that she was all curves and upmarket class. She was top-notch totty; the kind of girl he always went for. It was something to do with flying in the face of his father's prejudice against the middle and upper classes. But apart from that, Miss Maxine Stone was gorgeous. Almost as tall as him, and dressed in an impeccable black suit, her hair was tied back in a prim little bun, which he found wildly sexy. She was looking him straight in the eye (hers were green) and smiling confidently. With a slim briefcase hanging from her left hand (no sign of an engagement ring), she held out her other hand. He shook hands with her and, conscious that he hadn't yet uttered a word, said, 'Can I take you out for dinner and then to bed for dynamite sex?' That was what he wanted to say, but what he actually said was, 'Come on through; my mother's in the sitting room.'

His mother, always the perfect hostess, welcomed Maxine Stone as though she was a long-lost relative and bustled around making tea and arranging biscuits on a plate. It was some time before they got down to the meat of the matter – the fate of an ugly set of bedroom furniture – but Will didn't care. He couldn't take his eyes off this young woman. He reckoned she was about the same age as him, early twenties, and as she perched on the edge of the sofa with her elegant knees locked tight, he was mesmerised. Captivated. Slain. Call it what you will. He wanted her! He watched her face intently as she chatted amiably with his mother, who, if given the chance, could keep an unwary caller hostage for hours. Keep on talking, he willed his mother. Keep talking so that I can plan how to ask her out. 'Well, I find that hard to believe,' he suddenly heard his mother say. 'Don't you, Will?'

'Sorry,' he said, 'I was miles away.' He was mentally unpinning all that ash-blonde hair and running his fingers through it. 'What don't you believe, Mum?'

'That Maxine hasn't been snapped up by a handsome young man.' Only his mother could have been on first-name terms so soon with a complete stranger, openly enquiring about her marital status.

His eyes locked with Maxine's. 'Perhaps she's waiting for the right man,' he said as his mother went out to the kitchen to refill the teapot.

'Perhaps you're right,' Maxine said. 'Shall we go upstairs?'

'My, but you're a fast worker.'

'I was thinking of the bedroom furniture I'm here to value,' she said, her professional poise still firmly in place.

He smiled. 'So was I.' He got to his feet. 'I'll show you the way.'

'I'll bet you could, given half a chance.'

The room was practically zinging with their attraction for each other.

The wardrobe and dressing table were non-starters. 'Not the kind of thing we deal in, I'm afraid,' she apologised. 'I can recommend a man in Crewe who might be interested, though.'

More apologies flowed, this time from Will's mother, Ruby. 'I'm so sorry to have wasted your time. I wish I had something else to offer you instead.'

Two weeks later, when he'd come home for another weekend and was lying in bed with Maxine, he said, 'I know I'm a poor substitute for an ugly set of bedroom furniture, circa 1950s, but I do think we should do this more often.'

They were married two years later, after he'd finished his training contract and was fully qualified. Carlton Webb Davis made him an attractive offer and Maxine continued to work for her father, Christopher Stone. They were perfectly matched: both ambitious, both in a tearing hurry to make a name for themselves. For Maxine it was a foregone conclusion that she would take over her father's auction room and Will knew that she longed for that day to come. She didn't wish her father dead, but she did want him to retire and hand over the reins.

Meanwhile, things were really taking off for Will and he was climbing the greasy pole with chest-beating aplomb. It meant that he was rarely at home, but the more clients who kept him out till all hours, the more supportive Maxine was. Even when Suzie and Gemma came along, she never once complained that he wasn't there to change the nappies or read the bedtime stories. Not that she did a lot of that herself. They had help – a series of nannies whose names he could never keep up with. Maxine wasn't the easiest of employers and like him was rarely around to supervise them. The agency never minded; they had an endless supply of young Scandinavian and Spanish girls who were only in the country to learn English and have a good time.

As well as pursuing their careers, he and Maxine were climbing the property ladder and moved house as often as they could: it was all part of the master plan. His part in the plan, as a highly respected corporate lawyer, was to be the youngest ever senior partner at Carlton Webb Davis – not a bad ambition for a mere secondary-school boy who'd made good – and if anything was guaranteed to turn Maxine on, it was the thought of her man being the Big Cheese. The Numero Uno. The Honcho. Power, he came to realise, really was an aphrodisiac for her. She often joked that Lady Macbeth was her role model.

But when it all started to go wrong, when he began to morph from Superman into a snivelling burnt-out wreck, Lady Macbeth was not amused.

The day he realised he couldn't go on this way was one of the scariest moments of his life. For a while now he'd grown tired of sitting through sixteen-hour meetings just so that a roomful of tossers could flex their egos. It was like being back in the school playground, seeing who had the biggest conkers. Then late one night, after he'd sat through ten hours of client argy-bargy – my conkers are bigger than yours – he had suddenly banged his fist on the table and said, 'Will you just sign the sodding contract and have done with it? Some of us have better things to do with our lives than jerk others about.' He'd gathered up his papers, thrown them into his briefcase and walked out of the boardroom.

The following morning he was called to the fifth floor to explain himself. 'Trouble at home,' he'd lied.

'Then sort it, William. And sooner rather than later.'

For a few weeks he continued to play the game, keeping a tight lid on his cynicism and temper. Somehow he managed to be deferential when necessary and ruthlessly determined when fighting on behalf of his client. 'No hostages allowed' was what the firm believed in, but before long, Will realised there was a scared-witless hostage in their midst: him. He was a hostage of his own making and he couldn't go on. The price was too high. He wanted his life back. He wanted to spend time with his daughters, to sit on their beds at night and read to them, or in Suzie's case, sing her her favourite lullaby, 'Scarlet Ribbons'. But more than anything, he wanted to stop feeling so knackered he couldn't make it in bed anymore.

However, Maxine saw things differently. 'It's just a bad patch you're going through,' she said. 'You're tired, I expect. Why don't we go on holiday without the children?'

They went away together to a relaxing hotel in southern Italy, but all it did was give him some courage on his return to the office: without telling Maxine, he handed in his notice. He was immediately put on 'gardening leave' and for a full month he managed to keep Maxine in ignorance of this. He'd get up in the morning as usual, put on his suit, drive off in his BMW (a bag of clothing in the boot, ready to change into at a motorway service station) and then spend the day anywhere but in Manchester. He'd go across to North Wales, the Peak District, or up to the Lakes. He'd browse round bookstores and stately homes – Chatsworth House was a particular favourite. He also visited antique shops and attended a couple of auctions; to his surprise, he began to understand how addictive they were. No wonder Maxine got a thrill out of her work. Up until then, he'd been politely refused entry to the circles in which she moved. Dealers and valuers, he reckoned, were a bit like masons: secretive and prepared to close ranks if anyone tried to muscle in. Through regular attendance at the sale-rooms and with his keen observational eye, he soon learned about the dodgy goings on, like taking bids off the wall. Some places did it as a matter of course; others, the posher firms, frowned upon the practice of bumping up the sale price of a lot by acknowledging imaginary bidders but occasionally did it all the same.

He grew fond of playing truant and would return home

with a faint spring in his step. Maxine was delighted to see the improvement in him; as far as she was concerned they were now back on track, the glitch dealt with. There was even some bedroom action again.

But inevitably she found out, and when she did – he was spotted at an auction by one of her colleagues – she went ballistic. 'What's happened to you?' she screamed. 'You're not the man I married.'

He tried to explain how he felt, how futile and pointless everything had become for him at Carlton Webb Davis, and how ill he'd begun to feel. He couldn't bring himself to admit to his panic attacks, which forced him to go and sit in the loo until he calmed down. But all she was interested in was how they were going to manage financially.

It was a real enough concern. And while Maxine was prepared to ride out the storm sheltering in the safety of her father's cavernous wallet, Will was not. Christopher Stone was a formidable man, who had originally welcomed Will into the Stone family with a haughty coolness that gradually warmed to tepid approval when he realised what a clever, ambitious son-in-law he had. But when, overnight, Will turned into an indolent good-for-nothing, his hostility knew no bounds. The gloves were off and Will was told in no uncertain terms that Christopher Stone's biggest regret in life was that his only daughter had wasted herself on a thoroughly bad lot.

So fierce pride on Will's part had him steering his family further into the eye of the storm. They sold their expensive house and made drastic economy measures. The nanny was sent packing and he became a house-husband. Temporarily, he assured Maxine. Secretly, though, he enjoyed doing the school run, helping the girls with their homework, taking them swimming, and cooking the tea with one eye on *Blue Peter*. But it was no job for a real man, as Maxine would imply with one of her steely power-suited looks when she came home after a hard day's graft at the saleroom. One evening, when she was feeling particularly bitter that his selfishness had disrupted their lives so dramatically, she said, 'As far as I can see, you're of no use to the girls or me like this.' She was all for him getting off his backside and submitting his CV to whichever law firm would be desperate enough to have him. She missed the perks of having a husband who spent his every waking moment killing himself through stress.

That was when the affairs started. And for the record he'd like it to be known that he was a monogamous man by instinct, and only ended up in the mess he did by circumstances beyond his control. But maybe that's what all men say. The first affair was with one of the mothers he got to know at the school gate. Simply put, she was bored and he was desperate. If he had to defend himself, and he had tried to do so many times, his actions were those of a man trying to gain a modicum of self-respect: if his wife could no longer bear to look at him or regard him as attractive then he was sure as hell going to find the affirmation he needed elsewhere.

It was a mistake, of course. His self-respect had no intention of showing up while he was cheating on his wife. Even without knowing about the affairs, Maxine's loathing for him was growing on a daily basis. When he announced that he was going into business, and confessed exactly what line of business he was considering, she threw hot, scathing scorn at him. 'You, an antique dealer!' she crowed. 'You don't know the first thing about it.'

'Actually,' he said, 'I do. You've taught me all you know. For which I shall be eternally grateful.'

It was a cheap shot, but by this stage of their relationship there were few sweet endearments.

When their divorce was finalised and the money shared out, he took a gamble and opened an antiques shop, rapidly discovering that only throwing his gelt at a three-legged horse in the 2.30 at Uttoxeter would have been riskier. Nonetheless, he lived above his rented shop in Maywood, and began a new life of buying and selling. Given the right motivation he'd always been a fast learner, so he read up, did his homework and got lucky when he stumbled across an expert willing to share his knowledge. His name was Jarvis and he took a liking to Will, becoming his self-appointed mentor. He still was.

All these years on, his life could not be more different. But for all the aggravation and all the friends he'd lost – only Marty had hung in there with him – nothing would make him go back to those days of sitting behind a shiny desk in the soulless air-conditioned offices of Carlton Webb Davis. Not unless he was armed with a machete.

He was sprawled comfortably on the sofa that evening, having decided to take a break from unpacking, and was listening to R.E.M.'s *Up* – not the critics' choice, admittedly, but a favourite of his – when his mobile rang. He recognised the number at once. It was his eldest daughter, Suzie.

'Hi, Dad. How did the move go? How's the new house? And can you lend me some money? *Pleee-ase.*'

'The move went well,' he said. 'Marty helped. The house is horrible. And how much do you want?'

'How much can you spare?'

'For you sweetheart, my very last shirt button. What do you need it for?'

'My coke dealer's raised his prices.'

'Then tell him to stick it up his bum. You're paying through the nose as it is.'

'Oh, *Dad.*'

'No Suzie, I'm holding firm this time. No amount of wheedling from you is going to work. Can't you try something cheaper? Cannabis, for instance.'

Suzie laughed. 'One of these days I'm going to shock you and not be the respectable daughter you've always taken me for.'

He laughed too. 'So why do you want the money?'

'Promise you won't hit the roof?'

'Have I ever been that sort of father?'

'I've bumped the car and want to get it fixed before Mum sees it.'

'When you say bumped, you mean that literally, I hope? You're not about to tell me the car's totalled and you're in hospital covered in bandages, are you?'

'No, nothing like that. I reversed into a metal post and, well, the bumper kind of dropped off.'

'Mm . . . how fast were you going?'

'I was hardly moving at all. So will you lend me the money?'

'Why don't you do what the rest of us do? Get it sorted on your insurance. If I'm not mistaken, I already pay for that anyway.'

'Um . . . thing is, it . . . it wasn't my car. It was Steve's.'

'Steve's?' Will sat up. 'Hang on, let me get this straight. You mean to say that when you were hardly moving at all, and the bumper just *kind of* dropped off, you were driving PC Plod's brand new Jag? The *Shaguar?*'

Suzie's answer was so faint, he scarcely caught it. Or perhaps it was the sound of his laughter bouncing off the sitting-room walls that drowned out her voice.

'Dad, it isn't funny. They're back from Paris next week with Gemma and I need to get it fixed before Steve sees it. You know he'll be as mad as hell about it.'

Will was still laughing when he ended the call. He was picturing the expression on the face of his ex-wife's second husband when he saw what had happened to his precious new car. Steve Dodd, a.k.a. PC Plod because he used to be something big in the police force, had tried hard to be a model step-father to Suzie and Gemma, but he suspected that Steve was going to have his work cut out keeping his cool over this. Unless, of course, for Suzie's sake, Will could get it sorted before anyone was the wiser.

Ten minutes later, when he was hunting through the Yellow Pages for a suitable body shop, his mobile chirruped with a text message from Sandra saying the coast wasn't clear for the next few days. Sandra was a fellow dealer and had one of those open marriages that he thought only ever existed in people's heads. Seemingly her husband would be around for the foreseeable, so any nocturnal visits from

Will would be inappropriate. To be honest he was relieved. He was too tired for one of Sandra's sexual marathons. She might not demand any form of commitment from him, but physically she was the most exhausting woman he'd ever been to bed with. There was no such thing as a quickie for her.

Putting his mobile aside, he returned his attention to more important matters: finding a body shop for PC Plod's pranged car.

Chapter Seven

It was raining when Harriet arrived in Oxford. She let herself into her flat, went through to the kitchen, hung her keys tidily on the hook beside the breadbin and stood for a moment in the gloomy half-light, listening to the silence. The flat felt cold and empty, as if it had fallen asleep in her absence. Or . . . as if it had died.

She briskly chased the thought away and went round switching on lamps, filling the kettle, and checking there was nothing amiss, that a pipe hadn't sprung a leak or a window been jemmied open. Constant activity, she'd come to know, was the only answer.

She'd set off early that morning, trying to beat the worst of the traffic, but had still got caught in a two-mile tailback just north of Birmingham. Her father had offered to come with her, but knowing how tired her mother was, Harriet had suggested he ought to take the children out for the day to give Mum a break. It was obvious to them all that Eileen wasn't getting enough rest, and if that went on for too long, Harriet knew her mother would be stuck in bed for days. It was such a frustration for Mum; just as soon as she started to feel well and her energy levels increased she invariably overdid it and was back where she'd started, feeling ill again. She needed to avoid emotional stress and too much physical work, but they were there for her every day of the week. There seemed no let-up. Harriet knew that her mother would carry on until she dropped. 'Don't worry about me, Harriet,' Eileen had said to her only last night, 'none of us has the luxury of going to pieces, least of all me. I wouldn't do that to the children.' It seemed wrong to Harriet that the focus was all on the children, but maybe

49

that was because she didn't have a maternal bone in her body.

The first room she tackled was the bedroom. It didn't take her long. Most of her things from this room were already up in Cheshire; only a few winter clothes were left, which she had known she wouldn't need straight away. What little furniture she had was being packed up this afternoon by a removal firm and put into storage – there was no space left in Mum and Dad's garage.

From her bedroom she moved to the bathroom: the linen and towels from the airing cupboard took up no more than a couple of bin liners. The sitting room was next, and with the first shelf of her books packed, the buzzer for the intercom sounded.

Spencer.

She wanted to feel pleased about seeing him again, but her pride wouldn't let her. Let's not forget why he's really here, she reminded herself. During the journey down in the car she had wondered about getting in first, ensuring she was the one to end it between them. 'Look, Spencer,' she'd imagined herself saying, 'let's be adult about this. We had our fun, now it's time to move on.' She then imagined winning an Oscar for the most clichéd performance ever given in the history of hammy break-up scenes.

She buzzed him up and, fixing a smile to her face, opened the door. 'Hi, Spencer,' she said. If nothing else, he was going to remember her for being positive and upbeat. But the moment he leaned in for a kiss and she felt the dampness from the rain on his hair and cheek, and smelled the familiar scent of him, she wasn't so sure of herself. A flood of happy memories came back and she kissed him for a fraction longer than she'd intended. Hope surfaced, too. Maybe he would stand by her after all. Maybe he'd be there for her.

'You've been busy,' he said, taking off his wet coat and eyeing the narrow hall that was crowded with boxes and bin liners.

'You know me. If a job's got to be done, best to get it

over and done with.' Like ending their doomed relationship, she thought. Noticing the carrier bag he was holding, she said, 'What's that?'

'Lunch. I knew you'd be too busy to go out, so I called in at your favourite deli. Take your choice: avocado and bacon baguettes, coronation chicken sandwiches and a smoked salmon bagel.'

'How intuitive of you.' Of course, ending it in a restaurant would have been much too dangerous. An embarrassing scene might ensue.

'You carry on with what you were doing,' he said, 'and I'll set things up in the kitchen.'

Down on the floor with her boxes of books, she listened to Spencer as he unwrapped the parcels of food in the kitchen. He definitely seemed quieter than usual. *They always do when they're about to pull the rug out from beneath you. They need to concentrate. You know what men are like, can't multi-task like us girls.*

Stop it! She warned the crazy, paranoid woman inside her head. Perhaps he was just unsure how to treat her these days. Be too relaxed and jaunty with her and he might think she would accuse him of being insensitive.

'Ready when you are,' he called.

They sat opposite each other at the circular table. 'I'm going to miss Franco's Deli,' she said, helping herself to a baguette and ripping it in two. 'Do you want half?'

He shook his head. 'What else do you think you'll miss?'

'Just about everything.' She looked about her, indicating her precious home of the last fourteen months. 'This. Work. Oxford.' She paused and looked at him meaningfully. 'And you. Especially you.' She was throwing him a line. Cueing him up. But all he did was smile and take another bite of his sandwich.

That was when she knew for sure that it was over.

They ate in silence, like an ancient married couple who no longer had anything to say to one another. When she couldn't take the awkwardness any longer, she put down her baguette and said, 'I think we need to talk.' She cringed.

And the Oscar for most clichéd break-up opening line goes to Harriet Swift!

He gave her a nervous look.

'You said on the phone yesterday that there was something you wanted to say to me.' Once again she was throwing him a line.

He slowly finished what was in his mouth. 'It'll keep,' he murmured. 'Any luck on the job front yet?'

She would never have thought he was the cowardly type. He'd always seemed so objective and clear-headed. It was one of the things about him that had attracted her. Prepared to give him some slack, she said, 'I haven't had time to sneeze, never mind approach a job agency. No disrespect to my niece and nephew but they're incredibly time-consuming. There always seems to be something that needs doing for them. I'm worn out and in bed by nine most nights.'

'How are they coming to terms with everything?'

She really couldn't work out if he was genuinely interested or still prevaricating. 'They seem okay,' she said, 'but how do we really know what's going on inside their heads?'

'Have you thought about counselling?'

'They've been seeing a woman for a couple of weeks. I've no idea if it's helping them.'

'What about for you and your parents?'

She shrugged. 'Not really our thing.'

'So you'll just tough it out?'

'Isn't that what most people end up doing anyway?'

'I don't know. I've never been this closely associated . . .' he hesitated, '. . . this near to death before. Have you thought of keeping a journal?'

'Whatever for?' She could feel herself getting cross with him. If he'd never been this close to death before then perhaps he ought to shut the hell up with his half-baked advice.

'I once read about a man who'd lost his wife and he decided to work through his grief by writing everything

52

down. Whenever he couldn't cope, he turned to his diary. I reckon that's what I'd do in your shoes.'

Harriet couldn't think of anything worse. She'd feel too exposed and vulnerable putting down any of the thoughts she'd had since Felicity had died. She also felt that if Spencer knew the first thing about her, he wouldn't have made such a suggestion. Looking at him across the table as he reached for another sandwich, she felt like she was having lunch with a stranger. It hit her then, that that was the reality. Here she was, patiently waiting for him to come clean and say that it was over between them, when the truth was, there was no 'them'. How could there be? They scarcely knew each other. Theirs was a fledgling relationship, still in its early stages. They'd worked together, had been to bed together, but Spencer couldn't possibly know what really made her tick. Just as she didn't know the real him.

Seizing the moment, she said, 'Spencer, I think we should get this over with. I can't think of a single good reason why you would want to carry on seeing me now that my circumstances have changed so dramatically, so let's not kid ourselves that after today we'll be anything but friends.'

He stopped eating. She saw and heard him swallow. He looked a picture of awkwardness. 'You knew, then, what it was I wanted to say?'

'A smart girl like me? Of course I knew.'

'And you're okay about it?'

'Perfectly okay.'

'Thank goodness for that.' Letting out his breath and visibly relaxing, he said, 'I shouldn't have doubted you, really. You're always so pragmatic. Another girl would have called me every name under the sun for being so shallow and only thinking of myself.'

She looked at him steadily, resisting the urge to slap his face. 'We both know that's not my style.'

'But you do see, don't you? It's the children. I've never wanted any, and . . . well, if we're to continue seeing each other, if we were to get seriously involved, the children would be a factor. And I'm not convinced—'

'Please,' she interrupted him, 'you don't have to explain. Believe me, I know *exactly* how you feel.'

Driving home later that evening, Harriet realised that for all her brave toughing-it-out talk, for all her reasoning of the situation, she was more hurt and disappointed than she'd expected. But what hurt the most was the look of pure relief on Spencer's face when they'd said goodbye. Would it have cost him so much to have pretended to be more upset?

As she headed north, with each mile that she put between herself and Oxford, her anger grew. Rejection was an ugly thing. You could dress it up as prettily and as civilly as you wanted but it still boiled down to the same hurtful blow: the person on the receiving end was left to think they weren't good enough.

By the time she reached Keele Services on the M6 she had to stop and be sick. If ever she had needed her sister at the other end of the phone, or right here with her, this was it. Felicity would have bucked her up; she would have made her laugh and said all the right things. She would have told her Spencer was a shallow toe-rag of the highest order, that she was better off without him.

She emerged from the toilets and joined a queue for a cup of tea to take away the vile taste in her mouth. She had to admit that part of her anger lay in the misguided shred of hope she had clung to. Spencer had been the only thing left that symbolised the woman she had been before Felicity's death – the woman she still wanted to be. Losing him meant she had to sever that tie and submit to the only certainty in her new life: that her days as an independent, carefree woman were over. She was now a parent. A parent whose will had to be subjugated to the needs of the children in her care.

As she sat in the busy service station, surrounded by a coach party of raucous pensioners on their way home after a day out, she finally accepted that her old way of life was over. It was as dead and buried as Felicity. Feeling pathetically sorry for herself she thought of everything she'd lost – her sister, her home, her job, her identity, and now her boyfriend. What next? Her mind?

Chapter Eight

Carrie closed the door of the Wendy house, looked at Joel and frowned. He was sucking his thumb and rubbing his cheek with his silky. His silky was a pale pink scarf Mum had worn when he'd been a baby. He used to stroke it whenever she wore it and then one night she gave it to him to help him sleep. He was always carrying the scarf around with him, dragging it on the floor when he was really little. Carrie could remember the time they were going somewhere and couldn't find it. Joel had cried and cried and wouldn't get in the car until he had it. They found it under a pile of his toys. He wasn't a baby then, but he'd acted like one.

He was acting like a baby now, sucking his thumb and making that humming noise he made when he was tired or upset. None of the grown-ups seemed to notice that he was doing it more and more, but Carrie knew he had to stop. If he did it when he went to school, he'd be laughed at. Someone would have to tell him. And seeing as she was the only one who knew what he was doing, it would have to be her. She sat in the chair next to him and put her arm around his shoulders, just as Mummy used to whenever she had something important to say. 'Joel,' she said, 'do you remember Daddy saying that big boys don't suck their thumbs? It's something you grow out of.'

Joel unplugged his thumb, making a small popping sound. 'Mummy said I could do it.'

'Yes, but that was when you were very little. Now you're a big boy. You'll be five soon.'

He shook his head. 'But Mummy said it was all right. She

did.' His eyes wide, he clutched at his silky as though afraid Carrie might snatch it from him.

She tried to make her voice sound firm, like a grown-up's. 'I'm only telling you this for your own good, Joel. Because when you go to big school in a few weeks' time, you'll get laughed at if you don't act like all the other children. And if I'm not around to keep an eye on you, they'll pick on you.'

His eyes opened even wider. 'Then I'm not going to school.'

'But you have to.'

He shook his head and put his thumb back in his mouth.

Carrie took her arms away from him, folded them in front of her and tried to look stern. 'If you don't do as I say, I won't let you sleep in my bed with me.'

The thumb was out again. 'But I don't like sleeping on my own.'

'Then you have to do as I say.'

He looked thoughtful. 'Can I take silky to school with me?'

'No. You wouldn't want to lose it, would you? And someone might take it. I took a doll to school once and a girl stole it. She said she didn't, but I know she did. You see, Joel, not everyone's as nice as us.'

'Grandma and Granddad are nice.'

'That's true.'

'And Harriet. She's nice.'

Carrie wasn't so sure about this. For the last few days, since Harriet had come back from wherever it was she'd been, she hadn't seemed at all nice. She'd told Carrie off for not eating enough of her cereal yesterday morning and then had snapped at her because she hadn't tidied her room. 'You have to do your bit,' Harriet had said. 'You can't expect me or Grandma and Granddad to do everything for you.'

'Grandma doesn't mind tidying up; she told me she quite likes it,' Carrie had said.

'But Grandma can't do as much as she used to.'

'What's wrong with her?'

'It doesn't matter what's wrong with her; the point is you have to make sure you clean up after yourselves. And if you can remember to put the lid back on the toothpaste after you've finished spreading it round the basin, so much the better.'

It wasn't even as if her bedroom had been that messy. Just a few toys she and Joel had tipped out of the box and had been playing with.

Harriet could be so bossy with her and Joel. Maybe not so much with Joel. That was because he was still little. Probably, when he was bigger, Harriet would start telling him off too.

Carrie often wished that Harriet could be more like their mother. You'd have thought because they were sisters they would be the same. But they weren't. Other than being the same size, they weren't like one another at all. Mum had been kind and patient, and her voice had always been gentle and full of happiness, like she was about to burst out laughing. Carrie used to love it when Mum read to her; she did all the voices, even the funny deep ones. Harriet never did that. She always rushed it as if she was in a hurry to do something else. She could look pretty sometimes, like Mum, but not when she was cross; then her lips would go all thin and her eyes would screw up in a scowl, as if she'd eaten something horrible.

Carrie knew for a fact that Harriet didn't like children. If she did like them, she'd be married with some of her own. Maybe then it wouldn't be so bad for her and Joel. If they had some cousins to play with, there wouldn't be time to think about . . .

Carrie stopped quickly. She'd promised herself not to let her mind get confused with sad thoughts about Mum and Dad. She had to remember what Grandma had told her, that they were happy where they were. But then everyone knew that if you went to heaven you were happy, that you didn't have anything to worry about. There wasn't anyone there to tell you off. No one to tell you to tidy your room.

Carrie often wished she and Joel could be there too. But if that happened then she'd miss Grandma and Granddad, who were always nice and hardly ever told them off. Granddad had taken them to the garden centre the other day – the day when Harriet came home in a bad mood with her car full of bags and boxes – and he hadn't even told Joel off when he didn't make it to the loo in time and wet himself. Although he did sigh quite a bit when they were queuing for an ice-cream.

It was weird, but Grandma and Granddad were the only friends Carrie and Joel now had. They hadn't lived in their last house long enough to make any friends, and the friends they'd made before she couldn't really remember because they'd moved house millions of times. Although Harriet said it wasn't anywhere near that many. She said she should know because she'd stayed with them at least once in every house they'd ever lived in.

Deciding it was too hot in the Wendy house, Carrie got up and opened the two windows either side of the door. She liked playing in here; it was like having her own little house. She lifted the lid of the toy box and looked inside. There was the plastic tea set Joel loved playing with. 'Let's have a tea party,' she said, knowing that it would please him.

Joel sprang into life and got off his chair. 'Can we have real water like we did last time? Not pretend water.'

She passed him a matching teapot and milk jug. 'Yes. But only if you promise not to spill it everywhere. We mustn't make extra work for Grandma and Granddad.' And quoting her aunt, she added, 'Grandma isn't very well, so we have to be extra good.'

She helped him to place the things carefully on the table, four cups and saucers and four plates – he always insisted that it had to be four of everything. 'Is Grandma going to die like Mummy and Daddy?' he asked, putting the lid on the teapot.

'Don't be stupid. No one is going to die, Joel.' Carrie didn't know if this was true. She and Joel weren't supposed to know that their grandmother had anything wrong with her. But Carrie often listened at the top of the stairs when everyone thought she was asleep in bed and one night she had heard Harriet telling Grandma that she should rest more, that if she didn't, she'd make herself more ill than she already was.

'But Mummy and Daddy died,' Joel said, his voice shrill and persistent. 'Harriet says that everyone dies in the end. Harriet told me that even—'

'Oh, stop going on about it, will you?' Carrie snapped. 'You're just a silly little boy who doesn't know anything.' She wrenched the teapot out of his hands and grabbed the milk jug. 'Now stay here while I go and fill these.'

She didn't know why, but her legs were shaking when she stepped outside into the sunshine. She walked uncertainly across the lawn to the tap that was on the end of the garage. Blinking back tears, she wondered if this was how you felt just before you fainted. A boy had fainted at school once, on sports day, and everyone had crowded round him to get a look as he lay on the grass. She stood in the shade of the garage and felt her heart racing. It felt like someone was playing a drum inside her. Her throat felt tight and it was an effort to swallow. Maybe she had what was making Grandma ill. Maybe she was dying. She suddenly thought of Joel and how lonely and frightened he'd be without her.

At night, when her brother was sleeping next to her, his breath noisy and tickly in her ear, his silky wrapped around his thumb-sucking hand, she often worried about who would look after them if anything happened to their grandparents. Or Harriet. What if there was another car crash and she and Joel were left on their own? Who would look after them then? Or would they be made to stay in one of those places where children without parents had to live?

An orphanage.

Just saying the word in her head scared Carrie. She knew all about orphanages; she'd seen them on the television. Children were made to wear smelly old clothes that had been worn by hundreds of other children. They were all made to sleep together in one big room and had to get up in the middle of the night to mop the floors. Oh, yes, she knew what went on. She'd watched that film with the girl who had all that curly red hair. She and the other girls in the orphanage didn't look too unhappy, but they all wanted to escape, didn't they? They wanted to be with kind, rich people who loved them.

Suddenly Carrie's throat was so tight she was struggling to breathe. It only loosened when hot tears splashed onto her cheeks. She drew her forearm across her face and wiped them away. Just as Joel had to stop sucking his thumb, she had to learn not to cry. She had to be good, too. Because if Grandma wasn't well and they annoyed Harriet, their aunt might decide not to look after them any more and they'd end up in an orphanage wearing clothes that didn't fit and shoes with holes in them.

Perhaps she ought to explain to Joel what could happen if they didn't do as Harriet said.

She filled the plastic teapot and jug and went back to the Wendy house. When she pushed the door open, she found Joel lying on his side on the floor. He was crying, curled up into a ball, his precious silky pushed against his eyes. In her hurry to put the teapot and jug on the table, she splashed water down the front of her shorts and T-shirt, but hardly noticing it, she dropped to her knees. She pulled her brother onto her lap. 'What's the matter, Joel? Have you hurt yourself?'

He lifted his head from her shoulder. 'You . . . you shouted at me. You called me silly. And I'm not. Mummy said I was clever. She . . . she always said I was clever.'

'Oh, Joel, I'm sorry. Of course you're not silly. Please don't cry any more.'

But the more she tried to calm him – rocking him gently, patting his back – the more he cried, his tears making a cool, damp patch on her shoulder. He was shuddering and gulping in her arms and there was nothing she could do to stop him. She tried to think what their mother would have done if she were here. How would Mum have stopped him crying?

Then it came to her: Mum would have given him a drink. Reaching across to the table she poured Joel a cup of water from the teapot. 'Look, Joel,' she said, 'I've got you a drink. Sit up straight and you can have it.'

Within seconds he was calm and drinking thirstily. Still holding him close and wiping his eyes with his silky, she said, 'Don't worry, Joel, I'll take care of you. I'll always look after you.'

Cuddling Joel tightly, she knew what she'd just said was true. She would always look after her brother. She had to. There wasn't anyone else they could rely on. Mummy and Daddy had left them, Grandma was ill and would probably leave them too, and Granddad had a bad knee, didn't he? So that only left Harriet. And Harriet didn't really like them, did she?

Chapter Nine

It was probably a first, but for once the commotion going on downstairs had nothing to do with Gemma – it wasn't about her clothes, her hair, the hours she kept or her attitude – and, pushing her unpacking onto the floor, she lay on the bed with her hands behind her head. The way Steve was carrying on, anyone would think Suzie had done it deliberately. What a twat! Kicking up such a fuss just because his stupid car had been damaged. At least Suzie had come clean about it. Mind you, even Gemma would have done that, but only because she would have been gagging to see the expression on Steve's face. She'd also have made a better job of it – would have really trashed the car, maybe taken off a door or two. And she certainly wouldn't have bothered to get it fixed like her sister had. Unluckily for Suzie, the garage had cocked up big-time by bodging the respray.

Gemma smirked at the memory of Steve's face when he'd realised something was wrong. They'd only been in the house ten minutes when he'd looked out of the sitting-room window and nearly had a fit. Mum had told him he was imagining it, but when they'd all gone outside, it became pretty obvious that there was a patch of paintwork that looked different from the rest. Suzie's eyes had been a giveaway too. Mum had immediately taken Steve's side, as she always did these days. 'What the hell did you think you were doing, driving Steve's car, anyway?' she'd shouted at Suzie.

'I'd run out of petrol in mine.'

'And you thought that gave you the right to help yourself to mine?' Steve had blustered, his nostrils flaring.

'I was only nipping to the shops for some milk.'

'Oh, so that makes it all right. Well, I'll tell you this for nothing; I'm going to get it fixed properly and you're going to pay for it. Do you hear me? What's more, we'll stop your allowance.'

'Steve, calm down. Let me handle this.'

More nostril flaring. 'You mean you'll just let her off. I've told you before, Maxine, you're not firm enough with them.'

That was when Gemma had decided she'd had enough. She wasn't going to stick around while PC Plod, as her father called Steve, banged on about the teenagers of today. She'd tried to signal to Suzie to make her escape with her, but Mum had stepped in. 'Oh, no you don't, you stay right where you are. Gemma, go and do your unpacking.'

Bugger the unpacking, thought Gemma, as she continued to lie on her bed. She was knackered and didn't have any intention of moving for the next hour. The journey back from Paris, which should only have taken a few hours had been a total nightmare. French baggage-handlers had been on a twenty-four-hour strike. Or had it been traffic controllers? Either way it delayed them getting home by more than six hours. Mum had been all for getting the Eurostar and then the train up to Crewe, but Steve, in one of his I've-paid-for-this-we'll-bloody-well-stick-it-out moods, wouldn't listen. She'd left them to their bickering and went off to find something to eat.

Looking at her watch, she wondered what time supper would be. Maybe she'd pass on it this evening. She could wander into town and get something from the chip shop. In fact, a bag of proper chips swimming in vinegar would be just the job after all that French food. Using the remote control, she turned up the volume on Radiohead's *OK Computer* and drowned out the argument still going on downstairs. She closed her eyes, imagining herself back at Glastonbury, where she'd gone earlier in the summer with a bunch of friends when their AS exams were over. She hadn't really fancied lolloping around in the mud, but seeing as Radiohead were playing, she reckoned she could rough it for a couple of days. It had been the perfect wind-up for Steve. For an ex-policeman, a music festival was the ultimate social evil. The amount of drugs awareness lectures he'd subjected her to was a criminal act in itself. Wake up and smell the coffee, Stevie Boy! She didn't need to go all the way to Glastonbury to find a supplier. She could do that at school. Or here in Maywood. But the festival had been cool. The sun had shone and the bands had been great. She and Fay had shared their tent with Gus and it had been a right laugh the three of them trying to sleep together. Not that she'd told Mum and Steve about Gus sleeping with her and Fay. That would have brought on a heart attack for them both. It had been a shame that Gemma's best friend hadn't been able to join them, but Yasmin came from a strict Muslim family and Mr and Mrs Patel were very protective of their only daughter.

She closed her eyes and lost herself in the music. It was good to be home. The last two weeks had been exhausting. As part of the student exchange system the school ran, she'd been staying with the Leon family in Paris. In theory, Veronique Leon would be coming to stay with them next summer, but Gemma wasn't so sure she'd actually come. Veronique had been an all-round loser and way too serious. She hardly ever wanted to go out and only wanted Gemma there to improve her English. Okay, so that was the point of the exercise, but how school had reached the conclusion that they'd have anything in common was a mystery to Gemma. It hadn't been all bad: Veronique's nineteen-year-old brother, Marcel, had more than made up for any inadequacy on his sister's behalf. Home from university, and with his own transport – a noisy, back-firing motorbike – Marcel had offered to take her out. They'd gone to the cinemas, they'd sat around in smoky bars and cafés and one night they'd gone to a party and didn't come home until seven in the morning, having spent the last two hours lying on the dewy grass in the nearby park, watching the sun come up. Mum and Steve would have gone mad if they'd known.

But not half as mad as if they knew what else she'd been doing. Marcel had made it pretty obvious that he wanted to go to bed with her, and deciding that she quite fancied him, and that she might just as well get the whole virginity thing over and done with, she'd gone along with it. The first time had been the let-down she'd expected. It hadn't hurt, but then it hadn't been all that great either. But the second time had been okay. The third and fourth time she began to see what all the fuss was about.

When Mum and Steve had met her at the airport she'd been convinced that they would take one look at her and guess. But she should have known better. They were so cross – they'd just heard about the strike at the airport – that not even a sticker on her forehead with the words 'All Shagged Out' would have made them pay attention.

For some reason she thought of her father and, not having spoken to him for some time, she got off the bed, turned down the volume on *Karma Police* and dug around in her rucksack for her mobile. The one thing you could count on with Dad was that he always had time for you. She'd phoned him once when he was in the middle of bidding at an auction; he'd kept chatting with her and only asked her to hold on when the bidding got really serious.

Within seconds he answered. 'Hi Bobtail,' he said, 'how was France? Have you brought me back a present? A pretty little Lalique bowl would be nice.'

'I've got you a bottle of wine and a T-shirt with *Je Suis un Rockstar* on it.'

'Sweetkins, you shouldn't have.'

'I know, but I'm like that. All heart.'

'So come on, tell me all about the trip. How was chez Leon? Did they treat you well? Did you go up the Eiffel Tower? Have you come back stinking of Gauloise and Camel cigarettes and with a liking for incomprehensible black and white films shot from arty angles?'

'Easy there, Dad. You've got to handle those stereotypes

66

with care. How about I come round and see the new house and tell you all about it?'

'When do you want to come?'

'Now would be great but I don't think Mum would appreciate driving me anywhere tonight.'

'Tired after her romantic trip away with PC Plod, is she? That'll teach her.'

'No, it's got nothing to do with that; it's Steve's car.' She started to tell her father about Suzie being in trouble.

'Damn!' he interrupted her. 'I knew we wouldn't get away with it.'

'You knew?'

'Yes. Your sister asked me to lend her the money to get it put right and, thinking I could do better than that, I stepped in and organised for it to be fixed. Trouble was, the only garage that could do the job at such short notice wasn't exactly the best. On a scale of one to ten, how mad is Steve?'

'How would you rate six inches off the ground with incandescent rage?'

'Highly amusing if I didn't feel so sorry for Suzie. Does he know I had anything to do with it?'

'No. Suzie hasn't said anything. Well, not to my knowledge. But then I've been up here in my bedroom for the last half-hour, so for all I know, he might have got the thumbscrews out by now and be extracting a full confession.'

'Sounds like Suzie needs a good defence lawyer. Shall I just happen to be passing and call in?'

With the second load of holiday washing now in the machine, Maxine was staring into the freezer hoping for inspiration. It was the worst thing about coming home after a holiday – trying to summon up the enthusiasm to cook again. More often than not Steve cooked, but tonight he wasn't capable of boiling an egg. He was currently upstairs in the shower, trying to calm down. Maxine had never seen him so furious, and frankly, she didn't blame him. If Suzie had bumped *her* new car she'd be hopping mad. What the hell had Suzie been playing at? If it wasn't one thing with those girls, it was another.

And the shame of it was, she and Steve hadn't managed to get a week away together – just the two of them – in ages, and when they did manage it, it was ruined. You had to wonder if it was worth the effort. Perhaps they should have taken a week off work and just stayed at home. That way Suzie wouldn't have dreamt of borrowing a car she had absolutely no right to touch.

Paris had been Steve's idea. He'd wanted to celebrate their fifth wedding anniversary by doing something special, and when Gemma had come home from school with the letter about the lower-sixth French student exchange system, he had suddenly fancied France for himself, particularly Paris. 'We could treat ourselves to a decent hotel and really take our time exploring,' he said. 'It could be a second honeymoon for us.'

'But I've already had a second one,' she'd said, 'when I married you.'

'Yes, but did the first one really count?'

Steve didn't often badmouth Will – that was her job, especially if Will had been irritatingly stubborn over something – but she supposed that occasionally it was natural that Husband Number Two would feel the need to check his stock against that of Husband Number One. Not that he needed to worry. Will didn't compare at all. Steve was everything Will could never be. He was dependable, solid, hardworking, ambitious, organised and most importantly, all grown up. When Steve said he'd organise something he did it by the book and you could be sure it would happen. There were no embarrassing surprises or disappointments. If Will had suggested a trip to Paris it would probably turn out to be a long weekend to EuroDisney with Big Macs thrown in. Her idea of hell.

It transpired that the only week she and Steve could both get away coincided with Gemma's trip to Paris. 'I might know you'd find some way to keep an eye on me,' Gemma had said.

'Paris is a big city,' Maxine had mollified her, 'quite large enough for us to avoid bumping into each other.'

'I certainly hope so.'

As tempting as it was to look up Monsieur and Madame Leon in Paris and introduce themselves, they stuck to the arrangement that they would meet at Charles de Gaulle airport at the agreed time. It was then, when they discovered there was a strike on, that all the pleasure of the holiday started to fade away.

Maxine sighed, and deciding on chicken Kiev for supper, she closed the freezer door. After putting the unappetising lumps of breaded chicken into a dish and shoving them into the oven, she went over to the wine rack. A very large glass of wine was just what was needed. She had the cork almost out when the doorbell rang. If it was one of the girls' friends, a Jehovah's Witness or a double-glazing man, they were in for short shrift. She flung the door back in a way guaranteed to see them off.

'Oh, it's you.'

'Bonjour, ma cherie! Is that the pungent smell of a ripe Brie fresh from its travels across the channel? Or is it the smell of a daughter being roasted on the spit?'

Maxine frowned. 'It's really not a good time for one of your tiresome, not to say cryptic, stand-up routines, Will. I'm tired and likely to attack at the slightest provocation.'

From behind Maxine came the thundering of feet. 'Hey Dad, good to see you!'

'Wow! Look at you, Gemma, you're positively glowing. France obviously suited you.'

Maxine's head was beginning to ache. 'Okay, Will,' she conceded, stepping back to let him in. 'You've got twenty minutes, then our supper's ready.'

Chapter Ten

Will followed Maxine and Gemma through to the kitchen, glancing left and right, an imaginary rifle cocked and ready to go. *Come on you bastard! Where're you hiding? Come out and show yourself, you snivelling excuse of a man. I'll teach you to pick on one of my daughters!*

'Hello, Will, what are you doing here?'

Will spun round. He fired and blew a hole clean through Steve's head. *Boom! Job done.*

What Maxine saw in Steve was another of life's great mysteries. Okay, the man was seriously good for a few quid, but surely looks and personality had to count for something? As far as Will was concerned, Steve was too short, too ugly, too old, too hairy and much too successful. Five years ago, Steve had taken early retirement from being a desk jockey for the police force. He'd worked his way up to being a peaked-cap and gold-braid type of copper, where the only dangerous action he saw was the occasional paper cut. Then he started his own security firm, installing burglar alarms and CCTV systems. Will didn't know the exact figures involved, but he didn't need to be a mathematical genius to work out that business was booming – the prestigious double-fronted Victorian house opposite the park and the expensive top-of-the-range Jag (slightly damaged) told its own story. Combine that with Maxine's earnings from Stone's Auctioneers, which she now ran, and they were fairly rolling in it. Like a couple of porkers in mud.

Expert these days at keeping the animosity out of his voice and sounding sufficiently blokey, Will turned up the charm ready to smooth the waters. 'Hi, Steve. Good holiday?'

'Yes, but I have to tell you I'm not at all pleased with Suzie, she's—'

He was interrupted by the girl herself coming into the kitchen. 'Hey, Dad, I didn't know you were here.' She came over and planted a kiss on his cheek. He put his arm round her, and with Gemma standing the other side of him, it seemed the perfect moment to tell Steve the awful truth.

'Steve,' he said, 'I've got something to say. You won't like it, and I'm ashamed of myself for being such a coward, but . . .' he lowered his gaze to emphasise just how pitifully sorry he was, 'well, the thing is, I reversed into your car when you were away and—'

'But Dad—'

He tightened his hold on Suzie. 'It's okay, you don't need to cover for me any more, Suzie. I should never have got you to lie on my behalf. I don't know what I was thinking of.' He returned his gaze to Steve, noting Maxine's flinty look of suspicion. 'I'm really sorry, Steve. I tried my best to get it fixed before you came home, but if you want to get it done properly, just send me the bill.' The feeble bleating now over, Will held out his hand. 'No hard feelings I hope?' *Yes! An upbeat finale. Performance over. I thank you!*

It was anyone's guess how much he'd be down on the deal by the time Steve had shopped around to find the most expensive garage to exact his revenge, but Will didn't care. It had been pretty dumb of Suzie to borrow the wretched car in the first place, but he'd be damned before he'd stand back and let Steve punish her. And to hell with what any textbook said about step-children needing to respect their step-fathers. Baloney with knobs on! They were his children, not Steve's. End of story.

Instead of taking the road away from the centre of town, he drove into Kings Melford. A fraction smaller than

Maywood, but definitely more attractive, it had an abundance of black and white half-timbered buildings, and a quaint cobbled square that had been the original marketplace, going back to the time of Henry VIII when the town was given some kind of official status. Some Tudor duke geezer called Melford, who'd been a chum of the King, had taken a liking to the place – it was then no more than a village – and Henry had had it named in his honour. But if you really wanted to get down and dirty historically, you could do no better than visit the town's museum and read up on its Anglo-Saxon heritage.

The museum also had a section devoted to anything and everything to do with inland waterways. The Shropshire Union canal skirted the top of the town and when it was built it became an important part of the system for transporting salt out of Cheshire. Nowadays it wasn't the canal workers who stopped off in Kings Melford to stock up on provisions and fuel; it was the people cruising the waterways in their pleasure crafts. There was a purpose-built marina a short walk along the towpath to The Navigation – the best pub in the town, and Will's current destination – and a couple of boat firms, one of which still made the traditional crafts so beloved by narrowboat purists.

He passed Hart's Antique Emporium, just off the main road and to his left, and gave his most recent business venture a salute. Strictly speaking, it wasn't just *his* business: Jarvis owned the building and rented it out to Will for a nominal amount, on the basis that he took a percentage of the profits. Originally called The Tavern, it started life as an inn and during the early nineteenth century had been a popular stopover point for as many as eight coaches a day bound for Birmingham, London, Liverpool and Manchester. When the railways put coaching into a decline, Jarvis's grandfather, Elijah Cooper, bought the inn so that he could expand his flourishing boot-and shoe-making business. Now in his mid seventies, Jarvis, who hadn't followed in his ancestor's footsteps (no pun intended) could still remember watching his grandfather put the finishing touches to a pair of navvy boots.

Just as Will expected, and despite the warmth of the evening, he found Jarvis in his usual chair in the snug of The Navigation. He was alone and doing the *Telegraph*'s crossword. More often than not, he would be surrounded by a reverential group of visiting boating folk listening to his tales of the town and his long-standing family connection with it. By the time they left, having worshipped at the knee of the town's one true character and had their photograph taken with him, they would go away happy, but definitely poorer. Jarvis rarely bought himself a drink; after all, it was thirsty work spinning all those yarns.

Being one of the last great characters was a job that Jarvis took very seriously. A stickler for eccentric dress, he never left home unless he was wearing something off-kilter. This evening he was dressed to kill in olive-green corduroy trousers, a plaid shirt and purple waistcoat and a red silk cravat. Pretty standard stuff. But it was the burgundy monogrammed carpet slippers that really pulled the ensemble together.

'Another of what you're drinking?' Will asked.

Jarvis looked up from his near-empty glass. 'As ever, Laddie, your timing is of the perfection normally the reserve of the cavalry. I'll have a double of my usual malt. That's if funds are permitting?'

Will smiled. 'It's been a good week; I'll stand you a triple.'

When they were both settled with their drinks, and Will was wishing they were outside in the beer garden overlooking the canal in the balmy evening air, he said, 'I wasn't joking about it having been a good week. Your cut should be up nicely this month.'

Jarvis waved his comment aside, as only a man could who didn't have to worry where his next guinea was coming from. Having inherited well from those who had worried over the pennies, he had an enviably casual approach to work and money. The antiques trade had been his lifelong true love and had kept him conveniently off the streets, as he liked to put it. He'd never married and Will had absolutely no idea what his sexual orientation was. He was heartily robust and theatrically camp at the same time. The first time Will set eyes on him was when he'd been going through his breakdown phase. Will had been playing truant at an auction and had noticed a dapper man in a fedora. To make his bid, he would raise his chin no more than a hair's breadth and the auctioneer would notice him every time. His manner had such an air of authority that Will couldn't take his eyes off him. He saw him again at another saleroom in Shropshire, and then in Kings Melford in The Navigation, not long before he and Maxine split up. Will had introduced himself and discovered that the man was Jarvis Cooper, a local dealer. After buying him a drink, Will mentioned that he was thinking of getting into the business himself.

'Don't do it, Laddie,' Jarvis had said in the kind of voice Noël Coward had used to tell Mrs Worthington not to put her daughter on the stage. 'Buying and selling is like trying to satisfy an insatiable nymphomaniac; the more you give her, the more she'll take from you. She'll use and abuse you, then spit you out and move onto her next lover.'

'I rather like the sound of that. Where do I sign up?'

Jarvis had laughed and asked if he'd like to have a look at The Tavern. Thinking this was an invitation to join him on a pub crawl, he'd agreed. The Tavern turned out to be a rambling, three-storey Aladdin's cave. It was chock-full of goodies that ranged from fifties tat to exquisite pieces of porcelain. Jarvis had a particular weakness for Royal Worcester and there were cabinets of the stuff. 'Your first lesson,' he said, unlocking one of the cabinets and selecting a fragile cup and saucer. 'Put a value on that. Two clues: it's hand-painted, circa 1917.'

'I haven't a clue.'

'China not your thing, Laddie?'

'I was thinking more of specialising in furniture.'

74

'Ah, you think porcelain is for poofters and nancy boys, do you?'

'I didn't say that.'

'No, Laddie. It's implicit in the disinterested way you're holding that near piece of perfection. Give it to me. You see, Laddie, if you're to make your way in this business you have to *feel* it. You have to breathe in the workmanship. Picture the artist bent over his bench as he laboured over his work. Think of his family back in their terraced house in Worcester as they waited for their father, an unsung hero of his time, to come home with nowt but a few shillings in his pocket. These were painted by a true artist, but he was treated as little better than a factory worker on a production line. Even the great man himself, James Stinton, thought he was just a humble craftsman.' He sighed. 'I tell you, it's enough to make a grown man weep.'

Watching Jarvis cradle the porcelain, clucking and cooing over it, Will began to see a whole new world open up. He wanted to feel what Jarvis felt. He wanted that buzz that so clearly brought this old-timer to life.

Under Jarvis's tutelage, Will learned fast. He learned how to check out the goods at saleroom previews, how to study the catalogue and the importance of listing the prices the pieces fetched under the hammer. His days revolved around researching, collecting, buying and selling, and he soon realised that being in the antique trade wasn't about money. It was the buzz. The thrill of the chase. But it wasn't plain sailing; sometimes Jarvis deliberately set him up. Like the dud Jacobean oak coffer he promised would make Will a nice little turn. Turned out to be a fake. A good fake, mind. '*Caveat emptor*, Laddie!' Jarvis told him. Which was posh-speak for *buyer beware!* It was an important lesson. It taught him to listen to other dealers but not to trust a single word they uttered. Not unlike lawyers, really. 'Dealers are the biggest storytellers going,' Jarvis warned him. 'They can spin a yarn about the provenance of a fake that would be so convincing it would have you and all the other punters selling your grandmothers to raise the money to buy it.'

But the best story these yarn-spinning dealers had ever come up with was that Will was Jarvis's illegitimate, long-lost son. Will didn't object to the gossip; in fact he'd have preferred to have Jarvis as his father and not the miserable specimen nature had landed him with.

'The reason it's been a good week,' he said, bringing his thoughts back to the present, 'is that I've sold that pair of Charley Baldwyn vases; you know the ones—'

'The swans?'

'Yes.'

'I shall miss them.' Jarvis took a sip of his malt whisky and assumed the air of a man already in deep mourning. 'They went to another dealer, presumably? Who was it? Some London runner?'

'No. A couple looking for pension alternatives.'

'Ah, a familiar tale.'

It was true; a lot of their business was going this way. These days people were afraid to put their money in stocks and shares, so antiques seemed a safer bet. And they could be, providing you didn't go and fall in love with the pieces and couldn't bring yourself to sell when the time came.

After finishing his drink, Will left Jarvis to his crossword and drove onto his next port of call. Sandra had texted him earlier to say that the coast would be clear that evening. Her husband was something big in the world of piping – industrial piping as opposed to cake decoration – and was often away, leaving Sandra alone and bored. A dangerous combination for a woman in her forties, so Sandra claimed. 'I'm in my prime and I have my needs,' she said after one of their trysts. That's a woman for you, always needing to justify her actions.

He'd met Sandra at an antique fair in Harrogate. Their stands were opposite each other, and as with all dealers, they'd spent a good deal of time eyeing up each other's goods under the pretext of being sociable.

Fresh out of the bath, Sandra was wrapped in only a

towel and smelling of super-strength musk. She was in full frisky mood. Exchanging a few pleasantries – jacket and shoes off – she led the way upstairs. Afterwards, when she went back downstairs to make a post-coital cup of tea, Will stared up at the ceiling and thought of Sandra's husband. No guilt, he told himself. You know the drill; Sandra and her husband have an open marriage. For all you know, the man is probably in bed with another woman right now.

But deep down, Will knew it was wrong. Even in the most open of relationships people could get hurt. Having fun at the expense of someone else could only ever end in tears. It was selfish and irresponsible. His train of thought surprised him and he suddenly didn't want to hang around for anything else Sandra might have in mind.

He was halfway through pulling on his trousers when she appeared in the doorway. She was stark naked, her modesty partially concealed behind the contents of a particularly fine butler's tray. 'Oh, no you don't,' she said. 'David's back tomorrow, so I need to make the most of you while I can.'

'I wish I could oblige, but I have an early start in the morning. An auction over in Colwyn Bay.'

She put the tray down on the oak chest at the foot of the bed, revealing the glory of her voluptuous body. What man could resist such a tempting offer?

But he did. Sometimes he surprised himself. He tried to kiss her goodnight but she wasn't having it. 'You're not the only man I could have a good time with, Will,' she said petulantly. She was clearly offended and he was sorry for that.

He drove home, the windows down so that the cool night air would keep him awake. He was bone-tired. As he turned into Maple Drive, in the light cast from his headlamps he saw a figure in a baseball cap crossing the road. A young teenager out at this time of night? Or was he a lad out for a night of petty thieving? Will slowed his speed and drew alongside the boy, who was moving fast.

There was no obvious sign of any swag, but who knows what his pockets were filled with. Deciding to be a good neighbour and challenge the lad, Will leaned across the passenger seat to the open window. 'You're out late, sonny.'

The boy turned and gave him a look that could have cut through graphite.

It wasn't a boy. It was the daughter of the couple who lived opposite him. Or at least he thought she was their daughter. That and the mother of those two young children he saw occasionally. He hadn't spotted a father to the boy and girl, but who knows what went for a father these days. With the engine purring, he pursued her down the road – she'd made no attempt to slow her pace, let alone stop. 'I'm sorry,' he called out of the window, 'it was the cap. It makes you look like a boy.'

Still she didn't stop, and as she turned into the drive of number twenty without a word, he had to accept that his apology had compounded the insult.

As he got ready for bed he wondered what she'd been doing out so late, especially as, if his guesswork was correct, she'd emerged from his side of the road, where the footpath was. Surely she hadn't been down to the canal in the darkness on her own.

He knew next to nothing about his neighbours; he'd been so busy since moving in he hadn't had time to get to know them. Perhaps now, after his monumental gaffe, he ought to make more of an effort to be sociable.

Chapter Eleven

It was the last week of August and with only six days to go until the start of the autumn term, Harriet and her parents, plus Carrie and Joel, were meeting the headmistress of Kings Melford Junior School. There was an air of forced jollity as they drove the short distance and Harriet suspected that the children could see right through Bob and Eileen's attempts to reassure them that there was nothing to worry about. Joel's anxiety, as he twisted his silky round his hand and sucked his thumb, was all too evident; he hadn't eaten much breakfast and he'd wet the bed again last night. Perhaps it was a mistake to keep lifting him out of Carrie's bed and putting him in his own.

Privately Harriet was counting the days until the children would go to school. Once they were there, it would give her and her parents some much-needed breathing space, but more importantly it meant that Harriet could make a start on finding a job. She'd promised her parents she wouldn't do this until the children were settled at school and the pressure was off them all. There had been talk of Carrie attending school part way through the summer term, but rightly or wrongly, they'd decided against it. Splitting the two children at such a crucial time hadn't seemed a good idea.

Bob parked in an allotted visitor's space next to one marked 'Headmistress'. The school was just as Harriet remembered it. An expanse of depressing dark brickwork that shouted from its slate roof tops that you entered at your peril. The Victorians had a lot to answer for when it came to designing schools. Had they deliberately gone all out to make them seem like prisons? But despite its daunting appearance, both Harriet and Felicity had enjoyed their time there.

'Well,' said Eileen, when they were all out of the car and she was fussing with Carrie's skirt, which had got rucked up during the journey. 'Here we are then.' The breezy note was again too forced and completely at odds with the look on Carrie's face as she glanced up at the forbidding building.

'It looks horrible,' she said.

Yesterday, in a rare moment of loquacity, Carrie had talked about her old school – not the one in Newcastle, which she'd hardly got to know, but the previous one in Exeter. She'd told them how new and modern it was, and how there were carpets in the classrooms and hamster cages and fish tanks in the corridors.

'Well,' said Bob, echoing his wife. 'Shall we go in?'

Neither child moved.

Impatient to get on, Harriet took hold of their hands. 'Okay kiddos, let's get this over and done with.' She dragged them through the doors, ignoring the dead-weight reluctance in their bodies and the look of alarm on her parents' faces.

The headmistress, all bustling efficiency, greeted them with a handshake. Her name was Mrs Thompson. She was a plump woman in her mid fifties with a shaggy perm and gold, hooped earrings. She was wearing a navy jacket that was slightly too large for her, the cuffs dangling down as though she might one day grow into it. Pearly pink toenails peeped through open-toed sandals. Her lipstick was the same colour. 'And you two must be Carrie and Joel,' she said with excruciating cheerfulness, pushing her shaggy head into their faces. 'We're all looking forward to having you here with us.'

Carrie gave the woman a cool stare. Joel edged away.

'And now that you're such a big boy starting school,' she laughed, fixing her attention on Joel and giving his grubby silky a disapproving look, 'you'll be able to leave that at home, won't you? Now then,' she continued to the adults, still using the same patronising tone, 'I thought we'd have a little look around the school, and then stop for a little chat in my office.'

Where I might give you a *little* slap, you irritating woman, thought Harriet as they fell in behind her. She wished now that they'd got this over and done with sooner, but not wanting to rush the children into too much too soon, her parents had said that so long as Carrie and Joel had places lined up at the school, having a look around it could wait. It was immaterial anyway. This was the school they were going to, whether they liked the look of it or not. It was more or less on their doorstep, and there was also the link with their mother, which Harriet hoped would mean something to them, maybe even help them settle in.

She certainly hoped this was the case, because precious little else she was seeing gave her cause to hope that Carrie and Joel would feel settled. Reports of schools being woefully under-funded were always in the newspapers, but here was the reality. The building looked as if nothing had been spent on it since Harriet and Felicity had been pupils here. The corridors were just as gloomy and echoey. The walls were all bare and Mrs Thompson was currently explaining the reason for this. 'It's always a bad time to see a school between terms, but once we're underway next week, these walls will be beautifully decorated with children's artwork. The place will really come alive.' She pushed open a door and suddenly turned on Carrie. 'This will be your classroom.'

They dutifully trooped in and stood to admire the book corner, the freshly painted blackboard and the groups of desks. Harriet didn't know exactly how old she'd been, but this had been her classroom at some stage. She could remember being told off for talking when she should have been listening to the teacher read out some dreary poem. She'd been made to stand at the front of the class and recite her seven times tables. She'd recited them in seconds flat only to be reprimanded again for showing off. She then remembered who it was she'd been talking to: Miles

McKendrick. In those days he hadn't enjoyed English; like her he'd preferred maths and fiddling around with jars of water and food dyes in their makeshift science lessons. Ironically, he'd gone on to study English at university, as his brother Dominic had done, and he now ran Novel Ways, the bookshop over in Maywood. She kept meaning to get in touch with him, but since she'd moved back permanently the days had just slipped by. She was slightly hurt that he hadn't been in touch himself. His mother, Freda, had mentioned to Eileen something about him being away on holiday, so maybe that was it. She decided to give him a ring. Having an old friend around would go a long way to cheering her up.

Realising that the others were moving on to the next part of the tour, she followed behind. When they were back out into the corridor, she felt a hand slip through hers. It was Joel, and clearly something was bothering him; his eyes were brimming with tearful misery. Her heart sank. What now? 'You okay, Joel?' It was a stupid question, but what else could she say? But then he did something that inexplicably made her throat constrict. He leant against her, his head resting on her side, his face hidden. She knew he was trying hard not to cry. Leaving the others to go on without them, she prised him away from her and bent down to him. 'What is it, Joel?'

He raised his head. 'I want to go home,' he whispered, his lower lip trembling.

'Right now?'

He nodded.

'Any particular reason why?'

His eyes flickered to the far end of the corridor where the headmistress was opening another door.

'You don't like Mrs Thompson?'

He shook his head. Tears spilled down his cheeks. He buried his face in her silky.

Harriet had to steel herself. She hated it when he cried. It made her want to cry too. 'That's okay,' she said quietly. 'Promise you won't tell anyone, but I don't like Mrs

Thompson either. The good news is that you'll hardly see anything of her. She's a headmistress, which means she has to sit behind a big desk every day and write lots of boring letters and ring the bell for break-time and lessons.'

He peered over the top of his silky. 'Really?'

'For sure. Come on, we'd better catch up with the others.'

She should have felt relieved that yet another crisis had been averted, but all she felt was exhaustion. Was that how it was going to be for the next thirteen and a half years? Thirteen and a half long years until Joel was eighteen and legally no longer her responsibility. She'd get less for murder.

That evening, and while her mother was upstairs supervising the children's bedtime, Harriet helped her father clear away supper. The children were now at least eating and the return of their appetites did mean Harriet and her parents had one less worry.

The subject of school hadn't been discussed during the meal, yet it was clear it had to be very much on Carrie's and Joel's minds. Tomorrow Harriet was taking them to buy the necessary items of school uniform.

As the last of the plates was stacked in the dishwasher, Bob said, 'Harriet, I want to talk to you.'

It sounded ominous and at once Harriet was worried that it was about her mother. Was Mum's ME getting worse? 'What is it, Dad?'

'Don't look so worried. Come and sit down with me.'

She did as he said.

Sitting opposite her, he said, 'I don't want you to take this the wrong way, and your mother and I certainly aren't criticising you, but—'

The 'but' hung in the air.

'But what?'

He took a fortifying breath. 'Your mother and I are worried. We think that perhaps you're—'

Another hesitant pause.

Tired? Depressed? Thoroughly cheesed off that her life had hit the skids so spectacularly? Not to mention that she was homeless. Jobless. Boyfriendless. No, strike that one from the record. Spencer didn't come into it. Compared to everything else, his cowardly selfishness didn't even register.

'We think you're a little too hard on the children.'

Harriet sat back in her chair. What the hell did that mean?

'Oh, dear, we knew you wouldn't take it well. I told your mother—'

'Dad, it's not a matter of taking it well; it's a matter of understanding. I haven't a clue what I'm being accused of.'

'We're not accusing you of anything.'

'Sounds like it to me. So come on, tell me what I've done wrong.'

'It's your manner. You're so short with them. So brusque. We're worried that you're scaring them. Adding to their problems. There's a chance you might be making things worse. Especially for Joel.'

Just then the telephone rang. With a look of relief, Bob went to answer it.

Left on her own, Harriet stared at the table. The injustice of her father's remarks made her head throb, and claustrophobia crushed in on her. She stood up abruptly. She had to get out of the house. Within seconds, she was hurtling down the drive and across the road, heading for the footpath and the canal. As a teenager it was where she had always gone when she was annoyed or upset. The soothing stillness of the water usually calmed her.

Right now she was far from calm. Boiling over with fury, she could hardly breathe at the unfairness of it. After all the sacrifices she had made, her parents had the nerve to criticise her. How could they turn on her? Was it her fault that she wasn't the maternal type? Not for the first time she wondered why the hell her sister had thought she would be any good at raising her children.

At the end of the footpath she was about to go right but

changed her mind when she saw a row of fishermen, their lines cast, their nets and wicker baskets in place. Instead she turned left. From here it was a twenty-five-minute walk into town, and to the nearest decent pub, The Navigation. Drinking her anger into submission could be the answer, but having left the house without any money, she was resigned to walking it out of her system. She ground the path beneath her, her arms swinging, her hands tightly clenched into fists.

And if her parents really thought she was doing such a bad job, then perhaps she ought to go back to Oxford and leave them to it! How would that suit them? Or perhaps they wished it had been her who'd died. Doubtless that would have been easier all round, especially for her father. She'd always known that Felicity had been the special daughter for him, the one he idolised. It had never bothered Harriet before, this preference, but it hurt now, knowing that her death would have had dramatically less impact. Let's face it, she'd been dispensable; no ties, no commitments, no responsibilities. Well, all that had changed. Now she had commitments coming out of her ears. It felt as if she had the full weight of the world on her shoulders.

She was so deeply locked into her thoughts that she didn't notice the man sitting on the bench until she was almost upon him. It was their new neighbour, and with his legs stretched out in front of him, he was drinking from a bottle of beer. He smiled at her over the top of his sunglasses, which were set low down on his nose. 'You look different without the cap,' he said.

A week had passed since he'd mistaken her for a boy late at night. She had been too upset at the time to stop and put him right, having just spent the previous half-hour on the towpath trying to walk off the fear that she was destined to live out the rest of her days cooped up with her parents and two small children. She'd learned that afternoon that completion had taken place on her flat. The finality of it had left her feeling trapped and isolated. The very last cord had been cut. She now had no reason to return to Oxford.

And there hadn't been so much as an email or text message from Spencer – which shouldn't have surprised her; he was probably glad to be rid of her. Far worse, though, was the anger she suddenly felt towards her sister. Why did Felicity have to be so careless and die! If only she and Jeff hadn't gone out that night, they'd still be alive and Harriet wouldn't be lumbered with picking up the pieces. Appalled at her train of thought, Harriet didn't know who she hated more: the teenage boy who had done this terrible thing to them all, or herself.

Even if Harriet had had the nerve to blank their new neighbour and walk on by, she wouldn't have been able to. He was now on his feet, effectively blocking her path. 'Hi,' he said, removing his sunglasses and pushing back his hair. 'I'm Will Hart. I expect the neighbourhood's rife with gossip about me, but I'd like to put the record straight and say that it's all untrue.'

She was in no mood for small talk, but forced herself to say, 'How long are you taking the lease on for? The usual six months?'

'Actually, I've bought the place.'

'I didn't know it was for sale.'

'It didn't get a chance to go on the market. The previous owners are clients of a friend of mine and when they told Marty they'd decided to settle abroad, I nipped in sharpish and made them an offer. I don't suppose you'd like to join me in a drink,' – he held up his bottle of beer as though indicating what sort of drink – 'so that I can pick your brains about the neighbourhood? I've been so busy since moving in that I haven't had a chance to get to know anyone.'

Small talk over a beer? No. It was out of the question. With her parents' criticism still ringing in her ears, she needed to be alone.

'It would also give me the opportunity to apologise properly for the other night,' he added.

She remembered her earlier desire to drink her anger into

submission. Imagining herself gulping down a cold beer, she wavered.

'I have wine if you'd prefer. Or maybe a soft drink.'

All resolve gone, she said, 'Thank you, a beer would be nice.'

Down to his last two bottles in the fridge, Will snapped off the lids and put them on a tray, along with a glass – she was probably a refined sort who wouldn't dream of drinking straight from the bottle – and went back outside to the garden. He hoped she was feeling a bit less spiky now. When she'd appeared on the towpath she'd had a face like thunder. He wondered what she was so angry about. There was no mistaking her for a boy today. Her hair, which must have been tied up under her baseball cap that night last week, was shoulder-length and framed a small, pensive face with wide cheekbones.

'Here we go, then,' he said, pushing open the gate and joining her on the bench. He set the tray down on the grass and handed her a beer and the glass.

She shook her head. 'The bottle's fine.'

Amused he'd got that wrong about her, he wondered if she would prove him wrong on anything else. So far his guesswork told him that she was in her late twenties and he'd put money on a smile from her being rarer than an eclipse. She was small and delicately built (his mother would describe her as sparrow-boned), and dressed in close-fitting flared jeans. Her foot was tapping the ground – the knee going like a piston – and he suspected she was one of those high-energy people, who are always on the move, always looking for a way to wear themselves out. She needs to learn how to chill, he thought.

Watching her take a long, thirsty swig of her beer, he said, 'Can I ask the name of the person with whom I'm drinking?'

Without looking at him, she said, 'Harriet. Harriet Swift.'

'Well, Harriet Swift, it's good to meet you. Am I right in

thinking that you and your children live with your parents in the house directly opposite me?'

She turned round sharply. Blue-grey eyes stared back at him with laser strength. 'They're not my children. They're my niece and nephew.'

Ah, so that was it. The grandchildren were staying with the grandparents. Lucky them. 'So where are their parents? Whooping it up on holiday somewhere hot and exotic?' From the way her eyes narrowed, he knew at once he'd said something wrong. The foot had stopped tapping. The knee was still.

When she answered him, her voice was eerily flat. 'They were killed in a car crash in April. The children's mother was my sister. My only sister.'

Horrified by his blunder, he said, 'I . . . I'm sorry. I had no idea.'

'Please don't say you're sorry. You don't know me and you didn't know Felicity. So no platitudes. However well-meant.'

All he could think to say was, 'How old are the children?'

'Nine and four and a half.'

'Nice ages. I remember them well.'

She said nothing, just drank her beer and resumed tapping her foot.

'I have children,' he said, 'older than that, but no matter what age they are, they're still hopelessly young and vulnerable through parents' eyes. Mine live with their mother in Maywood.' Aware that her silence was making him ramble nervously, he tried another question. 'What are their names, your nephew and niece?'

'Carrie and Joel.'

She reminded him of a hedgehog curling itself up into a ball when under attack. Her clipped answers told him she didn't want to discuss the matter any further, that if he knew what was good for him, he'd back off. But he never did know when to back off. Watching her out of the corner of his eye, he acknowledged to himself that he'd done a first-class job of putting his foot in it so far. Time to change tack to a safer line of questioning – something innocuous and guaranteed to be non-controversial. 'I'm in the antique trade,' he said. 'What kind of work do you do?'

'I'm a computer programmer. And if you really want to know, I've given up a bloody good job to take care of Carrie and Joel, only to have my parents now accuse me of adding to their problems. Apparently I scare the children. How's that for gratitude! I've given up my flat, my career, my boyfriend, and for what?'

Was there nothing he could get right with this woman? He wasn't surprised she scared the kids; she scared the hell out of him.

Chapter Twelve

For days afterwards, Harriet felt the embarrassment of losing her composure in front of a virtual stranger. She had so very nearly cried. Had he realised that? Presumably he had. 'I'm not the best of company right now,' she'd said, on her feet, suddenly desperate to escape. She'd hastily mumbled some kind of goodbye and retraced the way she'd come, then took the path she should have gone in the first place, picking her way through the fishermen's paraphernalia. She walked and walked until the light began to fade and the evening air grew thick with insects and the sweet smell of dusk. Her chest began to tighten and, knowing she needed her inhaler from her bag in her bedroom, she turned for home.

Naturally, her parents told her she'd overreacted. 'All you need to do is be more patient with the children,' her mother had said. 'Particularly with Joel. He's such a gentle little boy. Miss Fryer says he misses the—'

'Oh, so now you're throwing Miss Fryer at me?' she'd retaliated. 'As if it isn't obvious what the children miss!'

Miss Fryer was the children's counsellor. For the last two months, every week Harriet had driven the children to her office, where they were encouraged to share their feelings with a woman they hardly knew. While they were doing that, Harriet sat outside in a small waiting room, idly flicking through magazines to kill the time.

'For goodness' sake, just try to be a little less stern with them,' her father had joined in, his voice sharper than she was used to hearing. 'We know it's not easy for you, Harriet. And we do appreciate all that you're doing, but snapping at Carrie for leaving her socks on the sofa won't help anyone.'

Then why are you snapping at me? she'd thought indignantly.

That had been three days ago, and since then Harriet had tried hard to do what her parents had suggested. But it wasn't easy. She kept catching herself wondering if what she'd just said or done with the children came under the category of being 'stern'. If she asked Carrie to put her empty cereal bowl in the dishwasher, was that a request too far? And if she called up the stairs, as she was about to now, to tell them to get a move on, would that be tantamount to child abuse?

'Come on, you two, I haven't got all day!'

Seconds later, the sound of the toilet flushing could be heard, followed by scuffling footsteps across the landing. Carrie led the way with Joel closely behind. 'Did you wash your hands?' Harriet asked them.

Joel held his out for inspection. 'We used Grandma's nice squirty soap.'

'Yes, I can smell it from here. Is there any left? Or have you splattered it—' She stopped herself short, remembering she was supposed to be St Harriet, the Patron Saint of the Meek and bloody Mild. 'Mm . . . well done you two,' she added. 'Right then, let's say goodbye to Grandma and get going. We've got a lot to do.' In her jeans pocket was a lengthy list of items they needed for the start of term: lunch boxes, notepads, biros, pencils, felt-tip pens, sharpeners, rubbers, glue sticks.

Harriet's mother was in the sitting room with Dora. The coffee table and the floor were covered with items of school uniform waiting to have name tags sewn onto them.

'We're off now, Mum. You're sure there's nothing we can get you?'

Eileen shook her head. 'I can't think of anything, darling. How about you, Dora? Anything Harriet can get you?'

'No, but I have something here for the children.' After a brief rummage in her handbag, she pulled out her purse.

'Here you are, you two.' She gave them each a couple of pound coins. 'You can't go shopping without a little something in your pockets, can you now?'

'You needn't have done that, Dora,' Eileen said when the front door had been shut and the house was quiet.

'I know, but I wanted to. They're such dear little children. Whenever I think about what must be going through their heads, well, I could just weep.'

Eileen picked up a bright-red sweatshirt and threaded her needle. All those years of labelling items of school uniform and here she was doing it all over again. She could remember doing Felicity's first uniform. She had sat up late into the night taking in the waistband of a pleated skirt feeling both proud and sad. It was such a milestone occasion, one's first child going to school. Felicity had been so excited she couldn't sleep, but in the morning she had lost her nerve and didn't want to go. She'd sat on the bottom step of the stairs and refused to put on her blazer. That was in the days of proper school uniforms. Not these cheap, foreign-made polyester sweatshirts that wouldn't last a term in the washing machine. After some gentle cajoling, Felicity had slipped on her blazer and they'd set off for school. In the end it was Eileen who had been more upset at the point of parting and on the way home, hiding her tears from Harriet, she had answered her youngest daughter's barrage of questions. What time would Felicity be home? How many hours was that? Would it be dark when they went back for her? Would she and Felicity have time to play together before bed? And how long would they have to play?

Even at such a young age, Harriet had wanted hard factual evidence before letting anything rest. She still did, which was why it had been so difficult trying to explain to her that she was being too sharp with the children. They had no actual evidence to give her that this was the case, only the fear that if she carried on as she was, Carrie and Joel might withdraw into themselves even further. Felicity had been a loving and affectionate mother and while Eileen knew no one could ever take her place, she and Bob, *and* Harriet, had a duty to offer as much love and tenderness as they could. It was the only thing that would help them to come to terms with their loss.

From across the room, Dora said, 'Now that we're alone, I can tell you all about last night.'

Eileen looked up from her sewing, thinking again how incongruous it was to see her friend with a needle and thread in her hands. 'Goodness, Dora, what have you been up to now?'

'Put the kettle on and I'll tell you. No, second thoughts, I'll make us some tea while you carry on here. I'm hopeless at sewing – all fingers and thumbs. I'm doing about one item to your five.'

'You haven't had enough practice, that's your trouble. It's a miracle I've got you helping in the first place.'

Dora had never had children and Eileen privately thought this was one of her friend's big regrets in life. Her first husband had left her for his secretary after eleven years of marriage and then her second husband had died six years ago. He'd been the love of Dora's life but with an admirable show of spirit she had picked herself up and bulldozed her way through her grief. Eileen could only hope that she and Bob would be able to do the same.

Dora was the only woman Eileen knew who had had cosmetic surgery, but her real claim to fame was that during her twenties she had been a model and became the 'legs' of a leading brand of tights and stockings. Her legs were seen on billboards, in magazines and of course, on the packets themselves. She hadn't made a fabulous amount of money, not like the models of today, but it had given her an independence a lot of women in those days never had. But for all her independence, Dora, at the age of sixty-two, couldn't imagine life without a man in it, and in her search for husband number three she had joined numerous dating agencies and answered scores of Lonely Hearts ads – always in the posh papers, like the *Telegraph* or *The Times*. Some of the men she'd been out with had been quite pleasant, but some had been absolute no-hopers. But after each failed date or brief relationship, Dora always bounced back smiling. She was one of life's great survivors and always believed that her Prince Charming was just around the corner. 'What I need,' she often told Eileen. 'is someone steady like Bob.'

Of course, Dora had no idea about Bob's affairs all those years ago and Eileen would never dream of telling her; that would be too disloyal. Every marriage had its secrets and Eileen wasn't prepared to divulge hers, not even to a good friend like Dora. What would be the point?

She reached for another name tag and thought of Bob. With each day that passed he was becoming more cool and distant. In bed at night he felt a million miles from her. Without kissing her goodnight, he'd switch off his lamp and lie on his side with his face turned away. It was useless asking him if he was all right, because she knew he wasn't. Which of them was? Things could never be as they once were, but Felicity was dead and no amount of grieving would bring her back. But Bob didn't seem able to move on. It was as if Felicity had died yesterday, not nearly five months ago. There were times when Eileen believed that Bob resented her because she was coping better than he was. But she was only coping because she knew she had to.

It had been the same three years ago when she'd suddenly fallen ill with a mystery virus. She'd woken one morning with a violent headache and had gone to work at the Oxfam shop as normal, but by lunchtime she was back at home and in bed. She was still there when Bob came home from work, by which time she suspected she was coming down with flu. Four days later she was no better and barely had the energy to sit up and eat. It was six months before ME was diagnosed and she was forced to change her way of life, accepting that some days her legs would feel like jelly and her back would ache so much at night that it would keep her awake. She had to learn to pace herself, to use efficiently what little energy she had. She had been prescribed a low dose of Prozac to keep her emotions on an even keel too.

'Tea's up,' announced Dora.

Rousing herself, Eileen made room on the table for the tray and, putting aside her sewing, she said, 'So, Dora, would I be right in thinking it was another date last night?'

Dora poured the tea, took her cup and saucer back to her armchair and once she was settled, knees and ankles together, she said, 'I've joined The Soirée Club.'

'Heavens, what's that? It sounds like something Hyacinth Bouquet would join. Do you have to give smart candlelit dinners?'

Dora laughed. 'As good as. Every other week there's a dinner party held in the house of one of the club's members and you simply sign up for whichever one you want to go to.'

'Does that mean you all have to take your turn?'

'Yes.'

'But what if you can't cook?'

'Like me, you mean?' Dora was known for her Marks and Spencer microwave meals for one. 'No problem. We're given a list of caterers we can use. As you'd expect, the gentlemen tend to use that service more than the ladies.'

'It sounds expensive.'

Dora stirred her tea. 'As I've always said, what cost the price of a good man?'

What cost indeed, thought Eileen.

Annoyed that she couldn't get everything they needed in Kings Melford, Harriet drove on to Maywood. The woman in the shoe shop had all but laughed in her face when she'd asked if they had any plimsolls. 'We sold out of them weeks ago,' she'd said. 'You could try Woolies; they might have a few pairs left.' But the Back to School racks and shelves in Woolworth's were practically bare. Another time and Harriet would know not to leave these things to the last minute. How long had it taken her sister to learn these tricks?

By the time they'd driven to Maywood, Joel had fallen asleep. His flushed cheeks were puffed out, and his head was tilted so far forward his chin was almost resting on his chest. It seemed a shame to disturb him. But it had to be done. Harriet called his name softly and as she unclipped his seatbelt, he stirred. With his eyes still closed, he reached out to her. 'Can I have a drink, please, Mummy?'

Harriet froze. She caught Carrie's intake of breath. 'I'll get you a drink when we've done the shopping, Joel,' she said in a tight voice.

His eyes slowly opened. They were dark with sleepy confusion. But giving him no time to dwell on his mistake, she lifted him out of his seat and he stood wobbling by her side as she hooked her bag over her shoulder and locked the car. 'Right,' she said, taking his hand, 'bring on your plimsolls, Maywood!'

'Who are you talking to?' Carrie's face was scornful.

'Myself as much as anyone. Don't you ever do that?'

'Not out loud.'

'Perhaps you should. It helps clear the mind.'

If only it was that simple, Harriet thought as they tripped along Crown Street towards Fuller's. Fuller's was the kind of old-fashioned shoe shop that stored most of its limited stock in shelves above the displays, and as they pushed open the door, they looked up to see an elderly woman balanced on a stepladder, sorting through a column of boxes. Some things never change, thought Harriet, remembering the countless times she and Felicity had been brought here by their mother to buy sensible school shoes – boring black, lace-ups. There were no other customers about and, not wanting to waste time browsing the shelves, Harriet asked the woman if she had any plimsolls.

'You've left it a bit late, haven't you?'

Harriet gritted her teeth. 'So I keep being told.'

The woman came nimbly down the stepladder. 'What size are you after?'

'Size one and—' But Harriet got no further.

Having eyed the measuring device in front of the row of

96

chairs, Carrie had kicked off her shoes. 'I'd like my feet measured, please,' she said.

'Carrie, we know exactly what size you are.'

'That's all right, dear, I don't mind measuring her. It's best to get these things right. We don't want her coming last in a race because she was wearing the wrong size, do we now?'

'But you do have some plimsolls?' Harriet couldn't bear to go through the palaver of having Carrie's feet measured only to be told there wasn't a single plimsoll to be had. Though why she should worry about a few lost minutes was beyond her. She'd lost the whole of her life; half an hour in a timewarp shoe shop was neither here nor there.

'Oh yes, we still have some stock left,' the woman said with a smile.

Joel tugged her sleeve.

'Can I have my feet measured too?'

Twenty minutes later they emerged from the shop with the children each carrying a plastic bag. Relieved that she could cross the last item off her list, Harriet said, 'Let's have that drink now, shall we?' She thought they'd earned it. She also thought she'd earned the right to a treat and so took the children into Novel Ways where she could have not only a caffé latte but also a rare, self-indulgent browse among the bookshelves afterwards. She hoped Miles would be about: she still hadn't got around to ringing him.

They queued up for their drinks, then found themselves a table. They'd only been there a minute or two – long enough for the children to have messed about with the sachets of sugar and spill some milk – when a voice said, 'Hello Harriet.'

It was Miles, looking his usual hurried self: carrying a stack of paperbacks, a pen stuck behind an ear, a piece of ripped paper sticking out from his shirt pocket. He was the only person Harriet had ever known who walked as fast as she did. They'd always marched on ahead together, leaving Dominic and Felicity trailing in their wake. 'Hello, Miles,' she said warmly. 'You look busy.'

He rolled his eyes. 'Tell me about it.' Then more awkwardly: 'I've been meaning to ring you for ages.'

She shrugged. 'Same here.'

'Mum and Dad told me you were back on a permanent basis now. Is that true?'

'It was the only answer.'

His gaze flickered over the children and Harriet was prompted to say something to bring them into the conversation. There were any number of memory joggers she could give them, like 'You remember Miles; he was at your parents' funeral,' or, 'You remember Miles; you met him most years when your parents came back to Cheshire for Christmas,' but what she said was, 'You remember Miles, don't you? His parents live in Maple Drive.'

Joel said nothing, just continued to suck hard on the straw of his milkshake, but Carrie looked thoughtful. 'Is this your bookshop?' she said.

'Yes, it is,' Miles replied with a smile. 'Do you like it?'

She frowned. 'I don't know. I haven't seen enough of it yet.'

'That wasn't very polite of you,' Harriet said when Miles had been called away to answer the telephone.

'I was only telling the truth. You're always saying we should be honest.'

Touché, thought Harriet. But then Carrie said something that surprised her.

'Did Mum bring us here?'

Joel stopped sucking on his milkshake and peered at Harriet beneath his eyelashes.

'I don't know,' she said carefully. 'She might have. Can you remember her bringing you here?'

Carrie lifted her shoulders and let them drop. 'Maybe it was another bookshop.'

This was as close as Carrie had got to openly discussing her mother, and Harriet didn't know whether she ought to pursue the matter. Was it enough that Carrie had said as much as she had, or was it a tentative signal that she was prepared to go further if given the necessary encouragement? But the moment was lost when Joel said, 'I need the loo.'

They hurriedly finished their drinks and after the obligatory trip to the loos, Harriet showed Carrie and Joel to the children's area. She told them to stay there until she came back for them, then went to find something to read for herself. Something totally absorbing in which she could lose herself. She was just picking the latest Tracy Chevalier off the shelf when Miles appeared again. This time he was empty-handed, though there was still a pen sticking out from behind his ear – a tuft of hair sticking up too – and an air of urgency about him. He was often taken for a young student, as she herself was, and she knew it irritated him, especially if he wasn't taken seriously. He had once tried to grow a beard to look older, but with his fair hair and smooth-skinned complexion, the attempt had taken for ever and had provoked people to ask repeatedly if he was unwell.

'Harriet, I don't suppose—' he broke off and swallowed nervously. 'And you would say if you thought it was inappropriate, what with Felicity and everything—' Again he paused, this time pushing a hand through his short hair and dislodging the pen. He picked it up and shoved it clumsily into his back pocket. 'Look, I just wondered if you'd like to go for a drink. That's if you're not too tied up with the children.'

Despite the reference to Felicity, and the painful awkwardness in Miles's face, she smiled. 'You mean a grown-up drink? In a pub, or a wine bar? A proper drink that doesn't include straws and endless trips to the toilet?'

He relaxed and smiled back. 'I guess that is what I mean.'

'Then you're on. When were you thinking?'

'How about Wednesday evening?'

'Perfect. I can't wait.'

And the extraordinary thing was; she meant it. For the first time in weeks, she felt she had something to look forward to.

Chapter Thirteen

While Eileen was busy with Dora, and Harriet was out shopping with the children, Bob was acting on an impulse he wasn't sure would be greeted with universal approval. Eileen would probably question the extra cost and work involved, but he didn't care, this was something for him.

He stared down at the abandoned one-year-old wire-haired fox terrier in the cage and saw not a rescue dog in need of a good home, but the means by which he would be able to plan his own escape. Walking a dog twice a day would give him the ideal excuse to be out of the house. It would give him the chance to be on his own. To think his own thoughts. To be himself.

'I'll take this one,' he said to the young woman who was patiently waiting for him to make up his mind. She'd let him inspect five dogs in all, but she'd said that this one would be the best around children, and had a lively but loving nature. As though understanding that he was about to be freed from the depressing dog refuge, the terrier got up and wagged its short tail.

The money side of things was soon dealt with, and using the tatty, worn-out collar and lead supplied, Bob walked the dog to the car. The terrier stayed close to his heels and Bob felt oddly comfortable with him at his side. Before Bob could decide whether to put him in the front or the back of the car, the dog decided for himself. In one easy movement he hopped up onto the driver's seat and then stepped across to the passenger seat. He sat back on his haunches, ears pricked, and looked steadily at Bob as if to say, Where to?

Home, was Bob's unspoken reply. If you can call it that, he added silently. Latterly, he'd started to feel a stranger there. More than that, a stranger in his own life. Everything seemed to revolve around the children. Any conversation he had with Eileen usually began and ended with Carrie and Joel. He gripped the steering wheel, vaguely ashamed of this admission. He was being selfish, he knew. But he couldn't help it. He loved the children, as any grandparent would, yet the strain of having them under his feet every single minute of the day was getting to him, making him feel claustrophobic. He longed for the old days, when he could trot out that old grandparents' line about being able to spoil the little darlings with sweets and ice-cream, then hand them back before they were sick.

But, of course, what he really longed for was his daughter to be returned to him. Some might say that he should count his blessings, that he did at least have another daughter. In fact, someone had actually said that to him. He racked his brains to remember who it had been. Some well-thinking fool who didn't have a clue what they were talking about. As a parent you're not supposed to have a favourite amongst your children, but Felicity had always been special. She'd been an important turning point in his life. He had never felt so close to Eileen as he had when she'd first handed Felicity to him to hold. He didn't so much as look at another woman from that moment on. It was as though the purity of his newborn baby's life had rubbed off on him and turned him into a better person.

The two affairs he'd had still haunted him. He wasn't proud of it, and he didn't know what he'd do if Eileen ever found out. He'd gone to great lengths to cover his tracks, to keep her from being hurt. He'd never been so stupid as to leave till receipts lying around or to get up in the middle of the night to make a secret phone call, as someone at work said he'd done, only to learn that his wife had picked up the extension in the bedroom and heard every word.

As a salesman, he'd spent the vast majority of his working life on the road, travelling from town to town, city to city. The opportunity to play away from home had always been there, and compared to a lot of reps he knew, he'd been the model of good behaviour by having only two affairs. The first one had lasted less than six months and the second one, two years later, had gone on for nearly twelve months. Both of the women concerned had had no idea who or what he really was. He'd lied to them both, telling them he was recently separated and felt too raw to commit fully to anyone new so soon. It was behaviour of the very worst kind and he'd hated himself when he was at home lying in bed beside Eileen. Unable to sleep, he would promise himself it would stop, that there was too much at stake. But he was weak, and within days he would be figuring out when he'd be able to get away next. It was only when he was with these other women that the pain of what he and Eileen were going through lessened. It was in their arms that he could forget the sadness they were forced to endure each time they lost yet another baby.

On both occasions, the affairs had ended because of his conscience. Deep down he loved his wife and didn't want to hurt her. When she fell pregnant and for the first time managed to get beyond the five-month stage, he made a promise to himself. If this baby lived, he would never put temptation in his way again by spending a night apart from his wife.

It was a promise he stuck to and no matter where in the country he was sent, no matter how bad the weather, he always drove home to be with Eileen and the family he was so proud of.

His wasn't an exciting job, working for a firm that sold industrial cleaning equipment, but he'd been with the company since the start, when it had been little more than a Portakabin office and a lock-up, and over the years it had given him a decent living, security for his family, and stability. On his retirement, last year, the firm celebrated forty years of business and boasted over a hundred employees with an office in Birmingham as well as the original one in Chester. He'd been the first of the long-term employees to retire and had been nicknamed the Daddy of the team. Jim Clark, the managing director, had made an amusing speech on the day of his retirement, and had presented him with a set of garden furniture. It was good-quality stuff, solid teak – the sort, so Jim had said, that would live for ever if looked after carefully. These days Bob couldn't look at that garden furniture without thinking, what was the point in it living for ever? Who gave a damn if a bloody bench outlived you? And why could a bench go on living when his daughter couldn't?

Some of his colleagues had been at the funeral. They'd brought flowers and cards, but not the ability to look him in the eye. They made promises to give him a ring, to take him out for a drink. But the phone had never rung.

He swallowed hard, kept his eyes firmly on the road, clamping down on the pathetic loneliness. Still, it was better than the days when he felt an uncontrollable need to tear out his own guts.

Eileen seemed to be coping far better than he was. It was irrational, but her one-step-at-a-time attitude annoyed him, as though her steady recovery somehow trivialised his pain, or worse, trivialised Felicity's death. She seemed perfectly happy to muddle through the days, focusing on the children or worrying about Harriet's handling of them. She didn't seem to need to make sense of what had happened. Perhaps she had the right idea, because as far as he could see, it was a hopeless task. Maybe he should start taking Prozac like her and sleep his troubles away. He instantly felt guilty for this thought. It wasn't Eileen's fault that she needed to rest in the afternoon.

He was almost home when it occurred to him that some dog food might not be a bad idea. He pulled up onto the kerb outside Edna's and nipped inside. Edna was behind the counter, giving a group of young teenage girls the beady-eye treatment as they crowded round the magazines, giggling and chatting much too loudly. It was yet another reminder that it felt like only yesterday when Felicity and Harriet had been doing the same.

He found the pet-food shelves, made a random selection

and took them to the counter. The shop was quiet now; the girls had left. Edna surveyed the tins. 'Dog food, eh?'

'That's right. I decided we needed a dog to cheer us all up.' Sometimes it was easier simply to provide all the necessary information, thereby short-circuiting Edna's interrogation.

'That'll prove a costly business, then, won't it?'

It will if I continue to buy the food from here, he very nearly said.

Back outside, the girls were grouped around his car. They were ooh-ing and ah-ing at the dog, who seemed to be enjoying being the focus of attention – he was leaping about the car like a performing circus dog. All he needed was a pointy hat and a ruffle round his neck to complete the picture.

Bob drove the short distance home, and letting the dog out of the car but keeping it on the lead, he went round to the back of the house, bracing himself for Eileen's reaction.

September

Each player must accept the cards
life deals him or her.

But once they are in hand,
he or she alone must decide
how to play the cards
in order to win the game.

Voltaire

Chapter Fourteen

It was the start of the autumn term, and the school gate and playground were thronging with activity. The sight of so many children made Harriet shudder. She had a terrifying picture of Carrie and Joel making friends with every man jack of them and inviting them all home to tea. But looking down at Joel's petrified face, and the grim set of Carrie's jaw, it looked more likely they wouldn't make a single friend. They'd be lucky to survive, never mind socialise.

It had been agreed during tea yesterday that the job of taking the children to school for their first day would fall to Harriet. Her mother, while doling out yet another child-friendly meal of reheated shepherd's pie and peas, had suggested to Carrie and Joel that since it was their 'special day' they should choose who took them. 'We could all go if you like,' Eileen had added. Feeling silently relieved that this was one task that wouldn't fall to her – no way in the world would Carrie and Joel want their horribly scary aunt with them – Harriet had been astonished to hear Joel say, 'I want Harriet to come with us.'

Even Bob and Eileen had looked askance. 'How about you, Carrie?' Bob had said.

Stirring her plate of food, without looking up, Carrie had said, 'I'd like Harriet *and* Toby to take us.'

Joel's face brightened. 'Oh, I didn't think of him. Can Toby come as well?'

Coming home out of the blue with a dog was the best thing her father could have done for cheering up the children. Eileen wasn't keen, though, and had said the house was full enough as it was with so many to feed and keep clean. 'And what about Harriet's asthma?' she'd asked.

'Mum, you know it's pollen and mould spores I'm allergic to, not animals,' Harriet had told her. Stress could also bring it on, but she saw no reason to mention that.

But seeing how the children instantly connected with the dog, Eileen had soon relented. 'Oh, all right,' she'd said, 'he can stay. But I can tell you for nothing, it won't be me who'll take it for walks in the wind and rain.'

'That will be entirely my responsibility,' Bob had stepped in. 'I promise.'

Carrie had thought of the name Toby and they had all agreed that it suited the dog perfectly.

Toby had to be left behind in the car while Harriet and the children walked across the playground, because it was against the rules to bring him into school, much to Joel's disappointment. Harriet was convinced, knowing how cunning children could be, that Carrie and Joel had chosen her for the task as some sort of punishment. Their grandparents would have made a far better job of it; after all, they were the experts, having done it twice before.

They were greeted in the noisy corridor by a tall, elegant woman who claimed to be Carrie's teacher, Mrs Kennedy. Amidst the kerfuffle of screeching children and gossiping mothers, they were shown where to hang Carrie's PE bag, then pointed in the direction of Joel's classroom further down the corridor. It was probably for the best, but there was no appropriate moment to say goodbye. Mrs Kennedy swept Carrie away with her and there was nothing else for it but to get the next bit over and done with. Joel was going to cry; Harriet just knew it. And she had no idea how to prevent it.

There were lots of small children milling around outside Joel's classroom; Harriet noted that one or two faces were not dissimilar from Joel's. Presumably they were in the same boat – their first day at school. Others, the confident, cocky ones who were charging on ahead to the classroom were, she imagined, old hands, having been in some kind of nursery class. They'd probably already sized up the potential losers who could be bullied into drug-running for them. Not funny, she told herself. There were one or two mothers who looked in bad shape, their faces hanging grimly onto what they doubtless thought was an encouraging smile. Harriet remembered Felicity saying how upset she'd been when she'd waved Carrie goodbye for the first time. Apparently she'd driven home in floods of tears and had spent the day playing with Joel, counting the hours until it was time to collect her.

Feeling the pressure of Joel's hand in hers, Harriet glanced down at him. His eyes were pools of tear-filled wretchedness. Once again she thought of Felicity, and how good she would have been in this situation. She would have known exactly what to do and say.

All the other children had disappeared inside the classroom, and now that the corridor was empty, Harriet spotted Joel's name above a coat peg. 'Here,' she said, 'we'd better hang up your plimsoll bag. Joel?'

He shook his head and pressed the bag to his chest.

'Come on, Joel, hand it over or we'll be late and in trouble before we've even started.'

Still he wouldn't do as she said. She bent down to him and he leaned into her. With his head resting against her forehead, he dropped the plimsoll bag and flung his arms around her neck. He held her tightly. So tightly he nearly pushed her backwards and onto the floor. He wasn't crying, but somehow that made it worse. She knew that when he was silent he was most upset. All she could think to do was put her own arms around him. It was then, with a shock of tenderness, as she felt the trembling within his small body, that she realised this was the first time she could recall ever really hugging either of the children.

'Hello there. I'm Miss Rawlinson and you must be Joel Knight. I was wondering what had happened to you.'

Disentangling herself from Joel's vice-like grip, Harriet stood up to greet her nephew's teacher. 'I'm afraid he's a little nervous,' she explained, at the same time taking in the woman, or rather the girl. Miss Rawlinson looked no older than a school-leaver. With her wide grin, her hair in high bunches, her gingham, puff-sleeved top, denim skirt and black PVC boots, she resembled one of those overactive children's television presenters that Carrie and Joel found so unaccountably absorbing. Surely she wasn't old enough to be in charge of so many children? Especially a child like Joel who would need extra support and encouragement. Suddenly feeling twice her age and unexpectedly reluctant to hand over her nephew, Harriet put a protective hand on his shoulder.

'Is this yours, Joel?' Miss Rawlinson asked, picking up the plimsoll bag.

Burying his face into Harriet's legs, Joel ignored her.

'Why don't you come and meet all your new friends? Everyone's waiting to meet you.'

His head moved from side to side.

'Don't you want to make lots of new friends?'

Another shake of his head.

'I think that's a no,' Harriet said. 'Perhaps we ought to give him a break and try again tomorrow?' She couldn't believe what she'd just said, but it seemed the simplest and kindest thing to do. His misery was too much for her.

But the young girl shook her head. 'It would be a terrible mistake to give in to him,' she said. Then lowering her voice to a confidential murmur, she added, 'It's usually better if the mother just walks away.'

Her voice equally low, and leaning over Joel, Harriet said, 'It's usually better if the mother isn't dead. My name's Miss Swift; I'm his aunt and legal guardian and I'd appreciate a little more thought on your part towards my nephew. Maybe you should acquaint yourself with his background.'

The girl looked flustered. Down on Joel's level once more, Harriet looked into his face. 'Joel,' she whispered, 'you've got to help me out here. I want you to be really brave and give today your best shot. I'll be back later this afternoon, and . . . and I promise I'll bring Toby with me.'

Pressing her mouth close to his ear, she said, 'What's more, I promise to bring him right into the playground so all your new friends can see him. I'll even have your silky waiting for you in the car.' She leaned back. 'Do we have a deal?'

After a lengthy pause, he nodded. But only just.

'Shake on it?'

He put out his hand.

'Okay, and remember, a deal's a deal. You make it through the whole day, and I'll be here later with Toby.'

She straightened up again and though it seemed all wrong, she handed Joel into the care of this complete stranger. She walked away, not trusting herself to look back.

Passing Carrie's classroom on her way out, she took a moment to glance through the glass panes of the door. She spotted her niece straight away. She was the one chewing on the end of her plait and staring absently out of the window. It could have been Harriet sitting there at the same age. She had a feeling Carrie was going to need watching. She was a bright girl and if she wasn't stimulated sufficiently, she would quickly grow bored.

When Harriet got back to the car, Toby was standing on his hind legs in the driver's seat, his front paws resting on the steering wheel as he peered through the windscreen. 'Have you got a licence for that motor vehicle, sir?' she asked him, waiting for him to swap seats so that she could get in. As she switched on the engine and put the car into gear, he butted her elbow with his head, reminding her of Joel, the way he often made his presence felt. Poor little devil, she thought. Turning to the dog, she said, 'Now listen, you'd better do your part and cheer Joel up this afternoon. And when you've done that, you can book me into the nearest loony bin. Talking to a hairy mutt must make me classic fruitcake material.'

He gave a polite little bark and turned away to look out of the window, his ears pricked as if ready for any further instructions. It was difficult to understand how such a smart dog had come to be abandoned. The first night he'd spent in Maple Drive, when Harriet was on bedtime duty reading to the children, Carrie had interrupted her and said, 'I'm glad Toby's come to live with us. It must have been horrible in the orphanage for him.'

'It wasn't an orphanage,' Harriet corrected her. 'It was a dog pound.'

'A pound?' Joel repeated. 'Like money?'

'No. It's a place where animals abandoned by their cruel owners are looked after until someone very kind, like Granddad, comes along and takes them home. Can we get back to the story now?'

Her father was in the kitchen putting cereal packets away in the cupboard when Harriet got home. Toby went straight to his water bowl and lapped noisily.

'Where's Mum?' she asked, picking up her post from the table.

'Upstairs in bed. She didn't like to say anything at breakfast, what with the children's big day, but she's not feeling so good. She's got that weakness in her legs again and her back kept her awake in the night.'

'She's been overdoing it, hasn't she?'

'You know what she's like.'

'I'll go up and see her, make sure she's okay.'

'I wouldn't; she was fast asleep when I looked in on her ten minutes ago. Better to let her rest. Coffee?'

Surprised by her father's good mood – this was the chattiest he'd been in a long while – she said, 'Yes please. Shall I make it?'

'No, you sit down; I'll do it while you tell me how you got on with Carrie and Joel. Were they okay? Were there any tears?'

'No real tears, thank God, but I wasn't impressed with Joel's teacher. She didn't even know that I wasn't his mother. What qualifications do they need these days to be a teacher? A GCSE in nailbiting?' She sighed and sat back in the chair. 'Things will get easier, won't they, Dad?'

*

It was first break and Carrie searched the playground for Joel. She found him in the sandpit. There were other children with him, but he wasn't joining in with them; he was just sitting there fiddling with a toy car and watching the other boys as they pushed a blue plastic lorry along a track they'd made. He didn't look very happy, but when he saw her his face changed, then he threw down the car and ran to her. 'Is it time to go home now?' he asked. 'Is Harriet here? She said she would bring Toby. She promised.'

Holding his hand, Carrie walked him across the field where earlier she had easily won a running race in a PE lesson. When no one could hear them, she said, 'Joel, we haven't had lunch yet. Look at your watch.'

He pulled a face. 'You know I can't tell the time.'

'But it's easy. Look.' She pulled the cuff back on his sweatshirt. 'There, the big hand's on the six and the small one is between the ten and eleven.'

'Where will the hands be when it's time for Harriet to come for us?'

'The big hand will be on the six and the little one will be between three and four.'

'How long will it be before that happens?'

Exasperated, she said, 'Ages!' Then: 'You haven't cried this morning, have you?'

He shook his head solemnly. 'You said I wasn't to do that.'

'Good boy. And no thumb-sucking?'

He looked less sure. 'Um . . . I might have.'

She sighed and put her hands on her hips. 'Joel, I told you, you mustn't do it. You'll get called names. You'll be called a baby.'

'But I'm not a baby!'

'Is he your brother?'

Carrie spun round. A group of girls from her class had appeared from nowhere and were staring at her and Joel. The one she'd beaten in the running race earlier said again, 'Is he your brother?'

'Yes,' she said.

'He looks really sweet. What's his name?'

'Joel.'

They moved in closer. One of them said, 'Is it true your mum and dad are dead?'

Carrie reached for Joel's hand.

'And is it true they were killed in a car crash and had their heads chopped off?'

Joel gasped. Carrie suddenly wanted to pick him up and run, but she knew she mustn't. She had to be strong. 'Yes,' she said. 'It is true. And do you want to know something else?'

They nodded.

She leaned in towards them. 'Their heads rolled out of the car and onto the road. There was blood everywhere. Puddles of it. Great big enormous puddles of blood.' Enjoying the look of horror on the girls' faces, Carrie wondered what else to say. But the bell sounded for end of break time, and everyone started to run across the field.

It was lunchtime and Joel was doing his best to do everything Carrie had told him.

Not to cry.

Not to suck his thumb.

Not to be a baby.

But he couldn't help himself. He felt sick and he badly needed the loo, and all he could think of was Mummy and Daddy's heads rolling around in the road. Did the police find their heads or were they still there somewhere in the bushes?

He shifted in his seat but couldn't hold on any longer and suddenly he felt the wet warmth spreading down his legs. On and on it went. There was nothing he could do to stop it. He began to cry. Now Carrie would be cross with him. And Harriet too. Carrie had told him they mustn't ever make Harriet angry because then they'd end up in a place like Toby had been in. But surely Harriet wouldn't do that to them. Harriet was nice. Look how she'd promised to bring Toby in this afternoon.

Through his tears, he looked under the table and saw that there was a puddle on the floor. The sight of it made him cry even harder. Perhaps Harriet would be cross with him after all.

Harriet was in a good mood. Well, it was all relative, but the day was turning out better than she had hoped. And the source of her happiness? The morning's post had brought her a party invitation from Erin. Out of the small circle of friends she'd had in Oxford, Erin was the only one who had stayed in touch, albeit intermittently. This didn't surprise Harriet. Once you were no longer a part of something, everyone moved on without you. She was also to blame. She hadn't made an effort to write to or phone anyone either.

The prospect of going down to Oxford for one of Erin's parties shone like a beacon in the wasteland of Harriet's pitiful social life. Erin had an eclectic mix of friends – a lot of high-minded academics from the university, some arty types from the Ashmolean where she worked as a picture restorer and a variety of trendy types from London. Erin knew all about Spencer dumping Harriet – she had shown up that day when Spencer had done his amazing Houdini act – and had written on the invitation that Harriet was more than welcome to bring someone. Harriet wondered about asking Miles but decided against it. Some of Erin's friends could be a bit full on, not Miles's type really.

She turned away from the kitchen window where she'd been watching her father meticulously dead-heading the roses while Toby dozed in the shade of the cherry tree, and went upstairs to work on her laptop. She wanted to tweak her CV and start hawking it round. Now that she had the luxury of some free time, she could get down to the business of landing a job. The long-term plan was that her parents would always do the afternoon school run for her (she would drop the children off early in the morning before going to work) and that if either of the children were ill, they would be there to look after them. This, in theory, should mean that no potential employer would be put off because she had two children to care for and might be unreliable. It seemed a flawless plan, and one that would, before long, give her the wherewithal to buy a house of her own.

She pushed open her bedroom door – Felicity's old bedroom – and went in, shutting it quietly behind her. Her mother was still resting in the room next door and she didn't want to disturb her. Harriet had assumed that when she moved back home she would have her old bedroom, but Eileen had suggested it would be better for her to have her sister's. 'I don't think it's a good idea for either of the children to sleep in their mother's bedroom. Who knows what their vivid imaginations might dream up?' It had seemed a bit far-fetched to Harriet, but she had gone along with it. As she had with so many things.

She switched on her laptop, flexed her hands in front of her and sat up straight. 'Now then,' she said out loud. 'Here go the finishing touches to a perfect CV, which will reel in the perfect job.' Cheshire had so many software companies in its midst that it was often referred to in the industry as Silicone Valley. That, together with her level of expertise, made her confident that she would soon be taking her pick of the best of the jobs available.

Chapter Fifteen

Outside Joel's classroom, where she was waiting in the corridor to speak to Miss Rawlinson, Harriet was keeping an eye on the children through a large picture window. They were in the playground, where Toby was trying to stick his nose into Joel's crotch.

'I'm sorry to keep you waiting.'

Harriet whipped round to face Miss Rawlinson. Without preamble, she said, 'Why didn't you ring to say there was a problem with Joel?'

The girl looked confused. 'I'm not aware of there having been a problem, Mrs Knight, I mean Mrs Swift.'

'It's *Miss* Swift. And if Joel wet himself it sounds to me like there was a problem.'

'But they nearly all do that at this age. It's nerves.'

'Really? Well, the least you could have done was change his trousers for him. That would have been the humane thing to do, instead of leaving him in that degrading state. Have you any idea how humiliated he must have felt?'

'Unfortunately there wasn't much we could do. It's the start of term so there weren't any spare trousers lying around. The lost property box is empty, you see. Perhaps—' She hesitated. 'Perhaps it might be helpful if you could send him in with a spare pair of his own trousers from now on. You know, just in case.'

I might even send him in with a spare grown-up teacher who can look after him properly, fumed Harriet as she banged the main school door after her and went outside to the children.

'Toby! Stop sniffing Joel like that! It's obscene.' She took the dog lead from Carrie. 'Come on you two, let's get out of here.'

Nobody spoke until they were sitting in the car and Harriet was once again telling Toby off for shoving his snout in Joel's crotch. Just as she was pulling the dog away from him, Joel said, 'I'm sorry, Harriet. It just came out. I ... I couldn't stop it.'

She looked at him in the rear-view mirror. Oh, hell, that face. That anxious little face. She lowered her gaze and turned the key in the ignition.

'Please don't be cross with him,' Carrie said. 'It was an accident. He didn't mean to do it. It's not fair if you're angry with him.'

Harriet yanked on the handbrake. She turned round to face them both. 'Whoa there! Who said anything about me being angry with Joel?'

The children exchanged glances. Carrie said, 'You looked cross when you were talking to Joel's teacher.'

'That's because I have a tendency to get cross when I'm talking to a numpty-head who doesn't know her arse from her elbow.'

Carrie's eyes widened. 'You're not allowed to say bad words in front of us.'

'I'll say what the hell I like in front of you. Watch out, because here I go again. *Arse!*'

Carrie began to laugh. Harriet laughed too. But looking in the rear-view mirror again, she noticed Joel wasn't joining in. If anything, he shrank lower into his seat. She saw him reach for his silky, which she'd only at the last minute remembered to put in the car for him as she'd promised.

'So did it go okay?' she asked, her question directed more to Carrie. 'Did you learn anything?' She'd decided she'd get more out of Joel when she'd got him home and he'd had a bath and a change of clothes.

But she was wrong. Joel remained as tight-lipped as ever. Even Eileen failed to get him to open up, and all during tea he just sat playing with his food, his eyes downcast, his legs swinging under the table. He was silent too during bedtime when Harriet read to them, and despite hovering by his bed for longer than usual, he still said nothing about his day at school.

Accepting there was nothing else she could do, she then got ready to go out. She was meeting Miles at his parents' house before going for a drink. For some reason his mother had expressed a desire to see her.

'I just wanted to say how desperately sorry I was that I was too ill to come to Felicity's funeral,' Freda McKendrick said. 'I was so disappointed not to make it.'

Harriet played along. She'd heard it all before; the list of mystery illnesses that had kept Freda away from every social engagement beyond her own doorstep was endless. 'These things happen,' she said lightly. Sitting next to his father on the sofa, Miles gave her a nod of gratitude, which annoyed her. And her annoyance annoyed her further. Miles didn't deserve her animosity. Yet why did he pander to his mother? Why was he content to let her fritter away her life? Why not just bundle her through the front door and stick her out in the road for a dose of cold turkey treatment? What did he think would happen? That she'd have a heart attack and die on the spot?

Freda pushed a pale, elegant hand through the fine strands of her hair – honey-gold hair that was cut, dyed and styled by a hairdresser who came to the house. 'And how are you all coping? Dear me, it seems like yesterday when you four children used to play together. Miles, dear, pass me that photograph of Dominic. It must be quite a while since Harriet last saw your brother. Here. Doesn't he look handsome?'

Freda's overly refined but vague manner had Harriet wanting to grab her by the shoulders and shake her. She wanted to kick at the cabinets of china figurines, to run her hand along the spotless mantelpiece, knocking every ornament and dried-flower arrangement to the floor then grind them underfoot. The house was a mausoleum of perfection.

Freda had turned housework into a vocation. Because, at the end of the day, it was all she had to stop herself going completely gaga. And that husband of hers wasn't much better. Harvey McKendrick had always given Harriet the creeps. There was something weird about his manner: so upright and formal. Harriet had never seen him without a tie. He was cold-blooded too. When they were children, he ran over a neighbour's cat by accident and couldn't understand the fuss everyone had made about it.

Harriet gave the photograph a cursory glance. It was of Dominic, *Dr Dominic McKendrick*, and he was dressed up to the nines in his Cambridge finery; black gown and fancy fur trim. The picture had probably been taken to commemorate some highly important occasion in his world of academia, but she couldn't be bothered to ask what. Freda was right about one thing, though. He did look handsome. But then he always had.

She muttered a suitable response, passed the photograph back to Freda and said, 'Well, Miles, shall we see what delights Kings Melford has to offer us?' She was on her feet before Freda could press them to stay any longer. She wanted to get out of the suffocating atmosphere this irritating woman was so reluctant to leave.

She had always been infuriated by the blatant favouritism that had gone on in the McKendrick household. Since for ever, Dominic had been considered the brightest son, the one destined for a stellar future. At the age of eleven he was sent away to boarding school where, apparently, his academic ability would be better nurtured. This might have left him isolated and excluded when he came home for the holidays, but there was no force on this earth that could hold, restrain or exclude Dominic McKendrick. From an early age he'd been convinced of his own brilliance and had believed the world revolved around him. The oldest within their gang of four – he was a year older than Felicity – he'd been their self-appointed leader. It had been him who'd got them all drunk for the first time, one night when both sets of parents had been out – this was in the days before

Freda's problems had started. He'd decided it would be a laugh to concoct the mother of all cocktails. They'd pooled their resources by pinching a selection of barely touched bottles from the back of their respective parents' drinks cabinets and had mixed them together. Net result, when Harvey and Freda came home, they found four teenagers in varying degrees of drunkenness. And undress – Dominic had also suggested a game of strip poker and they were all down to their underwear, with Felicity on the verge of removing her bra.

Harriet's face coloured at the memory. She wondered if Miles remembered that night, too.

'Seeing as it's such a nice evening, I thought we'd go to The Navigation,' he said. 'That okay with you?'

'So long as it's not pensioners' night and it's child-free, I have no complaints.'

The pub was heaving, and after queuing for their drinks, they spied a free table in the garden overlooking the canal and the bridge. Further along, the towpath was busy with people mooring up for the night. When they were settled, she noticed that Miles's attention was caught by one particular boat, a beautiful sixty-foot traditional narrowboat. Its paintwork – red, black and green – was immaculate, and the brassware gleamed in the low evening sun. It was in excellent condition, not a mark or scratch on it, which meant it wasn't a hire boat; it had to be privately owned, about a hundred grand's worth.

'Ever thought you'd like to have a boat and just cruise away?' she asked him.

He looked back at her. 'We all think that at some time or other, don't we?'

'So why don't we do it?'

He blinked. 'You mean you and me?'

She smiled. 'No, I was talking generally. People dream of escaping, but they rarely do it.'

'The vast majority of people aren't brave enough. And, of course, there are those who are too tied down to do it.' He glanced away, his gaze once more drawn to the boat he'd been admiring.

Harriet took a moment to observe him. He'd always been the quieter and more thoughtful of the McKendrick boys. He had a sensitive, intelligent face with pale blue eyes. In all the years she had known him they had never argued and she had never stopped respecting the way he'd handled living in the shadow of such a difficult and dynamic brother. Dominic had to be the ultimate pain when it came to older brothers. As a highly regarded English don with a couple of slim books of poetry to his name it wouldn't occur to him that Miles was his equal. Or that anyone else was, for that matter.

As children, the four of them had been extraordinarily close, to the point of being a tight, self-sufficient clique. They had no need of any other friends; they had all the friendship they wanted. To this day, Harriet was convinced that this was the reason she found it difficult to fit in with other people and make new friends – she just hadn't learned the necessary skills at the age when most others do. After they'd all been through university they'd drifted apart, each doing their own thing. Felicity got married, Harriet started working for a small software house in Newbury, Miles went to London to work for a large chain of bookstores, and Dominic was offered a teaching job in the States at the University of Chicago.

Thinking about what Miles had just said, she asked him, 'So do you feel tied down?'

Again he looked back at her. 'Yes.' The starkness with which he uttered that one word made her sit up.

'But why?' she pressed. 'You're not married and have no real commitments to stop you doing whatever you want. You could sell the bookshop and—'

'I have a mother who's ill, Harriet,' he interrupted, his voice perfectly level.

'You have a father who can take care of her. She's not your responsibility.'

'You think I should just walk away and leave them to it? Like Dominic has?'

'It's an option.'

He looked her straight in the eye. 'Presumably that's the same option you could take. You could leave your parents to look after Felicity's kids.'

For a moment she didn't know what to say. Miles was the first person to broach the subject with her. No one had ever suggested she had a choice. That she could turn her back on her family . . . could forget her promise to Felicity.

'I'm sorry, I shouldn't have been so blunt,' he said. 'But I'm right, aren't I?'

'I could walk away if I wanted to,' she admitted.

'You could, but you're missing the point. You won't walk because, like me, you have a strong sense of what's right and wrong.'

'That's not how I see it – right versus wrong.'

He dismissed her words with a wave of his hand. 'We're two of a kind; we both have an innate sense of duty. You're either born with it or you're not. It's called loyalty and it means we play with the cards we're dealt. We do the best job we can.'

She sat back in her chair and felt a rush of affection towards her old friend. Inexplicably, she felt like hugging him. It was great sitting here with no children, no parents, just the two of them having a proper, grown-up conversation that wasn't subject to countless interruptions. A conversation that meant something. 'You have no idea how refreshing it is to talk to someone who understands,' she said at length.

'I think I understand all too well. And I have nothing but admiration for you.'

Harriet took a long swallow of her lager and watched a pair of swans gliding past on the other side of the canal. When they disappeared behind the fronds of the willow branches dipping into the still, languid water, she looked up and noticed the sun was slipping lower in the sky, turning it hazy. 'People think that because I loved Felicity,' she said quietly, 'it must follow that I'm crazy about her children. But I'm not. I can't help it, but that's the truth. Children have never interested me. Does that sound as awful to you as it just did to me?'

'I have even less experience with kids than you, but my guess is the important thing is that you're there for them. That they know they can rely on you. They need stability and I reckon you'd be better than most at providing that. Okay, you might not be made from the conventional mother mould, but that might just work to the children's advantage.'

She suddenly smiled. 'You know what? I think we should do this again. You're good for me. To be honest, I'd been feeling guilty that I didn't seem able to—' She broke off, distracted by the sight of a tall, slim man on the other side of the beer garden carrying two glasses of wine in his hands and a packet of crisps between his teeth. There was something comical about the way he was weaving his way through the tables and chairs, and the way his hair had flopped down in front of his eyes and was adding to his problems. It was only when he'd reached his table and was able to remove the crisp packet from his mouth and push back his hair that she recognised him: Will Hart. He was with an attractive blonde girl who laughed when he kissed her on the top of her head. She had to be about half his age. Typical, Harriet thought with disgust.

'Someone you know?' asked Miles, following her gaze. She explained who it was. 'Do you know him?'

'I know *of* him. His ex-wife's an auctioneer in Maywood; she runs Stone's. Do you know it?'

'No. But I know he's into antiques.'

'He is now, but apparently he used to be a hotshot lawyer, had some kind of breakdown and then got into the antique trade. He has a place here in Kings Melford, took it over from a real old character, Jarvis Cooper. You must have heard of *him*.'

She laughed. 'Sorry, but the grapevine must have run out of branches; the news didn't reach me down in Oxford.'

'He's not new news, so to speak. He was around when we were kids. Hart's Antique Emporium is in what used to be The Tavern, the old coaching inn opposite the square; it's been owned by the Cooper family for years.'

Harriet vaguely recalled something about a shoe shop or a cobbler. But still thinking of Will Hart, she said, 'He doesn't look the sort to have a breakdown. He looks too . . .' She sought to find the right words. 'He looks too laid back and untroubled.'

'Perhaps he has life sussed. Doesn't feel the need to escape like the rest of us.'

'How do you know so much about everyone?'

'I own a bookshop where people congregate to gossip over coffee and occasionally contemplate buying a book. I always knew I'd end up doing some kind of community service.'

'Hey, no whingeing allowed! You know you love that bookshop.'

'Actually, I do. The customers are great, and surprisingly loyal. They like the individual touch we offer. The nothing's-too-much-trouble approach we small businesses are famous for still means something to a lot of people.'

'I'm glad to hear it.'

'Have you started looking for a job yet?'

'I spent today putting the finishing touches to my CV and now that it's polished to within an inch of its life, I'm going to email it out to as many agencies as I can.'

'You wouldn't consider a change of direction, then?'

'No chance. I love the geeky world of computer programming.' She put a hand to her heart. 'I always knew it was my destiny, darling.'

He smiled. 'Felicity used to be so proud of you, you know.'

'Really?'

He nodded. 'She once told me that she wished she had half your brains.'

Harriet frowned. 'When did she say that?'

'Earlier in the year when she was staying with your

parents. It might have been during February half-term. She had the children with her, so it probably was. She often used to come into the shop when she was home.'

Thinking that this tied in with Carrie's question about Novel Ways, Harriet said, 'Felicity was far smarter than me. She spoke three different languages, for heaven's sake. She was always in demand to do translation work. I don't know how she did it with the children around. Especially when they were really young.'

'She must have been very organised. Like you, I expect.' After a pause, during which he fiddled with his beer mat, he said, 'Does it upset you to talk about Felicity?'

'No. Funnily enough, it feels good. Like she's still with us. That I could look over my shoulder and there she'd be, her old smiling self.'

He nodded and looked thoughtful, staring off into the distance. 'I know what you mean. I still can't quite believe she's gone, but then . . . but then I remember the funeral and it hits me like a hammer. Dead. It's so final.' He swallowed and slowly turned his pale-blue eyes back to Harriet. She was surprised to see the depth of sadness within them. 'I don't think I shall ever forget that day at the funeral,' he said. 'You handled it so well.'

'I was on autopilot. In too much shock to cry. But I do remember how glad I was to see you there.' She also remembered how upset he was, and that he made no attempt to hide his feelings. She liked his uncomplicated honesty. He was the complete opposite of his brother, who was the most devious person she knew. Felicity used to say that Harriet judged Dominic too harshly, that she expected too much of him. 'He can't help being the man he is,' Felicity said. 'We're all the sum of our experiences.'

In that case, Dominic must have had some pretty awful experiences, because he always behaved abominably.

A burst of laughter from Will Hart's table had them both turning to look. Harriet rolled her eyes. What was it about middle-aged men – especially the moderately good-looking ones – and attractive young blondes? Changing the subject, she said, 'So how's your love life, Miles?'

He looked surprised by her question. 'Non-existent. And you? How's it working out between you and that guy you mentioned at the funeral?'

'It didn't. I can't think why, but I may have lost some of my appeal when I moved back up here to look after Carrie and Joel.'

'Then he's a fool. You're well rid of him. You deserve better.'

'My sentiments exactly.' She raised her glass to drink to this but found that it was empty.

'Another lager?'

'Why not?'

She watched him go back inside the pub. It felt good spending the evening with someone who knew her so well. She might not consider Miles to be the greatest judge of her character and abilities – he was too old and too loyal a friend and therefore biased – but she did value his down-to-earth support and encouragement. Maybe he was right when he said that what the children needed was someone they knew they could rely on. Perhaps that's what Felicity had been thinking when she'd made Harriet make that promise. She must have known that if the unimaginable happened, Harriet wouldn't let her down. Or more importantly, wouldn't let her children down.

It was a tall order, but as Miles had just said, she couldn't help but try and do the best job she could.

Chapter Sixteen

It had been a good day, with the prospect of getting better still. It was Will's birthday and he was driving back to the shop after a successful afternoon spent in Colwyn Bay at one of his favourite salerooms. He went there at least twice a month and it was always a pleasure. To top it off, he was looking forward to spending the evening with Gemma and Suzie. He'd suggested they eat out, but Suzie had said a meal in would be better. 'If you cook for us, I'll bake you a cake,' she'd said. 'How's that?'

Following the coastal road out of Colwyn Bay, he glanced to his left where the sea heaved and rolled. It reminded him of the sensation he always had in his stomach during an auction. He'd experienced the same thing earlier when the lot he'd come for had been announced. Crucially, he'd already checked out the stylish Art Deco clock online – a French piece, admittedly only silver plate, but all smooth lines and sexy curves – and had set his limit. His stomach had started to churn the moment the lot was held up by the saleroom porter, Hairy Joe. When Will first knew the porter he was called Metal Joe, then he became Country Joe, now he was Hairy Joe because of the grey ponytail that hung down his back. With his palms sweating, his heart hammering and his stomach pitching, Will had kept one eye on Hairy Joe and the clock and the other on the assembled company. It wasn't a big turnout but there were a few faces he recognised: a couple of interior designers from south Manchester; a pair of London runners (the Spearmint Boys as Will called them because their jaws were permanently working at chewing gum); a smattering of dealers from all over the north-west and a handful of casual punters hoping for a bargain. It was the kind of slow-moving day when a less scrupulous auctioneer might take a bid or two off the wall to bump up the prices, but not this one. He was as straight as they come, a staunch chapel-goer who would never incur the wrath of the Almighty through dodgy practice. With a wave of his catalogue, Will came in as a fresh bidder when things began to go quiet – when the interior designers thought they had the lot in the bag. He knew they'd have cash to flash, that their clients numbered footballers and soap stars, but like the rest of them, they had their budgets and if you knew what you were doing, you stuck to your limit. To his satisfaction, the interior designers bowed out and the clock was his. He made two further successful bids, one for a pretty Victorian fire screen, and another for a job lot of odds and sods that he'd had a quick squint at when he'd arrived. All in all, it was a good day's work.

Once he was beyond Chester, he stopped for some petrol and a Mars bar, then took the road for Maywood and Kings Melford. It was gone five thirty when he arrived back at the shop. Jarvis was on his own – the two part-time dealers to whom Will sub-let an area on the top floor had already left.

'And what treasures have you brought home today?' Jarvis asked, making a play of pushing back his cuffs and rubbing his hands. 'Aha!' His eyes lit up when Will removed the clock from its swaddling of bubble wrap. 'Excellent,' he crooned, rather like Fagin. 'You did well, Laddie. The face is a little ordinary, but those exquisite figures more than make up for the deficit.' He stroked the slender leg of one of the figures lovingly. 'Charming. Quite charming.'

'And even more charming,' said Will, 'I have a buyer lined up. Remember the woman from the Wirral?'

'Pushy madam, tarty red convertible, and a face like a flounder?'

'One and the same. She asked me to look out for an Art Deco clock just like this.'

'And like a dog retrieving a stick for his mistress, you did her bidding. Very commendable. And in the box?'

'Take a look.'

While Will rewrapped the clock, Jarvis examined the fire screen then sorted through the job lot of junk, issuing forth a series of dismissive grunts and snorts. 'Ah, what have we here?' He held up a piece of china. 'A Noritake powder bowl, complete with lid. Gilt still fresh and perky too. How much did you pay for the box?'

'Five quid.' Will took the Japanese porcelain back, knowing Jarvis only tolerated Will's interest in Noritake ware. It wasn't proper fine porcelain as far as Jarvis was concerned – 'It's hardly in the same league as Royal Worcester or Minton, Laddie, is it?' – but even Jarvis had to admit that it was a growing market that only a fool would ignore. This scenic bowl and cover would perform nicely. Eighty quid minimum or he'd eat one of Jarvis's grubby old hats.

After Jarvis had left, Will made a few phone calls, including one to the flounder-faced woman on the Wirral, and locked up for the night, making sure the burglar alarm was switched on. It was a state-of-the-art system, so PC Plod had told him when he'd installed it. Will had deliberately approached Steve to do the job for two reasons. One, he wanted to show how magnanimous he could be, and two, if it ever went wrong, he'd have the bugger fixing it no matter what time of day it was. And for free.

Which wasn't the case regarding Steve's car. Will had now paid twice for the wretched thing to be fixed. Steve had taken it to the Jaguar garage where he'd bought it and the quote that had been faxed to Will could have cleared the whole of the third-world debt problem. Yet there was nothing else for it but for Will to grit his teeth and divvy up the gelt. Suzie had taken him to task for taking the blame. 'I feel awful,' she'd said. 'You should have told him the truth.'

But he'd shushed her, saying, 'Give your dad a break. I'm

racked with guilt that you come from a broken home; this is my pathetic way to make it up to you.'

'Don't be daft, Dad.'

'Not even a little?'

'No. If you keep doing things like this, people will start calling me Princess Precious. They'll say I can't stand on my own two feet.'

'Rubbish. Anyway, there's plenty of time before you have to do all that boring grown-up stuff. How about you enjoy life a bit?'

Will would give anything to change what had happened to their family – bar live with the girls' mother again – but all he could do was indulge them now and again. In his opinion, they'd never once displayed a moment's Princess Precious behaviour. Unlike their mother, he thought less kindly. Perhaps that was Maxine's problem; she'd been too used to getting her own way as a young child and had come to expect it as her right. Her father had thoroughly ruined her, in Will's opinion; he had lavished everything he possibly could on her, all except for genuine, unconditional love.

Will had also been an only child, but his father had been the antithesis of the dad he wanted to be to Suzie and Gemma. William Hart senior had been a bitter man who'd worn his disappointment on the frayed cuff of his sleeve. A self-styled working-class hero, he'd been shocked when Will had shown a desire to do well at school. William senior believed in learning at the School of Hard Knocks and when Will had announced his intention of going to university to study law, he might just as well have said he wanted to become a ballerina. In his father's mind, he'd sold out. If working for British Rail had been good enough for him, it was certainly good enough for his son.

Will often wondered what he would have made of the son who'd sold out on his own highfalutin dream. 'Well, you buggered that one up, didn't you?' he'd probably have said. 'I could have told you you were making a mistake.'

Will's mother had borne her husband's moods and

criticism better than Will ever had. But as soon as she was widowed and free of the tyranny of constantly being judged, Ruby had blossomed and was finally able to be herself. Having been held back for most of her married life, she confided that she was now free to make all the mistakes she wanted without a word of criticism. Off like a hound after the hare, she filled her life with a job at the local supermarket, evenings at the theatre and cinema, and organised coach trips round Britain and Europe. In keeping with this new philosophy, she'd never once criticised Will. Not even when he messed up his marriage so spectacularly with a series of affairs. The worst she had done was to tut. But that small, apparently insignificant tut had done more to bring him to his senses than any screamed condemnation Maxine had flung at him. The 'tut' had been followed with: 'Are you sure this is what you want, Will?' And, of course, it wasn't.

Halfway down Maple Drive, he saw a small boy being dragged along by a wire-haired fox terrier. With his free hand, the boy was hanging onto a man. Behind the man was a girl. Recognising the group, Will gave a pip of the horn and a wave. Bob Swift returned it.

Will had met Bob one evening just as the light was beginning to fade. He'd been hacking back the jungle of bushes at the end of the garden when he'd heard a voice: 'Looks like you've got your hands full there.' Emerging from the undergrowth, Will had recognised his neighbour. Introductions were made and so that there could be no ambiguous awkwardness, Will had mentioned that he'd met Harriet and had learned of the family's loss. The other man's response had been: 'Harriet never said anything about meeting you.' Somehow this hadn't surprised Will.

He took a liking to the older man and they were soon chatting about the neighbourhood. Will was amazed to discover that the Swifts had lived there for so long. The McKendricks too. 'The four children literally grew up in each other's pockets,' Bob had explained. 'They were constantly getting into some scrape or other.' There had been several conversations since, all conducted over the gate and in the dusky half-light while Bob was out walking the recently acquired dog on the canal path. The dead daughter was never referred to again directly but her presence, he suspected, was a heavy one in Bob's heart. He couldn't begin to imagine how he would feel if anything happened to one of his girls.

Only a couple of packing boxes remained unopened, and stepping round these in the hall, Will carried the post through to the kitchen. One of the envelopes had Marty's familiar, neat writing on it. He opened the envelope and drew out a card depicting a grizzled old man behind the wheel of a Hillman Imp. 'If you're old enough to remember the car,' the caption read, 'you're too old to be driving!' Cheers, Marty, thought Will. The next card was from his mother. She'd also sent him a music voucher. She'd never been one of those mothers who religiously gave their sons M & S sweaters or socks. 'I know you wouldn't return them if they didn't fit,' she'd once said. She knew he'd hate to hurt her feelings. Which is why that 'tut' still resonated in his ears. 'Shame on you William Hart,' it said. 'I thought I'd brought you up better than to go screwing any woman you could lay your hands on.' Not that his mother would ever dream of using the word 'screw', other than when referring to cross heads or flat heads.

Will wasn't a great cook, but having lived on his own for as long as he had, he considered himself competent. Tonight he was knocking a chicken korma into shape. It was only at Suzie's insistence that he was celebrating his birthday. He'd been all for letting it slip by unnoticed, but Suzie had put her foot down. He was touched, but not happy that another year had been added to those already stacked against him. Forty-six. Who'd have thought it?

'Just get in the car, Gemma! Honestly, sometimes I could cheerfully kill you.'

Gemma banged the door shut.

'What's with the grumpy sister act?'

'I'm not grumpy,' snapped Suzie.

Gemma snorted. 'Not much. So come on, what's bugging you? Better you get it off your chest before we arrive at Dad's and spoil the evening for him.' To Gemma's surprise, her sister turned very pale.

After a long silence, as though she had needed to compose herself, Suzie said, 'I just wish you wouldn't deliberately wind up Mum and Steve the way you do.'

Gemma rolled her eyes. 'Like I give a toss what they think.'

'Perhaps you should. You know perfectly well that when you play them off against Dad, it's Dad who comes off worse.'

'All I said was seeing as Dad had more space in his new house, I wouldn't mind moving in with him.'

'But there was no need for you to say it so stroppily. You know they have a big enough downer on Dad without you adding to it.'

'Well, that's hardly my fault.'

'Nothing ever is!'

Gemma sank back into her seat and stared at the road ahead. She pursed her lips, annoyed. Something had rattled Suzie's cage and she couldn't for the life of her work out what it was. Still, it wasn't her problem. She dismissed her sister from her mind and thought of the letter she'd received that morning from Marcel. He'd written to say that he wanted to come and see her. Could he stay? The very idea of him under the same roof as Mum and Steve made her want to leave the country. Mum would have a fit if she clapped eyes on Marcel, with his shaggy, shoulder-length hair, his pierced tongue and his goatee beard. And if she ever, *ever*, knew what they'd got up to in Paris . . . well, it just wasn't worth considering. Gemma didn't object to a bit of boat-rocking, but she was smart enough to know that a capsize was counterproductive.

Suzie gripped the steering wheel, trying to keep calm. It wasn't easy. She was about to tell her father something no father wants to hear. She had deliberately engineered this whole evening, had rehearsed herself till she was word-perfect. But now that she was minutes away from telling Dad, she was losing her nerve. Perhaps she would be better leaving it until she went back to university in a few weeks, when she could decide more objectively what she was going to do. But even that frightened her. She couldn't bear the thought of her friends – one friend in particular – knowing about it.

Usually daughters turned to their mothers when faced with a crisis, but Suzie had always turned to Dad when there was something she couldn't resolve on her own. She supposed it stemmed from those days when he'd chucked in being a lawyer and was at home with her and Gemma. Many a time they'd have the kitchen covered in glue, cardboard boxes, painted cotton reels and glitter when Mum came home from work. Often she would go mad because the place was a mess and Dad hadn't done the ironing. Other days he'd take them out after school – tea at Nana Ruby's, or a trip to the library, or maybe a walk in the park. They'd frequently lose track of the time and Mum would get cross and say he was ruining the structure of the day for them. Bedtimes had always been great. He'd read to them for ages. There was always time for another page, another chapter. And when he'd done that, he'd sing to them. She still liked 'Scarlet Ribbons' even now.

She knew Dad had been far from perfect – especially for Mum, who liked everything done a certain way – but from a child's perspective he'd been fun. He still was. It might not have been a conventional childhood, and her friends had thought it dead weird that her father wasn't working, but it was better than a lot of other people's family life.

She swallowed. Could she be as good a parent as her father? She chewed on her lip. Oh, God, how could she have been so stupid? How could she have slept with a friend's boyfriend and ended up pregnant?

Chapter Seventeen

It was warm enough to eat in the garden so they'd carried the only table Will possessed – the kitchen table – outside. In the gathering darkness, listening to Gemma telling him and Suzie about something that had happened at school that day, Will thought of the birthday present they'd clubbed together to buy him: a pair of tickets to see Jools Holland at the Apollo in Manchester. Not exactly his first choice, but he appreciated it all the same. It was a marked improvement on all those years of Homer Simpson boxer shorts he'd had to endure.

'More to drink, anyone?' he asked when Gemma finally drew breath. Gemma held out her glass for some more wine, but knowing that Suzie was driving, he said, 'More orange juice? Or do you fancy something else?'

'Do you have any Coke?'

'Yes. I'll get you some. You okay? You look tired.'

'It's nothing. I didn't sleep well last night, that's all.'

While she waited for her father to come back with her drink, Suzie prayed that Gemma wouldn't start up again with one of her long-drawn-out stories. It was a risk deciding to break the news in front of her sister, but she was doing it because she hoped Gemma would defuse the shock. But that would only happen if Gemma would shut up long enough for Suzie to get a word in edgeways.

'Here you go,' her father said when he returned. 'I brought the bottle as well.'

'Thanks,' she murmured when he'd filled her glass and the Coke was fizzing loudly in the quiet. She waited for him to sit down and cleared her throat, ready at last.

'Hey, Dad, did you know that Steve's thinking about taking up golf?'

Suzie nearly screamed. What was it with Gemma and that great big mouth of hers?

'Really?' said Dad. 'How will they ever manage to measure his colossal handicap, I wonder? His handicap being his head.' Both he and Gemma laughed. Then Gemma was off again, something about that French guy she'd met in Paris and how he'd written to her. Suzie tuned out of the conversation and stared up at the darkening sky. Next thing she knew, Gemma was on her feet. 'Come on Suzie,' she was saying, 'time to bring on Dad's cake.'

Their father groaned when he saw it. 'That looks horribly like a forest fire of candles,' he said when Gemma placed it on the table. Suzie handed him the knife to cut it, but Gemma said, 'Not yet, we haven't sung to him. Happy birthday to you . . .' she began.

Suzie did her best to join in but her heart wasn't in it. Get it over and done with, she told herself.

'Happy birthday to you . . .'

What's the worst he could say?

'Happy birthday dear Dad . . .'

You know he'll be okay. He always is.

'Happy birthday to y-o-u.'

'Go on, Dad,' urged Gemma, 'blow out the candles. Don't forget to make a wish!'

Suzie watched her father take a deep breath and just as he was about to lean forward, she said, 'Dad, I'm pregnant.'

Will's breath came out in one long exhalation; all but two of the candles spluttered and died.

It was Gemma who spoke first. 'Bloody hell!'

Very slowly, Will wetted his thumb and middle finger and snuffed out the two remaining candles. He was giving himself time to think.

'Say something, Dad.'

He raised his glance and stared at Suzie. 'Are you sure?'

She nodded.

For the longest time the three of them sat round the table, their expressions blank.

'I'm sorry, Dad. And I'm sorry for spoiling your birthday. But I had to tell you.'

'Of course you did.' He swallowed, tried to keep the shock and disappointment from his face. 'Er . . . Gemma, I wonder if you'd give us a moment? Maybe some coffee would be a good idea.'

When they were alone, Suzie said, 'Are you very cross with me?'

He shook his head. 'I don't know what to think. I'm too stunned. I'd never have thought . . . I mean, you've always been . . .' He broke off, knowing how absurd he was about to sound.

'You were going to say sensible, weren't you?'

He nodded, reminded of the conversation they'd had on the phone not so long ago: 'One of these days I'm going to shock you and not be the responsible daughter you've always taken me for.' Had she known then what she knew now?

From inside the house came the sound of Gemma rattling crockery. Distracted, he said, 'Let's go down to the end of the garden. It'll be easier to think in the quiet.'

While Suzie sat on the bench overlooking the slick, unmoving surface of the canal, he lit the storm lantern he'd rigged up in one of the trees; at once moths appeared from nowhere. He joined her on the bench. 'Who's the father?' he asked. 'You haven't mentioned a boyfriend in a long while.'

'The father has nothing to do with it.'

Will raised an eyebrow. 'I think you'll find he does.'

'It's not that straightforward. He's the boyfriend of a friend of mine at uni.'

Anger stirred inside Will. 'Then what the hell was he doing with you? What kind of two-timing bastard is he?'

'Be fair, Dad, you could ask the same of me. What kind of friend was I?'

'I'm sorry,' he said. 'I'm probably saying all the wrong things. Making it worse for you. So . . . how many weeks are you?'

'Four months.'

He tried to hide yet another level of shock. 'As much as that? When did you find out?'

'Last week. I did a test then went to the doctor and had it confirmed. And before you ask, I hadn't sussed before because I'm not that regular. I never have been.'

Will reached for her hand, remembering the day she'd started her periods. They'd been on holiday – just him and the girls – and he'd had to get up early and go to the nearest shop that was open to buy the necessaries. Thinking of that day, when he'd realised his eldest daughter was growing up fast, his mind snagged on the disappointment he couldn't help but feel. Surely she was intelligent enough to know better. He said, 'Sex without precautions, Suzie, surely you knew the risks?'

'It was a mistake. A stupid, drunken mistake. We were at a party; Sinead wasn't there and, well—'

Suddenly squeamish, Will interrupted her: he didn't need to know any more; there were certain things a father shouldn't hear. 'It's okay, you don't have to give me the details. But are you sure you shouldn't be having this discussion with him?'

'No. It should never have happened between us. One bad decision on both our parts shouldn't mean his life is ruined. Or Sinead's; she's mad about him.' She hung her head. 'Oh, Dad, I feel so ashamed. I felt bad enough the day after, that I could go behind her back like that, but now . . . now it's as if the baby is a way to punish me.'

He put his arm round her. 'Hey, beating yourself up with irrational talk like that won't get you anywhere. What does your mother say about it?' As if he needed to ask. She'd be breathing fire.

'I haven't told her. I wanted to talk to you first.'

Will was concerned. 'She's your mother, Suzie; she should know.'

'I'll tell her when I know what I'm going to do.'

This was the crux of the conversation, the all-important area to which Will had been reluctant to stray. 'You mean whether you'll keep the baby or have a termination? Or even have it, then give it up for adoption?'

Suzie nodded and turned away. But not before Will saw her eyes fill. His heart went out to her. He drew her close. 'It'll be okay. Whatever you decide to do, I'll be there for you. You're not to worry.' She began to cry, and he held her closer still, wanting her to know that he meant every word. He wouldn't let her go through this alone. He wished, though, that she'd spoken to Maxine. Keeping Maxine in the dark would only infuriate her.

They decided to stay the night with their father, but as tired as she was Suzie couldn't sleep. She hadn't slept a full night since she'd plucked up the courage to buy the pregnancy test kit and known the worst. Standing at the bedroom window that overlooked the front garden, she rested her elbows on the sill and looked at the houses opposite. They were ordinary houses with ordinary gardens and she imagined the ordinary people who lived inside them, living their safe, ordinary lives. How she envied them.

Staying the night at Dad's had been a last-minute arrangement; basically she couldn't face going home to Mum and Steve. She'd cried so much that Mum would have taken one look at her and known straight away that something was wrong. Dad had phoned Mum to say that there'd been a change of plan and was it okay if they stopped the night with him. Ridiculous really, that at their age he'd asked for permission. Surely they could do what they wanted. 'Just keeping the peace,' he'd said when Gemma had pointed this out. 'We don't want any unnecessary antagonism.'

They'd stayed up late talking about the coming weeks. Her father had agreed with Suzie that it might be best to hold off returning to uni until she knew exactly what she was going to do.

'Do you want the baby?' Gemma had asked with her typical frankness.

'I don't know,' she'd mumbled, through yet more tears.

As if to lighten the mood, Gemma had then said, 'Just think, Dad, if Suzie does go ahead and keeps the baby, I'll become an aunt and you'll be a grandfather. How awesomely unreal does that sound?'

The obvious thing to do was to have a termination. Four months ago and she'd have advised any of her friends in this situation to do exactly that. Four months ago, she thought dryly, she should have taken a morning-after pill, but it hadn't crossed her mind. Well, she was paying the price now, wasn't she? Every time she thought that a termination would solve everything, she remembered the girl at university who had given such an impassioned speech at the debating society last term. An earnest pro-lifer, the girl had held the audience spellbound as she'd calmly laid out the facts. How the foetus was totally recognisable as a human form, how it was receptive to light and sound. 'And yet this fragile form of human life, this baby, yes,' the girl had said fervently, 'let's call it what it is, a baby, can be legally murdered. What kind of a society are we that allows this to happen? And what kind of woman,' the girl had said, her voice dropping for added emphasis, 'would willingly violate the sanctity of human life?'

A frightened woman, thought Suzie.

Chapter Eighteen

Marty had never forgiven Will for not confiding in him when his career and marriage hit the skids. He'd been horrified when he discovered how bad things were. 'Why didn't you tell me?' he'd said. 'I thought we were friends.'

'I was too screwed up,' was all Will could say.

It was with this in mind that Will, once he'd opened the shop next morning, phoned Marty. He had promised Suzie at breakfast that he wouldn't say a word to Maxine, and he'd stick to that, but Marty was a different matter.

'You sound serious. Everything's okay, isn't it?' his friend asked when Will enquired if he was free for lunch, because there was something he wanted to discuss. 'You're not about to pop your clogs, are you?'

'No. Nothing like that. So you can put your professional zeal back in its box. I'm not in need of a new will.'

'You're getting married and want a pre-nup, is that it?'

'When hell starts flogging ice-cream, that's the day I'll marry again and need a pre-nup.'

'Well, just you make sure you count me in on that deal too. Usual time and place?'

The shop was busy that morning, mostly with people who had no intention of putting a hand in their pocket. They were the time-wasters who said unimaginative things like: 'Oh, would you look at this! I remember having one of these when I was a girl.' Or, 'Twenty quid for this, my granny had a dozen of them! Talk about money for old rope.' Will knew a dealer down in Ludlow who had a sign in his shop that said: 'The only person interested in what your grandmother had is your granddad!' In contrast, the serious punters came in knowing exactly what they wanted and were prepared to pay the going rate, understanding that dealers had a living to make. It was extraordinary how many people genuinely resented dealers for earning an honest crust.

At ten to one, leaving Jarvis in charge, Will set off to meet Marty. It was market day, which meant the town had assumed a jaunty two-for-a-pound air. It also meant that the main car park was home to an eclectic mix of stallholders selling their wares, most of which had been made in the Far East. The original cobbled marketplace had long since been considered too small to be of use, and was now only used on May Day bank holiday and the Saturday before Christmas, when wooden Hansel and Gretel chalets were erected on it and the air was fragrant with the smell of Gluwein and German sausages.

Will and Marty's 'usual place' was a burger van on the edge of the market stalls. Brian, a Gulf War veteran, presided over his griddles and hotplates with regimented efficiency. Given that this was where Will and Marty often came to chat and clog up their arteries, they had nicknamed the burger van Chewing The Fat.

Marty was already there when Will worked his way through the crowds of shoppers picking over the spoils of pirate DVDs, Hoover attachments and cheap bedlinen. 'I've already put our order in,' Marty said, looking wildly out of place in his pinstripe suit, polished brogues and fob watch and chain. As a small-town solicitor in nearby Nantwich, he liked to dress the part. He reminded Will of an Agatha Christie character; the ever-loyal family solicitor. The fact that he was a resigned bachelor – the right woman had never come along – added to the illusion.

Brian gave Will a salute with his spatula. 'It'll be ready in a tick,' he said, scooping up an onion ring that had flown off the spatula and landed in a tub of margarine a foot square. True to his word, within seconds Will and Marty were clutching their cheeseburgers and polystyrene cups of coffee and commandeering the one and only table Brian provided for his customers. Once they were settled, Marty said, 'Come on then, what's the mystery?'

Straight to the point, Will said, 'It's Suzie. She told me last night that she's pregnant.'

Marty's eyes opened wide. 'Suzie?'

Will nodded.

'Bloody hell! But she's no more than a child herself.'

'Tell me about it. She's four months, apparently, which means in five months—'

'You could be a grandfather,' Marty finished off for him. He whistled. 'Boy, when I said it was time for you to think about growing up, Will, I didn't mean *that* grown-up. Does this herald a wedding? I can just see Maxine holding a Kalashnikov to the bugger's head.'

'No. There'll be no wedding. It was a one-off event. A mistake. Apparently the boy is going out with someone else.' Not meeting Marty's gaze, Will took a cautious sip of Brian's notoriously scalding-hot coffee, but still managed to burn his tongue. He was surprised how awkward he felt admitting that Suzie had had a one-night stand. Disappointed in himself, he said, 'The thing is, Suzie hasn't decided what she's going to do.'

They both fell silent. Then Marty said, 'Hypothetical question: what would you like her to do?'

'I don't think I have a right to think anything, do I?'

'Rubbish! As her father you have a gut reaction, the same as everyone else. Say it out loud. See how it sounds. Because I bet you've said it a thousand times in your head already.'

Pushing his half-eaten burger away, Will said, 'Okay, you're right, as ever. But my opinion counts for nothing, just remember that.'

'Get on with it.'

'Every ounce of my common sense screams out that an abortion would be best all round. But—'

Marty fixed him with a shrewd gaze.

'But I can't bear the thought of Suzie making a decision that might torment her for the rest of her life. Because once it's done, it's done. She has to live with that decision. And let's face it, we've all read or heard about women who never get over it. They feel haunted by the guilt.'

'What does Maxine say?'

Will explained Suzie's reason for not telling Maxine first. 'I guess she knows that her mother will overreact and she wants to feel more in control of any decision she makes. I can't say I blame her.'

'Poor kid.'

'My sentiments exactly.' He paused, then: 'Marty, think before you say anything, but do you suppose there's a chance that this is my fault? You know, the whole dysfunctional family bit.'

'What? Because you cocked up, ergo Suzie and Gemma are destined to do the same?'

'Yes.'

'That's the most absurd thing I've ever heard you say. Suzie's made a mistake, that's all. A mistake generations of girls have made before and will continue to do for years to come. Didn't we both take our fair share of risks when we were Suzie's age?' He pointed to the remains of the burger Will had allowed to go cold and uneaten. 'Eat up, Will, or Brian will flay you alive with his spatula. And that really will be the end of the world for you.'

Will knew his friend was trying to help, but he couldn't shift the growing fear that somehow this was his fault. Had he been blinded by his arrogance? Had he been deluded into thinking he'd done a reasonable job, when all along he'd let his daughters down, hadn't prepared them sufficiently for the traps and pitfalls that lay ahead?

Chapter Nineteen

After a run of bad days, Eileen was having a good one. The lethargy that had swamped her this last week had lifted and she was able to do more with the children. Carrie and Joel were now into their second week at school and the workload was considerably lighter. However, a new side to their lives had opened up. Now there was Carrie's homework to supervise. Last night's exercise had been to list five facts about each of the world's main religions. Thank goodness they had Harriet to turn to; she had shown Carrie how to find everything she needed on the computer. Both of the children were dab hands at playing games on the computer, which had belonged to their mother, but using it for homework purposes was new to them. In Felicity and Harriet's day the homework had been far more straight-forward. Helping the girls to learn their times tables and spellings had been a lot less stressful and time-consuming. Not for the first time since their lives had been turned upside down, Eileen felt out of her depth. Thank goodness Joel only had reading homework to do each evening. That much she could manage.

But Joel troubled Eileen. He was having nightmares. Night after night they were woken by his piercing screams. Every time it was the same; they'd find him petrified, in tears and huddled at the end of his bed, his back against the wall, his hands covering his eyes. Try as they might, they couldn't get him to say what he was dreaming of. Eileen regretted now that the children's sessions with the grief counsellor had recently come to an end. If the nightmares continued, perhaps they ought to think about Joel seeing the woman again.

In a rare moment of peace and quiet, while the children were at school and Bob was walking the dog, Eileen listened to Harriet moving about upstairs. She was packing for her weekend away. Guiltily, Eileen wished she was going with her.

Less than five miles from home and Harriet could feel an explosion of relief rushing through her body. As she left the slip-road and joined the M6 southbound, she felt as giddy as Toad of Toad Hall when he first discovered the joys of the motor car. 'Hurrah for the open road!' She laughed out loud, wishing she had a pair of goggles to hand. *Poop, poop!* A cap and a cape too. And gloves. *Poop, poop!* For the sheer hell of it, she honked the horn of her beloved Mini Cooper, which she'd bought brand new on her thirtieth birthday as a special treat, and sailed out into the middle lane. She felt no guilt that she was filled with this glorious sense of freedom. Two days of not having to answer questions like: *Why are bananas called bananas and why do they turn brown? Why do cats meow and dogs bark? Why is the sky blue?* Better still, there would be no hair to brush. No faces to wash. No teeth to check. No endless games of 'I Spy' to play. What bliss. And nothing, absolutely nothing, was going to ruin the next few days. She'd earned the break. It would also take her mind off the disappointment of not getting anywhere with her job-hunt. The agencies to whom she'd emailed her CV had all replied with more or less the same message: that there was nothing currently available but they would add her details to their records and get in touch when a suitable vacancy came their way. It was a classic don't-hold-your-breath response. So yes, she had every right to enjoy herself at Erin's party tonight and then lie on the sofa tomorrow with a skip-sized tub of KFC between them while watching non-stop, back-to-back *Sex and the City* DVDs.

So stop making it sound as if you're justifying it! she told herself. Forty-eight hours of self-indulgent behaviour was her deserved reward.

But then she went and spoiled it by recalling the look on Carrie's and Joel's faces when she'd told them that a friend had invited her to stay for a couple of days.

'How will we get to school?' Carrie had demanded, an uncompromising jut to her chin.

'You won't be going to school. I'm away over the weekend. And anyway, even if I wasn't here for a school day, Grandma and Granddad would take you then bring you home in the afternoon.'

'But you can't go! You have to stay here with us! I don't want you to go.'

This had been from Joel and the squealed vehemence of his words had taken Harriet aback. They'd been upstairs sitting on the floor in Carrie's bedroom, reading the latest Harry Potter before bedtime. 'I'll only be gone two days,' she'd explained patiently.

'But you will come back?' Everything Joel said these days was peppered with buts.

'Don't be silly, Joel,' Carrie had said, 'of course she'll come back. Won't you, Harriet?'

While her niece's steely gaze elicited a suitably reassuring reply – 'I'll be back before you've even missed me,' – Harriet had felt a twinge of irritation that her movements were being monitored so thoroughly. It was like being a teenager again and being grilled by Mum and Dad about what time she was expected home.

At breakfast this morning and during the journey to school, neither of the children had spoken to Harriet. She was surprised how hurt she felt.

But no matter. She refused to feel guilty. It wasn't as if she was going away for a fortnight's holiday. Two days off; was that so very bad? And she'd gone to great lengths to make sure that she'd covered all bases in her absence, reminding her mother that it was Friday and therefore sausage and chips night – the one meal Joel was guaranteed to eat – and that Carrie's weekend assignment (when did the word 'homework' become defunct?) was to make a Muslim prayer mat and that everything she needed –

coloured bits of paper, felt-tip pens and glue – was on the dining-room table. 'Why a prayer mat?' her father had asked, in an incredulous tone of voice that suggested the world had gone crazy. Harriet hadn't bothered to respond. She knew what her father meant: that breadth and ethnic diversity was all very well, but how about the basics? How about teaching the children to read and write good, honest, home-grown English? Just before she'd set off, she'd written a last-minute list for her parents:

1. Don't forget to buy Joel's favourite apple juice.
2. Also the muesli bars Carrie likes for breakfast – the ones with apricot, not raisins.
3. And remember to check their book bags for notes from school.
4. We're up to Chapter Nine of Harry Potter.

Enough! No more thoughts about Carrie and Joel. Or Mum and Dad. She was off the hook. She pressed down on the accelerator and swooped on towards Oxford and the life she'd left behind. *Poop, poop!*

Harriet suspected she was drunk, but not quite as drunk as the bleary-eyed bore she was talking to. With all the interrupted nights she'd had lately because of Joel's nightmares, if she spent another second in this man's company she'd nod off, no trouble. She glanced desperately around, hoping for some polite reason to extract herself without appearing rude. Someone choking on a peanut would be perfect. But there was nothing doing. Everyone else was either helping themselves to the plates of food she had helped Erin put out earlier or tossing back drinks as though any minute someone would call, 'Time gentlemen, please'. She decided simply to walk away. He probably wouldn't notice she'd gone.

She went to look for Erin. She knew Erin was embarrassed that only a handful of Harriet's friends had replied to the invitations and only two had bothered to turn up –

Gary and Paula who used to live in the house next door. Holidays were blamed, which only served to remind Harriet of the gap that now existed between her and her friends, or those she'd thought were friends. They could holiday out of term-time, whereas she was doomed for the rest of eternity to spend her precious time off with other young families in damp seaside cottages building sandcastles and pretending she was having a ball. Or worse, driven insane by staying at one of those purpose-built places in the middle of nowhere where she'd be forced to swim, cycle and hit balls from dawn to dusk. No more relaxing walking holidays in Tuscany or the Pyrenees for her. No more dreams of one day snorkelling in the turquoise waters of some faraway island.

Harriet suspected the real reason for her so-called friends not showing up was that she was still infectious, incubating a double whammy of those highly contagious germs of the recently bereaved and the out-of-work loser. 'Nobody knows you when you're down and out,' as Eric Clapton put it so succinctly. Well, to hell with them! If she'd become a pariah, it was their problem, not hers.

Erin was otherwise engaged when Harriet found her. Pressed against the combi boiler in the kitchen by a man who didn't look like a central-heating engineer, she waved Harriet away. Back into the crowded sitting room, Harriet pushed through the noisy mob of guests to help herself to another drink. Inspecting the bottles for something suitable for a girl hellbent on a good time, she found the ideal tipple tucked in behind the vodka and Bacardi Breezers. A bottle of Baileys: it was her and Felicity's favourite drink from way back when. They only ever drank it when they'd drunk too much already. Dominic used to call it their devil's homebrew of sugared cream and Benylin.

'Trust me; you don't want to touch that.'

Harriet swivelled round. Observing her as she struggled to unscrew the lid of the Baileys was a man who looked like he was straight off the cover of GQ. He was dressed in a navy-blue linen suit with an open-necked shirt and looked suspiciously like he was exceeding the weight limit in charm. Definitely not her type. Probably a banker. Or something that rhymed with it.

'Wouldn't you prefer a proper drink?' he asked with a smile that revealed two rows of perfectly even, white teeth. He produced a bottle of wine from somewhere about his person and began filling a pair of glasses that he'd also conjured up. 'I never trust the booze at these parties,' he said. 'Always wise to bring one's own. Here, try this.'

She was right about the charm. 'A piece of advice for you,' she said, refusing to take the proffered glass and annoyed at his arrogance. 'Never part a girl from her drink of choice. She might turn nasty.'

He smiled again. 'And what constitutes nasty in your book?' he drawled. 'A feisty little put-down learned at the Bridget Jones Finishing School?'

Oh, great! A smart aleck. Just what she needed. 'You know what, why don't we *not* do this? Parting, as they say, is such sweet sorrow, but I'm sure I'll get over it.'

She was about to turn and walk away when he said, 'Please, don't go. How about we start afresh?' He held out the glass for her again. 'I promise not to be such a git; it's just that these parties bring out the worst in me. You're the first girl I've spoken to since I arrived who's shown any intelligence. Please have a drink with me.'

What the hell, she thought. Maybe she had overreacted. He seemed contrite enough. After finding somewhere quieter to talk, he said, 'So tell me all about yourself. What's your name and what do you do? My name's Titus by the way, as in—'

'The hero of Mervyn Peake's *Gormenghast*?' she interrupted him. She was reminded of Dominic – it had been one of his favourite books as a teenager. 'Or perhaps your parents took their inspiration from the New Testament?'

He bowed. 'Your first guess was correct.'

'With a name like that I could almost feel sorry for you.' Beginning to relax, she pondered whether there was a chance he might turn out to be more than just a *GQ* pretty boy. 'I'm Harriet, by the way.'

'Pleased to meet you, Harriet.'

To her amusement, he leaned in closer, rested his shoulder against the wall and crossed his legs at the ankle, displaying a classic move from The Expert Flirter's Handbook: leave her in no doubt that she's the most fascinating girl in the room and that you're settling in for a long-haul conversation during which she will find you irresistible. 'So how do you fit in here?' she asked. 'How do you know Erin?'

'I met her through a friend. The last time I saw him he was in the kitchen with his tongue halfway down the host's throat. How about you?'

'I used to live in the flat downstairs.'

His glass hovered midway to his mouth. 'So you're the one whose sister snuffed – I mean died. Erin told me about it. What are you doing now?'

'I'm living in Cheshire looking after my sister's children.'

'Bloody hell. That's rotten luck. And living in the north, too. How long for?'

'For ever.'

'No, seriously, when do you come back?'

She stiffened. 'I *am* being serious.' How dare this patronising man denigrate what she was now doing. 'Children aren't like dogs,' she said sharply. 'You can't abandon them on the roadside like a bag of unwanted puppies.'

'Yeah, but they're not even yours.' He uncrossed his ankles and stood up straight, shaking his head wearily. 'God, your life is so over. Because let's face it, when you're done with those kids, there'll be the aging parents to wash and feed.' He stepped away from her and drank long and deep from his wine. She sensed him flicking onto page ten of The Expert Flirter's Handbook: unless you are a fully trained baggage handler, there is absolutely no point in wasting vital time and energy on a woman who comes with this much heavy-duty baggage.

'You know what,' she said, 'I think my first impression of you was right on the button. You're nothing but a shallow, gobby bloke who's just pushed me into mental meltdown.'

This time she did walk away, and not trusting herself to speak to anyone, not unless they were keen to have their head torn clean off, she kept on walking until she was standing in Erin's tiny spare bedroom, where she was spending the night. With enormous willpower – resisting the urge to slam it – she quietly closed the door behind her and leaned against it in the dark, giving herself time to calm down and steady her breathing. A stress-induced asthma attack was not what she needed right now. After several seconds of deep, slow breathing she realised she wasn't alone, and that what she could hear wasn't her lungs wheezing, but the unmistakable sound of two people mid-shag.

'Out!' she screamed. 'Out of my room!' She switched on the light, pulled the duvet off the semi-naked couple and pushed them into the hall, throwing their shoes and clothes after them before slamming the door shut. She noticed the remains of a coke-fest on the bedside table and wondered what the hell she was doing here. This was no longer her world. She had nothing in common with these people. They were more or less the same age as her, but she felt like an aged spinster aunt who'd accidentally gatecrashed a students' party. She'd actually had to stop herself from reprimanding Paula for knocking over a bowl of crisps, just as she would Carrie or Joel.

Harriet groaned and sank down onto the floor. Felicity had once told her that children made you grow up; that they made you act more responsibly and less selfishly. 'It must be a hormonal thing because it just happens,' she told Harriet. 'Once you've given birth you want the world to be a better place for your children, which means having to be a better person yourself.'

'Hormones be damned, Felicity!' she said out loud. 'It's nothing to do with them. It's something far more insidious.' She couldn't bring herself to say what it was, but after all the excitement of getting away, she knew she'd rather be back in Maple Drive than here. She'd much prefer to be sitting on the bedroom floor reading to Carrie and Joel – Carrie absently winding a lock of hair round a finger and Joel pressing against her, his small body fresh from the bath, warm and sweet-smelling.

She raked her hands through her hair and closed her eyes. But when it felt as if the room was spinning she snapped them open. She'd definitely had too much to drink. Coffee was needed. As she got to her feet, a muffled trilling sound came from somewhere in the room. She hunted through the tangle of bedclothes on the floor and clicked open the phone. It was ten past one – who the hell was calling her at this time of night?

At the sound of her father's voice, she froze. It was all too reminiscent of the night he'd called to say Felicity was dead. She sank onto the edge of the bed. Oh, God, what had happened now?

Chapter Twenty

'Thank goodness you're there, Harriet. We're at our wits' end. We didn't know what else to do. If he carries on like this we'll have to call a doctor out. We can't do anything with him. He's cried so much he's made himself sick. Your mother's exhausted and with all the fuss at school we—'

'Dad, slow down!' Harriet's head was spinning. 'Tell me what's happened. And take it slowly.' Her heart was hammering painfully and the knot of panic that had started in her stomach had spread to her chest. But at least it didn't sound as if anyone had died.

'It's Joel,' her father said. 'Well, it's Carrie too. She's the one who started it.'

'You're still not making any sense, Dad.'

'We've discovered what's been causing Joel's nightmares. We had a phone call from the headmistress this afternoon; apparently Carrie's been telling everyone at school that her parents' death was more gruesome than it really was. She's told them things like . . . oh, God, I can hardly think of it myself. No wonder Joel's been so terrified.'

'What exactly has she been saying?'

'That their heads were sliced off in the accident, that the police never found them and . . . because of that, Felicity and Jeff, dripping in blood, are forced to wander the streets at night searching for them.'

A chill ran down Harriet's spine. 'Carrie said all that? But why?'

'I've no idea, but she's said a lot worse. Stuff about her being able to make her parents haunt anyone she doesn't like. She's scared some of the children so badly that their parents have complained to school.'

'To hell with them. It's Joel I'm concerned about. Do you think he'll talk to me?'

'That's why I've called. He keeps asking for you. Perhaps if you speak to him, he might calm down and go back to bed. Will you do it, Harriet? You know, just talk him round so we can all get some sleep.'

'Of course, Dad. Put him on.'

'You'll have to hang on while I go upstairs; I'm on the phone in the kitchen.'

Waiting for her father to put Joel on the line, Harriet thought of the nights she'd found her nephew drenched in sweat, his damp hair sticking to his scalp, his eyes squeezed shut, and the duvet wrapped tightly around his body as though it would protect him. Knowing what they knew now, she could understand his terror. Her chest tightened and she coughed, instinctively trying to force oxygen into lungs that were threatening to close down. She fumbled for her inhaler at the bottom of her bag. With the mobile pressed against her ear, she could hear her father's voice and the racking, hiccupy sobs of Joel in the background.

'Harriet, are you still there?'

'Yes, Dad,' she wheezed. 'Put him on.'

There was a pause while her father told Joel to say hello. He didn't. But he had stopped crying.

'Joel, can you hear me? It's me, Harriet. Aren't you going to say hello?'

In the ensuing silence, she put her inhaler to her mouth, pressed down on the canister and breathed in sharply. It was always tempting to give herself two quick hits, one immediately after the other. But she knew better and instead imagined the chemicals rushing through the narrowing airways of her lungs, flushing them out like those pipes you see in a toilet-cleaner advert.

'Wassat noise?' a small, husky voice asked.

Progress, thought Harriet. 'It's my asthma inhaler, Joel.'

She heard a sob catch in his throat. 'Are you . . . ill?'

'No, of course not. I'm as fit as a fiddle. How about you? I hear you've had another bad dream.'

Silence again.

'Joel?'

'Are you coming back?' His voice was a dried-up raspy whisper. He'd probably cried his throat raw.

'On Sunday. Don't you remember we discussed all that?'

'Can't you come back now?'

'I don't know if you've noticed, Joel, but it's the middle of the night.'

'But I want you here. Why can't you come home?' He started to cry again.

'Oh, Joel, it's not as easy as that.' How could she explain that even if she wanted to leap into the car and drive all the way home, she couldn't because she was well over the limit? 'Listen to me, Joel,' she said as firmly as her breath would allow her. 'You have to go back to bed and get some sleep. It's not fair to Grandma and Granddad.'

'No!' he wailed. 'I don't want to.'

'I know you don't; I also know what's been causing the nightmares you've been having. But none of it's true. All that stuff Carrie's been saying – she was making it up.'

'But why would she say those things if they weren't true?'

'I haven't a clue.' And thinking it might help him to talk about the nightmares, she said, 'Do you want to tell me what goes on in your dreams?'

Her question went unanswered.

'Okay, I'll take the silence as a no.' She took another puff of her inhaler. Her heart was racing now, but she could feel her lungs expanding and the air getting through.

'Is that your inhaler again?'

'Yes.'

'You're not going to die, are you?'

His question shook her. 'Joel, now listen very hard. I've always told you the truth, and I'm not about to start lying to you now. I'm not dying, and your parents didn't die the way Carrie said they did. Ghosts don't exist and you have nothing to be frightened of. Unlike your sister, who's going to get a good talking-to from me when I get home.'

After a lengthy pause, he said, 'Harriet?'

157

'Yes?'

'Please come home. I want you to come back. I don't like it when you're not here.'

Not for a long time had Harriet allowed anyone to manipulate her, but this boy could do it every time. Stupid thing was, she realised she didn't care; her planned day of watching *Sex and the City* DVDs with Erin had lost its appeal anyway. 'I'll be home some time after breakfast,' she said. 'How does that sound?'

As if by magic, he cheered up instantly. 'Will you take me to the bookshop? The one where your friend works?'

'I will.' Then seizing her opportunity, she added, 'But you have to promise me you'll go to bed right now. This very minute.'

'Can I have a drink first?'

'A very quick one.'

Harriet was on the road by seven. Erin surfaced briefly, and yawning hugely like the Dormouse at the Mad Hatter's tea party, she said she completely understood that Harriet had to get home. 'No worries,' she said, 'we'll get together again soon.' But Harriet knew it wasn't ever going to happen. Those days had gone. And maybe, if it meant she never again had to meet the likes of that arrogant prat Titus, it was for the best.

It was while she was tearing up the M6 that yet another truth hit her. When it came to the children's sense of security, it appeared that the buck stopped with her. It had been her, last night, that Joel had wanted. Not her mother. Not her father. For the life of her she didn't know why this would be – especially given her parents' view that she scared the children by being too firm with them. Only a number of weeks ago and this realisation would have alarmed her, but today it didn't. It felt oddly reassuring, as if she was finally getting something right. Being able to comfort and reason with Joel on the phone last night had been of paramount importance to her. It still was. She couldn't bear to think of him being so upset ever again.

And what of Carrie in all this? What on earth had been going through that girl's head to make her say such ghoulish things?

Harriet knew from experience that most children – usually older than Carrie – go through a phase of being fascinated by death. Certainly when she and Felicity had been teenagers it was a topic of conversation that had cropped up with morbid regularity, and invariably with Dominic and Miles. Felicity had always been adamant that she wanted to be cremated when she died; she hated the thought of being buried. Harriet could remember one conversation in particular on the subject. It had taken place during late summer, the year Dominic had been offered a place at Cambridge. They'd been lying on the flattened grass in the corner of a field, just behind the hawthorn hedge along the towpath of the canal. On their backs, staring up at the clouds and trying to spot Margaret Thatcher's face, which Miles swore blind was there in the sky, Felicity had said that she wanted her body to be donated to medical science and that what was left had to be cremated. 'I don't want worms wriggling in and out of my eye sockets and centipedes crawling up my nose,' she'd explained, just a little too graphically.

Rolling onto his side and running his hand over Felicity's stomach then letting it linger on her breasts, Dominic had said, 'I've got a better idea: why don't you donate your body to me to research.' It had always amazed Harriet that Felicity could let Dominic touch her like that. It upset her because she knew he was only doing it to annoy his brother – Miles had always had a bit of a crush on Felicity.

'What's wrong with what we do?' Felicity said to Harriet when she tackled her about it one day. 'Dominic knows I like it when he touches me. It doesn't mean anything.'

'But it drives Miles mad, and that's the real reason Dominic does it.'

'Miles knows better than to be upset by anything his brother does.'

It wasn't often that Harriet questioned her sister's

judgement, but in that instance she did. Privately, she thought Miles minded a lot of things, especially the way Dominic would treat people. On one memorable outing to a club in Manchester, when Dominic was home from Cambridge for Easter, he had really excelled himself. Even Felicity, his constant champion, was cross with him. As a foursome, they were used to people staring at them when they went out, mostly because Dominic was so strikingly good-looking. With his black hair swept back from his broad forehead, his piercingly blue eyes and his easy nonchalance he had an aura of glamour that attracted attention wherever he went. On that particular night he was attracting the normal number of looks and stares, and after several drinks he suddenly announced that he was going to make someone's night. 'And it's that girl there,' he said, indicating the most under-dressed over-permed, and possibly ugliest girl in the club. To their surprise, he sauntered over to where she was standing and started chatting to her. The girl's friends drew close, clearly impressed.

'What the hell's he up to now?' muttered Miles. Minutes passed, then Dominic joined them where they'd been queuing for a drink. Leaning against the bar, he drained the remains of his Jack Daniel's and smiled. Intrigued, they then watched the girl come towards him. She tapped Dominic on the shoulder. 'Are you ready for that dance now?' she said.

Dominic swung round and said, 'Good God, you didn't think I was serious, did you? That I'd willingly dance with a fat cow like you? Why don't you try my brother; he's much more your type. Not so choosy either.'

It was like watching a balloon being popped. The girl burst into tears and fled.

It was one of the cruellest things Harriet had ever witnessed. Miles was so furious with Dominic that he dragged him outside, pushed him up against a wall and punched him hard. A fight broke out between them and only when a bouncer intervened did they pull apart. For days afterwards, Harriet and Felicity refused to speak to Dominic. In the end, in a typically over-the-top gesture, he stood beneath their bedroom windows late one night and read out a letter of apology. 'For the love of God, tell the bloody stupid fool that you've forgiven him,' Dad had said, as lights up and down Maple Drive switched on and windows were opened and pointedly banged shut, 'or we'll never get any sleep.'

That was Dominic all over. A clever, self-obsessed man who ruthlessly trampled others underfoot for his own pleasure and saw it as his right to be forgiven, no matter what the offence. On that occasion, Harriet and her sister let him stew for a further three days.

In danger of dozing off at the wheel – she'd only had three hours' sleep – Harriet stopped at Stafford Services. She bought a newspaper, a cup of coffee and a slice of toast. Half an hour later, feeling suitably revived, she went back out to the car park, ready for the rest of her journey home. But when she saw her car, she stopped in her tracks. The driver's window was smashed and the alarm was screeching. A panicky first glance told her that her laptop had been stolen.

Chapter Twenty-One

Carrie knew she was in big trouble. Grandma and Grand-dad had calmed down, but Harriet would be home soon and then she'd really get it. She just hoped that when Harriet started shouting at her she'd remember to tilt her head back and stare at the ceiling so that it was impossible for any tears to spill out. She'd learned to do this (and to blink a lot) when Mummy and Daddy had died and everyone kept asking if she was okay.

It felt like for ever since they'd died. Sometimes she had trouble remembering what they looked like. Part of her thought it might be easier to forget them, but then she'd suddenly think of something nice, like her birthday, when she'd unwrapped their presents and found the best one of all: Poppy. Poppy was an enormous fluffy polar bear and lying on the bed with her arms wrapped around her, Carrie suddenly wished that it was Mum she was cuddling. Mum had been nice to cuddle up to. She'd smelled nice and she always knew what to say or do to make her and Joel smile when they were upset. She was better at that than Dad. But then Dad was good at making them laugh; he'd tickle them or tell them jokes that didn't make sense. If only Mum and Dad were here now, they'd cheer her up. She hugged Poppy tightly. Harriet was going to be so cross. She reminded Carrie of Professor Snape sometimes, always scowling and looking serious. But then, just when you thought she was about to tell you off or be cross about something, she'd surprise you. Like that time in the car when she'd used that word Mummy said they weren't to say and had laughed her head off.

But there wouldn't be any laughing today. She shouldn't have told all those lies. She hadn't meant to but they'd just kept slipping out. She was sorry she'd frightened Joel, but she wasn't sorry about the others at school. They deserved it. Hadn't they started it by asking if Mum and Dad had had their heads chopped off? How would they feel if it was their parents who were dead? Burying her face in Poppy's white fur, she let herself quietly cry, safe in the knowledge that no one was there to see. Grandma was downstairs with Joel and Granddad was out walking Toby.

With Toby off the leash and snuffling on ahead in the bushes, Bob followed slowly behind. It was only the second week of September, but already there was a hint of things to come. There was a soft gauze of mist hanging over the surface of the canal and the air was both sharp and damp. Either side of the path, grass glistened with early-morning dew, and a scattering of fallen willow leaves, yellow and wet, lay like a catch of slippery fish on the ground. Pausing at Will's house, Toby peered through the hedge as if hoping for something to eat – Will often gave Toby a titbit while he and Bob passed the time of day. But there was no sign of Will this morning. It was Saturday after all; he was probably at work. Disappointed, Bob pressed on. After the night he'd had, he would have appreciated the opportunity to talk to Will. He struck Bob as being a good listener. Perhaps they ought to have him over for a drink. Maybe invite Dora and the McKendricks too – knowing full well, of course, that only Harvey would turn up. They could put on a sort of belated 'welcome to the neighbourhood' do. Except that would mean fuss and bother, something he couldn't face. For now it was as much as he could do to keep treading water, his chin just skimming the surface. It'll change, he told himself. Things *will* get better. They had to.

Following the towpath as it curved away from the last of the houses of Maple Drive and through the patch of elderberry trees, their branches heavy with beads of shiny black fruit, Bob watched Toby chase a startled moorhen out of the undergrowth. Worried the dog might hurl itself into the water after the bird, Bob called him to heel. At the sound of chugging, he turned. Coming towards them was a traditional tug-style narrowboat, its small brass chimney chucking out puffs of sooty smoke. Toby barked at the boat, and when it drew level, a well-wrapped-up woman with an arm resting on the tiller waved at Bob. 'Beautiful morning,' she said.

'I suppose it is,' he said. He couldn't remember the last time he had thought anything beautiful.

'You wouldn't give me a hand, would you?' she asked. 'I want to moor up for a brew. If I could just throw you a rope, it would make things a lot easier.'

Surprised at the request, and that she was apparently travelling alone, Bob went on ahead to the prow of the boat and kept pace while the woman steered it towards the bank. She then cut the engine and nimbly made her way to the front where she scooped up a neat coil of rope and tossed it to him. While he held the boat firm, she returned to the stern, stuffed some mooring pins into her jacket pockets and hopped out with a coil of rope in one hand and a rubber mallet in the other. 'You okay to hang on while I bang this one in?' she called to him.

'No problem at all.'

Toby went over to investigate, keeping a cautionary distance as the mallet rose and fell. Bob watched the woman; she clearly knew what she was about and had a purposeful weather-beaten look about her. He wondered why she was travelling alone. Or maybe she wasn't. Perhaps there was a companion sleeping soundly on board. He wondered what the interior of the boat looked like. He knew they could be very smart these days, all the mod cons thrown in: hot and cold water, carpets, log-burning stoves, toilets, even showers. Peering through one of the brass-rimmed portholes, he could make out a cabin that looked invitingly snug. He had often been tempted to go on a canal holiday but somehow it had never happened. The children had either been too young and therefore in danger of falling in and drowning or they'd been too old and in danger of being bored. There had also been the busman's holiday element to take into account; having the Shropshire Union Canal on their doorstep it hadn't seemed that big or worthwhile a change. Instead, they'd spent most of their summer holidays camping in France. Remembering the many child-friendly campsites they stayed at, Bob felt a pang of compromise and regret.

'Right then, that's the back end sorted; let's see about relieving you.' The woman was by his side now, and with Toby in obedient attendance, she pushed a mooring pin into the damp earth, then hammered it home. In no time at all, she had the rope expertly knotted and the excess neatly dealt with.

'You look like you've done this before,' he said when she was finished.

Hot from all the exertion, she pulled off the woolly tea-cosy of a hat she was wearing and revealed a head of curly salt and pepper hair. 'Just once or twice,' she said with a broad smile, unzipping her bulky jacket. Without the hat, she was less weather-beaten than he'd first thought. Slimmer and younger too. Late fifties he reckoned. She looked like an old-fashioned games mistress, cheerful and robust. 'Thanks for the help, by the way,' she said. 'I appreciate it.'

'It's a large boat to manage on your own.' He was blatantly fishing, curious to know if there was a companion on board who was too lazy to shift his weight and help.

'It's not as difficult as you'd think. I can do locks on my own quite easily, which was my biggest worry initially. With the centre rope, it's not too bad.' She smiled again, revealing, he thought, a hint of pride. 'Although, being an opportunist at heart,' she went on, 'I'm quite happy to grab a useful pair of hands if they're available.'

'Then I'm glad I was around.'

A flurry of movement from the other side of the canal had them both turning. A pair of moorhens was scuttling noisily out of the bushes, but as if knowing they'd been spotted, they adopted a more leisurely pace, slipped into the water and swam sedately away.

'Well,' he said, 'I'd better leave you to your brew.'

She laughed – a happy, carefree laugh. 'I'm afraid that was a euphemism for wanting the loo.'

'In that case, even more reason for me to take my leave. Come on, Toby, stop sniffing round that rope.' The dog looked suspiciously like he too needed the loo and was about to raise his leg.

Normally Bob would walk Toby as far as the bend just before The Navigation, where there were official mooring places, but this morning, knowing that Harriet would be arriving home soon, he cut short their walk and within a few minutes was returning the way he'd come. 'It's got nothing to do with chatting to that woman again, then?' He asked himself.

The mist had cleared when he spotted the boat. It was still moored where he'd left it, but a different chimney, one in the middle of the boat, was now sending out a thin plume of smoke. Sniffing the air, he recognised it as woodsmoke. He hadn't noticed earlier, but there were gaily painted pots (decorated with the traditional narrowboat rose motif) of flowering chrysanthemums on the roof of the boat, which he now saw was named the *Jennifer Rose*. The flowers suggested that the woman was a live-aboard, as the boating fraternity described people who lived on the waterways, and not a casual holidaymaker. He pictured the curly-haired woman sitting in the cabin, cosily insulated from the outside world and planning where to go next. He suddenly wished he could do the same. Oh, to leave all those painful reminders of Felicity behind so that they couldn't hurt him any more. How much better it would be to pretend he was someone else, that he had never known Felicity. The thought was such a betrayal of his love for his daughter that he had to fight to keep his composure.

A tapping sound had him looking to one of the windows. Holding up a metal teapot and a china mug, the woman was inviting him to join her in a cup of tea.

'You'll tell her you haven't got time,' he said to himself, 'that you're expected home.'

But he didn't.

Chapter Twenty-Two

Harriet knew it was pointless to be so angry; it only made her feel worse. It was three days since her car had been broken into – it was now back from the garage – and she felt completely lost without her laptop. Rightly or wrongly, the theft had superseded her shock at the gruesomely sensational tales Carrie had been spreading at school. Maybe it was for the best, because who knows what she may have said or done to Carrie in the heat of the moment? It was still a mystery to Harriet and her parents why Carrie had felt the need to tell such lies – no amount of careful questioning could make sense of any of the muttered answers the girl gave them. In the end, Harriet had concluded that her niece didn't know why she'd done it; she had promised, though, not to do it again. After a brief telephone call to the headmistress at school, it was accepted that in view of the circumstances, no more would be said on the matter. However, the subject was not entirely closed; Harriet had been on the receiving end of some strange, not to say hostile looks from some of the mothers at the school gate.

This morning had been no exception, but with so much else on her mind, she didn't let it get to her. Back home, while she opened a letter regarding her motor insurance, she made the mistake of cursing the thieving bastard who had broken into her car. For some inexplicable reason it provoked her father to snap at her. 'This is what happens when you rely so heavily on modern technology,' he said. 'You become obsessed with it and think you can't manage without it. For God's sake, it was only a plastic box of chips and memory boards.'

'Thank you, Dad, for that helpful comment,' she said dryly, both annoyed and taken aback at his outburst.

'And as I've told you before,' he went on, 'you're more than welcome to use my computer.'

'No offence, but that would be like offering a kite to an astronaut to get him to the moon. Your machine's hopelessly antiquated.'

'Oh, well, if you're going to be like that, I'm off. Toby? Come here, boy. Let's go in search of more convivial company, shall we?'

'That dog's going to be worn out if you take him for any more walks,' Eileen had muttered from the sink, where she was trying to remove Biro ink from one of Carrie's school sweatshirts.

'Nonsense. A dog needs plenty of exercise.'

Despite what her father thought, being without her laptop really was a major upheaval for Harriet. She regretted taking it down to Erin's; she'd only taken it because she had wanted to check her emails in case a job offer came through while she was away. But it wasn't just the hassle of buying a new one and dealing with the insurance company that irritated her, it was the loss of so much vital information and the sense of violation that really bothered her. It was the personal stuff that affected her most; all those emails she and Felicity had exchanged. It was like losing a precious photograph album. In the weeks after Felicity's death, Harriet had spent many sleepless nights comforting herself by rereading the emails they had written to each other. Staring into the blue-white glow of the laptop screen, and hearing Felicity's voice brought vividly to life in the amusing exchanges, Harriet could almost believe that in the morning there would be a new email waiting for her.

In the meantime, before Harriet could buy a replacement laptop, she was using Felicity's computer in Carrie's bedroom. Harriet had helped her sister to buy it last autumn when her old one had become unusable, and had also installed all the software Felicity had needed for her translation work, along with games and pseudo-educational stuff for the children. Jeff hadn't been into computers; he'd used them at work but that was as far as his interest had gone. Felicity, on the other hand, freely admitted that she was an email junkie, that she couldn't go to bed without checking her Inbox.

Harriet switched on Felicity's computer to access her own emails, hoping to hear from one of the job agencies. In her heart, she knew that if there was a job going, they would be in touch by phone. Nonetheless she still felt disappointed when she saw there was no news from any of the agencies. She felt a failure. She missed work so much; it was her identity, she supposed. She missed the office culture, the trade in put-downs and jokes. She also missed the way computers didn't answer back, unlike children. She used to tease Spencer that at worst, computers were like men: they just stared vacantly at you, waiting for an instruction.

Resigned to another week of scanning the pages of *Computer Weekly* and waiting for the phone to ring, she sighed heavily. 'Oh, Felicity, why did you have to die? Why did you leave me in this mess?' She sat for a moment gazing absently at the computer screen and, suddenly filled with longing to feel closer to her sister, she wondered if it would be so wrong to read an email Felicity had sent to her – just to hear her voice, to feel her presence. In her heart she knew it would be like poking around in another person's personal diary, but she justified her need by telling herself that it wasn't the same, that reading something Felicity had already sent to her was perfectly all right.

She knew Felicity's password and had no trouble accessing her sister's Outbox. The list of sent emails was in date order and Harriet felt a chill run through her when she saw the last email had been sent the day before Felicity and Jeff had died. She also saw that the email address was Harriet_Swift@yahoo.co.uk. She stared at the address and those preceding it. Scrolling back over the preceding weeks and months, there was an obvious pattern. And one which intrigued her. There were two names that appeared more regularly than any others. The Harriet_Swift@yahoo.co.uk address and the MissTechie@btinternet.co.uk address were about evens in frequency. A strange feeling crept over Harriet. She was all too familiar with who MissTechie was – it was her email address – but who was Felicity messaging under the name of Harriet Swift? She'd never had a Yahoo account.

There was only one way to find out, but should she do it? Her hand hovered over the mouse.

Click.

Whatever she'd expected, it wasn't this. The text was brief and made no sense. It appeared to be scrambled. But as Harriet scanned the block of text she saw it for what it was: a code. And not any old code. This one had been used by Harriet and her sister when they were children. She hadn't thought of it in years, but it all came flooding back and she recalled how the two of them had been sitting on Harriet's bed one rainy Sunday afternoon when she had devised the idea. Hardly up to Bletchley Park standards, the trick had been not to leave any gaps between the words or use any punctuation or capital letters. Also, the letters of each word had to be substituted with the following letter of the alphabet – for instance, THE would be written as UIF. It had been an instant success and they had spent hours writing secret letters to each other.

Harriet knew, as she looked at the text, that there could be only one reason why Felicity had used their childhood secret code: she had wanted this kept private. She thought of Miles's words about her having a strong sense of right and wrong. 'Sorry to disappoint you, Miles,' she murmured, getting up from the chair and crossing the room to shut the door – she sensed this wasn't something her parents should walk in on. She helped herself to a pen and a piece of paper from Carrie's desk drawer and began the painstaking process of decoding the email. When it was done, she sat back in the chair and read it through.

I dreamt of you last night. We were wrapped in each other's arms but you were crying. You said your heart was breaking. That I was breaking it. Tell me that's not true. I couldn't live with myself if I ever thought I was causing you such unhappiness. You know how very much I love you – you always have – but you have to be patient. Trust me, please, it won't be long now. Just give me a little more time. You mean everything to me. EVERYTHING.

The sound of a door banging shut downstairs had Harriet snapping forward in the chair and closing the email. She then hurriedly switched off the computer and folded the piece of paper she had written on and slipped it into her pocket.

What a discovery. Felicity had been having an affair. It was inconceivable. Her very own sister, who she'd thought had never kept anything from her.

Harriet's first thought was that she should format the hard disk and wipe the computer clean. No one else must ever stumble across what she had. It would kill her father if he ever knew that Felicity had been leading this double life, that she had been less than perfect.

Her second thought was to wonder who Felicity had been seeing. She racked her brains to think of a name that might have come up in conversation more frequently than any other. But nothing came to mind. Knowing it went against her nature, Harriet knew she would have to read more. She wanted to know who had mattered so much to her sister. Who had meant *everything* to Felicity?

Chapter Twenty-Three

Normally one of the more attentive students in the class, Gemma was having trouble concentrating on that afternoon's philosophy lesson on Descartes' rationalism.

It was two weeks since Suzie's revelation, but Gemma still couldn't believe her sister had made such a mess of things. How could she have got herself pregnant? How dumb she had been! But even as she asked herself the question, Gemma knew the answer. Hadn't she and Marcel taken a similar risk in Paris? Each time she thought of that occasion – when they'd realised he'd run out of condoms – she shuddered. They'd been upstairs in his bedroom and suddenly so desperate for each other that they were prepared to do it while Veronique had been in the bathroom next door. She'd told him it would be okay, so long as he came out at the crucial moment. It had only happened the once – all the other times they'd been careful – but of course, once was all it took. How crazy could she have been? Well, one thing was for sure, she'd never make that mistake again. No way. And to make doubly sure there was no danger of her feelings for Marcel getting the better of her, she'd replied to his letter saying there was too much going on for him to visit. 'It would be better to put your trip off until next year,' she'd written. She was slightly ashamed of herself that she'd taken this step, because it looked like she didn't trust herself to be in the same room as him without wanting sex. Maybe the sensible thing to do was to go on the pill and have done with it.

Next to her, Yasmin was sitting bolt upright. Her friend's attention was fixed firmly on what Mr Sheridan was saying. She was one of the most focused people Gemma knew and she couldn't imagine Yasmin being stupid enough to have unprotected sex. For one thing her parents and brother would kill her. For another, Yasmin didn't want anything to get in the way of the career she had in mind. She wanted to go to Oxford and then be a fund manager in London. Gemma knew that Mr and Mrs Patel were disappointed by this; they wanted their daughter to go into the family mobile-phone business. Gemma wished she was as focused as her friend. She didn't have a clue what she wanted to do. Some days she wondered why she was even considering university. Mum sometimes said that she was too much like her father and lacked the grit and determination for which the Stone family was famous. But Gemma thought her father was more determined than Mum made him out to be. To have done what he did – jack in a good job at his time of life, and with a young family – took a lot of guts.

But the million-dollar question was what Mum would say about Suzie's pregnancy, other than going mental and screaming the full nine yards about safe sex and what a right Horlicks Suzie had made of her life. She'd probably ask what Suzie had thought she'd been doing having sex in the first place.

But tonight was the night. Suzie had told Gemma and Dad that she was going to break the news to Mum during a family dinner, which Suzie would cook and to which Dad was invited. This meant one thing and one thing only: they were in for an evening of pure over-the-top melodrama.

Maxine was suspicious; she knew in her bones that something was going on. She called through to the en suite bathroom where Steve was brushing his teeth. 'The last time Suzie went to this much trouble and cooked for us it was my fortieth birthday. I haven't missed an important date on the calendar, have I?'

Steve joined her in the bedroom and stood behind her as she finished applying a fresh coat of mascara to her daytime make-up. He'd changed out of his suit and was casually dressed in a pair of Ralph Lauren chinos and a pale green

Tommy Hilfiger shirt. He was twelve years older than her but still looked good. He knew how to dress and how to keep the weight off – he went to the gym three times a week and played tennis as often as the weather permitted. 'I think you should just relax and enjoy yourself,' he said. 'Maybe this is Suzie's way of apologising for what her father did to my car. Take it as an olive branch.'

He kissed her neck and placed his hands around her waist, something Maxine wished he wouldn't do. She always felt as though he was sizing her up, checking to see if she'd put on any weight. And dammit, she had. Ever since Paris, when they'd overindulged, her clothes had felt too tight. There was nothing else for it; she'd have to go on a diet, and soon. Joining a gym was out of the question. She simply didn't have the time. Hell, she didn't even have time to go out and buy any new outfits. When did she last spend a leisurely hour or two browsing round her favourite shoe shops? Or have lunch with friends? Her life was so hectic. But then it always had been. She wouldn't have it any other way.

Work was crazier than ever at the moment; the saleroom had never been busier. She blamed that David Dickinson and his programme *Bargain Hunt*. Not that anyone with any real sense would think there was a correlation between what went on in that programme and the real world of buying and selling. Still, sales were up and the punters, victims of first-time auction fever, kept on coming. It was their lookout, not hers. She liked to think that Dad would have been proud of her, that he would have approved of how she'd carried on the business, making it even more successful than he had. And if everything went to plan, she'd soon be acquiring a second saleroom; one in Stafford. The deal was agreed in principle, and now it was down to the paperwork between the lawyers and accountants. It was a shame her father wasn't around to see what she'd achieved. He'd worked so hard himself, and she would have liked him to know that she really had been cut from the same cloth as him. It gave her a warm glow of satisfaction knowing that her ambition easily matched his.

But work was no excuse for letting herself go. She knew she wasn't overweight, not really, but at her age she couldn't afford to carry too many excess pounds. Will used to say she had the best curves this side of a Stradivarius violin, but Steve didn't like the 'comely wench' look, as he referred to any woman bigger than a size twelve. Just as well he'd never seen her when she was pregnant with the girls. She'd been enormous then. Will used to pretend he couldn't get his arms around her, but then he'd kiss her, and suddenly his hands and arms would be all over her and they'd end up in bed. For a lot of couples, pregnancy puts a stop to sex, but it didn't for them. In those days, she and Will couldn't get enough of each other.

What a lifetime ago that was. And how pig-headedly, how selfishly and how recklessly Will had thrown it all away. If she lived to be a hundred, she didn't think she would ever forgive him for what he did to her and the girls. She cringed at the embarrassing memories of trying to pretend to her friends and work associates that all was well at home, that her husband was merely taking time out to consider an exciting career change. She would sooner have died than let anyone know that he was at home drinking endless cups of coffee and watching hour after hour of mind-rotting daytime telly while she was out grafting from dawn till dusk.

Realising that Steve's hands were still on her waist and that he was saying something, she came back to the present with a jolt. 'Sorry, darling, what was that?'

'I was just asking if you remembered how tough the chicken was that Suzie cooked for you on your fortieth. She must only have been fourteen. It makes you wonder where the time goes, doesn't it?'

Maxine snapped the lid back onto the tube of mascara, and refusing to let the past spoil the evening or her mood, she said, 'I prefer to think about the future and what that has in store for us. Come on, let's go downstairs and see how the chef's faring.'

'Absolutely not. Suzie said we're under strict instructions to wait in the sitting room with Gemma until we're summoned to the dining room.'

The doorbell chimed. 'That'll be Will,' she said. 'I wonder if he knows what this evening's all about. I certainly don't buy your olive-branch theory.'

Will had promised Suzie that he'd be on his best behaviour. 'Don't worry,' he'd told her when she'd said what she was planning. 'I won't crack a single joke in poor taste.'

As they sat round the late nineteenth-century French mahogany dining table and rested their bums on a set of Victorian rosewood parlour chairs (all genuine, no fakes or repro here), with everything glowing lusciously in the tinkling light cast from a rococo-style ormolu chandelier above their heads, Will's light-heartedness was all a front. Beneath the gossamer-thin surface of apparent joviality, he was a bundle of nerves. He knew Maxine would have him strung up by his privates before the night was through. God, he wished Suzie had told Maxine before him. 'That's what comes from being Mr Approachable,' Marty had told him. 'And thank your lucky stars that Suzie does trust and love you. Not many fathers would get such treatment. So stop whingeing and buckle down.'

'Cheers, Marty, you're a real pal,' he'd said. 'Just promise me this: as my solicitor you have to make sure my wishes are adhered to at my funeral. R.E.M.'s 'I've Been High' has to be played when you help carry in the coffin. Okay?'

'Stop being such a coward. So what if Maxine does have a go at you for being first to know? That's more a reflection of her character, not yours.'

'Being first to know isn't the problem. It's the fact that I knew and didn't tell her. I'm going to be shredded.'

Nina Simone singing 'My Baby Just Cares For Me' smooched her way into the dining room from the CD player in the sitting room – the entire ground floor of the house was rigged up to Steve's state-of-the-art system – and for a welcome moment of distraction, Will listened to the lyrics about Nina's baby not caring for shows or clothes, or cars and races or high-tone places. *Ding, dong!* Irony alert, he thought. Maxine and PC Plod were obsessed with the superficial frippery money could buy.

Registering that an ominous silence had fallen on them, and terrified Suzie might feel now was the time to explain why they were all here, Will said, 'So, Steve, how's tricks? People still wanting to have their houses wired up like Fort Knox?'

'More or less. Did Maxine tell you I'm in the middle of negotiating for an American company in the Midwest? It'll be quite a deal if we can pull it off.'

'No she didn't.' Will glanced across the table to Maxine. He'd heard on the grapevine that she was expanding Stone's and buying a saleroom in Staffordshire, but Steve's plans were news to him. Just how much money did they need? 'Perhaps she was sparing my feelings,' he said carefully. 'Me being such a pauper.'

Maxine cleared her throat. 'If you're a pauper, Will, you have only yourself to blame. Anyway, the truth is that I was waiting to tell you when it was official.'

'I doff my cap to your thoughtfulness, your ladyship.'

'It's only a small company,' Steve said as though imagining he could ever smooth the waters, 'just to give us a foothold in a wider market.'

'Hey, you kick ass and go as global as you like. The poor will always be here to remind you of what you left behind.'

'Dad!'

Damn! He'd broken his promise. 'Sorry, Suzie,' he murmured, giving her the briefest of apologetic smiles. He didn't dare risk looking at her properly. If he did then he'd really feel the pathetic loser he turned into when he was around Maxine for too long. When the heat was off him, and Maxine had eased back on the dirty looks and Steve was changing the CD, Will took a moment to snatch a sideways glance at Suzie again. All things considered, she didn't look too bad. There was no obvious sign that she was pregnant, although to the discerning eye, maybe the loose-fitting top she was wearing was a bit of a giveaway. Unlike Gemma, whose midriff was permanently on display no matter what the weather, Suzie's was well covered up.

Will and Gemma were still in the dark about what she was going to do regarding the baby. Gemma reckoned that Suzie would keep the baby and a small, indefinable part of him hoped that she would. Unbelievably, the idea of being a grandfather had grown on him. Simplistically, the child he had helped to create, the child who carried his genes, now carried another extension of himself. Wasn't this the whole point of the human existence? The continuation of the species.

He suspected Maxine wouldn't see it quite this way. Moreover, he fully expected her to find a way to blame his defective genes for bringing this on Suzie and, more importantly, on the Stones' good name.

They were halfway through their desserts when Suzie announced that she had something to say. His heart thudded and he put down his spoon and fork. This was it, then.

Suzie took a deep breath. All day as she'd chopped, sliced, mixed and marinated, she'd rehearsed what she was going to say. She said it now: 'Mum, you'd better pour yourself another glass of wine; you're going to need it. I'm pregnant.'

Her mother didn't reach for her glass, as Suzie had thought she would, but her jaw did go slack. 'Oh, my God!' she muttered. Then more loudly: 'I don't believe it. How? I mean, how could you be so bloody stupid?' And louder still: 'You stupid, *stupid* girl!'

This was exactly the response Suzie had expected, but even so the sharpness of her mother's tone made her feel like a naughty child. Swallowing back the lump of fear that had been lodged in her throat all evening, she sensed her father sitting up straighter in his seat. 'Maxine,' he said firmly, 'just once in your life will you show a little compassion?'

'Wishy-washy compassion isn't what's called for right now,' Maxine fired at him, her eyes blazing, her shoulders squared. 'Cool-headed detachment is what's needed. That's what will get this sorted out.'

Oh, God, thought Suzie, this was just what she wanted to avoid. Then why had she planned to tell her mother this way? Because, coward that she was, she'd wanted to hide behind as many people as she could. Especially her father. Her mother's eyes were on her again. 'How pregnant are you?' she demanded.

'Four and a half months . . . nineteen weeks to be precise.'

Maxine paused to take this in. 'Okay,' she said, 'that still gives us time to deal with this mess. It needn't be the disaster it sounds. Presumably the father isn't going to make any trouble and insist on his rights or some such crap.'

Suzie winced. She didn't like hearing the baby referred to as a mess. She was about to say something, but Dad beat her to it: 'Maxine, do you think you could sound just a little more like a mother and not the hard-bitten chairman of the board trying to—'

He got no further. Maxine rounded on him. 'The day you have something sensible to say, Will, I'll be in touch. For now, I suggest you leave the matter to me.'

'What about Suzie? Doesn't she figure in this?' piped up Gemma.

Maxine turned her attention to Gemma. 'Well, of course she does.' She hesitated. Switching her gaze to Will and then back again to Gemma, she said in a more measured voice, 'Hang on, you two don't look or sound at all shocked by what Suzie's told us. Why's that?'

A crashing silence roared around the table. Gemma and Will both stared at Suzie, and knowing it was down to her, she said, 'Mum, I know you're trying your best to cope with this, but—'

'They already knew, didn't they?' Maxine interrupted her. For a second, she looked genuinely hurt. And oddly vulnerable. Something Suzie would never have thought possible. But it was only a flicker of emotion, then once more her mother was on the attack and Suzie was bracing herself. 'When did you tell them?'

Honesty seemed the wisest option. 'Two weeks ago.'

'And you didn't think to mention it to me?'

'I . . . I wanted to be sure in my mind what I was going to do before I spoke to you. I didn't want you worrying unnecessarily.'

'You're not telling me you've had to deliberate over this, are you? How the hell do you think you'll carry on at university with a baby hanging round your neck? And don't imagine for one second that I'm going to step into the breach and take care of it; I've got the new saleroom to cope with, on top of everything else. And as for your father, he's already proved how inept he is when it comes to shouldering responsibility.'

'For God's sake, Maxine! Do you have to be so insensitive?'

'Dad's right, Mum,' joined in Gemma, 'you're out of line, talking like Suzie doesn't have any choice in the matter. It's her baby; only she can decide what she's going to do.'

'Gemma, I'd rather you didn't speak to your mother like that.'

'This is a family matter, Steve, so I'd rather you did us all a favour and kept quiet,' said Will.

'How dare you speak to Steve like that? Please remember that you're here as a guest in our house.'

'Oh, as if I could ever forget.' Will flung down his napkin and got to his feet. 'If you can't be civil,' he said, pushing back his chair, 'then I give up.'

Feeling tearful now, Suzie had to shout to make herself heard above the din. 'Please!' she yelled. 'Please, will you all just calm down. And Dad, don't even think about leaving. I have more to say and I want you to hear it.' She waited for her father to sit down again. 'Now,' she said, when she had everyone's attention. 'This is what I plan to do.'

Chapter Twenty-Four

It wasn't until Will was home that he trusted himself to replay the scene. Maxine had been breathtaking in her ferociousness. Riding roughshod didn't come close. She'd spoken in terms of 'the right thing to do', 'the only sensible option' and 'the best thing all round'. But not a word did she say of the emotional stress this had to be putting on poor Suzie.

He poured himself a generous glass of Glenmorangie and went outside. It was a cool, clear night and the sky was pricked with diamond-white stars. He took a gulp of his drink, then walked the length of the garden. The gate creaked noisily in the hushed stillness. He sat in the moonlight on the old bench and swished another swig of whisky round his mouth, letting it dull his senses. It was a long time since he'd experienced this level of animosity towards Maxine and the strength of his feelings alarmed him. But what scared him most was his reaction to Suzie's decision. She had opted to have a termination and he was staggered how disappointed he was. Stupidly, he'd already pictured himself kicking a ball around with the little lad. Taking him for walks. Hunting for conkers together. Explaining to him why R.E.M. were the greatest rock band to come out of America. Teaching him the ways of the world: that it was the law to put HP sauce on bacon butties, that a woman will always think her bum is too big no matter how much you say it isn't, and politicians will always lie to save their own necks.

And yes, he'd imagined a grandson.

The son he'd never had.

He drank some more whisky.

But it wasn't to be. And rightly so, he told himself. Suzie was much too young to go through motherhood. Why the hell should she want to sacrifice the best years of her life and all the wonderful opportunities on offer in order to bring up a child she'd never planned to have?

He raised the glass again. How had it happened? How the hell had he allowed himself to get so attached to the idea of a grandson?

Maxine, on the other hand, had been obscenely quick to support Suzie in her decision. So damn quick Will wouldn't have been surprised if she'd rolled up her sleeves and carried out the abortion there and then on the dining-room table. He groaned and hung his head, shocked that he could think of something so monstrous.

He was overreacting, he knew. He'd allowed himself to become too emotionally involved. He had to step back and be more objective. Because let's face it, when he'd been nineteen, the last thing he'd have wanted was a girlfriend telling him she was pregnant. He'd like to think he'd have stood by and that the two of them would have made a go of it, but Suzie was alone. The father – never to know about his part in this drama – would not be on hand to share the load. So of course it made sense for Suzie to get rid of the baby, to put the whole business behind her, carry on with her studies and be glad that she'd been given a second chance.

All this, while Steve and Gemma had made themselves scarce, Maxine had put in her own inimitable way. She'd then gone on to say that she would go to the doctor in the morning with Suzie; that, in her own words, they'd 'get things moving'. Will was too stunned to speak. Too stunned because it felt as though he was already going through some kind of weird grieving process for a child he would never know.

For the first time ever, he felt distanced from one of his children, sidelined by the very fact that he was a man and this was women's business. He was clearly not needed. This was something that was going to take some getting used to.

One of Maxine's favourite weapons that she frequently loosed from her deadly arsenal of killer complaints was: 'You always make me out to be the bad parent, the villain.' He'd once sniped back at her that he didn't need to do that; she made a tidy job of it herself. Another complaint was that he deliberately left her out in the cold when it came to the girls. Not true. She'd left herself standing on the wrong side of the door, always claiming that she couldn't pick up the children from school or attend a parents' evening because she had an accountant to see, a meeting to chair. He'd sympathised with her to a degree; after all, it wasn't easy juggling those slippery balls of selfish ambition, but now, when it was him standing the wrong side of the door, he could feel the icy chill of exclusion swirling around and he didn't like it.

He drained his glass, letting the last of the liquid slide down his throat and dull what was left of his senses. He wondered, cruelly, if the real reason Maxine didn't want Suzie to go through with having the baby was because it would turn her into a grandmother. A concept that would be anathema to her.

Far away in the distance, he heard the sound of a church bell striking the hour – just the one mournful chime. Aware of something moving along the path, he leaned forward to peer into the silvery darkness. A fox perhaps?

He smiled. It was the Hedgehog, and beneath the peak of her baseball cap she looked as prickly as ever, hair tied back in a ponytail, her shoulders hunched. What was she doing out at this time of night when all sensible people were tucked up in bed? 'Hi,' he said, making his presence known so that she wouldn't be startled by suddenly coming upon him.

'Where are you heading? An illegal after-hours drink at The Navigation.

She studied him intensely before saying, 'I fancied a walk.'

He raised an eyebrow. 'At this time of night?'

'I couldn't sleep.' She glanced at the empty glass on the

arm of the bench. 'Whenever I see you, you have a drink in your hand.'

'It's the neighbourhood; it's driving me to it.'

He waited for her to say something, but she didn't, just kept on standing there, her hands pushed into the pockets of her baseball jacket, her shoulders up somewhere around her ears. She looked like a rebellious teenager. She also looked tired. 'Well, don't let me keep you from your moonlit stroll,' he said. 'But you know; you really oughtn't to be out on your own so late at night.'

Her cool blue-grey eyes locked with his. 'I'm not a child.'

'And luckily for you I'm not a crazed psycho on the lookout for a fresh victim, but who knows what excitement lurks further down the towpath for you?'

'I can take care of myself.'

'I'm sure you could, if you were attacked by a one-legged midget with both arms tied behind his back.'

She bristled; every one of her hedgehog spikes was up and ready to repel him. 'A one-legged vertically challenged individual is the correct term, I think you'll find.'

He laughed. 'Priceless! The PC approach. I heard on the radio the other day that we're not allowed to say children are naughty any more; we have to say their behaviour is challenging.'

'Children are challenging, full stop,' she said with feeling.

'But also very rewarding,' he countered.

The shoulders relaxed, came down to about jaw level. 'I wouldn't know about that. So far, it seems to be nothing but one drama after another.'

'Take it from me, the reward is that when you've moved onto the new drama, the one you've just recovered from seems like light relief in comparison.'

Again she made no comment and, distracted from his own problems, Will suddenly felt sorry for this young woman. Knowing more of her background from the conversations he'd had with her father, he said, 'Any luck on the job front, yet?'

'No.'

185

He admired her candour, the fact that she didn't give out any bull about there being any number of offers she was currently considering – the kind of face-saving remark he might have made in his former life. 'By the way, I was being serious when I said you ought to be careful walking along the canal late at night.' He received a look that seemed to dare him to go on and annoy her further. Which, of course, he did. 'If you'd like, I could trail you by skulking along in the shadows and act as your bodyguard. I've got an old CIA raincoat somewhere I could wear. Along with the regulation sunglasses.' This at least elicited a smile. Possibly the first he'd seen on her face.

'And there I was, thinking you were only good for sitting on benches and making out you were a dedicated wino,' she said.

'That's me; Jack of all trades.'

'I heard you used to be a lawyer. Why did you give it up?'

A question from the Hedgehog? This was a new phenomenon. 'I had to,' he said. 'I was beginning to imagine myself running amok in the office with a machete and massacring anything with a pulse.'

She raised an eyebrow. 'So much for not being the crazy psycho on the lookout for a fresh victim.'

'Ah, but I'm all cured now. I put my unstable past behind me when I became a convert to the school of thought that believes tomorrow is but a dream and yesterday no longer exists. What matters is today and seizing the opportunities that come one's way. As a lawyer you can't live like that; the two aren't mutually compatible. Would you like to sit down?'

She shook her head. 'Carpe diem is a bit passé, don't you think?'

'Tell me that when you're all grown up. Meanwhile, I'll give you my personal philosophy on life; I've discovered it's nothing but a very tricky egg and spoon race.'

'You're very patronising, you know.'

'I'm sorry, I don't mean to be. It's just that you look so young.'

'I'm thirty-two.'

He smiled. 'Okay, so you're older than I thought you were by a few years, but I guarantee one day you'll remember this conversation and think what a wise sage I was.'

'I think you're living in a fantasy world. One simply can't live without planning tomorrow.'

'Ah, but as Jung said, "What great thing ever came into existence that was not at first fantasy?" You sure I can't persuade you to let me keep you company on your walk?'

'Thanks, but I need to think.'

'Tell me about it. That's what I was doing before you showed up.' Torn between wanting to respect Suzie's privacy and suddenly feeling the need to talk about his rotten evening, he chose his next words carefully. 'Someone very close to me has got herself pregnant and, well, the thing is she's very young and has decided to have an abortion. And for reasons I'm almost ashamed to confess, I hate the thought of her doing that. I know it's selfish, that the decision is hers, but I can't help it.'

'You're right, it is selfish of you. You can't dictate her life.'

'But what if she regrets the abortion?'

'That's the price of choice. *Her* choice.'

'Do you always see things so dispassionately?'

'If you mean do I always view things rationally and with an objective eye, then yes, I do.'

He folded his arms across his chest, beginning to feel the cold. 'You'd have made an excellent lawyer.'

'And you'd probably have hacked me to death.'

He smiled. 'There's still time. Anyway, I'm going in now; the cold's getting to me.' He stood up. 'It was nice chatting with you. We must do this again, but maybe in the warm and at a more sociable time of day. Take care.'

Closing the gate after him, Will thought that if there

were any psychos out there on the towpath, they were the ones who might need to take care. She was one formidable girl.

Chapter Twenty-Five

At last Harriet had a job interview. It had come her way not through an agency, but by word of mouth. Adrian, her old boss down in Oxford, called to say that he knew of a company in south Manchester that was desperate for someone with her level of expertise and in particular, her specific knowledge of AVLS – automatic vehicle location systems. 'Howard Beningfield, who runs the company, is one of the brashest, most straight-talking men I know,' Adrian had said. 'Get on the right side of him and he'll be your friend for life.'

'And the wrong side of him?'

'You'll be out on your ear.'

'He sounds a regular charmer.'

'That's the funny thing; he is. What do you think? Shall I give him a ring and put in a good word for you?'

'Absolutely.'

Adrian had one final piece of advice for her. 'Whatever you do, Harriet, don't underestimate Howard. It's his favourite trick, fooling people into thinking he's an idiot.'

So here she was, looking for the road that would lead her to a small business-park on the outskirts of Crantsford. This way lies my sanity, she told herself. Once she had a job, she would soon be back on track. It wouldn't solve everything, but she'd have her self-respect up and running again and she'd be able to start making plans for the future. She was desperate to get a place of her own. Or rather, a place for her and the children. The thought of taking on the full weight of responsibility for Carrie and Joel still terrified her, but biting bullets was what she did best. Dodging had never been an option. Wasn't that why Felicity had entrusted her with the task in the first place?

A week had passed since Harriet had read the first of her sister's secret emails and she was still shocked at what she'd discovered. Felicity's had been no lightweight affair, the kind of fling that quickly runs out of passion and burns itself to dust. It was obvious that Felicity had been involved with whoever it was for some time.

A lot of the emails they'd written to each other had been near-pornographic in content and Harriet had baulked at reading some of them, but curiosity had won out. Wanting to discover the identity of Felicity's lover, she had forced herself to go on, hopelessly trying not to imagine her sister's voracious appetite for this man. And all the while, she kept thinking of Jeff. Had he been such a terrible husband that he had driven his wife to these lengths? Harriet didn't think so; she'd always liked him. Perhaps he'd been a little staid – steady was what Mum and Dad had called him – but he'd been devoted to Felicity in his quiet, measured way. Felicity had always claimed that she fell in love with him the moment she set eyes on him, when they were at university. 'That's the man I'm going to marry,' she had said in a loud voice when they were standing in the dinner queue during a ball up in Durham. 'His name's Jeff Knight and he's my knight in shining armour. He doesn't know it yet, but he's going to sweep me off my feet.' It was nearly the end of the summer term and Felicity was drunk, as they all were – Miles and Dominic were spending the weekend with them – and they'd laughed at her, thinking her quite mad.

'But darling,' Dominic had said, his voice overtly camp and booming through the stratosphere so that the student in question, further up the queue, turned round, 'he looks like one of those frighteningly hale and hearty types. Not our sort at all. Where's the aesthetic content? I ask myself.'

As soon as Dominic had made the transition from boarding school to university, he'd come out as gay and delighted in shocking those who were uneasy about such matters. Including his parents. *Particularly* his parents. Had

Harriet not heard his lurid tales about the gay bars and clubs he frequented in London, or seen for herself a set of moody black-and-white photographs of him lying naked in the arms of a man a good deal older than him, she would have said it was another of his affectations.

'He's exceptionally hearty,' Felicity had said proudly. 'He's a rower and has the most wondrous legs. He has muscles you McKendrick boys can only dream of.'

'I can't speak for my brother,' Dominic had drawled, 'but for myself, I'm rather partial to something with a brain.'

'He has one of those too,' Felicity crowed. 'He's a third-year maths scholar.'

Dominic shuddered. 'Another maths bore, just like Harriet. How extraordinarily dull.'

'I don't care what you think of him. He's the man I'm going to marry. What's more, I'm going to ask him right now if he'll dance with me when dinner is over.'

True to her word, Felicity sidled up to him and introduced herself. Her reward was a smile of such tender embarrassment that Harriet had felt sorry for him. You don't know what you're getting into, she thought.

This was during their first year at Durham. Felicity had suffered a prolonged bout of glandular fever during her A-level year and had to repeat the upper sixth, which meant that she and Harriet started university together. Everyone had thought they were mad both opting to go to Durham, but to them it seemed perfect. Dominic was still at Cambridge and thinking of extending his stay by doing a doctorate; Miles had taken a gap year before taking his place at Bristol. No way in the world would he have contemplated going to Cambridge. 'Not even to rub Dominic's nose in it?' Harriet had asked him. 'To prove the point that you made it without all the advantages he'd been given?'

'Tempting, I agree,' Miles had said, 'but the thought of following in his footsteps holds little appeal.'

The night of the ball, when Felicity had declared her

intention to marry Jeff Knight, Miles had slept on the floor of Harriet's college room, while across town Dominic had slept alone in Felicity's bed. The last they'd seen of her had been as she'd disappeared down to the river, hand in hand with her shy husband-to-be, her dress trailing in the damp grass.

So where had it gone wrong? thought Harriet. The only clue was that Felicity's new life as a wife and mother lacked the excitement of the life she'd led before. Whoever the lover was, he filled that gap. If Felicity was to be believed from the way she wrote to him, he made her feel whole again. But this conclusion didn't make Harriet feel sympathetic towards her sister. She was furious with Felicity for being so deceitful and for jeopardising so much. What about the children? Where had they fitted in? Where were they when she was secretly meeting her lover? And had she really planned to leave Jeff? That last email certainly implied that she wanted to: ' . . . *you have to be patient. Trust me, please, it won't be long now. Just give me a little more time.*'

But it wasn't only Jeff who had been cheated on. Harriet felt betrayed, too. She hated knowing that despite the closeness between them, Felicity hadn't confided in her. It was a hurtful blow, and it left her wondering if she had ever really known her sister. It seemed as if Felicity had been even more reckless than Harriet had thought. By having an affair, she'd deliberately sought out a knife-edge on which to balance herself precariously. Why on earth had she done that?

Shock and bewilderment was causing Harriet to think less than kindly or rationally about her sister. In her mind, Felicity's secret, wilful behaviour had become entwined with her death, as if she had in some way been deliberately negligent to the point of causing her own death and the subsequent disaster that was now Harriet's life.

She entered the modern offices of ACT – Associated Controlled Technology – with five minutes to spare and was shown through to an office by a receptionist with the most amazing multi-coloured acrylic nails and a miniskirt that did her chunky legs no favours. She told Harriet that Mr Beningfield would be with her in a minute. 'He's just on the phone. Would you like a cup of coffee while you wait?'

'Thanks. White, no sugar.'

Left on her own, Harriet regretted the sharpness of her reply. Come on, she told herself, you need this job. Be nice to people. When the girl returned with a wobbling, over-filled cup and saucer in her hand, Harriet smiled sweetly in order to get on the right side of her. After all, if she got the job, she'd be seeing this girl on a daily basis. The last thing she needed was to be labelled the Snotty Bitch before she'd even started.

It was some time since she'd experienced the nerve-racking ordeal of a job interview and Adrian's description of Howard Beningfield hadn't done much to put her mind at rest. As well as being brash, he was apparently garrulous and jocular, but a 'bit much' at times. 'You have to stand up to him,' Adrian had said. 'He likes nothing better than a good sparring partner.'

At breakfast that morning, the children had presented her with a good luck card that they'd made. Presumably her mother had been behind the gesture, but even so, Harriet had been touched by their efforts. Joel had pointed out the bits that Carrie had allowed him to colour in, and she'd found herself getting stupidly choked up when he'd solemnly apologised for smudging part of it. 'It's perfect,' she'd told him, kissing his cheek and then going round the table to thank Carrie.

Now that the dust had settled on Carrie's handiwork at school, Joel's nightmares had stopped and he was sleeping properly. He was also opening up a little. Not much, but enough to convince Harriet and her mother that they had things under control again.

Harriet had to wait half an hour before Howard Beningfield walked in. Offering no apology for keeping her waiting, he fiddled with the air-conditioning unit on the wall. In his mid fifties, he was one of those men who are as broad as they are tall, with arms sticking out as though he had two invisible basketballs nestling in the undergrowth of his armpits. The way he moved his enormous frame around the desk to the black leather chair suggested he hadn't quite evolved. He plonked himself down – the chair exhaling a sigh of resistance – then looked up. 'Well then, Harriet,' he said, 'may I call you Harriet?'

She nodded.

'You come very highly recommended. Why's that, do you think?'

'Because I'm very good at what I do.'

He leant back into his chair, clasped his hands behind his enormous head and laughed. The chair groaned. 'That's what I like about you modern girls: more front than Blackpool and Southport put together.'

Oh brilliant! He was one of those suffer-the-little-women-unto-me types. In other words, he was a honking great sexist pig. Adrian had omitted to mention that. Feeling like she was taking part in an episode of *The Office*, she reminded herself, once again, how badly she needed this job.

Slowly rearranging himself, Howard sat forward and slid a thin file across the desk. He opened it and revealed Harriet's CV. She knew it was well above the usual standard he'd see; the computer industry was currently overflowing with bright young things of the useless variety, but highly skilled programmers like her were rare and in demand. He scanned it briefly, the tip of a finger running jerkily along the page, then with excruciating theatrical pomposity, he ripped it up. 'So much for the blah-di-blah,' he said. 'Let's get down to basics.' He fired off a salvo of questions which she returned with equal gusto, outlining various large-scale applications she'd been in charge of, paying special attention to the vehicle-tracking interface she'd written most recently, until finally he said, 'We'll only know if you're any good when you've worked here for a while. The proof will be in the pudding, so to speak. When do you want to start? Adrian explained that you're keen to get going a-s-a-p.'

Wondering what else Adrian might have explained – had he mentioned the children and their obvious consequences? – she said, 'I'm available as of tomorrow. Is it possible to have a chat with the people in the department I'd be working in?'

'No problemo.' He reached for the phone on the desk and punched in a number. It was then, as he waited for someone to pick up, that he said, 'I'll be straight with you, Harriet. Adrian told me to look no further than you, but I don't want to hire you if in nine months' time you waltz in to my office and announce that you're pregnant. And don't give me any of that equal rights in the workplace crap. I'm running a business, not a charity.'

Harriet knew that now was the moment she should raise the matter of being Carrie and Joel's guardian, that there might be times when, quite possibly, if her parents couldn't cover for her, she would have to take time off. But she didn't. Self-preservation made her keep quiet. No need to put herself at an unnecessary disadvantage, was there? Nor did she feel inclined to point out the glaringly obvious, that Howard Beningfield was committing the cardinal sin of discriminating against women who wanted to combine motherhood with a career. He could be hung, drawn and quartered for such a remark. Indeed, another woman in this situation might well already be out of the door girding her loins to take him to court but, while it pained her to admit it, the dreadful man had a point. If it was her company, Harriet would feel exactly the same way; why employ a woman when you could take on a man who wouldn't demand Tampax-dispensing machines and maternity rights? The sisterhood was all very well, but she'd never felt the need to be a part of it. Pinning that particular badge to one's breast seemed the surest way to imply a weakness of some kind. It was as good as turning oneself into a moving target. Felicity had once said of her that she never made a fuss because she was an honorary bloke anyway.

'Mr Beningfield,' she said, adopting a firm but deferential tone, 'I think we can safely say that there is about as much chance of me becoming pregnant as the Pope.' Well, he hadn't asked straight out if she already had children, had he?

An hour later, after considering all the pros and cons, her mind was made up. The overall package was marginally more generous than her last job, and the range of clients and prospective clients looked interesting and challenging. Moreover the company was expanding, hence the need for another senior analyst with her level of experience.

She drove away with a verbal job offer under her belt; a written offer would be in the post forthwith. She couldn't wait to get home and share her good news. Better still, she'd be able to have a celebratory drink that evening with Miles – they were now meeting regularly for either a drink or a meal, depending on how busy he was.

It was gone six when she turned into Maple Drive and parked alongside her parents' Rover. Across the road, she saw Will Hart getting out of his car. There was a young blonde girl with him – the same girl she'd seen him with at The Navigation, and presumably the 'someone very close' to him who was pregnant. Harriet hadn't been fooled by that guarded speech of his. Honestly, why didn't he just come right out and admit that he was having a relationship with a girl young enough to be his daughter and had got her pregnant? And what about his children? It was all very well him pontificating about the rewards of parenting, but she'd never once seen him with kids. Practise what you preach, matey!

Letting herself in at the back door, all set to announce her good news, Harriet froze. She could hear a voice coming from the sitting room. A voice that was all too familiar. Knowing that her arrival had gone unnoticed, she stood for a moment in the kitchen observing her parents and their visitor through the gap in the door. But as though gifted with a sixth sense, their visitor stopped mid-sentence and slowly turned round. 'Hello, Harriet,' he said, 'how long have you been standing there?'

Her first thought was that he still had the same effect on her. But just as she had taught herself all those years ago, she stamped on the emotion. Stamped on it hard. She would rather die than let him have the pleasure of knowing she'd spent the best part of her childhood hero-worshipping him.

'Hello, Dominic,' she said. And wanting to hurt him, to twist the knife round in his heart just as he had with her so many times, she added, 'We missed you at the funeral. What happened? A college crisis that was more important than saying goodbye to your oldest friend?'

Chapter Twenty-Six

Will could hear Suzie being sick upstairs. It was the third time that morning. Unable to finish his coffee, he poured it down the sink. He was almost sick with nerves himself. He glanced at his watch. Another five minutes and they would have to go. The clinic had told them to be there for ten o'clock.

Originally Maxine had insisted that she would be the one to accompany Suzie, and he'd had no complaints with that. Coward that he was, he had been glad for once that Maxine had taken charge. But then yesterday all hell had broken loose. He didn't know the full story, but Suzie and her mother had had one almighty row. The first he knew about it was when Suzie rang him at work to ask if she could stay the night at his place and said she wanted him to take her to the clinic. When he'd turned up to fetch her, Maxine had said, 'Suzie's got some stupid idea into her head that I'm treating her like a child.'

'I expect it's a combination of anxiety and hormones,' he'd replied, noting how unusually tired and fraught Maxine looked.

'She says I'm a control freak. Her exact words were: "Leave me alone you controlling bitch."'

For the sake of keeping the peace, for Suzie's benefit if nothing else, he said, 'Come off it, Maxine, we all have our moments if we're honest. Let it go. This is perhaps the one time in Suzie's life when we can allow her to behave as badly as she needs to.'

'Oh, that's so typical of you, isn't it? You always have to take the girls' side.'

'It's not a matter of taking sides; I'm just suggesting we try to keep things in perspective.'

She blew her nose, making him realise that she was close to tears. He said, 'If you want, I'll try and talk her round. Make her realise that it would be better if you took her to the clinic.'

'Don't even think about it, Dad.'

Startled, they both turned to see Suzie. She had a patchwork duffel bag slung over her shoulder and despite the firm defiance in her voice, Will could see she'd been crying and looked ready for a fresh bout. Getting her away from Maxine probably was the best thing to do.

It was raining during the journey to the clinic and the wipers, long since past their best, squeaked and juddered in the awkward silence. Will couldn't remember a time when he and Suzie hadn't had a hundred and one things to chat and laugh about. But what could they discuss today? Anything, other than what Suzie was about to go through with, would seem trivial and insulting. He'd never been good when it came to medical problems – to his shame he'd once fainted at school during a biology lesson and had been teased mercilessly for weeks after – but stupidly, late last night when Suzie was in bed, he'd gone on the Net to read up on the procedure for an abortion. It was ignorant of him, he supposed, that he didn't know the full details, but twenty minutes of browsing and he knew enough to wish he'd never clicked on SEARCH. Just as well he'd stuck to the plain medical facts. Had he scanned any of the anti-abortion websites, he'd probably have been spark out on the floor. He reminded himself that it was a straightforward procedure these days, that nothing could go wrong, and turned to look at Suzie in the passenger seat. Her head was back against the headrest, her eyes closed, her hands clasped on her lap. She's so beautiful, he thought, his heart bursting with love. She didn't deserve this ordeal. If there was a way, he'd willingly bear the fear and pain of it himself. He could remember thinking the same when

Gemma had had to have four teeth out before her brace was fitted. How long would he go on wanting to protect his girls? he wondered. The answer was easy. For ever. That's what parents did. Didn't his own mother still phone him up to make sure he was eating properly? He smiled and started to hum to himself.

Suzie opened her eyes.

'Sorry, love, were you trying to sleep?'

She shook her head. 'What made you pick that song?'

'I don't know; it just came into my head.'

'Sing it properly, with all the words. Like you used to when Gemma and I were little.'

For the rest of the journey, the mournful tune of 'Scarlet Ribbons' filled the car.

From the outside, the clinic looked more like an upmarket country hotel: cool, aloof and just a little splendid. That was private health-care for you. As they stood on the step and Will rang the bell, he put his arm around Suzie. 'Okay, Bobtail?'

She gave him a wobbly smile. 'I think so.'

Everyone spoke in hushed tones and was very nice and reassuring. The paperwork was dealt with amongst bowls of sweet-smelling pot pourri, vases of cut flowers, soft-tread carpets and gentle background music. So efficient and professional were the members of staff, Will hardly noticed his daughter being spirited away, and as he settled in for the necessary wait, he flicked idly through a glossy car magazine. It could have been written in Swahili for all the sense it made. Unable to concentrate, he flung it back onto the table irritably. He considered going outside to call his mother, who had wanted to be kept informed of how things went, but the rain was coming down even harder now. Before picking up Suzie yesterday, he'd called in on his mother as he did every other week – while she cooked him supper he got on with any odd jobs that needed doing on the house – and he'd told her about Suzie's pregnancy, and that she was having a termination. Her immediate concern was that Suzie hadn't been coerced into her decision and then she said, 'I suppose that's why she hasn't been to see me recently. I thought perhaps she had gone back to university.'

'I think she's been keeping her head down.'

'Well, that's very understandable; it's been an emotional time for her. Give her my love, won't you, tell her I'll be thinking of her tomorrow and that just as soon as she wants to, she's to come for tea.' Ruby had then gone on to discuss more practical matters. 'Presumably, when she feels ready, she'll be returning to university. Has she missed much already?'

'Just the first week. I'm sure she'll be able to catch up.'

'Of course she will; she's a bright girl with everything ahead of her.'

That was what was so great about his mother: nothing fazed her. She was a full-on optimist.

He was just considering having another go at the car magazine when the door opened and Suzie came in. One of the nurses he'd seen earlier was with her. He leapt to his feet, nearly knocking the table over. Surely it couldn't have been done already?

The next thing he knew, Suzie was in his arms, sobbing. 'I'm sorry, Dad, but I couldn't do it. I just couldn't get rid of it. I'm so sorry.'

Catching Will's eye, the nurse quietly shut the door and left them alone. 'It's okay, Suzie,' he said, his voice cracking. 'If this is what you want, it'll all be fine. Don't you worry about a thing.'

Chapter Twenty-Seven

Some things never change. Dominic had only been back in Maple Drive a matter of hours, but within no time at all he'd made himself the centre of attention. Harriet's drink with Miles had been postponed because Freda was in the mood for playing happy families and had insisted on both her sons sitting round the dinner table that evening. 'Sorry about this,' Miles had apologised on the phone, 'I'll make it up as soon as he's gone. He won't be here for long; he never is.'

But strangely Dominic was in no hurry to return to the rarefied atmosphere of his Cambridge college. Five days after his surprise arrival, he was still around, casting the shadow of his ferocious presence on their lives.

Harriet's parents had taken her to task over the sharpness of her greeting to Dominic. 'There was no need to be so rude,' her mother had said. 'Especially as he'd gone to the trouble to call in and apologise to us about missing the funeral.' They might have succeeded in making her feel churlish had it not been for the fact that she knew Dominic better than they did. He revelled in making people eat their words. One minute he'd make people hate him, the next he'd be so contrite that he'd be instantly forgiven, somehow instilling a sense of guilt in those who had been so quick to misjudge him. 'I'm a cruel man,' he once declared, 'but who will save me from myself?'

Plenty had tried. Or rather, he had allowed plenty to think they could do it. It was another of his games: send out the bait – his twisted, cruel-mannered charm – then reel in the poor, hapless fool.

Harriet had observed this since childhood, hating it when

she had been reeled in. Humiliating people was what he did best. Harriet had often told him what she thought of him, and on one occasion she said to his face that he was a narcissistic bastard who didn't care who he hurt. All he'd done was laugh at her and say that if you were old enough to play the game, you were old enough to pay the emotional cost of getting hurt. 'People aren't as fragile as you think,' he'd told her, 'and anyway, as Byron put it so succinctly, "The heart will live on brokenly."'

It turned out that even children weren't immune to his charm; Carrie and Joel were fascinated by him. With his tall, lean frame, his Prince of Denmark attire – black polo-neck sweater and black leather trousers – and his formidably short dark hair (as a student he'd worn it long and tied it back with a black silk ribbon; now it was short like his temper) and his propensity to swear at random, he was irresistibly charismatic. The children had met him several times before, but they'd been too young and had no memory of him – something that probably pierced Dominic's ego more than they would ever know. But once Carrie realised he was Miles's brother and had been a friend of her mother's, she wanted to know everything they had ever done together. Any of the stories Harriet and her parents had told the children were now forgotten, redundant in the face of this golden-tongued storyteller in their midst. Harriet couldn't blame them, after all; when was the last time they'd been exposed to someone who exuded so much glamour and excitement? Many years ago Dora had said that Dominic had the smile of an angel, but the mind of a devil. It was one of the most apt descriptions Harriet had heard.

'Did Mummy really get caught for shoplifting?' Carrie was now asking Dominic, her face more radiant than Harriet had ever seen it. Joel was listening too, his eyes rapt with wonder.

'You bet to buggery she did! We all did; Harriet, my brother Miles, and me.'

It was Saturday morning, and they were in the kitchen.

Shortly after Mum and Dad had gone to the supermarket, leaving Harriet to supervise Carrie's homework, an autumn montage of leaves and twigs, Dominic had called round. 'I'm bored to death,' he'd said. 'Let me in and talk to me. If you don't I shall have to shoot myself. Here, these are for you.' He thrust an extravagantly large box of champagne truffles at her. 'I thought you deserved something expensive and frivolous. And these are for the children.' From his coat pocket he produced a box of Maltesers. His thoughtfulness brought to mind equally unexpected gestures of kindness he'd made in the past – the large bouquet of flowers he'd arranged to be sent to her mother when he'd heard about her being diagnosed with ME; the amusing card he'd posted to Dad on his retirement; the housewarming gift of a luxury food hamper that had turned up for Harriet when she'd moved into her flat in Oxford. She smiled her thanks and took his coat.

Now, as Harriet listened to Dominic answering Carrie's question, giving a riveting account of Edna Gannet catching the four of them as they'd tried to sneak out with their pockets bursting with Cadbury's creme eggs and threatening to box their ears, she wondered why he was here in Kings Melford. Why had he come home when it was normally the last place on the planet he wanted to be? He'd said his rooms in college were being decorated before the start of term and the smell of paint was making him ill, but Harriet's suspicious mind doubted this. True, he didn't look that well – his handsome face was thinner and sharper and he looked older than when she'd last seen him, scarcely a year ago – but she was more inclined to think that his protracted visit was to do with something completely different.

'I hear you and Miles are practically inseparable these days,' he'd said after he'd caught up on local gossip at Freda's enforced family get-together.

'We've been out for drinks and the occasional meal, if it's any of your business,' she'd said. 'But I suppose in your world that would signify a deep and meaningful relationship.'

'By that sharp little riposte, I assume you're referring to my renowned promiscuity. Is it serious, then?'

'Is what serious?'

'You and Miles. I always thought you two should get it together. You're perfectly suited.'

'Why? So that you could take pleasure in tearing us apart like you used to pull the legs off spiders?'

He had sighed. 'I'm getting bored with the diva bitch thing. Whatever's happened to you? You never used to be quite so touchy.'

'Losing the person who meant the most to me has changed me more than you'll ever know,' she'd said.

'Ah . . . Felicity,' he had said stiffly, sounding like the desiccated academic he was destined to be. 'I miss her too.'

She gritted her teeth. How glib he could be.

Tuning back in to what Dominic was now saying, Harriet did a double-take. To her astonishment, he was helping Joel to pull on his socks and telling Carrie to forget about her homework so they could all go for a walk.

'Keep away from the bank,' she yelled at the children as they scampered on ahead in their Wellington boots, squealing and laughing and throwing sticks for Toby. Honestly, what had got into them? They were as high as kites. They never normally made so much noise. Perhaps it was all those Maltesers they'd scoffed.

The morning was bright and fresh, the sky clear as if washed clean by the heavy rain overnight. The air was damp and earthy, the towpath slippery with leaves that had been shaken from the trees. The sight of Dominic's sartorial elegance wrecked by a pair of her father's old gardening boots brought a smirk to her face.

'What's so sodding funny?' he demanded.

'Nothing.' She rearranged her face. 'When are you going back to Cambridge to pore over all those dusty old books?'

'When I'm ready.'

'What about the start of term and freshers' week? Won't you miss the first pick of budding undergraduates to corrupt?'

'I dare say they can manage a few days without me.'

'But I thought the world revolved around you, Dominic.'

'It does. Which is why I can decide my own comings and goings. A bit like masturbation, you could say.'

Again she smiled to herself. The same old Dominic; buried in amongst all the faults and flaws was his sharp wit and diverting turn of thought. 'What brought you home?' she asked. 'I'd have thought you'd have preferred a few days somewhere more cerebrally challenging than Maple Drive.'

He shrugged. 'I accepted a long time ago that an occasional foray into my home town of Sodom and Gomorrah would be the cross I'd have to bear. Tell me about this job you've been offered.'

Quite used to the speed at which he could change the subject, she complied. 'It's with a software house in Crantsford. I'll be head of a team of four and my main responsibility will be to provide the means to interface between AVLS systems and road haulage systems.'

'My God! Could you have picked anything more boring?'

'Oh, shut up!'

They walked on in silence, passing Will's house. Harriet wondered if his young girlfriend had had her abortion yet. Wondered too what its consequences would be on their relationship. If indeed they really had one in the first place. She thought of Felicity and her secret relationship. What would her sister have done if she'd got pregnant by her lover? Passed the baby off as Jeff's? It occurred to Harriet, stealing a quick glance at Dominic, that maybe, because they'd been such close friends, he was the one person in whom Felicity might have confided. She had come to the conclusion that her sister hadn't told Harriet because she was too close and too fond of Jeff. Whereas Dominic had never really liked Jeff and therefore wouldn't have judged Felicity. It was all supposition, but Harriet was tempted to ask Dominic if he knew anything. Before that, though, she had something else she wanted to sort out with him.

'I still think you were a complete shit to miss Felicity's funeral,' she said.

He slowed his step, but didn't speak.

'Why didn't you come?' she pressed. It rankled that he hadn't bothered. That he could have been so cavalier.

After another pause, he said, 'She wouldn't have wanted it.'

'You mean *you* didn't want it. Funerals, after all, must be so wearisomely pedestrian for a distinguished don such as you; strictly for the masses, the plebs. All that cheap dry sherry and polite chit-chat to get through. If only it could be more civilised – Mozart's Requiem played, some dreary piece of poetry recited. Women wailing. Men flaying themselves.'

He suddenly turned on her, his face so savage that she took a step back – looking into his eyes was like staring down the loaded barrel of a gun. 'Don't be so bloody patronising!' he roared. 'Is it too much for you to understand that I wanted to remember my oldest and closest friend the way she was? That I didn't want to watch her mutilated corpse being shoved into a hole in the ground? Is that really too difficult for you to grasp?'

'Liar! You're too selfish and vain to grieve for anyone but yourself. It's always about you, isn't it? You, you, *you*! And for the record, she was cremated and her ashes buried. She was not *shoved* into a hole!'

'You picky little cow! But at least I have a heart. More than you have. You're nothing but an analytical machine. You're like Miles: incapable of feeling anything from the heart.'

'And what would you know about my feelings? It's not just Felicity I've lost. It's everything. My home, my job, even my boyfriend.'

'Well, bully for you. But just remember this; there are no exclusive rights to grief.'

He turned and stalked off the way they'd just come. Her

eyes brimmed with hot, stinging tears, and she rushed on to find the children. *Bastard!* Why had she allowed him to get to her? And how the hell had he managed to grab the moral high ground?

By twisting her words, that's how.

October

Love may be a fool's paradise, but it is the only
paradise we know on this troubled planet.
Robert Blatchford
Taken from My Eighty Years

Chapter Twenty-Eight

It was the middle of October, and what had so far been a gentle and relatively mild autumn now consisted of strong wintry winds coming in from the north, which shook the curling leaves from the trees, sending them rattling along the streets. A fence panel had blown over in the night, and under normal circumstances Bob would have been straight out to the garden to fix it. But as he stood at the kitchen window looking at the damage, it couldn't have interested him less: he had other things on his mind this morning. He had an appointment to keep. A rendezvous, you could say. He had been secretly counting the days and now that it was here he was doing his best to act normally. It was always possible, of course, that something had happened to change her plans, but he wouldn't let himself dwell on that worry. Or maybe she simply said things she didn't mean. No. Jennifer wasn't that kind of woman. She'd said she would be coming back to Kings Melford and he had no reason to doubt her. Moreover, she'd said she wanted to photograph this stretch of the canal when autumn had really settled in.

That day when he'd accepted her offer of a cup of tea and climbed down into the snug warmth of the saloon had been a turning point for Bob. A powerful moment when he'd started to think about something other than the emptiness of his life.

'Grief's a terrible thing,' she'd said matter-of-factly when not long afterwards he'd told her about Felicity – the words had come out before he could stop himself. 'I lost my husband two years ago,' she said, 'and for months after his death I could hardly bring myself to get up in the morning.

Some days I didn't bother. I just stayed there howling under the duvet.'

'What changed?'

'You mean, how did I pull myself together? It sounds vaguely absurd, but I simply ran out of tears. I had none left. Unlike a lot of people who bottle them up, I let it all go in one long, horrid outburst. My children were probably on the verge of having me sectioned; they thought I'd lost it completely. And it's not something I'd recommend for everyone. There were a few moments when I thought I'd lost it too. It was a very scary time. Have you cried much?'

'Er . . . a bit.'

'In private, I'll bet.'

'Mostly at night,' he'd confessed, avoiding her gaze by bending down to Toby and scratching the top of the dog's head. 'I go and sit inside the Wendy house I made for my daughters when they were little,' he further admitted. 'It's the only place I can be alone.'

When he'd raised his glance, she'd said, 'Oh, that's so sad.'

'It's pathetic,' he shot back, his voice too loud and harsh.

'No, you mustn't ever think that. You do whatever it takes. I've discovered the hard way that you never get over grief; you learn to live with it. It's like having an arm chopped off and learning to manage without it. Excruciatingly painful but not impossible.'

After pouring him a second mug of tea and passing him a tin of custard creams, she said, 'How's your wife coping?'

'Better than me. She has her friend Dora to talk to. It seems to make all the difference for her.'

'Of course it does. Don't you have any friends you can talk to?'

'I have work colleagues but . . . but since I've retired, well, you know how it is, the link isn't there any more.'

She surveyed him over the rim of her mug. 'If I'd died first, my husband would have been in the same situation as you. He spent all his life working and didn't bother to make any real friends. It's a terrible mistake.'

Moving the subject on, he'd asked her what she was doing, cruising the inland waterways on her own. 'I'm satisfying a long-held ambition. Actually, it was something my husband and I had planned to do together, but when he died and I'd come out from under the duvet, I thought, what the heck, I'm going to do it anyway. I sold the house we'd lived in for more than twenty years and moved to an isolated bungalow where my only neighbour is a grumpy old farmer who is much too busy to bother me with pitying looks. And then I bought this boat and took off. So here I am living the dream. I've been away from home for four months and I'm having the time of my life.' She pointed to an expensive-looking camera on a shelf. 'I'm trying my hand at being a photographer. I want to put a book of pictures together. Maybe even have a go at getting it published.'

'Where are you heading next?' he'd asked, scarcely able to keep the envy out of his voice. Take me with you, he wanted to say. Take me along for the ride.

'I'm staying here for a few days, but I'm on my way up to Yorkshire. I have some friends just north of Hebden Bridge whom I haven't seen in a long while. They swear the run of locks up that way will finish me off, but I can't wait to prove them wrong.'

'Will you be passing this way again?'

Once more she'd looked at him shrewdly over the top of her cup. 'Yes. Why do you ask?'

'I'd be interested to hear how you get on with all those locks.'

Changing the subject, she said, 'I'm going to moor the boat this side of a pub called The Navigation. Do you know it?'

'You could say it's my local.'

'Is the food any good?'

'It's ages since I've eaten there, but I hear it's reasonably wholesome. Their chip butties are well known round here.'

'Sounds heavenly.'

As he'd known it would have, the next day when he was

out walking Toby, the *Jennifer Rose* had moved on. Approaching the mooring points in the stretch that led to The Navigation, he saw that its owner was on the roof of the boat, sweeping the leaves that had fallen from the nearby trees. She'd told him yesterday that she'd named the boat after herself; it was what her husband had planned to do. When she saw him, she straightened up and leaned against the broom. 'Hello,' she said, and without referring to her watch, added, 'it must be about time for a cuppa. Why don't you go down below and put the kettle on?'

In all, she stayed moored in the same spot for four days. He visited her every morning and late afternoon. He came to believe that she was part of his healing process. Or was that too fanciful? He never once thought about touching or kissing her – he'd never make that mistake again – he just wanted to be with her, to sit and talk. She understood his pain because she'd experienced something similar.

At night, after she'd moved on for Yorkshire, he would lie in bed picturing Jennifer cocooned in her cosy bedroom at the prow of the boat. She'd given him a full tour of the *Jennifer Rose* and he was as fascinated by the clever design of the craft as he was with her courage to change her life so dramatically. What would Eileen say if he announced that he'd like to blow their savings on a second-hand boat and leave Maple Drive?

Now that Harriet was working, it was his job to take the children to school, and after he'd done that he poked his head round the bedroom door. Eileen was having a lie-in; she hadn't slept well that night. 'I'm just off out with Toby,' he said softly. 'See you later.' Getting no reply, he assumed she was sleeping and crept quietly downstairs.

If he had been a younger and fitter man he would have sprinted to the towpath, but as it was, he lumbered along at his usual pace trying to keep the eager anticipation from showing on his face.

The wild wind that had blown overnight had settled, leaving twigs and bits of broken branches scattered on the ground but, annoyingly, the damp chill of autumn was aggravating his knee and he was forced to slow his pace yet more. He'd have to keep quiet about it; he didn't want Eileen worrying. Or Harriet thinking that it was another nail in the coffin. Now that she had a job, he knew she was keen to find a place of her own and move out with the children. Was it so very wrong of him to want that too? Eileen would shush him if he ever dared to say that he was tired of having the children around, but he longed for the day when he didn't have to worry about tripping over some toy or other left on the floor, or he could use the bathroom knowing there would be plenty of hot water. He resented his home not being his own. And he refused to feel guilty about it. He was being honest, which was more than Eileen was. She kept saying she was feeling better but he knew she wasn't. Her afternoon naps were getting longer and sometimes she was reluctant to leave the house. If Eileen wasn't careful, she'd turn into another Freda. He shuddered at the thought that he too might turn into a carbon copy of Harvey McKendrick: trapped and never saying a word, bitterly resigned to living a life of pretence.

He sighed, realising how angry he'd made himself. It wouldn't do. He thought again about Harriet and the houses she had started to view. The solicitor had already made arrangements for part of the children's trust fund to be made available and added to Harriet's money from the sale of her flat so that should the right property become available she could go ahead and buy it. As a cash buyer, she was in an enviable position, so the solicitor had said.

The words *enviable position* echoed inside Bob's head. It was hardly how Harriet would describe her situation, he suspected. He just hoped her new job would work out, because if the unthinkable happened and she was made redundant, having taken on a mortgage, what then? She'd have to dip into the trust fund, he told himself firmly. Or he would have to help out. Anything so long as it meant Harriet and the children didn't move back in with him and Eileen.

He stood for a moment to rest his knee and examined the

way his thoughts had gone. He was shocked how easily he'd turned his good mood upside down. I'm turning into a bitter old man, he thought miserably. This is what Felicity's death has done to me.

He pressed on, calling Toby to heel, determined to think more positively. Today was the day Jennifer had said she would be back in Kings Melford. And sure enough, as he rounded the curve of the canal, there was the *Jennifer Rose* moored just where it had been last month. At the sight of a plume of smoke rising from the chimney his spirits rose, and ignoring the grinding pain in his knee, he quickened his pace.

'Hello stranger,' she said, when she emerged from the engine room, her face dotted with soot. 'I'm having a bit of trouble with the engine. Don't suppose you're any good with such things, are you?'

It was just as if the intervening weeks had never passed. 'Put the kettle on and I'll take a look,' he said.

As she listened to the other girls chattering and laughing the other side of the toilet door, Carrie slid her fingernail under the gummed-down section of the envelope and opened it. She knew without reading it what it would say. With trembling hands and her heart hammering in her chest, she unfolded the piece of paper and took a deep breath.

Nobody likes you because you're a nasty show-off. We don't want you here. We wish you were dead like your parents.

It was the same as the last note. And the one before that.

Carrie waited for the school bell to ring for the end of morning break and when she'd heard the last of the girls bang the door shut after them, she ripped up the letter and dropped it into the loo. Next she did the same with the envelope. She tugged hard on the toilet handle and watched the bits of paper swirl round and round before disappearing.

With her eyes fixed on the ground, she marched out of the toilets and kept on walking towards her classroom. But as each step took her nearer, her heart beat a little faster. She felt hot all over. And sick. She wished she was at home. Anywhere but here. But she *was* here and she *had* to be strong. She couldn't let them see her cry. She was just passing the main entrance when she noticed the door was open. Usually it was shut and anyone wanting to come in would have to press a button, which would be answered by the school secretary, whose office was opposite. Carrie suddenly felt drawn to the door, and saw that Mrs Miller was sitting at her desk and talking on the phone. How easy it would be to slip away! To sneak out and spend the day wandering round the shops. Or maybe she could walk down to the canal and chat to the nice people in their boats who always waved and smiled at her and Joel. They might even invite her on board. It would be better than staying here listening to those spiteful girls calling her names and whispering about her every time she answered a question or was asked to read out something.

A glance over her shoulder told her that Mrs Miller was still talking on the phone. It gave her the courage to take a small step nearer the door. And another. Two more steps and she'd be out in the playground. If she was fast enough, she'd get to the gate before anyone saw her. And she was fast enough. She could beat anyone in her class at running. Even the boys. That's why they didn't like her. She was better than them at everything, especially maths. Harriet had taught her a special way to learn her times tables – a better way than Dad had – and she knew them all easy-peasy. No one else in her class could do that. They were all babies still trying to work out what three times three was. Most of them couldn't even do joined-up writing. They were useless. Well, she'd show them.

Her head zinging with excitement, she slipped quietly through the open door and made a dash for it. She kept on running until she was beyond the gate and out onto the pavement. On and on she ran, her shoes slapping on the ground, her plaits flying out behind her, the blood pounding in her ears. She'd done it!

Her first mistake, she realised, was not to have brought her coat. Now that she wasn't running, she was cold. Her school sweatshirt and grey skirt was also attracting attention. One woman had already asked her if she should be at school. 'I'm waiting for my mother,' she'd told the woman. 'She's in the cake shop.' Which was where she was now standing, her stomach growling for food. It would be lunchtime at school, and as she stared at the rows of iced buns, doughnuts and chocolate-dipped gingerbread men and breathed in the smell of freshly baked bread, Carrie knew that the next time she would have to bring some money with her.

Across the road, she saw a scruffy man in an anorak giving her an odd look. Carrie would have liked to stick out her tongue and pull a face at the nosy man, but she didn't think it would be a good idea. Deciding she ought to keep moving to keep warm, she wandered down the main street and came to the cobbled area where Harriet had told her the original market used to be. Turning to her right, and walking along a short, narrow alleyway, she came to an area she'd never noticed before. It was cobbled like the old marketplace and was a bit dark. It reminded her of Diagon Alley, where Harry Potter goes to buy his wands and books. Ahead of her was a building that she knew had to be very old; it had black beams criss-crossing all over it. There was a green and gold sign above the door that said 'Hart's Antique Emporium'. She knew exactly what an emporium was; it was somewhere big and fancy that sold lots of nice things. It would also be warm, she thought. She was just making up her mind whether to go inside and have a look when she heard footsteps behind her. She spun round, suddenly scared that it might be the scruffy man in the anorak.

But it wasn't him; it was the man who lived across the road from them.

'Hello, Carrie,' he said, 'what are you doing here?'

She swallowed. 'Um . . . I'm just waiting for Grandma.' She looked in the direction of the emporium, hoping it was the kind of place her grandmother would go in.

He looked surprised. 'Why did she leave you outside?'

Carrie began to get flustered. 'Because . . . because I didn't want to go in.'

'Well, you look frozen to death. Come on in out of the cold.'

She held back. 'It's okay. I'll wait here. I'm sure she won't be long.'

He smiled and she suddenly wished she wasn't lying to him. He was too nice to lie to. She saw that he was carrying two paper bags; one had a greasy patch on its side. She could smell food. A pasty? Or maybe a sausage roll? When she looked back at his face, she saw that the smile had gone and he was frowning. 'Your grandmother's not in there, is she, Carrie?'

How had he known she was lying? She shook her head and looked hard at her shoes.

He bent down to her. 'And you're not in school where you should be, are you?'

Again she shook her head. She noticed one of her shoelaces was fraying at the end.

'Tell you what; I'll trade with you. You tell me what you've been doing and I'll share some of my lunch with you – half a sausage roll and an iced bun. How does that sound?'

She raised her eyes. 'Will you tell on me?'

He stood up and took her hand. 'Not exactly. But we will have to tell a few people where you are as otherwise they'll be very anxious and call the police. If they haven't already. Just think how upset Harriet and your grandparents will be if they think you're missing.'

She tightened her grip on his hand. She was beginning to realise how much trouble she was in. But she had a worse fear. 'I don't want to go back to school,' she said.

He smiled. He had a nice smile, she decided. It reminded

her of Dad. 'Don't worry,' he said, 'I'll make sure you have the rest of the day off.'

He led her inside the emporium and at once she forgot all about being in trouble. She'd never been anywhere like it. Everywhere she looked there was furniture – tables, chairs, bookcases – and china and sparkling silvery things and lots and lots of ticking clocks. There were mirrors, too. And those lights made of diamonds that hung from the ceiling. She could hear music playing. Sleepy piano music. It made her want to curl up in a chair and close her eyes. 'What kind of place is this?' she asked.

'An antique shop. Do you like it?'

'Yes. Is it yours?'

'Not entirely.'

She let go of his hand and wandered over to a chest that had a glass dome on top of it. Inside the dome was a brightly coloured bird. It was a kingfisher. She knew because Granddad had pointed one out to her down by the canal. 'Is it real?' she asked.

'In a manner of speaking. It died a long time ago. It's stuffed.'

'What with?'

'Do you know, I haven't a clue?'

'Hello, hello, hel*lo*, and who have we here?'

Carrie turned round to see a very peculiar man coming towards them. He was wearing a suit the colour of Ribena with a spotty bow tie. On his feet were the strangest slippers she'd ever seen; the fronts were very pointed and curled like pigs' tails.

'Carrie, let me introduce you to Jarvis. He might look like something from another world, but he's quite harmless. Jarvis, this is Carrie Knight, a friend of mine. She's got herself into a bit of a fix and I'm going to sort things out for her.'

'Well my dear, any friend of Will's is a friend of mine. How do you do?' He leaned forward and held out his hand. Carrie giggled and held hers out just as she knew she was expected to. 'Enchanted,' he said. 'Now correct me if I'm wrong, but did I hear you enquiring with what this splendid creature is stuffed?'

She nodded, at the same time trying to get her giggling under control. He really was the funniest man.

'Permit me to explain. You see, what you have to bear in mind is that the Victorians believed this to be a form of conservation. Of course, these days, we have a very different approach to that.'

From inside his office, Will watched Jarvis carefully lift the glass dome off the kingfisher. He reached for the phone book on the shelf behind him and within seconds was ringing the local primary school. The next call he made was to his neighbours, Bob and Eileen. There was no answer.

Chapter Twenty-Nine

Harriet switched off her mobile and leapt to her feet. This couldn't be happening. What had got into Carrie? First she'd tried to scare the other children at school half to death, now she'd turned truant. What next? Drug dealer?

Shutting down her computer and gathering up her bag and jacket, she forced herself to take a deep, steadying breath while she thought how to make an exit from her office without attracting attention from her new boss. She would have to feign illness, and not some girly stomach ache or headache, or she'd be branded Princess PMT from here on. An asthma attack would be better. A nice unisex illness, the kind that even a great lump like Howard Beningfield might suffer from.

A knock at her door made her jump. It was Dave Carter, one of the junior analysts – a decent enough bloke if you forgave him his big buckled belt and cowboy boots, and the two lost causes in his life: real ale and Manchester City. His office nickname was Dangerous Dave on account of him being as action-packed as a loaf of stale bread. 'How's it going?' he said. 'I just thought you might like . . . Hey, you okay? Only you look a bit pale.'

Pale? It must be the shock. She covered her face with a hand and staggered a little as though she might faint any second. 'I'm really sorry,' she rasped, 'but it's an asthma attack. I'm going to have to call it a day. I'm so sorry.'

'Will you be okay to drive?'

'I'll manage,' she said, already out of the door and making for the reception area. 'I'll be in extra early tomorrow,' she called over her shoulder, 'if anyone asks.'

By the time she was driving out of the car park, she was

beginning to worry that she really did have an asthma attack looming. There was a niggling tightness in her chest that didn't bode well. But she couldn't reach her inhaler – it was in the bag on the back seat where she'd thrown it in her haste.

Once Crantsford was behind her, she tried to relax. There was nothing to worry about, she told herself when she had to stop for some traffic lights and was tapping the steering wheel impatiently. Carrie was quite safe. Admittedly she wasn't where she should have been, but she was safe. That was what was important, as the headmistress had pointed out on the phone. Apparently school hadn't been able to get hold of Mum and Dad when they realised Carrie was missing, and when she'd tried Harriet's mobile there'd been no answer because, until ten minutes ago, she'd switched it off while she was in a meeting. But thank goodness their neighbour, Will Hart, had spotted Carrie in town and taken her in, then phoned school. She would for ever be grateful to him. Even if he was now probably sitting in judgement on her and wondering how a child in her care had so nearly come to harm.

I'm doing my best, was all she could say in her defence. Then suddenly it wasn't Will to whom she was defending herself, it was Felicity, and her sister's presence was so palpable she felt her scalp prickle. 'Oh, Harriet,' she imagined her sister saying, 'I thought you'd take good care of Carrie. I trusted you. My precious baby could have been snatched by some vile perverted beast while your back was turned. She could have been tortured. Tortured, then murdered! Her violated body tossed into the canal. Her short life snuffed out because *you* didn't care about her.'

'But I do care about her!' Harriet said out loud, a rush of panicky sickness consuming her as the reality of what could have happened to Carrie sank in. 'She's safe, Felicity. Please don't make me feel any guiltier than I already do.'

She grasped the steering wheel and groaned. Oh, God, she was going mad. She was arguing with her dead sister.

She parked as near to Hart's Antique Emporium as she

223

could – which wasn't close at all – and ran all the way. The tranquil scene that greeted her was totally at odds with the state she was in – sweating and out of breath, her chest heaving and wheezy, her mouth dry. But there on the other side of the shop was Carrie, sitting in a wing-back armchair with a wooden tray on her lap, her legs sticking out in front of her. She was polishing a silver teapot, concentrating hard on its spout, and humming along to a piece of music that was playing. Nearby, a couple were smiling at each other in amusement.

'You must have driven like the wind.'

She turned to see Will sitting behind an untidy desk in a small, cramped office, a pile of paperwork before him. There was something different about him. Then she realised he was wearing glasses, a smart frameless pair that made him look more like the corporate lawyer he had been. Removing the glasses and tossing them onto the desk, he came towards her. 'The kettle's just boiled; would you like a cup of tea? You look like you could do with one.' His kindness was too much, and overcome with relief that Carrie really was okay, she felt foolishly tearful and sank into the nearest chair. The tightening in her chest had worsened to such an extent that she fumbled for her inhaler in her bag. But she'd gone too long without it; her fingers were numb with pins and needles. She felt light-headed too and knew that she must have been hyperventilating for some time. Panic kicked in, which made her throat constrict even more.

Will was concerned. 'What is it, Harriet? What can I do?'

'Asthma,' she wheezed. She pointed to her bag. 'My inhaler. It's in there.'

Not wanting to waste any time, Will tipped the bag upside down onto the floor, scattering pens, tissues, personal organiser, lip gloss, tampon, cheque book, wallet. And finally, an inhaler. He passed it to her.

'Okay?' he asked, when she'd pressed it to her mouth for a second time and he'd put everything back in her bag.

'I will be,' she rasped.

'How about a drink?'

She shook her head. 'I should take Carrie home.' They both looked over to where Carrie was oblivious to anything but the shiny teapot in her hands.

'I hope that's not too valuable,' Harriet mumbled, getting to her feet.

'Silver plate, circa yesterday.' He thought Harriet looked in no state to be going anywhere, and that maybe she ought to calm down some more before dealing with her niece. 'It's no trouble, you know, that cup of tea.'

'You're sure?'

'Come into my office and relax while I keep an eye on Carrie from the doorway.' She did as he said and after he'd moved some papers from a chair and flicked the switch on the kettle, he said, 'Carrie's really been no bother and I realise it's none of my business, but I made a bargain with her. I said she wouldn't get into too much trouble if she told me exactly what she'd been up to.'

'Well, of course she's in trouble. She can't expect to skive off school at her age and not realise there are serious consequences.'

He let it go. It wasn't his place to tell someone else how to go about the sticky business of parenting. Privately he thought Harriet and her parents would need to get to the bottom of what Carrie had done. She struck him as a good kid, not the sort who would ordinarily get into trouble. 'Milk and sugar?' he asked.

'Splash of milk, no sugar.'

When he'd dunked a teabag and stirred in some milk, he handed her the mug. 'Feeling any better?'

'Getting there. I'm sorry for snapping just now. It was rude of me. You've been very kind. I haven't even thanked you for taking care of Carrie.'

Her words were in the shape of an apology, but her tone was so stiff it sounded more like she was reading from a script. 'Oh, shucks,' he said good humouredly, 'now you're embarrassing me.' He expected her to smile, but to his horror her face crumpled and she began to cry.

'I'm a failure,' she murmured, her head lowered. 'A total failure. I haven't got a clue how to bring up children and today's proved just how bad I am. I feel so guilty. So useless.'

He looked about him for some tissues, but could only find a pack of muslin he used for polishing. He pulled out a sheet, knelt on the floor and passed it to her, at the same time taking the mug of tea from her shaking hands. 'You're not a failure,' he said, 'you're a hero for what you're doing. Your sister would be proud of you.'

She shook her head at his words. 'You're wrong. I've let her down.' She pressed the muslin to her eyes. 'I'm a rotten sister and an even worse aunt, guardian, mother, whatever it is I'm supposed to be. Oh, God, I don't even know who I am any more. What am I doing wrong? You're a parent; tell me how to do a better job.'

He put a hand on her shoulder. 'Don't be so hard on yourself. You're just on the steepest learning curve of your life. It'll get better, I promise.'

'That's okay for you to say; your children don't even live with you.'

Surprised at the vehemence of her words, and the implied criticism, he said nothing, just kept his hand on her shoulder.

In the silence, another voice spoke up: 'Will, have you got anything else for me to polish? Oh . . . hello, Harriet.'

Harriet shrugged off Will's hand and blew her nose hard as Carrie stepped into the office nervously. 'Are you crying, Harriet?'

'Don't be so silly. I've got something in my eye. That's all.'

'Is it me? Have I made you cry?'

Will could see that Harriet was fighting to keep what little composure she'd reinstated. 'You aunt's just relieved to find you in one piece,' he intervened. 'Now then, Carrie, why don't we let Harriet finish her tea while I find you something else to polish? How about a candlestick? If you do a good job, I'll let you come another day and you can polish all the other bits and bobs I have. But preferably at the weekend,' he added with a wink.

'Really?'

'I don't see why not.'

Leading the way, he glanced back to check if it was okay with Harriet. But she wasn't looking his way. He thought he'd never seen anyone look more miserable.

Later that afternoon, in Maple Drive, Harriet was conscious that they were all behaving strangely.

They were sitting round the kitchen table for an early tea and it was difficult to know who looked the most distracted and uncomfortable. Mum was fiddling with the salt and pepper pots, repositioning them every ten seconds. She always did this when she was anxious or cross – Harriet and Felicity used to call it Tea-Time Chess. And Dad, well, frankly, Dad looked as though he'd been caught with his fingers in the till and couldn't apologise enough for not having had his mobile switched on that day. Meanwhile Joel was swinging his legs under the table and playing with his supper but not eating it, and Carrie was sitting like a statue in her seat as though afraid that if she moved someone might notice her and start asking questions all over again.

They'd already had the Big Scene, during which Carrie had been cajoled in as many different ways as they could contrive to explain what had got into her. But all they'd learned was that she'd been bored and fancied a walk. Harriet had decided it could well be true; she had entertained the same thought countless times when she'd been at school.

When the ordeal of tea was over and Harriet was upstairs supervising bathtime, Carrie said, 'Harriet?'

'Yes.'

'Are you going to punish me?'

'Do you want me to?'

Carrie plunged the strawberry-shaped sponge under the water. 'No.'

'But I'll tell you what I do want you to do. I want you to write a letter of apology to school saying that you're very sorry for what you did and for causing so many people to worry. I think you might even write a thank-you note to Will. He was very good to you.'

At this, Carrie's face brightened. She reached for the toy plastic duck behind Joel and filled it with frothy bathwater. 'I like Will. Do you like Will, Harriet?'

'I've never really thought about it. He's just one of our neighbours.'

'Why was he hugging you when you were crying?'

Taken aback, Harriet said, 'I wasn't aware that he was hugging me. *Or* that I was crying,' she added hastily, noticing Joel looking at her with his luminous dark eyes. He hadn't said a word since asking to get down from the table.

'He had his hand on your shoulder,' Carrie carried on blithely. 'I think he likes you. Maybe he could be your boyfriend.'

'Oh, don't be absurd! He's much too old for me.'

'How old is he?'

'Ancient.'

'He doesn't look *too* ancient.'

'Well, he is. I reckon he must be about forty-five, forty-six, perhaps even older.'

Without a second's thought, Carrie said, 'If he's forty-six, that makes him fourteen years older than you.'

'Hah, Miss Carol Vorderman! That proves my point exactly. And besides, he has a girlfriend already.'

'Does he? That's a shame.'

Joel couldn't sleep that night. Outside his window he could hear the wind rustling in the trees. He didn't like the sound the leaves made; it was like people whispering. They whispered at school. They were always doing it. Sometimes it upset him, but usually he ignored them as Carrie had told him to.

He drew his legs up to his chest and hugged them tight. Why had Carrie tried to run away from school? And supposing she did it again and disappeared completely? What if he never saw her again? He'd be all alone. No one to cuddle up to in bed when he couldn't sleep. No one to tell him stories about Mummy and Daddy. And he really wanted to hear those stories because he was already beginning to forget what it used to be like.

With tears running down his cheeks, he slipped out of bed and tiptoed across the landing to Carrie's bedroom. He could tell that she was asleep because she was snoring. She said she didn't snore, but she did. Sometimes she did that strange thing with her teeth – scraped them against each other, making a horrid grinding noise. As quietly as he could, he slid under the duvet next to her. Comforted by her warmth, he was asleep within minutes.

Disturbed by the sound of Joel creeping into Carrie's bedroom, Eileen stirred. She was a light sleeper at the best of times, but these days the least noise woke her. She lay for a moment on her side, contemplating the day she'd had. She wished now that she hadn't taken up Dora on her offer to join her for a coffee and then lunch. It had been a mistake, and not just because if she'd been at home to answer the phone Harriet wouldn't have been bothered at work and rushed home and given herself an asthma attack.

But what Eileen most regretted was what she'd told Dora. It was wrong of her. Very wrong. It wasn't as if she had any proof, just a gut feeling to go on. And a history. Dora couldn't hide her shock that Bob, of all men, could have an affair. 'But how do you know?' she'd asked.

'I don't. All I have is a nagging sense of déjà vu.' She explained about the two affairs during the Wilderness Years and how she could see a pattern repeating itself. 'It's the way he always leaves the house making sure I have everything I need. It's his desire to please that is such a bad sign. That and the long absences.'

'But he's out walking the dog, surely?'

'Oh, Dora, don't you think I'd rather I was imagining it?' she'd said. 'Don't you think it would be easier? But I just know. You see, there were days, last month, when he was out with Toby for hours at a time and he'd come home almost cheerful. Then, I don't know why – perhaps she was away on holiday – the walks got shorter and he was permanently in the garden no matter what the weather, as if he was avoiding me. But this morning he was out for ages again, almost two hours. I'm certain he's seeing someone. He couldn't be out that long just walking on his own.'

'It's possible, isn't it? Perhaps it's his way of coping with his grief. Wanting to be alone.'

Thinking of all those miscarriages Bob had grieved for, Eileen knew that her husband wasn't capable of grieving alone.

Conscious that she couldn't hear Bob breathing beside her, she turned over to look at him. But the other side of the bed was empty. Perhaps he was downstairs making himself a drink. She could do with one herself. She pushed back the duvet and got slowly to her feet, feeling like a lead weight.

Downstairs, the kitchen was in darkness and there was no sign of Bob. The kettle hadn't boiled recently, either. She was about to go and see if he was in the sitting room when a glow of light in the garden caught her eye. Focusing her eyes on the Wendy house, she tried to make sense of what she was looking at: Bob was sitting in the Wendy house in the light of a candle. Her heart sank. What was he doing out there? Talking to his lover on his mobile?

Chapter Thirty

A week later, as she drove to work, Harriet knew she needed to make two apologies, neither of which she was looking forward to. Curiously, the two men to whom she needed to say sorry had become Carrie's favourite people. Hardly a day went by without Carrie singing their praises in one form or another. If she was watching television and an antique programme came on, she would hurl herself into a long monologue: 'Ooh, look, that's just like Will's shop. Except Will's shop is much nicer. He's got so much stuff in it, too. Will says that Jarvis used to run the shop but now he does. When I grow up, I want to do a job like Will's. It must be lots of fun. Not really like work at all. Do you know what Will—?' On and on she'd twitter until finally one of the others, usually Harriet, would change the subject.

Unfortunately Carrie's other hot topic of conversation was Dominic McKendrick. To everyone's amazement, Dominic had sent Carrie an old photograph of Felicity accompanied by a brief handwritten note:

> Carrie,
>   I wondered if you would like the enclosed.
>   Dominic.

'Good heavens, what a curious choice of photograph,' Eileen had said when they'd all taken a look at it. The picture was of Dominic and Felicity done up as a couple of teenage punks – gelled hair, bondage trousers, ripped T-shirts and scowls this side of a held-back smirk. Harriet could remember Dominic having his ear pierced specially for the occasion – someone's eighteenth birthday party –

but when it later turned septic, he'd vowed he'd never let anyone else mutilate him. 'Self-mutilation is the most satisfying path to nirvana anyway,' he'd quipped.

The photograph immediately became one of Carrie's most treasured possessions. She begged Harriet to buy her a frame for it and she placed it on her bedside table, next to her other framed photograph, the one of her parents. She then wrote and thanked Dominic. Harriet had no idea what her niece had put in the letter. She hadn't read the note Carrie had written to Will, either, but she did know that Carrie had spent an inordinate amount of time decorating the single piece of paper, colouring in a border of pink and mauve flowers interspersed with tiny red hearts. The masterpiece was then finished off with a flourish of glue and glitter. Harriet hoped that Dominic would acknowledge the effort that had gone into it before he rolled his eyes and dumped it unceremoniously into the waste-paper bin.

When by return of post a further piece of correspondence for Carrie arrived from Cambridge – a postcard depicting a college gargoyle picking its nose, causing Carrie to hoot with laughter – Harriet began to have second thoughts about Dominic. Was it possible that he was finally showing a more sensitive side to his nature? A more genuine side that made him want to please a nine-year-old girl? If this was the case, then she owed him an apology. Within minutes of that awful scene on the towpath when she'd accused him of being incapable of real grief, she had regretted her words. But there had been no opportunity to say sorry; he'd caught a train back to Cambridge that very afternoon. Harriet was all too aware that he'd been equally vitriolic in his attack on her, but she had been the one to start it, and had deliberately provoked him. Who was she to dictate how he should publicly mourn Felicity? Especially when they had been such close friends. It had been a friendship that Harriet had, at times, been jealous of. But she'd loved Felicity too much to allow something as petty as jealousy to spoil things between them. So what if Dominic always favoured Felicity? she'd told herself. Why should she care when she had Miles? Miles was infinitely kinder than his brother and much easier to be around.

Although there was so much going on in Harriet's life just now, what with her new job and house-hunting, her thoughts were never far from wondering who Felicity had been seeing behind Jeff's back. Could it be a neighbour from the past, perhaps? Or maybe a work colleague? There was no one obvious who sprang to mind. She had now transferred all of Felicity's emails onto her new laptop and was systematically going through them late each night, looking for clues as to the man's identity. She had gone way beyond feeling guilty about her actions. She was now on a quest. Intriguingly and annoyingly, neither Felicity nor her lover had used their names in any of the messages. Why all the subterfuge? Harriet wondered. They already had a code to hide behind, so why the extra mile?

For the most part, the emails were intensely serious and highly passionate. There were times when Harriet could see what Felicity saw in this man; his adoration must have been powerfully addictive. *'What woman could resist such sensual words of love?'* Felicity had written and Harriet had to agree. The emails even resurrected those old feelings of jealousy Harriet had known all those years ago. What must it be like to be loved so devotedly? Certainly no relationship she'd experienced had ever been so intense or so intimate. *'Erotic is a much misused word these days,'* Felicity's lover had written, *'but you provoke every erotic instinct within me. I want you here with me now. I want you in my bed every night; I'm tired of our snatched moments. I want more.'*

It was evident that while Felicity wanted to be with her lover, she was not about to walk out on her children. *'If we're to be together,'* she wrote, *'I have to bring my children; they're a part of me.'*

'I know that,' he replied. *'And what's a part of you is a part of me.'*

'You write as though it will be easy to wrench them away

from their father. Believe me, it won't be. They love him and he loves them.'

'But you have to believe me when I say that this agony I'm in is far worse than anything he might feel. His feelings cannot compare to the pain of my not being with you.'

The arrogant, self-absorbed nature of this reply made Harriet think of Dominic; without a doubt he fitted the profile perfectly. Except for the small matter of his sexual preference. True, he had spent part of his adolescence experimenting with Felicity – as Felicity had described what had passed between them – but his lifestyle, since those days, was all too clear. Many years ago, Harriet and Felicity had visited Dominic in Cambridge and they'd met for themselves his lover – Dominic always used the word *lover* and never *partner*; he claimed it implied a degree of permanency he wasn't interested in. The man in question was a beautiful young music scholar from the Ukraine with startlingly pale skin and long blond hair. 'You'll be amused to know that Uri has a temper worse than mine,' Dominic had said when Uri left them alone to go and prepare for a music recital. 'He also has a fondness for too much vodka. But I tolerate him because he keeps me company. For the time being, anyway.' A slight lifting of his shoulders suggested weary indifference. Thinking of this comment now, Harriet wondered just how lonely an existence Dominic led. Was it an inevitable fate for the promiscuous and self-obsessed?

All this Harriet put aside when she skirted Crantsford and headed towards the business park. Her journey into work had quickly developed its own routine and gave her time to readjust from the chaos of Maple Drive. One of her greatest skills, she liked to think, was her ability to compartmentalise her life. Work was work and her private life was exactly that; private. Spencer had been the only exception to this firm rule.

The good news was that she loved her new job. It was early days, but work with ACT was proving to be interesting and stimulating, even if she did still have months of settling in and learning the products ahead. Realistically, it would be some time before she had a firm grip on the large-scale applications going on. Until then she had to grit her teeth and make do with what she called the Noddy jobs: the simple applications she could be trusted with in the meantime.

However, her efforts to find a house were failing miserably. The details the estate agents were sending her were either grossly misleading or well out of her price range. That was the trouble with wanting to stay in Kings Melford, where she would be close to school and her parents. The latter was imperative; she just wouldn't survive if Bob and Eileen weren't within a two-mile radius. If nothing else, they were her safety net.

Although they hadn't been much of a safety net when Carrie had performed her disappearing act at school. It still appalled Harriet to think what might have happened to her niece if Will hadn't come across her. Which brought her full circle: Will Hart. Other than his taste in young girlfriends, he seemed a nice enough bloke and there really hadn't been any need for her to make that barbed comment about his children not living with him. It had been unnecessarily rude of her, given that he'd been so helpful with Carrie and herself when she'd been having her asthma attack.

Feeling decisive, she made a mental note to give him a ring at his shop during her lunch break. She would apologise and get him off her conscience. When she'd done that, she would ring Miles and ask him for Dominic's phone number so that she could wipe that slate clean as well. She might also ask Miles if he fancied a drink that evening.

Dangerous Dave poked his head round her office door just as she'd made a breakthrough on a particularly satisfying piece of programming and was leaning back in her chair, her feet up on her desk, a fist punching the air.

'Hiya, Harriet,' he said. 'If you've got a minute, the Big Man says he'd like a word with you.'

'Oh, hell. Any idea what he's on the warpath for today?'

Yesterday it had been a tedious bean-counting exercise – 'Keep the fiction out of your expense claims or you'll be working on your obituaries,' he'd told the assembled staff.

Expecting there to be a similar gathering as yesterday, Harriet was surprised to find it was just her who had been summoned to the Big Man's office.

'Ah, there you are. How do you fancy a trip over to Ireland?'

'A potential client?'

Howard nodded and pointed to a chair. 'That's right. But don't be getting your hopes up and thinking it's that leather-clad clog-dancing pretty boy Michael Flatulence. I want you to convince the haulage company I've been chasing for some months now that we're the boys to give them what they want. They're the reason I employed you.' He got to his feet and jangled some loose change in his pockets. 'Presumably there's no reason why you can't go?'

'No reason at all. When were you thinking?'

Back in her office, Harriet dug out her personal organiser and pencilled in the days she would be away. Looking ahead, assuming there wouldn't be a problem with her parents handling things in her absence, a couple of days guzzling Guinness and eating out seemed okay.

Her stomach rumbled, reminding her that it was now lunchtime. Which in turn reminded her that she had two phone calls to make. Will's number was engaged, so she tried Miles.

'You're lucky you caught me,' he said when one of the girls in the bookshop had located him. 'I'm just off for lunch with one of the publishing reps. How have you been? The new job going well? The kids okay?'

'Yes to all of the above. I shan't keep you, but have you got Dominic's phone number to hand?'

'I have, but what on earth do you want that for?'

'I need to speak to him. Actually, I need to apologise. I was pretty hard on him when he was up here and I've been feeling bad about it ever since.'

'Well, don't. Dominic's never felt bad about another

living soul. Besides, he won't know what to do with an apology, apart from pour scorn on it.'

After she'd rung off, having arranged to meet for a drink next week – Miles was busy tonight – Harriet tried Will's number again and got through. 'Hi,' she said, 'it's Harriet Swift, your neighbour from across the—'

He cut her off with a laugh. 'It's okay, I know exactly who you are. What can I do for you? Oh, by the way, how's your asthma? No further attacks I hope.'

Harriet stalled, picturing herself making an embarrassing fool of herself wheezing and crying in his office. She must have looked and sounded a total mess. An apology over the phone, though convenient, suddenly didn't seem entirely appropriate or adequate. More to the point, it might make her look weak and cowardly. If she had any bottle at all, she'd do it in person. 'What time do you finish work?' she asked.

'Hey, didn't you know? I'm the big honcho round here; I finish work whenever I want to.'

'And in the real world?'

'About six. Why? Do you want to negotiate a fair wage for Carrie when I put her on the payroll? I'll warn you now; there'll be occasional chimneys for her to clean as well as the odd Spinning Jenny to crawl under.'

'I'm sure my niece is more than capable of sorting out her own financial package without my intervention.' Harriet steeled herself. 'If you're around this evening, I wondered if I could nip across and speak to you. I won't keep you long.'

'You can keep me as long as you like. I have nothing planned for the evening.' He laughed. 'Or for the rest of time, come to think of it. Why not have that drink I've been threatening you with?'

Mm . . . she thought, when she'd said goodbye, idly moving the cursor about on her computer screen. It sounded like the pretty blonde girlfriend was no more. Was she pushed, or did she go of her own accord? And was there a danger, if Will was used to pulling girls much younger than himself, that he might try it on with Harriet?

Let him try!

Chapter Thirty-One

It was a while since Will had had anyone other than Suzie and Gemma to the house, and after a hurried tidy-up and a blitz round with the Dyson and a duster, he deemed the place verging on the half-decent. I'm letting myself go, he thought, pushing the Dyson back into the under-stairs cupboard. But then lately he hadn't had much time for the pinny and rubber-glove routine. If he wasn't chasing his tail with the shop, driving hundreds of miles every week to auctions and being called out by people who'd watched one too many episodes of *Bargain Hunt* and *Flog It* and now believed they had a stash of priceless *objets d'art* languishing in the attic, he was keeping the peace between Suzie and her mother. A full-time job in itself.

When he'd driven Suzie away from the clinic, he'd brought her back to his house before taking her home to Maywood. She'd cried for most of the journey and it was only when he'd settled her in the armchair in the sitting room and had made her a hot drink that they talked about the baby. 'You don't have to justify why you changed your mind,' he said. 'It's your decision, no one else's.'

'But Mum's going to kill me.'

'Nonsense. She doesn't handle change too well, that's all. Once she gets used to the idea, she'll be fine. She'll start organising the mother of all nurseries for you. The whole shebang.'

But Maxine was far from fine when Will drove Suzie home and explained the situation while Suzie rushed upstairs to her bedroom. 'But she can't keep the baby!' Maxine had screeched. 'She's only nineteen. What about university? How does she think she's going to manage? Has she figured that out yet? Oh, this is madness!'

Unable to keep his temper in check a moment longer, Will turned on Maxine. 'I'll tell you how's she going to manage: she's going to have all the love and support she bloody well deserves. And if you're not prepared to do it, I'll do it alone.'

'Oh, there you go again. You always have to be the good guy.'

'Change the record, why don't you?'

She glared at him. 'I blame you. If you'd been firmer with her at the clinic she wouldn't have backed out. I wouldn't be at all surprised if you deliberately engineered this just to put her against me.'

'For God's sake, Maxine, listen to yourself! Where's your love and compassion? This is our daughter. She's just made the most crucially important decision of her life and you're twisting it round to make it proof that I'm some kind of bastard. What's the sense in that?'

'Don't you ever question my love for Suzie. It's because I love her that I want the best for her and that doesn't include being a single mother at nineteen.'

'I agree it's not ideal, but this is the choice she's made and I for one am going to help her all I can.'

Steve had arrived home from work at that point and Will had taken it as his cue to exit stage left. Since then, Maxine had calmed down but Will knew Suzie was hurt that her mother had pointed out several times that it wasn't too late for her to change her mind and have a termination. She was also repeatedly warning Suzie of the difficulties that lay ahead.

Will was also worried about the numerous practicalities Suzie would soon be facing. His primary concern was where Suzie and the baby would live and what they'd live on if Maxine didn't have a change of heart. Benefits would be available, he supposed, but parental pride and something horribly middle-class in Will made him feel he'd be letting Suzie down if this was what she was reduced to.

Plan B was to invite Suzie to move in with him and somehow he'd earn the extra money needed. He'd be damned if he'd go cap in hand to Maxine. But he couldn't believe that Maxine wouldn't finally come round and be there for Suzie.

He gave the sitting room a final checking over for dust and cobwebs, then opened a bottle of Merlot, which he fancied for himself, and made sure there was also a bottle of white and some beer in the fridge. He then decided the house felt a bit chilly, so he went out to the garage and set about making a fire with logs from the diseased apple tree he'd chopped down at the bottom of the garden. The previous owners had had lousy taste in décor, but thankfully they hadn't got rid of the fireplace in the sitting room. It was small but effective and he soon had a good blaze going. Washing his hands at the kitchen sink, he wondered what the Hedgehog wanted to discuss with him. What was so important that she couldn't have said it over the phone?

Harriet went downstairs after reading Joel his bedtime story. Her mother was in the kitchen emptying the children's lunchboxes of half-eaten apples and muesli bar wrappers and her father, yet again, was nowhere to be seen. Toby's basket next to the washing machine was empty. 'Dad out with Toby again?' she asked.

Eileen slammed the lid of the bin shut. 'Looks like it.'

Her tone was as stark as the overhead striplight that for years Harriet had wished her parents would get rid of. In its harsh brilliance, she could see how tired her mother looked, how pale and gaunt her face was.

'You look ready to drop, Mum,' Harriet said, going over to her and taking Carrie's lunchbox out of her hands. 'Let me finish that for you. You go and sit down.'

'I will later, when Carrie's finished watching *Top of the Pops*. I didn't mind sitting through it with you and Felicity, but I'm past it now.'

'I know what you mean. Even to my ears the music all sounds the same and the girls look like cheap hookers.'

'You don't suppose we should stop Carrie watching it, do you?'

Harriet shook her head. 'It's too late for that. Anyway, she says Jeff and Felicity used to let her stay up to watch it.'

Eileen sighed, alerting Harriet once again to the worry that perhaps her mother was overdoing things. She hadn't yet mentioned the trip to Ireland and she was suddenly concerned that she might have taken too much for granted. What if her mother's illness was getting progressively worse? What then? Would her father be able to look after Mum *and* babysit the children when required? The obvious answer was to hire a childminder, she told herself firmly, squashing flat the concern before it got out of hand. 'Are you all right, Mum?' she asked.

'I'm tired, that's all. Nothing to worry about.'

But Harriet was worried. After she'd said goodnight to Carrie and was crossing the road to see Will, she sensed it wasn't only her ME and Felicity's death that was bothering her mother. There was something else going on; something she'd missed. But what? She was no good at subtexts. It was another reason why she often preferred computers to people. You knew exactly where you stood with them.

While Will was in the kitchen fetching their drinks, Harriet took the opportunity to prowl round his sitting room. Other than the television and CD player, there was nothing modern in the room. Everything looked to be Victorian, but there again, being a compulsive minimalist with a liking for contemporary furniture, she wouldn't know the difference between Regency and Edwardian. But to her surprise, she liked what she saw. The battered leather chesterfield sofa and high-backed chair to one side of the fireplace looked homely and comfortable and the grandfather clock, with its rhythmic, resonant tick-tock, created an elegant but restful atmosphere. At the far end of the room, there was a writing desk with attractive barley-sugar twist legs and above it a pretty watercolour of cattle grazing beneath a setting sun. She was just about to pick up one of a pair of silver-framed photographs on the desk when Will came in with their drinks.

'Feel free,' he said, when she put it back guiltily. 'I'm totally biased, of course,' he went on, 'but I think they're beautiful.'

Harriet looked at the two little girls, dressed in what looked like their best party frocks. Their blonde hair was long and fine and Harriet had to admit they did indeed look beautiful. 'How old are they?'

'In the picture?'

'Yes.'

'Two and four.'

'And now?'

He set their wine glasses on the green-leather-topped desk and picked up the other photograph. 'This was taken of the three of us last Christmas. Suzie's nineteen and Gemma's seventeen.'

Harriet took the photograph from him. She studied it closely, paying particular attention to the taller of the two girls. She suddenly felt very stupid. The girl she'd thought was his girlfriend hadn't been anything of the sort.

'Something puzzling you?' he asked.

She returned the frame to its place on the desk. 'I don't know why, but I'd imagined your children were younger; early teens perhaps.'

'Ah, that will be on account of me looking so devilishly youthful for my age. Come and sit down. I'd recommend the armchair; the sofa has a mind of its own and can skewer the unwary with its armoury of wonky springs.'

Settling herself by the fire, Harriet's thoughts were still with the error she'd made about Will's eldest daughter. She was anxious that she might have said something to offend him. Oh well. If she had, it was another apology she owed him.

'How's Carrie?' he asked. 'No more breakouts, I trust?'

'Thankfully her attempt last week seems to have been a one-off.'

'Did you get to the bottom of why she did it?'

'She said she was bored.'

'And you believed her?'

Perched on the edge of her seat, Harriet bristled. Was he questioning her judgement? 'Why wouldn't we? She's a bright girl and probably isn't being stimulated enough.'

He opened his mouth to say something but then seemed to change his mind. He took a gulp of his wine and said, 'My mother once told me that becoming a parent provides you with the opportunity to make more mistakes than any other way she knew.'

'Are you saying I've made a mistake with Carrie?'

'Not at all. I'm suggesting, as I did before, that you shouldn't be so hard on yourself.'

Harriet didn't want to think about that day too much. Blaming herself for Carrie's behaviour now seemed slightly silly, an overreaction, but seeing as he'd brought up the subject, she said, 'You were very good to Carrie . . . and me, which is why I'm here. I want you to know that we're all really grateful for what you did. I don't think I expressed myself very well at the time.'

He waved a hand at her words. 'You were upset. I quite understood. Anyway, your father's already thanked me.'

'He has? He never said anything. When did you speak with him?'

'We often pass the time of day when he's out walking Toby and I'm at the end of the garden wielding a pair of shears.'

This was news to Harriet. Not once had her father mentioned that he and Will were on speaking terms. 'Oh well,' she sighed, 'it just goes to prove what I've always suspected: nobody ever tells me anything. But the apology still stands; there was no excuse for what I said to you.'

He raised an eyebrow. 'Remind me what you said.'

If she didn't know better, she'd say he was enjoying himself at her expense. 'I accused you of not knowing what you were talking about because your children don't live with you.'

'It's a reasonable enough accusation and one my ex-wife would be only too quick to agree with.'

'That's as maybe, but I had no right to suggest it. I'm sorry.' There. She'd done it. Mission accomplished. Apology made. Now she could relax, finish her wine and go home. She sat back in the chair, crossed one leg over the other and tapped the air with her foot.

'You don't like apologising, do you?' he said after a moment's silence.

Unnerved by his perceptive observation, she said, 'Does anyone?'

'Me, I love it. I've made a career out of saying sorry. I'm always blundering around and having to make amends for some faux pas or other. So, tell me how the new job's going. But before that, tell me how the hell you can do what you do. What's a nice girl like you doing in the yawn-inducing world of computers?'

She rolled her eyes. 'And if I had a pound for every time I'd been asked that crass question, I'd be richer than Bill Gates.'

'Sorry to be so unoriginal.'

'Don't worry, I'm used to it. But first off, to be a really good analyst, you have to have a certain mindset. There's a theory that only a limited number of people are genetically predisposed to be programmers.'

'And you're one of them?'

'It would seem so. It's not a matter of intelligence as such, more a way of thinking.'

'Sounds a bit precious to me.'

She smiled. 'It can be, yes. Another commonly held view is that the computer industry is growing faster than any other.'

'It isn't?'

'No. For the simple reason that there aren't enough of the right brains out there. Sure, there's an abundance of bright young things of the useless variety, but highly skilled programmers are like gold dust.'

'So what's the fascination? They're just machines.'

'To you, maybe. But for someone like me, it's the perfect interaction. Computers don't answer back; they only give out what you put in. You tell it what to do and it does it, no questions asked.'

'In my limited experience that isn't always the case.'

'That's because you're not giving it the right instructions. The fault is yours. You see,' she shifted forward in her seat, 'what you have to remember is that a computer has no nuances, no intuition, and no initiative. A computer never doubts or questions itself. Computers are very literal and as a programmer you get used to taking things, and people, at face value.'

'So if a Johnny Quick Banana came along and tried out something subtle on you, like a compliment, you'd blow a fuse and flash up, "Sorry, can't compute!"'

Knowing that he was making fun of her, she said, 'Except there wouldn't be the apology.'

He smiled. 'Unless you were feeling particularly remorseful about something.'

'Are you trying to extract another apology out of me?'

'No. I think you've done splendidly in that department already. How about some music?'

'Depends what you're going to suggest.'

Going over to his CD collection, Will said, 'You can have whatever you like, so long as it isn't bubble-gum pop.'

'Do I look like that kind of girl?'

'No, but I was just making sure. How do you feel about R.E.M.?'

'Bring it on.'

'Hey, you mean you're old enough to appreciate quality music?'

'Now *that* I recognise as an insult. A patronising one at that.'

'Wrong! It was a compliment.'

Will put *Reveal* into the CD player and went back to the sofa. He decided that once you got the Hedgehog onto safe ground, once she was relaxed and had the foot-tapping down to a minimum, she was excellent company. Her enthusiasm for her work was charming. Yet it occurred to him, remembering how upset she'd been that day in the shop, that the way she treated Carrie and Joel was probably a reflection of the way she worked – she expected them to behave logically, like a computer would. And as any parent could tell her, kids just don't do that. Did he dare tell her this? No. He was enjoying himself too much to want to spoil a pleasant evening by antagonising her.

'I've got a confession to make,' she said, interrupting his thoughts, which had started to run along the lines that with her guard lowered she was really quite pretty; her cheekbones seemed less sharp and her eyes softer, less wary.

'A confession,' he repeated. 'That sounds ominous. What have you done?'

'It's part of another apology I think I owe you. You see, one of the reasons I snapped at you last week was because I'd taken something at face value and misinterpreted it. I thought your eldest daughter, Suzie, was your girlfriend and that it was her you were referring to when you said someone close to you was pregnant and considering an abortion.'

'You're kidding!'

'I'm afraid not.'

'Bloody hell, I've done some shitty things in my time, but chasing girls less than half my age is not one of them. You must have thought the absolute worst. You did, didn't you? You thought I was a randy old git who couldn't keep it in his trousers.'

'I did. And I'm very sorry.'

He let out his breath. 'Wow. I don't know what to say, other than to put you straight and tell you that I go for women with a few more miles on the clock than that. And just to make it absolutely clear, Suzie is definitely my daughter and she's definitely pregnant, but not by me.' He saw a look of surprise pass across Harriet's face.

'Your daughter's pregnant?' she repeated. 'But she's—'

'So young,' he finished for her. 'Yes. I'm all too aware of that.'

'And the abortion?'

'She changed her mind. She's not going through with it.'

'That's brave. And the boyfriend? Where does he fit in?'

'There is no boyfriend.'

'That really is brave.'

'You're telling me.' Then, hearing the change of track on the CD, he said, 'Listen to this. Isn't it the best?'

'What's it called? I'm not familiar with it.'

He pulled a face. 'I knew you were too good to be true. It's "I've Been High". Now close your eyes and breathe it in.'

Harriet watched Will close his eyes and tilt his head back against the sofa cushion. What a surprising man he was.

Chapter Thirty-Two

The following Sunday Harriet took the children to see a house the estate agent had described as being ideally situated and extremely good value. It was within walking distance of Maple Drive, and sounded too good to be true.

It was. Harriet could see from Carrie's and Joel's faces when they pulled up outside the three-storey Victorian semi that they weren't impressed with the gloomy exterior and broken front-room window. Things got a lot worse when they rang the doorbell and were shown inside. There were about two dozen cats in residence, along with a whiskery old man in carpet slippers and a badly stained cardigan. The air was thick with rancid milk, cat hairs and poached fish. Within minutes Harriet made their excuses – 'Sorry, we were looking for something with a bigger garden' – and drove on to Maywood where they were meeting Miles for Sunday lunch at Casa Bellagio. 'Bring the children if you like,' he'd said. 'It'll give your mum and dad a rest.' Selfishly Harriet had wished it was she who was having the rest but quickly chided herself: Mum and Dad deserved some time to themselves. She was looking forward to lunch with Miles, but hoped Carrie and Joel would behave, and that the restaurant's lack of face-painting facilities, ball pits, tables of Lego and obstacle courses wouldn't lead them to run amok through boredom. Like most grandparents, Bob and Eileen took their grandchildren to mini theme parks to eat. Harriet had a theory about this: in the future there would be generations of adults who would be unable to sit for an entire meal without leaping up every five minutes to career about the place in a screaming frenzy.

'We're not going to live in that horrible house, are we?'

Harriet looked at Joel in the rear-view mirror. 'Not a hope. I wouldn't live in that dump if you paid me a million pounds.'

'A million pounds is a lot of money,' said Carrie thoughtfully, looking out of the side window. 'You could knock the house down and build a brand new one in its place.'

'That wouldn't be the same,' replied Joel. 'You only get the money if you live in it as it is. And what would you do with all those smelly cats?'

'I'd get Toby to chase them away.'

'Some of the cats were nearly as big as Toby; they might chase him.'

Harriet left them to their hypothetical debate and thought about how her efforts to apologise to Dominic had so far come to nothing. She had rung his number countless times but had run aground on an answering machine each time. Her messages for him to call her back had all been ignored and she'd decided not to waste any more energy on him. She had quite enough on her plate without worrying about Dominic. Work was picking up and next week she was off to Dublin. Her trip coincided with half term so it meant that there were no early starts for the children or her parents. However, it did mean that Bob and Eileen would have to entertain Carrie and Joel all day. Will had very kindly offered his daughter as a babysitter.

'Now that Suzie has definitely quit university, she might be glad of something to do,' he'd said, adding, 'It might also give her something else to think about.' Harriet had thanked him and said she would bear his offer in mind.

It was tempting to think that life was beginning to get easier, but Harriet was reluctant to get her hopes up, in case some new drama befell the Swift family. However, it was good to know that there were people close by to whom she could turn for help: Miles and Will, to name but two. In contrast, those she'd once counted as friends down in Oxford had all gone quiet. Even Erin; she hadn't been in touch since their disastrous weekend.

Will had also recommended a good friend of his who was a solicitor and who could act on her behalf when she was ready to buy a house. It certainly made sense to use a local guy rather than the firm she'd used in Oxford. Having got to know Will better, Harriet now realised just how unfairly she had judged him, especially when it came to bringing up children. He'd told her about his house-husband days. 'I can't tell you how much I enjoyed being at home with the girls,' he'd said. 'Call me a soppy big girl's blouse, but the thing about kids is the utter devotion you feel for them. It's the purest, most uncomplicated love you'll ever experience; one hundred per cent unconditional.'

'I'll have to take your word on that,' she'd said, recalling that Felicity had said something similar when Carrie was born.

Miles was already at the restaurant when they arrived. 'Have you been waiting long?' Harriet asked him.

'Just a few minutes.' He helped her to divest the children of their coats and small rucksacks containing puzzle and colouring books and felt-tip pens and anything else Harriet hoped would keep them amused. When they were settled, Miles produced two small Novel Ways carrier bags. He passed them across the table to Carrie and Joel. 'I thought you might like these,' he said. Their faces lit up when they each pulled out a book. 'That was very kind of you,' Harriet said, after the children had thanked him and started to turn the pages. They looked up briefly, minutes later, to decide what they were going to eat and to unwrap a breadstick each, then returned to their books, leaving Harriet and Miles free to talk. She suddenly felt enormously proud of them. Compared to the family on a nearby table, where the children were squabbling amongst themselves and flapping their menus about while their parents tried to ignore them, Carrie and Joel were models of good behaviour.

'Did you manage to speak to Dominic?' Miles asked.

'No. I've left several messages but I think he's deliberately ignoring me.'

'I wouldn't be at all surprised. He can dole out the insults, but he can't take any himself.'

'What can't Dominic take?'

This was from Carrie. Despite there having been no more postcards or letters from Cambridge, Carrie still regarded Dominic as a favourite person. Harriet was saved from answering by the arrival of a basket of garlic bread. When the waitress had left them alone Miles said, 'We're having a special Halloween event on at the shop next week during half term; I don't suppose you'd like to come, would you, Carrie and Joel? We're making pumpkin lanterns followed by a story hour. Everyone has to dress up as a character from a book. I'm thinking of dressing up as Dumbledore.'

Two eager faces stared at Harriet across the table. 'Can we go, Harriet?'

Harriet still found it weird that she was the one whose decision was sought on such matters. 'I don't see why not. What day is it, Miles?'

'Friday afternoon. You can come along as well if you like. If you can get away from work an extra pair of hands could be useful with all those pumpkins.'

She pulled a face. 'How tempting you make it sound.' But then with a smile, she said, 'I can't guarantee it, but I might be able to join you. I'll be flying back from Dublin that morning and skiving off early could well be justified.'

They decided to walk off lunch with a stroll in the park. They'd sneaked out a couple of half-eaten bread rolls in their napkins and were on their way to feed the ducks. There was a biting chill of approaching winter in the air and after the comforting, garlicky warmth of the restaurant, they buttoned up their coats and quickened their pace. As usual Carrie and Joel ran on ahead, kicking madly at the fallen leaves on the path. Anyone looking at them would have taken them for the perfect nuclear family. The thought, which not so long ago would have horrified

Harriet, gave her a curious feeling of pleasure. She slipped her hand through the crook of Miles's arm. He turned and smiled. 'Cold?'

'A little,' she lied. But it wasn't the cold she was feeling. Being with Miles like this gave her a sense of hope and optimism. There was something very right about the four of them being together. As crazy as it sounded, she could picture Felicity looking down on them and nodding her head approvingly.

By the time they'd caught up with Carrie and Joel, a greedy crowd of ducks had gathered at the edge of the pond. Some were out of the water and had formed an intimidating tight circle around the children, causing Joel to squeal with nervous excitement as he flung them crumbs of bread with panicky, jerky movements. When they'd run out of bread, they wandered over to the play area. At Miles's insistence they all clambered onto the see-saw, Harriet and Carrie on one end and Miles and Joel on the other. The children screamed each time they were jolted high in the air, and seeing the look of happiness on their faces as they ran off to the roundabout, it was hard to imagine they'd so recently gone through the trauma of losing their parents. They're moving on, Harriet thought as she watched Carrie telling Joel to hang on tight. It's really happening.

Breaking into her thoughts, Miles said, 'They're great kids, aren't they? They've coped so well.' He stood beside her and put his arm round her shoulder. 'Felicity would be proud of them.'

'Jeff too.' She was beginning to realise how easy it was for everyone to forget her brother-in-law. A man she was feeling increasingly sorry for.

But there was another man she had started to feel sorry for. A man she didn't even know. She had no idea why she hadn't thought of it before, but Felicity's lover must have been distraught when he found out she was dead. How he'd discovered, Harriet didn't know, but the emails had stopped the day of the crash. Somewhere there was a man in deep mourning for Felicity. How was he coping? How was he dealing with his grief? Did he have friends he could turn to? Or was he in so much pain he had been unable to do this? He had become so very real to Harriet that she had actually taken the step of sending an email to the address Felicity had been corresponding with. She had decided that if he wanted to talk to someone, to pour out his grief, without fear of recrimination, he could do it with her. Very briefly, she explained that she was Felicity's sister and that she knew about the affair. It came as no surprise to her, though, when her email came bouncing back. The account she'd messaged had been closed.

A squeeze on her shoulder made Harriet look up at Miles. He said, 'We should spend more afternoons like this.'

She smiled. 'I'd like that.'

He held her closer. 'And if you'd let me, I'd like to do more to help with Carrie and Joel. They feel like family to me anyway.'

Harriet thought about this later that evening when she was looking for a clean nightdress for Carrie in her chest of drawers. Remembering the look on Miles's face when he'd kissed her goodbye – a light kiss on the mouth – something stirred in her and she felt a lightness of spirit. Was it possible that she and Miles could be more than just friends?

She was on her way out of the room when she caught her foot on the waste-paper bin. She bent down to tidy the mess and noticed a screwed-up ball of paper in amongst the pencil sharpenings and used tissues. Without knowing why, she picked it up and smoothed it out. What she saw horrified her, and she cursed under her breath. 'The nasty, foul-mouthed little bitches.' Right. This called for tough measures. She quickly folded the piece of paper and stuffed it into the back pocket of her jeans. She then recalled Will's words about getting to the bottom of Carrie's actions. Once again her respect for the man went up a degree. It also explained the reluctance Carrie had started to display on Sunday evenings about going to school the next morning.

And the occasional mutterings of stomach aches and sore throats at breakfast time.

She said nothing about the note or what she was going to do about it to Carrie when she tucked her into bed that night, but she found herself giving the girl an extra big hug.

'I enjoyed today,' Carrie said. 'Did you?'

'Yes, it was fun. And you've got Friday afternoon at the bookshop to look forward to now, haven't you?' She was conscious that Carrie needed as many things to look forward to as possible. School must have become a nightmare for her.

'You will try and be there too, won't you?' Carrie asked. 'Miles invited you as well.'

'I can't promise anything, but I'll do my best.'

'Will you help us to make some costumes?'

'I've got a much better idea: why don't we ask Grandma to do that? You know she's better at that kind of thing than me.'

Carrie smiled and held out her arms. 'Can I have another hug, please?'

When Carrie was sure Harriet had gone downstairs, she got out of bed and tiptoed through to her brother's bedroom. 'Are you awake, Joel?'

He turned over and sat up. 'What is it?'

She closed the door after her and got into bed with him. 'Do you think Miles is Harriet's boyfriend?'

He shrugged. 'I don't know. What do you think?'

'I saw them holding hands in the park. *And* I saw them kiss. If Harriet married him we wouldn't have to live in a horrible house that smelled of cats. We could live with Miles in Maywood. I bet he has a lovely house. And we'd always have lots of books to read.'

'Would it be like having a proper mummy and daddy again?'

'Sort of. If we moved to Maywood, we'd have to change schools. You'd like that, wouldn't you? A new school with nicer people in it.'

Joel hugged his sister tight. If Carrie was right, and she always was, then everything would get better. If Carrie was happy in their new school, she wouldn't think of running away again and he wouldn't have to worry about being left all alone.

Chapter Thirty-Three

Bob knew it was selfish and unworthy of him, but he couldn't wait for half term to be over and the children to return to school. So long as they were around, it was difficult for him to slip away and see Jennifer. Any walk he went on, any errands he needed to do, they clamoured to go with him. They were bored, he knew, but couldn't they amuse themselves just occasionally? He'd thought he'd got it cracked yesterday when he'd taken them shopping and had stocked up on bargain-priced videos, along with some bottles of fizzy drinks, popcorn to go in the microwave and a selection of sweets from Edna Gannet's. But the result was that by late afternoon they were bug-eyed and climbing the walls, the slightest thing setting them off. Totally out of character, Carrie had actually turned on Joel and snatched his silky from him. When Eileen had managed to make her give it back, Joel had become hysterical because Carrie had ripped one of its corners. It was at that moment Harriet had come home from work and found Carrie refusing to come out of her bedroom and Joel wailing like a siren. She had suggested that maybe the children needed more variety and less sugar to their days. Easy for her to say when she was safely out of the house each day. What he wouldn't give still to be working! Still to be on the road chasing the orders, feeling the buzz. Being himself.

That was what he liked about Jennifer; she made him feel his old self. She had planned to move on earlier in the week, but the problems she'd experienced with the engine on her arrival back in Kings Melford had worsened and she had to stay put until it was fixed. The chandlery at the marina was doing its best to get hold of the necessary parts, but there had been a mix-up at the factory in Germany and the wrong parts had been sent out. A further order had been placed, but the chandlery, so Jennifer said, was doubtful it would arrive before next Tuesday.

It was fate. He knew it. She was meant to stay.

He'd managed to see her a few times this week, either early in the morning when walking Toby before the children were up, or at night when they were in bed. His feelings for Jennifer had intensified but not in the way he might have anticipated. She had made it very clear that she was not the sort of woman who would have an affair with a married man.

'That's not what I want,' he had said, taken aback by her candour, but at the same time, relieved. He didn't want there to be any ambiguity to their friendship. 'I find I feel better about myself when I'm with you,' he told her. 'You make all the bad stuff go away. All the anger. All the hopelessness. Am I making any sense to you? Or do I sound like a man going nuts?'

'You sound like a bereaved man who needs a friend,' she'd said simply. 'So long as we're both clear on that score,' she'd added. 'I'd hate for your wife to get the wrong idea about us.'

Today had started badly, as far as Bob was concerned. It had been raining so hard first thing that when he'd whistled to Toby and reached for his lead, the dog had stared at him in disbelief and hunkered down inside his basket. 'You're surely not thinking of going out in this weather,' Eileen had said. There was something in her tone and the look she gave him that had him shrugging and saying, 'Perhaps not.'

The rain had stopped and now, at Eileen's suggestion, he was driving them all to the garden centre. He would have preferred to come on his own, but Eileen had said that while she was deciding which daffodils bulbs to buy, he could treat the children to a ride on the miniature gauge railway train that ran through the garden centre. The train ran every day during the summer, but for the rest of the year it was Sundays and school holidays only.

They split up at the garden centre; Eileen inside to mull over the vast choice of bulbs, and Bob and the children to the wooden-built ticket office for the train. Carrie was wearing her I'm-too-grown-up-for-this face, but Joel was eager to be first in the queue. There was no queue, and they were greeted by a young lad whom Bob recognised as the boy who had carelessly sprayed him with a hose the last time he was here. 'Two kids and an OAP?' the boy asked, glancing up from a huge pair of breasts in the newspaper he was looking at on his side of the counter.

Bob hated being categorised as an OAP and had often lied about his age, preferring to pay the full rate rather than be labelled a poor old duffer. 'Just two tickets for the children,' he said, handing over a five-pound note.

The lad passed him the tickets and change, and grinned. 'Better to play it safe. You don't want too much excitement at your age, do you?'

The urge to ram his fist down the cheeky sod's throat was so strong, Bob had to take a moment to compose himself before giving the children their tickets. He was vaguely aware that Carrie was asking him a question. She was always asking questions. Occasionally numbness set in and he ignored her.

'Grand*daad*!'

Pulling himself together, he gave her his full attention. 'There's no need to shout, Carrie. What is it?'

'Why was that man looking at a picture of a naked lady, Granddad?'

'Because he's a perfect example of the kind of low-life scum this world is full of. Now then, here are your tickets. Carrie, you make sure you sit next to Joel.'

'Aren't you coming with us?'

'No, Joel, I'm not.'

'But what if I fall out?'

'Carrie will hold on to you.'

Joel looked at his sister doubtfully. Perhaps, thought Bob, the memory of his ripped silky was still too fresh in the boy's mind.

The train came into the miniature station and a handful of small children with their parents stepped out of the four-seater carriages. The driver waited a full five minutes before tooting his whistle and letting rip with a blast of coal-fired steam. Carrie and Joel were the only passengers as the train set off on its mammoth eight-minute trek. They waved at Bob – Carrie's hand barely moving, but Joel's waving frantically – and all at once he was overcome with a desperate sadness. Never had his grandchildren seemed more alone. Oh God, he thought as he returned the wave, I'm going to cry.

Carrie wished it could be like this always. No school, no horrid letter, no spiteful girls, just lots of lovely days out. After the train ride at the garden centre, and a beans and sausage lunch in the café, they were now going into town. While Grandma was having her hair done, Granddad said he'd take them round the shops.

'Can we go and see Will?' she asked when they'd dropped off Grandma at the hairdresser's and were parking the car.

'Good idea; it's a while since I've seen him.'

But Will wasn't around. The man called Jarvis, who'd worn the funny slippers that day she'd run away from school, told them Will was at an auction. 'Oh, well, tell him we called,' Granddad said.

From there they went to what Granddad said was his favourite type of shop. 'The thing about charity shops,' he said, as he pushed open the door, 'is that you never know what you might find.'

Carrie wrinkled her nose. 'What's that smell?'

'The smell of too many things squeezed into too small a place. Do try and keep your voice down, won't you? Now listen, there's a section over there with books and toys; why don't you both go and have a rummage?'

'Where will you be?' Joel asked.

'I'll be right here, sorting through this lot.'

Carrie looked uncertainly at the pile of junk her

grandfather was already inspecting and took Joel up a step to the back of the shop, to the children's area. 'Look, Joel,' she said, pointing to a low shelf, 'it's a train like the one we've just been on.'

'No it isn't. It's broken. And it's not the same colour. And it's ... ooh, look what I've found.' He held up a clockwork mouse. He turned the winder, then let the toy loose. It scuttled across the dirty carpet, and kept on going until it disappeared into a small, curtained area. They chased after it and dived under the curtain to find themselves looking up at a pretty blonde girl; she was just pushing an arm through the sleeve of a jacket. 'I think it went under my bag,' she said with a friendly smile. Embarrassed, they both slid out the way they'd just come. Within seconds the girl appeared and handed them the clockwork mouse. 'I know you two, don't I? You live over the road from my father.'

Carrie smiled. 'We've just been to see him at his shop, but he wasn't there.'

'Tell me about it. I was supposed to be having lunch with him, but an auction came up. I'm Gemma by the way. I hear that my dad's offered my sister's services as babysitter for you two.'

'Really?' asked Carrie.

'Don't look so scared. She's quite friendly. See you.'

Carrie watched the girl go and pay for whatever it was she'd been trying on in the changing room. 'She was nice, wasn't she?' she said to Joel.

'Why do we need a babysitter? We've got Harriet and Grandma and Granddad. We don't need anyone else.'

Carrie sighed. She was getting fed up of Joel's constant worrying. 'Even when we had Mum and Dad, we still had a babysitter,' she reminded him. 'Don't you remember Mum used to say it was important she and Dad went out without us sometimes? She called it grown-up time. Come on, let's ask Granddad if we can have this mouse.'

As they went to find their grandfather, Carrie had a sudden memory of her mother getting ready to go out one night. Dad had been away, and Carrie had been surprised that her mother was going out on her own. 'This is Mummy time,' she'd said with a happy laugh. 'Do I look nice?'

'You look lovely,' Carrie could remember saying. 'Where are you going?'

'To see a friend. A special friend. Kiss me goodnight and be extra good for the babysitter.'

That night seemed a long, long time ago.

They were leaving the charity shop when Carrie saw someone she recognised from school, and panicked. Emily mustn't notice her! But before she had a chance to slip behind her grandfather, Emily looked across the road and saw her. Their eyes locked and, in an instant, the day was ruined.

During the drive home, Joel sat behind Grandma, whose hair was all stiff and smelling of hairspray and kept thinking about what Carrie had said. That their parents used to go out without them. He had only one memory of them going out at night, and that was the night they never came back. Then, from nowhere, he recalled something he must have forgotten about that night. Dad had been angry about something. But what could Daddy have been angry about?

'Have you and your wife ever thought about bereavement counselling?'

Bob closed the door on the wood-burning stove, stepped over Toby and sat down on the bench seat. At the other end of the table, Jennifer was mixing herself a hot toddy. He'd been here for less than ten minutes, but already the strain of the day was slipping away. And it had been one hell of a day. First there was his anger with the ignorant oik at the garden centre, then the heart-wrenching sadness he'd felt for the children, and then, for no reason at all, Carrie had turned into the monster from hell, refusing to eat her tea and kicking up the dickens of a row when Eileen said she wouldn't be allowed to go to Maywood to the bookshop on Friday if she didn't behave. But here, on board the *Jennifer Rose*, he at once felt rested and calm. 'No,' he said finally in answer to Jennifer's question. 'Eileen wanted to, but . . . but I couldn't bring myself to discuss something so personal, not with a stranger.'

'But you've done it with me.'

He thought about this. 'This may sound odd, but you've never felt like a stranger.'

She stopped what she was doing and looked at him. 'That's probably one of the nicest things anyone's ever said to me. Thank you.' She went back to stirring the hot toddy, then took a cautious sip. He could smell the whisky from where he was sitting.

'If you're not feeling well, I ought to leave you,' he said.

'Perhaps you're right. I do feel rather tired.'

He reluctantly got to his feet. Toby stirred, rose up on all fours, arched his back and shook himself out, ready for action.

'Don't we all wish we could do that ourselves,' Jennifer said. 'Just shake all our troubles away.'

'Don't bother to see me off,' he said, as she moved towards the door of the saloon and the engine room. 'Stay in the warm. Is there anything I can fetch you in the morning?'

'I'll be fine.'

'Milk? Bread?'

She laughed. 'Stop fussing. It's nothing but a cold.'

He kissed her for the first time. Just a fond peck on the forehead. 'Sleep well.'

Out on the towpath, the chill of night seeped into his bones. He buttoned up his coat and walked as briskly as his knee would allow. When he was level with Will's house, he looked up at the house and saw a bedroom light on. There were no curtains at the window and it was embarrassingly easy to make out the two figures and what they were doing. Feeling uncomfortably like a peeping

Tom, Bob hurried on. Good luck to them, he thought, with a stab of envy.

Will was doing his best. But after the day he'd had – a fruitless auction and a wild-goose chase covering most of Shropshire for an oak dresser that didn't exist, it later transpired – he just couldn't summon the energy for what Sandra expected from him. Disentangling himself from her voluptuous body and coming up for air, he rolled over onto his side.

'Oh no you don't,' she said, 'you come back here.'

'I need the bathroom,' he lied. Before she had a chance to grab hold of him, he hot-footed it out of the bedroom and across the landing. Just to be sure, he locked the bathroom door and leaned against it in a drowsy fog of exhaustion. He wondered what the hell he was doing. Why had he agreed to see Sandra again, after they'd both admitted that the fun had gone out of their . . . their what? Their fling? Their mindless coupling? Oh, come on, he told himself, now standing in front of the mirror, what man in his right mind would turn down the chance of uncomplicated sex? He turned on the tap and splashed cold water onto his face.

But uncomplicated sex, he decided, was not without its complications. Hearing Sandra calling to him, he closed his eyes and tried to prepare himself for a convincing performance.

He didn't know whether to be humiliated or relieved when twenty minutes later Sandra was throwing on her clothes in a huff of frustration. 'You know what your trouble is, Will? You're getting old. You're past it.'

'I think you might be right,' he murmured as she was clattering down the stairs and shouting that she never wanted to hear from him again.

He stood in the shower till the scalding water ran cold. In his bathrobe, he went and stood on the landing by the window that overlooked the front garden. The light from the street lamps cast an attractive glow over the road. Further up was Dora Gold's house with its showy plumes of pampas grass in the front garden, which somehow seemed so appropriate from what he knew of the woman. And then there was the McKendricks' house, where the severely pruned bushes and shrubs looked as austere as Harvey McKendrick had appeared to Will when he'd come over one day to welcome him to the neighbourhood – he'd been civil enough, but no more.

Will had long since decided that he liked living in Maple Drive and probably wouldn't sell the house on as quickly as he'd originally planned. Fast bucks were a bit like uncomplicated sex – easy come, easy go. What he wanted in his life was something with a bit of permanence and substance to it. He smiled and thought how proud Marty would be of him for making this alarmingly grown-up leap of maturity.

Looking across to number twenty, he wondered how Harriet was. He'd enjoyed their evening together. Compared to the one he'd just had it seemed perfect. He wondered if he could get away with asking her out for dinner.

Why not? he asked himself.

Because she's so much younger than you, you idiot!

It would only be dinner, he argued back. Just dinner.

But even as he thought this, his body betrayed him with a stirring that would have solved all his earlier problems with Sandra.

Shocked, he turned away from the window, tightening his bathrobe. What the hell was going on? Harriet Swift was not his type at all.

She was too young.

She was too thin – where were the sexy curves he always went for?

She wasn't blonde. Not even a pretend blonde.

So what was it, then?

He remade his bed and lay on top of the duvet, his hands clasped behind his head. Okay, she was smart, pithy and honest, attributes he did like in a woman. She was also fiercely detached, which he found oddly touching. And, of course, there was that whole hedgehog thing he'd found so amusing initially, and which he now found endearing, knowing that her prickliness was actually due to a need to disguise how vulnerable her new situation made her. She took her role as Carrie and Joel's guardian very seriously – perhaps too seriously at times. It meant that occasionally her judgement was clouded. Nevertheless, he couldn't help but admire her. She had real guts.

So was that it? Did it all boil down to being in awe of her?

There was only one way to find out. He had to get to know her better. Would it be pushing his luck to say he had a spare ticket for the Jools Holland concert next month? He could always make out he was being neighbourly.

Why not? And anyway, the age gap wasn't *that* big.

Chapter Thirty-Four

That night Harriet dreamed she was in a pine forest, lost. She wasn't scared, but she was concerned; she couldn't remember where the children were. She'd had them with her a moment ago, but now they were gone. She ventured further into the heart of the forest and could hear her name being called, faintly at first, but then louder and more distinctly as she drew near its source. She came to the edge of a clearing where sunlight filtered through the towering pine trees and where the ground was soft and blanketed underfoot with pine needles. In the centre of the clearing, sitting on a wooden picnic table with her legs swinging, was Felicity. 'There you are,' Felicity said. 'We were waiting for you.'

'We?' asked Harriet. She wasn't at all surprised to see her sister.

Felicity laughed. 'You didn't think the others would forget, did you?'

Thinking that her sister was referring to the children, Harriet relaxed. Carrie and Joel were safe. Felicity suddenly jumped down from the picnic table and revealed a large birthday cake. Behind it stood Dominic and Miles. Harriet was confused. She was sure it wasn't her birthday. Dominic came towards her. 'Happy birthday,' he said, and then he kissed her hard on the lips, his tongue deep in her mouth, his eyes open and glittering, as if taunting her, daring her to enjoy what he was doing. But she *was* enjoying it, and kissing him back – breathlessly, passionately. She held him tight until, without warning, he pushed her away with a laugh. 'Sorry, Harriet. You must be mixing me up with my brother.'

Confused, she went to Miles. 'I'm sorry,' she whispered. He bent his head and kissed her lightly on the cheek. 'No,' she said. 'Kiss me properly. Like Dominic.'

He did as she said, his eyes closed, his arms around her, holding her firmly. 'I need to know what to do,' she said when she drew away and searched his face to see what he was thinking. 'Tell me what to do.'

'Everything will be fine,' he murmured, before slowly turning away and joining Felicity and Dominic at the picnic table.

The piercing pipping of the alarm clock woke Harriet and she lay for a moment in the darkness. Listening to the gurgling of the central-heating pipes, she considered the dream. It was one of those dreams that could persuade you it held some vital truth or significance. She dismissed the obvious, that once again Miles was being compared to Dominic, and thought hard. As irrational and absurd as it seemed, she was sure there was something it was trying to tell her. It was that comment – 'I need to know what to do' – that chimed like a faint, echoing bell. What had she been referring to?

By the time she was in the shower and thinking about the day ahead – her trip to Ireland – logic had kicked in. Of course! The anxiety in the dream had been about Carrie and school. Harriet still hadn't said anything to her parents about the letter she'd found or how she was going to deal with it. She didn't want them to worry. Especially not her mother, who worried Harriet almost as much as Carrie's latest problem. She was convinced there was something going on that Eileen was keeping to herself. Perhaps her illness was getting worse and she was holding out on Harriet and her father. It would be so typical of Mum to soldier on in stoic silence. Harriet considered speaking to Dora; it was possible that Eileen might have confided in her old friend. But all that would have to wait. Today there was Dublin to concentrate on.

The children were already up when she went downstairs

to grab a quick cup of coffee before driving to the airport to meet Howard. They were in the sitting room on the sofa, still in their pyjamas, when she popped her head round the door. Unaware of her presence, they watched the television, transfixed by the young presenter who appeared to be dressed for a photo-shoot for the front cover of some lads' magazine. The girl gabbled on in what passed for English in TV-land these days, and Harriet wondered what had happened to the girl-next-door look she and Felicity had grown up with. I'm growing old, Harriet thought. I'll be criticising Carrie's taste in friends and clothes next. Was that what parenting did to you? Brought out all those instinctive prejudices you never knew existed but which would eventually turn you into your own mother and father.

Joel saw her first. He took his thumb out of his mouth and wrapped his silky round his hand, as if keeping it for later. 'You look different, Harriet,' he said.

Carrie wrenched her gaze away from the television. 'You're wearing a skirt,' she said, a mixture of accusation and disbelief in her voice.

'Correction. I'm wearing a suit.'

'Why? You never wear skirts.'

'I am today.'

'Are you going somewhere special?'

This was something else she'd learned; children only ever remember what's going on in their own world. 'Don't you remember I'm flying to Ireland today?'

Joel's eyes grew wide. 'How long for?'

'Come on, Joel, we discussed this yesterday. I'm only going to be away for one night.' She went and sat on the sofa next to him. To distract him, she said, 'You haven't forgotten about going to Maywood tomorrow to see Miles at the bookshop, have you?'

Carrie hugged her knees. 'Grandma says she'll finish our costumes today. Do you think there'll be a prize for the best one?'

'You'll have to wait and see.'

'You will be back in time, won't you?' There was an anxious tremor in Joel's question.

Harriet said, 'I'll try very hard to make sure I am. But I'm afraid I can't promise anything. If my flight's delayed or the traffic's bad, it's out of my hands.'

'But you have to be there!'

This was from Carrie. Surprised that her niece was being so insistent, Harriet stood up. 'Like I say, I'll do my best.'

When she was leaving the house and saying goodbye, her mother said, 'Try not to let the children down about tomorrow. They really want you to be there.'

Harriet could never understand why people felt the need to reiterate the same point. One clearly made instruction was all it took.

It was when their Aer Lingus flight had landed at Dublin airport that Harriet realised she was in for the most embarrassing business trip of her life. Howard had already insulted one of the stewards by calling him Mick, even though his badge clearly said his name was Declan, and he was now engaged in what he probably thought was friendly banter with the man in the seat next to him, but which Harriet feared would turn out to be highly offensive. Impatient to get off the plane to catch a connecting flight, the fellow passenger was pulling on his jacket and gathering up his newspaper and briefcase.

'Don't worry, mate,' Howard said, 'we're on Irish time now. Your flight probably won't leave until tomorrow anyway.'

The man flashed him a look of pure venom. 'I think you'll find we're a lot more efficient here than you presume.' He shot off down the aisle.

To his credit, though, Howard didn't stint when he travelled and after hiring a car and negotiating Dublin's heavy traffic they arrived at their hotel opposite St Stephen's Green.

'I couldn't get us in at the Shelbourne,' he said, 'but here's apparently the next best thing. Shall we say fifteen minutes to freshen up, a cup of coffee in the lounge and then on the road?'

They were in neighbouring rooms. Harriet would have preferred a bit more distance between them – such as two floors – but after unpacking her few things she decided she was being churlish. Howard might be a self-inflated chauvinist, but he didn't seem the sort to try knocking on her door late at night suggesting a nightcap. According to office gossip he was happily married, even if it had taken him two bites of the marriage cherry to get it right. The only thing that gave her cause to worry was the expression on his face when she'd met him at the airport, and the way he'd surreptitiously eyed up her legs throughout the flight. In fairness, he was more used to seeing her in trousers and a T-shirt, her classic work uniform. She did wear skirts, but only very rarely. To her shame she'd given in to Howard's not-so-subtle suggestion that she might like, in his words, to 'look the biz' for their trip.

'I don't do feminine charm and guile,' she'd said. 'I'm a boffin. A techie.'

'Can you be a sexy boffin?' he'd asked, his face poker-straight.

Playing him at his own game, she said, 'You mean wear a white lab coat then peel off my thick-framed glasses and let my hair down to reveal my—?'

'Steady on, we're not making an adult movie!'

She only agreed to play the part he wanted of her because she badly wanted to prove her worth, and if a skirt helped her cause, then so be it.

Harriet was impressed. Howard was performing like a pro. She realised now that Adrian hadn't been exaggerating when he'd told her that Howard was sharper than he'd have you believe. He knew his stuff and was taking his time with the prospective client. There was no sign of the patronising buffoon she'd sat next to on the plane. 'What I suggest we do now,' he said, casting a look in her direction, 'is for Harriet to outline the kind of application we could do for you. That way you can get to know the expert who will look after the job for you.'

Several hours later, after she'd swapped email addresses with the AVLS supplier and he'd agreed to send her a specification for what was needed, she and Howard were heading back to their hotel. Harriet was looking forward to pampering herself in a hot, bubbly bath and then lying on the bed to watch telly and call room service, but Howard was having none of it when she declined his offer of a drink. 'Don't be a bore, Harriet,' he said. 'Let's go for a drink to celebrate.'

'We haven't got the contract yet.'

'Are you always this optimistic?'

'I think—'

'No, I'll tell you how you think,' he said, forcibly leading her through to the bar. 'You think too literally. You programmers are all the bloody same. Now sit on that stool and let me buy you a drink.' He attracted the barman's attention. 'A bottle of champagne. And don't fob me off with your house stuff. I'll have Veuve or Moët.'

Welcome back the real Howard, Harriet thought with a smile as she tried to make herself decent on the stool – her skirt had ridden up somewhere on a level with her knickers.

'Stop wriggling,' he said, 'and leave your skirt right where it is. It suits you.'

She blushed. 'Do you treat all your employees like this?'

He gave her a wink. 'Only the ones for whom I have high hopes.'

Their champagne arrived and Howard insisted on pouring it. 'Cheers. And well done for today. You did brilliantly. Just as I knew you would.'

She accepted the compliment with as much good grace as she could muster and tried not to worry what kind of high hopes he had for her. Stop being so paranoid, she told herself. Just drink up and relax.

Howard was a fast drinker and while she had no intention of keeping pace with him, Harriet drank more than she'd intended. Getting drunk with her boss didn't seem the best of ideas.

'How about dinner?' he asked when he'd drained the last of the bottle into their glasses. 'Shall we eat in or go exploring?'

Thinking that she could do with some fresh air to clear her head, she suggested they ate out. It was a mistake. Howard decided they had to experience a real Irish pub. 'I want the whole fiddle-scraping shebang,' he said. 'Draught Guinness, jigs and diddle-dee music.'

They made their way down to the Temple Bar area and Howard dragged her inside a pub producing the loudest music. It was packed, but only with tourists; it was an *Oirish* theme pub, as far removed from the real thing as could be. There was sawdust on the fake cobbled floor, upturned barrels as tables and tatty long-johns and pitchforks hanging from the rafters like something out of *Angela's Ashes*.

'Any minute and there'll be a Riverdance troupe performing for us,' she said to Howard as they were shown to a table worryingly close to a small stage.

His face lit up. 'Do you think so?'

Her prediction was proved right. Half an hour later, just as they were tucking into their crab cakes, hammering hard shoes descended upon the stage, causing their pints of Guinness to jump on the rickety barrel table: any chance of conversation was gone. Howard clapped and whooped along with the rest of the crowd, which seemed to be made up largely of raucous Brits. Harriet's fear now, was that audience participation would be foisted on them. 'Let's make those buggering eejit Brits look as stupid as possible,' she could imagine the dancers thinking.

'I'm going to the loo,' she shouted at Howard.

'Don't be long,' he yelled back. 'You don't want to miss a second of this.'

On the way back from the loo, she took a wrong turning and found herself in a small room where a man playing the guitar was singing to a quiet, dignified audience. Judging from the voices around her, this was where the local guys came to drink. The singer smiled at Harriet and she felt compelled to stay. Howard wouldn't miss her for five minutes, she decided.

But five minutes turned into ten and then into twenty. The singer, whose repertoire included Elvis and Beatles songs as well as traditional folk ballads, had a rich, mesmerising voice that could easily have lulled her to sleep. She closed her eyes, letting the music wash over her. The memory of that morning's dream came to mind and she thought of Miles. She also thought how nice it would be if he was here with her instead of Howard.

Howard! She'd forgotten all about him. She hurriedly found her way back to where she'd left him, and got there just in time to see him stepping down from the stage. The audience was giving him a standing ovation.

'Harriet,' he said, red-faced and breathless, 'you missed me. Where were you?'

'I'm sorry, I got waylaid. Another drink?'

'That's okay,' he said, 'I'll get them in. I've never before let a woman buy me a drink, and I'm not about to start now.'

She shook her head and watched him go. By the time he had returned, the entertainment had come to an end and a CD was playing in the background. 'Now tell me, Harriet,' he said, 'are you having fun?'

'Of course I am,' she lied.

'Good. I thought this trip would do you some good. You need some light in your life. You're much too serious for a girl your age.'

'Excuse me? Are you my therapist now?'

He laughed. 'No. I'm your boss and don't you forget it. Cheers.' He wiped the froth of Guinness from his lips with the back of his hand. 'There's something I want to say, Hat. Can I call you Hat?'

Suspecting that he was drunk and she could get away with it, she said, 'No. No one ever calls me Hat.'

He smiled. 'Well, Hat, I think you're doing a great job.'

'Thank you.'

'And I'm not just talking about work. I'm referring to the job you're doing at home.'

She tensed, but said nothing.

'I think it's brilliant, what you're doing, bringing up your sister's children. Can't be easy. And you've never once let it get in the way of your job.'

'How did you know?'

He tapped his nose. 'Adrian. He told me everything.'

'Before or after my interview?'

'Oh, definitely after your interview.'

'You didn't trust me?'

'As it turns out, I was right to think there was more to you than met the eye. So why didn't you tell me about the kiddies?'

'I didn't want them to jeopardise my chances.'

'You rate me pretty poorly then, don't you?'

'It was you who said you didn't want to employ one of those devious girls who'd get herself pregnant then sting you for maternity leave.'

'That's quite a different matter, Hat.'

'Please don't call me Hat.'

'How old are the kiddies?'

'Nine and almost five.'

'And how are you managing childcare wise?'

Seeing as he seemed genuinely interested, she told him about her parents and how she was now trying to buy somewhere to live.

'You've been on a hell of a learning curve. Now, Hat, I want you to promise me something.' He leaned in close. Looking at his bloodshot eyes, Harriet wondered if he'd remember much of this conversation in the morning. 'I want you to know that I'm not one of those bastards who doesn't stand by his employees. I'm a fair man. If you need the odd afternoon off to pick up the children for some reason or other, just make up the hours another day. Okay?'

'Thank you, that's very . . . very kind of you,' she said,

and seizing the opportunity, added, 'Can I do that tomorrow afternoon when we get back?'

'Sure. Anything you say.'

The next morning, Harriet was awake early. Unable to get back to sleep, she decided to go for a walk in the park opposite the hotel. It would be another two hours before Howard was meeting her for breakfast. It was a frosty morning – cold enough to see her breath in the air – and with her scarf wrapped around her neck and her hands pushed deep into her pockets, she set out to explore the park. Last night's conversation with Howard was on her mind. She supposed she shouldn't have been too surprised that Adrian had told Howard about her circumstances, but she hoped it wouldn't mark her out for special treatment. The important thing was that she was doing the job she'd been employed to do, to the best of her ability. When they were walking back to the hotel, Howard had said, 'You know, Hat, Adrian warned me there was a danger your dignified self-containment would get up my nose.'

'And does it?' she'd asked. If she ever saw Adrian again, he'd better watch out!

'Nah. I knew you'd be putty in my hands.'

'If you weren't my boss, I'd thump you for that.'

'Just as well I'm your boss, then.'

Harriet hadn't been walking for long when she noticed a figure on a bench ahead of her. Bundled up in a thick overcoat, he was leaning forwards, his elbows resting on his knees. He looked like he was deep in prayer. As she approached him, a prickle of recognition caused her to stare even harder at him. To her astonishment, she was looking at the only man other than Howard who had got away with calling her Hat.

Chapter Thirty-Five

'Dominic?'

'Good God, Harriet. Is that really you, or am I dreaming?'

'Perhaps we're both dreaming. What brings you to Dublin?'

He waved a hand airily. 'I'm ransacking Trinity's library for a paper I'm doing on Yeats. The poet,' he added.

She sat on the bench next to him, noting how tired and dishevelled he looked. Like a man who hadn't been to bed perhaps. Certainly not his own bed. Same old Dominic, then. 'Yes, Dominic, I am aware who Yeats is,' she said tightly. 'I'm not quite that thick, you know.'

He ignored the jibe. 'So what are you doing here?'

'Work. I'm here with my boss. We're staying in the hotel just over there.' She pointed across the park, through the thinning trees where the early morning sun was melting the frost on the grass. 'We leave this morning,' she added.

'Who's looking after Carrie and Joel while you're away?'

'Who do you think? Mum and Dad, of course.'

'And they're well?'

These questions from Dominic enquiring about someone else wrong-footed her. So often it was only his own welfare he was concerned about. 'Sorry. Who?'

He turned sharply. 'Just what exactly is your problem?'

'I'm not aware I have a problem. All I was wondering was who you meant specifically.'

'Is it entirely beyond the realms of your feeble understanding that I might ask after the children as well as your parents? Or have you imposed some kind of embargo on whose health I might be interested in? Just as you have when it comes to displays of grief.' He shook his head. 'Who'd have thought you'd turn into such a fascist?'

'And who'd have thought you'd turn into an even bigger bastard than the one we thought you were destined to be.'

He glared at her, then suddenly tipped his head back and laughed. 'I'm disappointed in you. How could you have ever underestimated me? I'd have hoped you of all people wouldn't make that error. Me, I'm the biggest bastard going.'

'Not entirely. You were very sweet to write to Carrie. And there were those chocolates you gave us.'

He shuddered. 'I knew that was a mistake. And if I ever hear you call me sweet again, I shall have to kill you. Now shut up, you obnoxious harridan, and give me a hug. I'm in dire need of one.'

Surprised to find herself wrapped in his arms, Harriet breathed in the smell of his woollen overcoat and the remnants of aftershave and shaving cream – just for effect, he'd always used an old-fashioned cutthroat razor. He held her fiercely then let her go, grazing his stubbly jaw against her cheek. She saw that his eyes were moist and bloodshot.

'You okay?'

'As it happens, no I'm not. I'm under siege.'

'Am I allowed to ask why?'

'I think I'm on the verge of a breakdown.'

The directness of his words shocked her. She didn't know what to say, and waited for him to go on.

He slumped forward, adopting the same position he'd had when she first saw him, elbows resting on his knees. 'I've been doing a lot of thinking,' he said softly. 'I've come to the only possible conclusion: that nothing much matters. Everything's so damned futile. Life has as much point to it as a mote of dust.'

'You mean in the light of Felicity's death?' she asked.

His head snapped up. 'Well, of course I do! What the hell else could I be referring to?'

'Look, if you're going to bite my head off every time I say

something, then there's no point in us talking. I might just as well leave you to—'

He suddenly reached out to her. 'Please. I'm sorry. Don't go flouncing off in a huff. I couldn't bear it. You don't know how much it means to me bumping into you like this.'

His voice was unbearably contrite and Harriet felt a wave of compassion for him. 'Okay. But be nice to me or I'll walk.'

Grinding the heel of his shoe on the tarmac beneath him, he nodded. 'Thank you. I'll do my best to behave.'

After a lengthy pause, she said, 'So tell me why you think everything's so futile.'

'I'd have thought that was obvious. It's because I'm completely and utterly alone in this world. If I was to die tomorrow, who would mourn my passing? Who would even care?'

'Aren't you forgetting your parents and Miles? And what about me? I'd miss you. There'd be no one to fight with,' she added lightly, hoping to lift the conversation.

But her attempt went unnoticed. 'I'm talking about love. Real love. The kind of all-consuming love Yeats understood too well.' He stared straight ahead. '"And who could play it well enough if deaf and dumb and blind with love? He that made this knows all the cost, for he gave all his heart and lost."'

'You don't have the monopoly on not being loved, Dominic. I don't exactly have a queue of people lining up to worship the ground I walk on.'

'But you have Carrie and Joel who rely on you. They *need* you. Who the hell needs me? What difference do I make to the world?'

'You have your work. Your students. Your poetry.'

He shrugged. 'It means nothing. Trust me. Come on, let's walk.' He grabbed her hand and pulled her to her feet.

They linked arms and as they strolled along the path, a squirrel shot out from under a bush. Harriet felt Dominic start at the suddenness of it. Hearing him curse violently under his breath, she wondered, and not a little sadly, if he had been speaking the truth when he said he was on the verge of a breakdown. 'How long have you been feeling like this, Dominic?' she asked.

'All my life.'

'I'm being serious,' she said.

'So was I. I've always felt as though I was on the verge of something. Madness. Greatness. Whatever.'

'Have you seen a doctor?'

'No, but I have seen a priest. I'm worried about my spiritual welfare.'

She laughed, but immediately wished she hadn't.

'Sod you, Harriet. I was being serious again.'

'It was so unexpected hearing you speak like that. I'm sorry.'

'So you should be. That was the difference between you and Felicity. Felicity was perfectly in tune with me. She never misinterpreted anything I said. She could always read between the lines.'

Harriet came to a stop. 'You know what? I'm sick of people criticising me.'

'Then do something about it.'

'I can't. I'm me. I'm Harriet Swift. The way I think is the way I am. Why can't people accept that?'

'They probably do. But it doesn't make it any less irritating. Jung said that the unconscious part of our own personality may be our best friend or our greatest enemy. Go figure.' He gripped her arm and dragged her on. 'So who else has been having a go at you, besides me?'

Thinking that he was the second person to quote Jung at her – Will had been the first – she told him about Howard saying she thought too literally, not realising until now just how deeply his comment had resonated with her. 'Do you think I'm too literal?' she asked Dominic.

'Of course you are. You always have been.'

'Is it a bad thing?'

'Yes. You lose sight of the wider picture. You see only the detail.'

'I've always been like it. It's how I function.'

'Then stop whingeing about it.'

'Why are you always so unpleasant to me?'

'I'm unpleasant to everyone; you're not a special case, Hat. And why, I'd like to know, are we talking about you, when it's me we're supposed to be discussing?'

She smiled. 'Because I'm far more interesting. Where are you staying?'

'I have rooms in Trinity. Do you want to come and see them?'

'Are they worth the effort?'

'Not particularly. I'm hungry. Let's go to your hotel for some breakfast.'

Glad that he was sounding less manic, and amused at the abrupt turnabout in the conversation, Harriet allowed him to steer her back in the direction of her hotel.

It was still early when they pushed open the door of the dining room; only a handful of guests had made it down. There was no sign of Howard.

'How perfectly ghastly,' Dominic said as they sat at a table overlooking the main street.

'What?' asked Harriet.

'The other guests. They're so ordinary-looking. Corporate wage slaves the lot of them, in their rolled-up shirtsleeves and brightly coloured ties.'

'We can't all be like you, Dominic. And anyway, who are you to criticise with your dishevelled, unshaven, haven't-gone-to-bed look?' She had to admit, though, even in his current state, he still outshone every man in the room.

He eyed her over the top of his menu. 'How very observant of you.'

'And correct?'

'Unutterably *in*correct.'

'What were you doing in the park so early, then, if not on your way back to Trinity after a night of debauchery?'

'The same as you, presumably. I couldn't sleep.'

When a waiter approached their table, they broke off

from their conversation and ordered eggs Benedict for Dominic, scrambled eggs and bacon for Harriet and a pot of coffee with two rounds of toast.

Alone again, Dominic said, 'Tell me something to cheer me up. How's my brother? Behaving himself, I trust?'

'The children and I spent the day with him on Sunday. We had lunch in Maywood then went for a walk in the park.'

'Ye Gods! It sounds like something out of *Mary Poppins*.'

'Hey, it might not sound very exciting to you, but it's the most fun I get these days, so quit the snide comments.'

He held up his hands in mock defence. 'I apologise. I'm sure you all had a very jolly time of it.'

'We did.'

'Good. But take a tip from me, Hat. Please indulge yourself more. Treat yourself to some sinful pleasure now and then. It'll do wonders to thaw that frosty streak of self-denial that's ruining your life.'

She folded her arms and stared out of the window, her left knee twitching convulsively under the table. Why did he always have to spoil things? More to the point, why did she let him do it? She went on the attack, as she usually did whenever she was in his company. 'Why haven't you returned any of the messages I left you?'

'I've been too busy.'

'Liar. Aren't you the least bit curious to know why I wanted to speak to you?'

'Not especially. At last, here's breakfast.'

When their waiter had left them alone, Dominic poured the coffee while Harriet buttered herself a piece of toast. 'This is very domestic, isn't it?' he said. 'I feel quite the husband.'

'That'll be the day,' she muttered, still cross with him.

He glanced at her. 'It must be exhausting being such a bitch. No wonder you're single; it must be impossible to love anyone when you're carrying that amount of hatred around with you. Why do you have such a problem with my lifestyle?'

'I've never been bothered by your sexuality; it's your promiscuity I have trouble with.'

'There's nothing illegal about the way I conduct my sex life. There's no law that says I can't sleep with as many men as I want to. You know me: high on charisma, low on morals.'

'Sounds to me like you're justifying what you get up to. How's your spiritual self squaring up to your immoral self?'

He stirred his coffee. 'People have sex for myriad reasons. Often it has nothing to do with the other person involved. I enjoy perfunctory sex, which I've always pre-ferred over hate-filled sex, or self-loathing sex. Good sex is what makes me know I'm truly alive. But I'm curious; why should you concern yourself with what a raging queer like me gets up to?'

She winced at his words. 'I'm not concerned.'

'You are. It's coming at me in great waves of disapproval across the table. Let's face it, you always were a prude. You used to hate it when Felicity and I went off for one of our experimental romps.'

In spite of herself, Harriet blushed. She hated knowing that he still had the power to do this to her. 'What if I did?'

'Was it because you were jealous? Jealous that it wasn't you I was experimenting with?'

His tone was uncharacteristically gentle, but even so she could have thrown her plate at him, then ground it hard into that handsome face of his. Summoning all her dignity, she said, 'I know you've always had a high opinion of yourself, Dominic, but really, take it from me, I'd have to have been two shades of crazy to fancy you.'

He chewed meticulously on what was in his mouth. 'I'm sorry if I've embarrassed you, but actually it was Felicity who told me you were jealous.'

'Never! Never in a million years would she have said that.'

He continued with his breakfast in silence, leaving

Harriet to contemplate the inconceivable – had Felicity betrayed her to Dominic? Could she really have done such a thing? Harriet picked disconsolately at her scrambled eggs. Everything she'd believed in, when it came to Felicity, was falling apart. There were too many acts of betrayal going on. She glanced up at Dominic, and watching him unobserved as he now stared out of the window, she wondered just how many more confidences Felicity had shared with him. Was it possible that he knew about Felicity's affair? Had he even encouraged it? She decided to test the water.

'Do you think Felicity was happy in her marriage?' she asked.

His fork halfway to his mouth, he said, 'What do you think?'

'I asked first.'

He placed his knife and fork either side of the plate, rested his elbows on the table. 'Well,' he said slowly, 'let's consider the facts.' He steepled his hands against his chin, but then snapped back in his chair, his hands crashing down on the table and rattling the crockery. 'Good God, Harriet, why are you doing this? The poor girl's dead. Have you no respect?'

Determined to make him answer her, she said, 'Do you think she was capable of an affair?'

He sighed. 'We're all capable of doing the unthinkable. Even a sexually repressed morality guardian like you. But I feel certain that if Felicity had been unhappy she would have done something about it. Cheating on her husband wasn't her style. She was above such behaviour.'

He resumed eating as though the matter had been neatly dealt with. But still hurting from the assertions he'd made about her, Harriet wanted to get her own back, and the best way to do that was to openly criticise his precious and beloved Felicity. 'I know for a fact that Felicity was seeing someone behind Jeff's back,' she said. She watched his face closely for a reaction. But unusually, his expression was fixed.

'I don't believe it,' he said.

'It's true. I promise you.'

'Who was it? Who was she seeing?'

'I don't know. I haven't worked that out yet.' She told him about the emails and the nature of them, taking a perverse pleasure in knocking down the plaster-saint illusion Dominic had created.

His reaction was not to defend Felicity, as she'd expected, but to lean across the table and say, 'And you really can't think who her lover might have been?'

'I told you. I don't have a clue.'

He narrowed his eyes. 'How strange, because I have a strong suspicion.'

'Really?'

'Come on, use that analytical brain you're so proud of. Who always had a thing for your sister? Who hated it whenever I embarrassed him in front of her. Who—?'

'You don't mean—'

'I do. Okay, I admit it's a shot in the dark from where you're sitting, but I know my brother and I know that he was always crazy about Felicity.'

'But . . . but she was never crazy about him. And surely Miles just isn't the type?'

'Are you saying my brother is too dull to fall in love with anyone, or that he's not worthy of being loved? I'm shocked; you're worse than me for condemning people out of hand.'

'I didn't say that. All I meant was, Miles isn't the sneaky sort. He's level-headed. And he's certainly not a home-wrecker.'

'How perfectly good you make him sound.'

'That's exactly it. He is good. He's kind and thoughtful. He's—'

'He's a man,' Dominic interrupted. 'He's a man with as great a sexual appetite as the next. Gay or straight.' He pushed his unfinished breakfast away and leant back in his chair, crossing one leg over the other. 'Have you looked through Felicity's things for proof? There must be diaries, letters, or *billet doux* you can mull over.'

'No. We got rid of most of the stuff like that. There are a few boxes left in the garage, but my guess is I won't find anything. Felicity and her lover went to great lengths to keep their relationship secret, so she wouldn't have been silly enough to keep anything that would give them away.'

'But you said the more recent emails indicated she was going to leave Jeff. If that was her intention, there would be no need for secrecy. Their love for each other was about to come out into the open.'

'You really believe it's Miles?'

'Yes. In fact, the more I think about it, the more certain I am. Call it instinct, but it fits.'

'So why hasn't he confided in me? Or even you? Why, now that Jeff and Felicity aren't around, does he want to keep the secrecy going?'

'Apart from wanting to avoid any unnecessary ill feeling and disapproval, perhaps it's a final act of devotion to Felicity. In his mind, it would be something they'd both take to the grave with them. I could quite imagine him doing that. You know how intense he can be.'

Harriet thought about this. Dominic was right; Miles was intense. Her thoughts then turned to his unconcealed distress at the funeral when he'd made no attempt to hide his grief. Was his sadness out of proportion for mourning a friend? Seeing his face before her, a more recent memory came into Harriet's mind. It was of her and Miles in the park in Maywood when she'd begun to think that maybe, after all these years, their friendship was developing into something deeper. That it was meant to be. And what of that comment he'd made about wanting to do more for the children, that they felt like family to him? Confused, she poured herself another cup of coffee. None of it made sense. If he'd loved her sister, why did he now want to spend time with her?

Dominic, listlessly drumming his fingers on the table, broke into her thoughts. Disappointed that the reaction she'd sought had fallen flat, Harriet said, 'You don't seem very shocked by what I've told you. After all, you did just say you thought Felicity was above such behaviour.'

'You expected me to be shocked? How odd. No, the truth is, the imbroglio of a love triangle that included my brother is quite intriguing and I—' His words stopped abruptly and his gaze shifted. Staring into a space just above her head, he said, 'Don't turn around, Hat, but there's the most hideous man looking this way. *Harriet!* I said don't turn round.'

Oh, Lord, it was Howard. Acknowledging that he'd spotted her, he raised his hand and started to come over. 'Dominic,' Harriet whispered, 'that man's my boss. Be nice or him or—'

'Or what?'

She didn't have a clue. That was the trouble with Dominic; he didn't have an Achilles heel like most normal people. She'd learned a long time ago that you can't threaten a man who has no morals.

Chapter Thirty-Six

While the girl with the dangling, light-up pumpkin earrings read to them, Joel watched the door anxiously. He wished Harriet would come. He also wished Grandma hadn't made him wear the wizard's hat she'd made; it was too big and kept slipping down over his eyes. One of the other children had laughed at him earlier and another boy kept trying to knock it off his head. He raised his hand to suck his thumb, but quickly changed his mind. Instead he shuffled closer to Carrie on the floor, even though she'd been nasty to him at breakfast and had called him a baby for not letting Grandma put his silky in the washing machine. He looked around the bookshop, searching for Miles. Miles was nice. Carrie said they had to be extra specially good when Miles was around. Because if they were naughty, he might not want to marry Harriet.

Once more he thought of Harriet and wished she was there. He pushed the cuff back on his jumper and tried to work out what time it was. But he couldn't. And anyway, he couldn't remember what time Granddad had said Harriet might get there. He would have liked for Grandma to come with them but she needed to rest and when he'd asked Granddad to stay, he'd said, 'Nonsense, a big boy like you doesn't need his grandfather hanging about. You go on and enjoy yourself. Be good now.'

Maybe if he closed his eyes, held his breath and counted to ten, the door would open and Harriet would be there. He tried it. Then tried again, this time counting to twenty. But when he got to sixteen he opened his eyes with a thought so terrifying it made his heart beat faster. What if Harriet wasn't coming? What if she was never coming because she'd had an accident like Mummy and Daddy? His bottom lip began to tremble. He pressed his fists to his mouth and squeezed his eyes tightly shut and tried to think of something nice. But he could only think of nasty things.

Bob left the car in The Navigation's car park and took the steps down to the towpath, the carrier bag of shopping he'd fetched for Jennifer weighing heavily from his right hand. With no Toby to slow his progress by rootling around in the undergrowth, he made it to the *Jennifer Rose* in a matter of seconds. He tapped on the side of the boat and was about to let himself in through the hatch doors as he usually did, when he heard the sound of a man's voice. Perhaps it was someone from the marina with news about the engine parts? He stepped into the saloon and was surprised to see a man shutting a large briefcase and handing over a piece of paper. But the bigger surprise was seeing how ill Jennifer looked. She appeared to be a lot worse than yesterday, when he'd insisted that she must stay in the warm and let him do her shopping for her.

Before he had an opportunity to apologise for bursting in, Jennifer said, 'It's okay, Bob, come on—' But her words were cut short by a racking cough that made her shoulders shake. 'Excuse me,' she managed to say, before disappearing to the prow of the boat where Bob could still hear her coughing painfully.

The man, clearly a doctor, and one Bob didn't recognise from his own surgery, looked at him. 'Are you the friend she says is looking after her?'

'Yes. How is she?'

'Not good. Ideally, she needs to get off this boat. She has a chest infection and the damp will only make things worse.'

After the doctor had left, Bob filled a hot-water bottle for Jennifer and helped her into bed. 'You need to do as the doctor says, Jennifer; you must go home to get well.'

She shook her head. 'No. I'll soon pick up. Once I've

started the course of antibiotics he's prescribed, I'll be on the mend.'

He looked at her doubtfully. 'If you're worrying about the logistics, don't. You can leave the boat here and I'll drive you home.'

A small smile appeared on her washed-out face. 'You're very sweet, but I couldn't possibly put you to so much trouble.'

'It wouldn't be any trouble. Warwick is no distance. You could be home by this evening. It's much better to be ill in your own bed in your own home.'

Again she shook her head. He wondered why she was so reluctant. 'Wouldn't it be better to be amongst your friends and family?'

'They all live miles away.'

He then remembered how she had deliberately cut herself off from everyone by living in the middle of nowhere. 'What about your children? Couldn't you go and stay with them?'

'Goodness, Bob, it's only a chest infection. I'll be fine.'

Not easily defeated, he said, 'I know, why don't I drive you to your friends in Hebden Bridge? That's not far.'

'They've just gone off on holiday to Bali. Now, please, stop fussing. But if you want to be useful, you could make me a drink.'

'I wish I could do more to help,' he said ten minutes later as he handed her a mug of tea. 'And for the record, I still think you'd be better off at home. The doctor said the damp will make things worse.'

She put the mug on the shelf behind the bed, then, to his surprise, reached for his hand. 'But if I went, I'd—' Gripped by a bout of painful coughing, she covered her mouth with a hand. Finally, she rested back against the pillows.

'What were you going to say?' he prompted.

'No,' she said breathlessly. 'It's better I don't say it.'

He stroked her hand. 'Please tell me what it was.'

Her fingers became entwined with his. She met his gaze.

'I'd rather be ill here and still see you than go home to an empty house.'

Bob's heart quickened. He had to swallow away the tightness in his throat before he could speak. He murmured, 'But I can't bear to see you so ill. Let me take you home. You know it's for the best.'

Harriet was cutting it fine, but so long as the traffic kept moving, she'd make it to Maywood and catch the last half-hour with the children at Novel Ways. Howard had been great; he'd told her to shoot off the moment they'd got through passport control. 'I'll catch up with you on Monday,' he'd called after her as she'd sprinted away. 'Have a good weekend.' He'd surprised her in so many ways during the trip. Behind the crass, overtly chauvinistic exterior, was a reasonable and approachable man. Why did people do that? Hide their real self behind another?

The other surprise had been Dominic showing up in Dublin. However, the extraordinary coincidence of their paths crossing hadn't amazed her as much as the content of their conversation had. Could Felicity really have told Dominic that Harriet had fancied him? Maybe, if she'd been drunk – Harriet didn't want to believe her sister could have let her down when she'd been stone-cold sober. It was too hurtful to contemplate Felicity deliberately betraying her, laughing with Dominic over something Harriet had scarcely been able to admit to herself: that there had been a time when she had secretly, *stupidly*, longed for Dominic to love her. The thought of Dominic crowing over such a confidence hurt Harriet to her core. She had sat through the rest of breakfast after Howard had joined them – Dominic had actually behaved himself – mortified that he knew something so intimate about her. She felt vulnerable, as if he had some kind of hold over her. What if he now intended to remind her of it, just to twist the knife when it so pleased him?

But far worse than any of that was Dominic's assertion that Miles could be Felicity's mystery lover. Surely it just wasn't possible. Or was it? Hadn't Dominic criticised her for losing sight of the bigger picture, of seeing only the detail? If that was true, then maybe something really had been going on right under her nose. When she'd said to Dominic that maybe she'd drop a few hints to Miles, just to see what his reaction was, he'd smiled and said he'd pay good money to see that. His parting words, when Howard had left them alone to go and settle the hotel bill, were, 'I wish you luck, but I doubt you'll succeed in getting Miles to admit to his affair with Felicity. He's probably so besotted with keeping her memory pure and unsullied he'd never confess to what they were up to.'

'Whereas if it was you?'

'Oh, I'd be right out there announcing it to the world.'

'I would have thought your feelings for Felicity would have made you extra-protective. In fact, I'm surprised you don't want to kill Miles in a fit of jealous love.'

'You mean, if I can't have her, no one can? Least of all my brother? Oh, Hat, what a precious little darling you are. That's the most romantic notion, if totally misplaced, you've ever come up with.' Pulling on his overcoat, he'd then gathered her into his arms and pressed his lips against hers. 'Thank you for breakfast and for cheering me up. Now why don't you hurry home and read yet more of those delicious-sounding emails and let me know what else you unearth? See if you can't prove me wrong about Miles. A hundred pounds says I'm right.'

He's mad, she'd thought as he hurried away and disappeared through the revolving door of the hotel.

She arrived at Novel Ways in time to see Carrie being awarded a book voucher for her vampire costume – gelled-back hair with widow's peak care of Superdrug; full-length black cape care of Eileen; and blood-tipped fangs and white make-up care of the joke shop in Maywood. She'd beaten an amazingly extravagant witch into second place and the witch's mother looked furiously robbed. She'd probably spent weeks making the costume and didn't take kindly to second place.

'I sincerely hope that was a clear-cut case of nepotism,' she said to Miles, slipping in at the back of the applauding parents.

'Harriet, you made it!' The pleasure on his face gave her a warm glow. But then she thought of everything Dominic had said and the feeling passed. Miles and Felicity. Felicity and Miles. The more she said their names together, the more possible their affair seemed. But where did it leave her? Where she'd always been, she supposed. Miles's friend. She'd been stupid to imagine anything else. Perhaps the reason he'd grown closer to her recently was because he'd desperately needed the proximity of another person to take away the pain of his grief.

But there was no time to reflect on this. Joel hurtled across the shop and threw himself at her. He held on tightly, his arms locked around her waist. 'You mustn't go away again,' he said breathlessly, when she finally managed to release his hands and could bend down to him.

'Whyever not?' she asked.

'Because you might die. Just like Mummy and Daddy did.'

She looked into his tear-filled eyes and felt something like an earthquake inside her.

November

Pleasure's a sin, and sometimes sin's a pleasure.
'Don Juan', Lord Byron

Chapter Thirty-Seven

On Monday morning the children went back to school and just as soon as she had a free moment, Harriet took a break from work to ring Mrs Thompson, the headmistress. 'She'll be free in about fifteen minutes if you'd like to call back,' the school secretary told her.

A meeting, face to face, was probably a better way of dealing with the matter, but Harriet didn't want to take any more time off work unnecessarily. Nor did she want to take the easy way out by telling her parents what had been going on and offloading the problem onto them. When the culprits had been dealt with, then she'd tell them. Or maybe she wouldn't. Just now her parents seemed distant and unreachable. Particularly her father. On Saturday he announced at breakfast that he was spending the day with an old work colleague who was going through a rough patch and needed taking out of himself. Harriet found it hard to believe that in his current frame of mind her father would be good for taking anyone out of themselves. But he must have done some good because he didn't come home until gone midnight.

When fifteen minutes had passed, Harriet hit the redial button on her mobile. Top of her agenda, when she finally got to talk to Mrs Thompson, was to stress that Carrie must never know that Harriet had got involved. She wanted Carrie to think she'd got through this without anyone else's intervention.

'Sorry to keep you,' Mrs Thompson said when she finally came to the phone. 'What can I do for you? Is it about the parents' evening next week?'

'No, it's not that,' Harriet said, scribbling a note on her

pad in front of her. Damn! How had she forgotten that? 'I'm ringing about an altogether different matter,' she went on. 'I'd like to know what your policy is for dealing with bullies.' She heard a small but unmistakable intake of breath down the line. 'I'm assuming you do have one.'

'Can you be more specific?'

'Yes. Carrie has received what I can only describe as hate mail. I suspect, given her behaviour recently, that it isn't the first Carrie has received.'

Her office door opened and Dangerous Dave poked his head round it. She raised her hand, indicating she'd be all his in five minutes. He scuttled away. 'I'm sorry,' she said to the headmistress when the door closed, 'but I'm not at all sure this is a storm in a teacup situation. My niece is being victimised and I want the culprits dealt with.'

'Do you still have the letter?'

'Yes.'

'If you bring it in, I can take it from there. In my experience, a small but firm word in the right ear is all that is required.'

A small but firm rap round the right ear seemed more appropriate, but Harriet let it go. 'I think we can safely say that this explains why Carrie skipped out of school the other week,' she said, 'so please, I'd appreciate it if you kept a close eye on her and made sure that the time she's in your care is a happy time.'

'I like to think that goes for all our pupils, Miss Swift. But we have to face facts. As unpalatable as it may seem, some children do single themselves out for treatment which is far from being socially acceptable.'

Harriet wasn't going to stand for this. 'I hope you're not suggesting that Carrie has brought this on herself because her parents are dead.'

'All I'm saying is that invariably there's a reason for these problems. Carrie didn't help herself with those terrible stories she told about her parents. We have to view the wider picture at all times. Have you talked to Carrie about the letter and that you were going to talk to me about it?'

'No. I didn't want her worrying that the bullying will get worse because I'm intervening.'

'Mm . . . I'm not sure that's the best thing to do. But for now, as I said earlier, bring in the letter and we'll take it from there.'

Harriet knew a dismissal when she heard one. She rang off and considered the headmistress's comment about the *wider picture*. Was someone trying to tell her something? Until recently, she had never before thought of herself as being short-sighted or blinkered, but was she?

Before long, though, these thoughts were pushed to the back of her mind, and she immersed herself in what she'd been doing before the phone call. It was nearly an hour later, when she'd finished compiling a code, that she remembered Dangerous Dave had wanted her for something.

The thing about R.E.M., Will thought as he drove out of town on Tuesday morning with the volume turned up on his outmoded cassette player, was that you could tie yourself up in Michael Stipe's lyrics. Some made no sense at all, while others were diamond-bright with the strength of their clarity. Those were the lyrics you had to think about. That was often when Stipe was being his most enigmatic and was fooling you into believing you'd got him sussed. Which was how life was, Will had come to realise. One minute you had it all in place and the next you were flailing around helplessly.

Ever since his spectacular fall from grace, his life had jogged along quite nicely. The trick, he'd frequently told Marty, was to keep things simple. And he'd done that to great effect. Until now. Now there were complications coming at him from all sides. The biggest one was Suzie. She was six months pregnant and Maxine was still struggling to come round to the inevitable. She had taken to ringing Will to discuss Suzie's future. Or lack of it, as she saw it. 'Steve and I were looking forward to that day when we'd have the house to ourselves,' she said on one occasion. 'Now we're going to have a baby living with us. And for how long? It's not fair to Steve. He didn't marry me only to end up with a baby permanently under his feet.'

Will could sympathise; he enjoyed his freedom after all. 'Suzie's more than welcome to move in with me,' he'd said.

'How very magnanimous of you,' Maxine had replied stiffly. 'But I somehow don't see Suzie forgoing her comfortable bedroom and en suite bathroom to rough it with you in Maple Drive.'

'Thanks a bunch.'

'Oh, please don't start; you know what I mean.'

'Aren't you forgetting we started out in far less salubrious surroundings? When you're young you can rough it without even realising it.'

'Thank you for reminding me that I'm getting older.'

'It happens to the best of us, Maxine. Or should I say Granny?'

The attempt at humour hadn't gone down well. But grandparents they were about to become, whether they liked it or not, and the sooner Maxine got used to the idea, the better for them all. He couldn't exactly say he was thrilled at the new persona he was about to adopt: Grandfather. It put at least another twenty years on him, which he'd rather not feel right now. And that brought him to the other equally unexpected complication in his life.

Harriet.

He wasn't used to being turned down by women and he wasn't sure he could handle it if Harriet said no. He still hadn't plucked up the courage to ask if she'd like to come to the Jools Holland concert with him. Part of him reasoned that if he left it to the last minute, he could convince himself that if she turned him down it was because she already had something else arranged. But he really wanted her to say yes, and not just to please his vanity. In a way he wanted to test himself and see if he really was as intrigued by her as he thought he was.

It would serve him right if she said yes and then made him wear a bag over his head like John Hurt in

The Elephant Man. 'You didn't actually think I'd be seen out in public with you, did you?' he could imagine her saying.

Every time he thought of Harriet – which he did frequently – he was reminded of that tough, determined spirit of hers. There was something quite magnificent about her, he'd decided. Heroic even.

He was five minutes early for his eleven o'clock appointment, but it didn't bother the elderly lady who answered the door of the terraced house. She ushered him through to the sitting room, where there was a tea tray awaiting his pleasure, and a coal fire that was hissing and spitting noisily. 'I've only just made the tea,' she said, 'so we'll let it brew, shall we?'

Will preferred his tea weak – like gnat's pee, Marty joked – but he said, 'That'll be perfect.' The old ladies always made tea for him and he always made a point of drinking it politely, no matter how stewed it was. 'Do you want to show me the cabinet you mentioned on the phone?' he asked. He'd already clocked the furniture in the sitting room; mostly post-war utility, which in itself had a market, but not one Will was interested in.

He followed her back out into the hall, which now felt like the Arctic after the heat of the small sitting room, and then along the narrow passage to a dining room. Whenever he dealt with the SOLs – the Sweet Old Ladies as Jarvis called them – he kept in mind one of his mentor's apocryphal tales. 'Beware Laddie,' Jarvis had warned him, 'of the helpless old dear who gives you the sob story about her husband dying from lung cancer and how she doesn't know how she's going to scrape together the money for the funeral. It's the oldest scam going. You look at the woodworm-riddled bit of tat she wants to sell and you know it's worth thirty quid tops, but you feel so sorry for her you divvy up sixty. Meanwhile, round the back is her son, dusting down the next piece of heartbreaking tat.'

'It belonged to an aunt,' this particular old lady said now as she pointed towards a cabinet that was packed to the gunwales with pieces of china and silver. Strictly speaking it wasn't a cabinet, it was a *credenza* – trust the Italians to come up with a posh word for a side cabinet with display shelves at either end. This was a very fine Victorian example – burr walnut with a marquetry frieze, a central panelled door flanked by two glazed doors, tapering columns with gilt metal borders, a plinth base and bun feet, and only a modicum of wear and tear. The patination of the wood was exquisite and he ran a hand up and down one of the elegant columns. A shiver ran through him. Without inspecting the back or even opening the door, he knew he was looking at four thousand pounds' worth, give or take.

'What do you think of it?' the woman asked anxiously, as though he was judging a favourite child.

'I think it's beautiful. But do you really want to part with it?'

'Oh, yes. My friends and I are planning a holiday and I thought this might help pay for it.'

Will could hear Jarvis hissing in his ear. *Beware Laddie! Remember those SOLs!* 'Where are you and your friends thinking of going?'

'A coach trip to Scotland. My husband, when he was alive, wasn't much of a traveller, but now I'm on my own, I've decided to have some fun. Do you think this might pay for a few nights in a guest house?'

Thinking of his mother's fondness for travel since she'd been widowed, Will said, 'I'll be dead straight with you. This will pay for more than a coach trip to Scotland. You could go on a luxury cruise with the proceeds.'

'Oh, dear me no. That would never do. I get seasick just having a bath.'

He smiled. 'What I'm trying to say is that this is a really fine piece of furniture. Its value is about three and a half thousand pounds. Maybe a tad more.'

'Really? Are you sure? It just belonged to my aunt. She was nothing special.'

'I don't know about your aunt, but this I am sure about.'

'Well, in that case, we'd better have that cup of tea. Goodness. What a day it's turning out to be.'

Two cups of tar-strength tea later, he was on the road with the *credenza* in the back of his car. He'd given the woman a fair price and knew that Jarvis would be frothing at the mouth when he laid eyes on it. It was a beauty. The kind of find that brightened the darkest of days.

He drove back to Kings Melford, where he was meeting Marty for lunch at Brian's burger bar. For once, Marty was late and Will chatted to Brian about the weather, the lack of punters and the cock-up the government was making of everything. 'It's all them spin-doctors,' was Brian's considered opinion as he slapped two burgers about on the hotplate. His conviction was such that Will didn't feel inclined to argue with him. Instead he wrapped his fingers around his polystyrene cup and scanned the market for Marty's approaching figure. It wasn't like Marty to be late. Perhaps a client had overrun and kept him. He took a sip of his hot chocolate, glad of its sweet warmth.

The forecast was that winter was on its way. Just as it should be. It was, after all, bonfire night in two days' time. He thought of all those years he'd put on monster displays of fireworks for Gemma and Suzie. There'd been times, looking back, when perhaps he'd been a little reckless. One year he'd nearly blown his hand off. Maxine had gone berserk, screaming that he was out of his mind and that he could have got them all killed. Very calmly, despite the searing pain in the palm of his hand, which he was trying to subdue with a packet of frozen peas, he'd said, 'I think I'll just pop along to the hospital if that's okay with you.' That was the year he'd spent seven hours in casualty and a week off work. He still had the scar and sometimes, when he stretched his hand open too far, he was reminded of what an idiot he'd been.

He caught sight of Marty hurrying over and waved. 'Sorry I'm late,' Marty said, his face flushed red from the cold.

'No worries. Difficult client I presume?'

'Yeah, something like that. Have you ordered?'

'Naturally.' He turned to Brian. 'How are the burgers doing?'

'Ready when you are.'

They took their lunch and strolled through the market – Brian's only table and set of chairs were already occupied. 'How's Suzie?' Marty asked, as they stood absently browsing a CD and DVD stall.

'Other than not liking how pregnant she now looks, she's well. The sickness has eased off.'

'And Maxine?'

'Not too much change there yet.'

'She'll come round.'

'Even for a lawyer you sound unfeasibly sure.'

Marty shrugged. 'People just need time to adjust.'

'My, you're philosophical today.'

When Marty didn't respond, Will said, 'You okay? You don't seem your usual self.'

Marty picked up a CD of an old Sex Pistols album. 'Do you remember us thinking this was the last word in world-changing music? How we ever fell for it, I'll never know. It'll take more than a few clever lyrics and bashed-out chords to change the world for the better.'

His voice low, Will said, 'Put the CD down and tell me what's wrong.'

Marty frowned. 'Who said anything was wrong?'

'It's written all over your face. Is it work?'

'No.'

'What, then?'

They walked on. 'It's no big deal,' Marty said quietly. 'I've just come from a doctor's appointment. That's why I was late. Sorry I lied. And please, no jokes about lying, cheating lawyers.'

'Hey, never mind the apologies or quips. What's wrong with you?'

'I have a lump where us chaps would prefer not to have such things.'

'Oh, shit!'

'No, we're not quite in that yet. But who knows.'

'So what did the doctors have to say?'

'He confirmed what I already knew: that I had a lump. He's now organising a visit to the specialist for some tests.'

'Are we talking cancer?'

'Too early to tell. That's what the tests are for.'

Will threw the remains of his burger in the nearest bin. 'It'll be fine,' he said. 'No worries. Absolutely no worries.'

'Now who sounds unfeasibly sure?'

Chapter Thirty-Eight

She was not depressed, Eileen told herself firmly. Run down, maybe. Overwhelmingly fatigued, most certainly. Angry, yes. But depressed, no. She had pills to deal with that. It was Bob who was depressed. It should be him sitting here in this stuffy waiting room queuing to see the doctor. It was him who needed help. Not her.

She'd only agreed to come because of Dora. 'You're worrying me, Eileen,' Dora had said. 'You've told me yourself you're not sleeping properly and that you feel completely done in. Perhaps, you know, in view of everything you're going through, you need some stronger medication. Just to tide you over.'

Eileen didn't think stronger drugs were the answer. It was courage she needed. Courage to confront Bob and make him talk to her and to hell with the consequences.

She reached for another magazine and flicked through the glossy pages, envying the young women their slim figures, their perfect faces and their come-hither eyes. She had been pretty once. Not eye-catchingly beautiful, as Dora had been, but attractive in an easy-going, homely kind of way. Attractive enough to catch Bob all those years ago, that much was true. But now she felt old and dowdy. She felt worn out most days, exhausted with the daily grind of just staying on top of things, of not letting the ME take control entirely. If she fully enjoyed a day it was always at the expense of another. She had to pace herself continuously. If she went shopping today, then tomorrow she would have to rest. If she didn't, she would end up paying the price and be forced to rest for two days. And there was always the worry that this was it, that she would never get better. Statistically, though, she knew that there was a good chance she would; she just needed to be patient.

More impossibly perfect bodies passed before her eyes. She stopped turning the pages when she came to a piece about a grandmother of two having a make-over. Eileen stared hard at the before and after pictures. The transformation was more subtle than she might have expected, but it was a transformation all the same. There was a sparkle in the eye of the woman, a lifting of the corners of her mouth and chin. '*I did this for me*,' the caption read beneath one of the photographs of the grandmother posing with her hands on her hips, shoulders back, head held high. '*Not for my husband, or my family. For me.*'

Dora would strongly approve of this woman, Eileen thought. Dora who rarely left the house without full make-up, matching handbag and shoes, and a pashmina tossed casually around her shoulders. Wonderful Dora who, despite the heartbreak in her life, always came bouncing back. She was currently bursting with happiness over a new man she'd met through her Soirée Club. 'You have to meet this one,' Dora had gushed. 'He's just the sweetest man alive.'

'There have been sweet men before,' Eileen had pointed out cautiously.

'Ah, but this one is the real thing. And so very interesting. He used to run his own wine-importing business. He wants to take me to Barcelona for a long weekend.'

For the first time Eileen felt envious of her friend. What did she have to look forward to each week, other than a husband who hardly spoke to her these days? She and Bob could sit in the same room together, watch the television together, even share the same bed, yet all the time they were separated by a distance that was growing wider every day. If only he would share his grief with her.

But that was never going to happen. Not now he'd found someone else to do that with. Another woman.

A buzzer above the receptionist's hatch went off. Eileen looked at the blue disc in her hand, back at the flashing light and registered that it was her turn to go through to the doctor. She remained in her seat though, suddenly aware that she was on the brink of an important decision. The way she saw it, she had three options. She could go and sit in that doctor's dull, cramped room and pour out her problems and admit she was terrified her husband would leave her. Or she could simply lie and hold out her hand like a good little girl and accept those magic sweeties in the hope they would turn her head to cotton wool. Or, she could simply walk out of here and . . . and do what, exactly?

She was still pondering this question outside in the cold November wind as she waited for Dora's car to appear round the corner. When it did, Dora said, 'You were quick. The surgery not busy today?'

'I didn't see the doctor. But I think I did see a chink of light. And I need your help.'

Bob would give anything to leap in his car and drive down to Warwick and see how Jennifer was. But he couldn't. In half an hour, when he'd finished cleaning the gutters, he had to fetch the children home from school, and then later he had to get things ready for the firework display he was putting on for them. It had been Harriet's idea to have fireworks. 'You always used to put on a good show for us, Dad,' she'd said. He'd noticed how she'd winced as she said the word 'us', and felt the sting of it himself. When the girls had been small, he'd loved seeing the joyful delight in their faces as they'd written their names in the darkness with sparklers. One day he might be brave enough to unearth the collection of cine films he had from those days. But that day, if it ever came, was a long way off. The pain of seeing his darling daughter projected onto the blank wall of the dining room – moving, laughing and staring straight into the camera lens in that bold, challenging way she had – would bring him to his knees. A position from which he was terrified there would be no recovery.

Climbing down the ladder, he stood on the patio and

looked at the mess he'd created. Slimy, rotting leaves lay scattered all around him. He began sweeping them up and loading them into the wheelbarrow to take down to the compost heap. When he'd been working all hours and driving a thousand miles a week, he'd longed for days like this, when he could do nothing but potter in the garden, treating every day as a weekend. He must have been mad. How could he ever have thought that this nothingness would suit him? Where was his identity? Who the hell was this half man he'd become, who spent his days wandering the wastelands of garden centres and DIY stores and doing the school run? Where in God's name had Bob Swift gone?

Jennifer would have the answer. She always seemed to be able to answer his questions. When he'd left her on Saturday night he could have wept. She'd been close to tears herself and if she'd said the words 'don't go' he would have obeyed without a second thought. Instead, he'd made sure she had everything to hand, including his mobile number.

She had finally given in to common sense – and a rising temperature – on Friday evening and told him she was going home. 'You were right,' she said.

'In that case, I'll drive you home.'

'What will you tell your wife?'

'I'll think of something.'

'We are going to be sensible about this, aren't we?' she'd said when they were halfway through the journey and she'd woken from a deep sleep.

He'd kept his gaze on the road. 'I'm not sure that I can cope with being sensible any more,' he said.

'But your marriage? You mustn't do anything to wreck that.'

'Perhaps it's wrecked already.'

They didn't speak again until she was directing him to where she lived – a bungalow at the end of a pot-holed farm track. Its isolation worried him, despite her saying that the farmer on whose land she lived was only a phone call away.

She was exhausted from a severe coughing fit when they arrived, and after he'd settled her on the sofa, covered her with a throw and had figured out the central-heating system, he made her some tea then drove to the nearest shops and stocked up on essentials. He knew she wouldn't eat much, but he bought what he thought might tempt her. It was strange buying food for someone he hadn't known for long. Did she like mushroom soup? Did she prefer white or wholemeal bread? Butter or margarine? But in all other ways, he felt he knew her so well.

After unpacking the shopping and filling a hot-water bottle, he insisted she went to bed. They both knew they were minutes away from saying goodbye and not knowing if they would ever see one another again. 'I'll ring you tomorrow morning,' he said. 'And don't worry about the *Jennifer Rose*. I'll arrange for her to be taken to the marina.' He sat on the bed and hugged her briefly. It was a wrench to let go.

Her last words to him were: 'Be kind to yourself, Bob. As kind as you've been to me.'

Harriet arrived home to find Joel and Carrie helping Eileen to butter some rolls. 'We're making hotdogs,' Joel told Harriet importantly. 'Granddad's in the garden setting up the fireworks.'

She put her bag down on the worktop. 'Anything I can do to help, Mum?'

'That's all right, love. We've got it all in hand. Carrie, a little less Flora; too much and the sausage will slide out. How was your day, dear? Oh, I nearly forgot, I've invited Will. I thought it was time we had him over for a drink. Dora said she'd pop in as well. We'll be quite a little party. Oh, and there's some post for you. It looks like estate agents' details.' She pointed to the microwave and the pile of mail on top of it.

Harriet wondered if she'd come home to the right house. Her mother was a different woman from the one she'd said goodbye to that morning. There was a sense of purpose about her that had been missing these last few weeks. Harriet hoped that by pulling out all the stops this evening, her mother wouldn't feel too shattered tomorrow.

She took her mail upstairs and while she exchanged her work clothes for something suitable for standing around in the freezing cold, she checked out the house details two agents had sent her. One house in particular caught her eye; a small end-of-terrace cottage overlooking the canal, on the outskirts of Kings Melford and on the Maywood road. It was at the top end of her budget, but on paper it looked promising. It had already been renovated and had a small extension added onto the side. It was too late now to make an appointment to view it, but it would be first on her list of jobs to do in the morning. She finished dressing, grabbing a scarf and her favourite old black beret, then went downstairs to see if there was anything she could do to help.

With Marty's news still fresh in his mind, Will wasn't in the mood for a party, even a low-key firework party. But he reasoned it would be better than mooching around on his own.

'Some things you never see coming,' Marty had said to him when they parted in the market. 'This is definitely one of them.'

'You will keep me posted, won't you?' Will had said. 'And if you fancy some company for any of the sessions with the consultant, you'll be in touch?'

'You'll be uppermost in my mind.'

Marty's stoicism really got to Will. If it had been him, he didn't think he'd behave so calmly. It seemed worse, too, that Marty was going through this alone, not having a wife or girlfriend to fuss over him. But then who the hell would fuss over Will? When it came right down to it, apart from his mother, he had only Marty and Jarvis to count on. There were people in the trade whom he occasionally had a drink with, and even the odd couple from his married days who stayed in touch by Christmas card, but no one other than Ruby, Marty and Jarvis who he would want to call on if the chips were down. It was a depressing thought.

He'd been told not to bother knocking on the front door, but to go round to the back. It was there he found Bob lining up a row of rockets; with difficulty he was pushing the sticks into the ground. 'It's so cold; the ground's freezing,' he said.

'No buckets of sand, then?'

'Sorry, not that organised.'

Will looked around the garden, his gaze coming to rest on a children's sandpit on the patio. 'How about we move that to the middle of the lawn and stick the rockets in the sand?'

'Already thought of that. The sand's not deep enough.'

'Nothing else for it: we'll have to push them into the ground as best we can.'

They worked steadily together and had just finished the task, having only snapped one of the rocket sticks, when Carrie and Joel appeared, each carrying a can of beer. 'Harriet thought you would like these,' Carrie said.

'Or would you prefer something else?' Harriet said, following behind. 'A glass of wine maybe?'

'No, this is great,' Will said. Better than great, he thought, unable to take his eyes off Harriet. She looked totally irresistible in that beret. Cute. Sweet. Sassy. But most of all, incredibly sexy. He popped open his beer and told himself to behave. Hitting on your host's daughter was not the done thing.

If there had been any doubt in his mind that he had imagined his attraction to Harriet, the matter was now settled. Now all he had to do was convince her that an older man in her life was just what she needed.

Chapter Thirty-Nine

Maxine's greatest regret in divorcing Will was the effect it had had on her relationship with his mother. Ruby Hart was one of the nicest and most straightforward women Maxine knew and had always gone out of her way to make her ex daughter-in-law still feel a part of her family. Initially Maxine had been reluctant to accept any of Ruby's invitations to get together, convinced that they were made out of a sense of duty. She was, after all, the mother of Ruby's only grandchildren. But in time she came to realise that the invitations were as sincere as Ruby herself. 'Don't be a stranger,' she used to say. 'You know where I am if you fancy a cuppa and a chat.'

Today, while Steve was at home watching the rugby, she and Suzie and Gemma were taking Nana Ruby out for afternoon tea. Maxine turned into the estate and parked in front of the neat little bungalow. Give him his due, Maxine thought, as she walked up the path with the girls, Will did his best when it came to his mother; he always kept an eye on her as well as doing whatever odd jobs needed doing around the house. She knew this because Ruby was inordinately proud of her son and was never shy in singing his praises to Maxine. Maxine had long since realised that it wasn't an act of rubbing her nose in it, just an act of love. But as devoted to her only child as she was, Ruby had once told Maxine that she wasn't blinkered when it came to his faults. 'I'm not one of those silly mothers who thinks the sun shines out of their children's behinds. Far from it. But I do believe Will's a good son and an excellent father.'

Dressed to the nines in a smart knitted suit with a glittery brooch on the lapel, Ruby greeted them with hugs and kisses and her usual stream of compliments and keen-eyed observations: 'Maxine, what a stunning trouser suit, but how tired you look! You must be working too hard ... Gemma, how colourful your hair is! How I wish I could be as daring.' But the biggest whoop of pleasure was reserved for Suzie. 'Ooh, look at you, Suzie! You must have doubled in size since I last saw you. You look just like your mother did when she was pregnant – wonderfully voluptuous, just as nature intended! Now sit yourselves down while I finish switching handbags.'

Maxine recognised the handbag that Ruby was exchanging for her everyday one, and was touched; it was the bag she'd given Ruby for Christmas last year, the price of which would horrify the older woman if she ever knew. Maxine never begrudged a penny she spent on Ruby, not when she'd been such a loving grandmother to the girls.

'What do you think of this lipstick?' Ruby was saying to Gemma and Suzie, while puckering her lips. 'A bit too young for me, do you think?'

'No way, Nana,' Gemma said. 'It looks great on you.' The generosity of the comment gave Maxine a prickle of envy. Gemma never said anything nice about her appearance. But then rarely could Maxine think of anything nice to say about her daughter's attire. Last night Gemma had spent an hour in the bathroom ruining her lovely blonde hair by applying garish pink streaks to it. And despite having asked her to dress appropriately this afternoon, Gemma had deliberately put on her worst clothes: an ill-fitting skirt that was so long it was practically dragging on the carpet and a raggedy old jacket that looked like something Che Guevara might have worn. Maxine just hoped the hotel where they were having tea wouldn't turn them away.

Will occasionally accused her of rampant snobbery, but was it so wrong to want better for, and of, her daughters? Was it so wrong to wish that Suzie's life didn't now revolve around ante-natal visits and maternity wear, and that her youngest daughter wasn't such a surly, ungrateful mess? In the coming months Gemma would be going for university interviews. What on earth would they think of her? What chance did she have of securing a place at a decent university? It was beyond Maxine how her daughters could be so wantonly careless with their lives. When she'd been their age she'd always striven to do her best and to be the best. What's more, if she'd been given the opportunity to go to university she would have grabbed it with both hands and made her parents proud of her. She hadn't cared at the time that her father wanted her to go straight into the business and forego her chance of studying, but just occasionally she had, over the years, experienced a tweak of regret that she'd missed out. As a teenager she had once harboured a dream of studying Art History and spending time travelling round Italy visiting galleries and museums. But it was not to be. Which was why she'd been so damned determined her girls wouldn't lose out.

Gemma had always loved coming to the Maywood Grange Hotel. Dad used to bring her and Suzie here when they were little. She didn't know at the time that he couldn't really afford it, but he'd always allowed them to have whatever they wanted. The waiters and waitresses would make a big fuss of them, explaining carefully what all the sandwiches contained and pouring out their tea, never minding if anything was ever spilt or knocked over. It was the first time she could remember feeling grown-up; she'd loved being treated as an adult.

Her mother could do with learning that. Gemma took a bite out of her scone and glanced across the table at her mother; she was boasting to Nana Ruby about the saleroom she'd recently bought and the building work she was having done. She doesn't care about anything but work, Gemma thought bitterly. Suzie and I don't mean anything to her. All because we haven't conformed to what she thinks is perfect daughter behaviour. Well, tough luck. If being perfect means turning out like her, then no thank you!

Gemma couldn't remember the last time she'd seen her mother happy. Even Steve was regularly getting his head bitten off these days. If Mum wasn't careful, she'd soon be looking for husband number three. Not that Gemma had any intention of sticking around to see that. She'd be long gone. Once she got to university, that would be it. After deciding to read Philosophy and Politics, she had applied to universities not on the strength of their courses but on distance; she wanted to be as far away from home as possible. Her first choice was Durham followed by Edinburgh and then Exeter, where Suzie had gone. She supposed that she probably would want to come home now and then, but only to see Dad. Oh, and Nana and Suzie. And the baby – her niece, or nephew. She turned this thought over and looked at Suzie, who was sitting next to her and spreading great dollops of jam and cream onto yet another scone – she really was eating for two!

Gemma had written to Marcel, telling him about her sister being pregnant, and how she was going to be an aunt next year – 'How totally weird is that?' she'd written. He'd replied almost straight away, inviting her to come to Paris for Christmas. She hadn't answered his letter yet, but she knew that there was no way her mother would let her go. But Christmas in Paris with Marcel would be just the coolest thing. She pictured the two of them walking through the Tuilerie Gardens eating hot chestnuts and then going to a bar and meeting up with Marcel's friends. But it would never happen. Mum would see to that.

While Mum was off paying the bill and Gemma was in the loo, Suzie watched her grandmother dig around inside her purse for a tip for their waitress. She did it every time, despite Mum telling her that she would see to it.

'So how are you, Suzie?' Nana Ruby said, slipping a two-pound coin underneath a saucer.

'I'm okay,' she said.

'Are you eating lots of spinach and broccoli? You must have plenty of iron.'

'I'm taking supplements.'

'Good. Now, I didn't like to say anything in front of your mother, but I've been knitting some baby clothes for you. You won't believe how many you'll get through and how quickly the baby will grow out of them. You know, I'm so excited about this for you. I can't believe I'm going to be a great-grandmother. My friends are all so envious.'

Suzie felt a rush of affection towards her grandmother. It was lovely to be with someone who wasn't telling her how awful her life was going to be. She was sick of her mother's comments and of the hurtful remarks her supposed friends from school and university were making, none of whom had shown the slightest effort to hide their shock. For a start they couldn't believe she was pregnant, but mostly they wanted to know why she hadn't done the sensible thing and gone through with the abortion. They were also all sickeningly desperate to know who the father was. Sinead had pressed her the hardest. 'Go on, Suzie,' she'd said on the phone, 'you can tell me. I won't tell anyone. Not even Richard. Was it someone here?'

'No,' she'd told her friend. 'It wasn't a student.' She would do anything to keep the truth from Sinead. And from Richard. She sometimes wondered if he'd put two and two together. If he had, he'd made no attempt to get in touch with her. She hoped he'd remain silent when the baby was born, that his conscience wouldn't get the better of him or that he'd become curious about the child.

Running her hand over her bump, she said, 'I wish Mum could be as pleased as you, Nana.'

Nana Ruby snapped her handbag shut. 'Not to worry; she has a lot on her mind at the moment. She works so hard.'

'You're always so fair, aren't you?'

'When you've lived as long as I have, you know there's usually more than one way of looking at a thing.'

'That's what I keep trying to tell Mum, but she doesn't listen. I told her I couldn't get rid of the baby and run the risk of thinking in years to come that today my child would have been starting school, or, today my child would have been learning to drive. I don't want a life of what might have been.'

'And what did your mother say?'

'She said I already had that to look forward to, and that I would forever ask myself what might have been if I hadn't got pregnant.'

Gran looked thoughtful. 'I wonder if your mother often asks herself a similar question?'

'What? If she hadn't had Gemma and me?'

'No, of course not. But maybe there are things your mother regrets not having done.'

Chapter Forty

It was almost two in the morning, and with her bedroom door shut, Harriet was once again decoding her sister's emails. It was the first opportunity she'd had to look at them since getting back from Dublin and she'd decided, in order to tackle the job in a more methodical manner, to go right back to the very first email Felicity had exchanged with her lover. It had taken the best part of two hours to read six messages – three written by Felicity and three sent by her lover – and so far she hadn't come up with a single clue as to the man's identity. Had they set out to be deliberately careful? Or had it been part of some elaborate game that added a further frisson of excitement to what they were doing? What she'd read tonight was mostly about a night spent together in a hotel; how much it had meant to them and how long before they could be together again.

There were numerous references to Felicity's state of mind, mostly how unhappy she had become in her marriage. Trapped was a word that appeared again and again, not with regard to the children, as Harriet might have supposed, but by the lack of choice she had in her life. '*I see my life as nothing more than an existence,*' Felicity had written. '*If it wasn't for the children – and you – I would question why I bother at all.*'

Harriet was shocked. She had never heard her sister speak in this manner. It was as if she was reading a stranger's letters.

'*I have tried so very hard to be more like the girl Jeff married,*' Felicity had also written, '*but I can't do it. I'm not the person I was then. Some days I feel such contempt*

317

for him, that he doesn't see how unhappy I am or how unfaithful. He just doesn't seem to notice me any more.'

The depth of her sister's unhappiness was more disturbing to Harriet than the original discovery of the affair.

But was the affair with Miles? That was the question. Frustratingly, the emails had yielded nothing of any use and she was no nearer the truth. Nor had there been a chance to see Miles recently so that she could subtly drop hints into the conversation and watch his reaction. If she was honest, in the light of Dominic's assumption she felt uncomfortable imagining herself in his company. She had always been so fond of him, but now she couldn't view him in the same way. As well as being embarrassed that she had misinterpreted his friendliness towards her for something deeper, she also felt angry with him, having come to the conclusion that he might have been using her. Was being with her his way of still being close to Felicity? If so, it was sick and she was having none of it.

But all this was pure conjecture. There was always the chance that Dominic was wrong. That he'd leapt to a wildly off-beam conclusion. In which case, it was important to keep an open mind. And her distance. Miles had phoned her this afternoon and invited her out to dinner. 'I've got this insatiable desire for some poppadoms and a deadly-strength vindaloo,' he'd said. 'Do you fancy joining me?'

She'd used the children and her parents to put him off, giving some feeble reason why she had to be at home, then she tried to deflect him by saying she had an appointment to view a house tomorrow. 'I'm quite excited about this one,' she told him, 'it really seems promising.'

Except it had backfired and he'd said, 'Why don't I come with you? Another pair of eyes to check out the place might be useful.' It would have been churlish to say no, so she had agreed to meet him at the property in the morning.

Still staring at the laptop screen, she yawned and rubbed her eyes. Another twenty minutes and she'd call it a day. If she didn't get to bed soon, she wouldn't make that appointment later this morning. Just as well it was Sunday.

She pulled up another email but tiredness was turning her brain to mush and her thoughts slipped away from her once more.

When Carrie had learned that Harriet had seen Dominic in Dublin she'd wanted to know when he was coming to see them again. 'He didn't mention anything,' Harriet told her gently, 'and I know he's very busy at the moment.' It had seemed too cruel to tell Carrie the truth – that it was unlikely Dominic would show his face in Maple Drive for at least another twelve months.

'Do you think he'll come home for Christmas?' Carrie had persisted. 'He'd probably want to be with his parents and his brother, wouldn't he?'

'I expect you're right,' Harriet said. Again it would have been unkind to point out that it was years since Dominic had spent the festive holiday in Maple Drive. He once told her that Cambridge was at its bleakest during Christmas – bitterly cold and devoid of twittering students – and that nowhere else could offer him such brutal solitude.

At the same time as fielding Carrie's questions about Dominic, Harriet had done some probing of her own, trying to ascertain how things were going at school. She had posted the bullying letter through the letter box at school on Tuesday, on her way to work, well before the children had set off for school with their grandfather. She'd put it in an envelope marked Private and written a brief accompanying note. Later that afternoon she'd received a phone call from the headmistress saying that it hadn't been difficult to work out who had been behind the letters and that the group of girls involved had been spoken to, as well as their parents. That the matter had been dealt with so readily should have pleased Harriet, but she hadn't shared the headmistress's confidence that it was now behind them. 'Isn't there the small but vitally important business of building bridges to get on with?' she'd asked. 'Carrie has been made to feel like a social outcast. How are you going to rectify that situation?'

'It'll take some time, but let me assure you Miss Swift,

we'll get there, together.' Harriet had just picked up on the emphasis of the word *together* when Mrs Thompson said, 'It might help if you got more involved with school, mixed with the other parents and got to know them. Have you thought of joining the PTA? I know they're always crying out for extra helping hands. Never more so than right now, what with the Christmas fayre and the nativity play coming up next month.'

Harriet didn't think there was a PTA in the world that was ready for her particular brand of helping hands and said, 'I'm sorry but I don't have the time.'

'Well, maybe you could take advantage of the parents' evening next week and meet some of the other parents. The PTA will be there providing coffee and biscuits for everyone.'

From what Harriet had so far seen of the parents, she thought she'd rather cover herself in raw chicken livers and get to know a tank of piranhas.

Once again she was left with the uneasy feeling that the onus was back on her. Was that what being a parent was about? Always feeling that it was down to you to solve everything?

She had raised the topic of school several times with Carrie in the hope that her niece might toss her plaits and say, 'I had such a great day at school today. Everyone was *so* friendly towards me.' But all she shoe-horned out of Carrie was that she was bored at school. This didn't come as a surprise to Harriet. Despite not fully understanding what key stages Carrie was supposed to be achieving, Harriet knew her niece was quite bright. Will had said much the same the other night when they'd had their firework party. After a few glasses of wine, while the children were tucking into hotdogs and getting themselves covered in ketchup, Harriet had found herself confiding in him about the bullying letter. He'd suggesting having an all-out heart-to-heart with Carrie: 'Give her the opportunity to get it off her chest,' he'd advised.

'But I wanted to give her the sense of having coped with it by herself. I thought it would be more empowering.'

He'd frowned and said, 'Is that because that's how you always do things? Single-handedly taking on the world? It can be a tough and lonely business being such a courageous pioneer.'

It was an odd comment to make, but what he'd come up with later, when he was leaving, surprised her even more. 'I have a spare ticket for the Jools Holland concert at the Apollo in Manchester next week; I don't suppose you'd like to go, would you?'

Dora had been hovering at the door with them as Will had offered to walk her home, and she gave Harriet an embarrassing wink, at the same time giving Will a nudge with her elbow and saying, 'If Harriet doesn't want to go, I'm sure I could make myself available.'

Will had laughed in that easy way of his and said, 'I wouldn't want to come between you and Derek.' During the course of the evening, Dora had talked at length about Derek, her wine-importing boyfriend, making them all laugh with her plans to snare this one before he got away. Somehow Will had left without Harriet giving him an answer to his question. She hadn't seen him since and because he hadn't gone to the trouble to ask her again, she was left to think that he'd thought better of his invitation.

She rubbed her face hard and focused her thoughts on the coded email in front of her. It was a particularly long one; perhaps it would be better to leave it until another night. But steeling herself, she began the painstaking process of deciphering Felicity's lover's words. It was Miles whom she now pictured as the writer. And as before, his language veered through a stellar gamut of emotions, from euphoria that Felicity should want to be with him, to desperate and heart-wrenching despair that she might regret what they had got themselves into. Harriet had to wonder what it was about Felicity that could have brought a man to his knees like this. She couldn't imagine anyone feeling the same for her.

Scrolling down, she came to a paragraph that had her senses on full alert. She slowly pieced together the coded words, pressing a finger to her lower lip as she often did when concentrating. When she'd finished, she stared at the screen, then grabbed a pen and a piece of paper. She jotted down the words and read them through one more time.

Do you remember that sweltering hot day when the four of us were lying in the cornfield and you were threatening to take off all your clothes and jump into the canal? That was the moment when I knew I loved you. You seemed braver and more vibrant than anyone else alive. It's how I've always thought of you.

It was difficult for Harriet to believe that she had finally found the proof she needed. But there it was; the evidence proved that it really had been Miles with whom Felicity had been having an affair. What's more, she could clearly remember the day in question. She could also remember telling her sister not to be so stupid. How boring she must have seemed in comparison to Felicity. In her heart, she'd known that Dominic had been right. He'd said he knew his brother and he clearly did. Better than Harriet did.

The next thing she did was to hit the delete button and wipe the disk clean. She had achieved her objective. There was no need now to keep a single word of what had passed between Felicity and Miles. As she sat back in her chair and pondered what she'd discovered, her cheeks suddenly burned fiercely at the thought of Miles and Felicity in bed together.

Ever since Dublin, she had tried to suppress this train of thought, but now that she knew the truth, she couldn't. She was surprised how much it hurt. She had only fantasised about Miles for a blink of an eye, but once more it was as if Felicity had spoilt things for her – first Dominic, now Miles. Oh, she'd never truly believed that Dominic would love her when they were teenagers, but if Felicity hadn't been there, well, who knows, he might actually have paid her more attention, perhaps treated her as an equal and not as the younger sister permanently cast in the shadow of the prettier and more interesting older one. And now it had happened all over again with Miles. He had been heart, body and soul in love with Felicity, therefore Harriet could only ever be second best in his eyes. She wouldn't have believed it possible, but she suddenly hated her sister. And Miles.

Her thoughts turned to the coming day, when she would be seeing Miles. She decided it would be better to take the children with her. She had thought she would view the house without them, that maybe it was unsettling for them to see too many potential homes, but now she thought they would make a convenient shield to hide behind. If she spent any time alone with Miles it was almost inevitable that she would end up telling him she knew about him and Felicity. In her current frame of mind, she didn't think this would be a good idea. She needed time to think about what she now knew. Would it, for instance, be better for the children's sake if their mother's secret remained exactly that, a secret? Given the measures Miles and Felicity had taken to hide their affair, it was probable that Miles had never confided in anyone, which in turn meant the only other person who knew about it was Harriet. So long as she remained quiet no one else would ever find out.

But with a jolt, she suddenly remembered Dominic and sat up straight. Dominic was the last person on earth whom she should have told. Even if he was merely armed with the suspicion that his brother had been having an affair with Felicity, he'd be capable of almost anything. With a sickening sense of misjudgement, she covered her face with her hands. What had she done?

She went to bed and passed a night of chaotic and violent dreams. Of Miles making love to Felicity while Dominic looked on furiously. Of Dominic fighting Miles, like he had that time outside the club in Manchester. Of Jeff threatening to kill himself if Felicity ever left him.

She woke in the morning exhausted and taut with

anxiety. Should she talk to Miles after all and warn him about Dominic? No, she decided. She had meddled enough.

Harriet and the children arrived at number one Lock Cottage ten minutes earlier than the appointed time. Harriet had wanted to look at the outside of the property unhindered by Miles's presence or the estate agent's representative.

The end-of-terrace cottage was empty, the owners having already moved out due to a company relocation, and after parking the car on the small gravelled area at the front, she took the children round to the back, which was the aspect of the house she knew they would appreciate most. Her parents had both declared her mad even to think about it, reminding her, as if she hadn't already given it her consideration, that children and water made a dangerous mix. But the thought of living in such a picturesque setting was irresistible to Harriet. Both children let out shrieks of delight when they saw that beyond the small, south-facing back garden, just the other side of the boundary wall, was the towpath and the canal.

Carrie was tall enough to see over the wall, and after hoisting Joel up so that he was sitting on top of it, his legs dangling over the side, the three of them took in the view. It was a glorious autumnal morning, a day so still it was as if time had been stopped in its tracks. After the last few days of frosts and freezing temperatures, the weather was unexpectedly mild. The sky was the palest of blues, and the shadows were long and ethereal. Unlike the stretch of canal at the back of Maple Drive, which was densely lined either side with trees and banks of hedgerows, the aspect here was open and exposed. Freshly ploughed fields, their rippled surfaces illuminated by the golden sunlight, undulated gently into the distance. Away to the right there were crows gathered in the tallest branches of a lone beech tree, their noisy cawing the only sound to be heard. Bob and Eileen would probably think the view was too bleak, but Harriet thought it was beautiful. She turned round to look at the cottage and thought of the views the bedrooms at the back would offer. A flicker of movement at the window in the next-door property had her hoping the natives were friendly. Because without even taking a step inside the cottage, she knew this was where she wanted to be.

'What do you think?' she asked the children. It was important to her that they shared at least half her enthusiasm.

'Could we have a boat if we lived here?' asked Joel.

She lifted him down from the wall. 'Maybe a very small rowing boat. The cottage does have its own mooring rights.'

'We'd be like Ratty in *Wind in the Willows*,' joined in Carrie. 'We could go for picnics in the boat. And Miles could come with us, couldn't he?'

'He could indeed,' Harriet said guardedly. She'd been aware lately how frequently Carrie brought Miles into the conversation. Hearing the sound of a car, she said, 'Come on, that'll either be Miles or the person who's going to show us round.'

It turned out to be both arriving in convoy. Miles greeted Harriet with a kiss on the cheek and the man, about the same age as her father, brandished a set of keys and house details, saying, 'This is my first day on the job, so if I can't answer any of your questions, I do apologise. Now then, let's see if we can get the front door open. I was warned it could be a bit tricky. Ah, that's got it,' he said, after applying his shoulder to the solid wood door. He stood back to let them all go inside. 'Of course, it's always better to view a house when it's lived in,' he said, 'so you'll have to fill in the blanks for yourselves.' Harriet was grateful for his running commentary; it meant she didn't have to speak to Miles.

Despite the echoing emptiness of the rooms and the dirty smudge marks on the walls where pictures had once hung, Harriet wasn't disappointed with what she saw. Leading off from a small hallway there was a downstairs cloakroom and a good sized sitting room with a view of the tiny front garden, but it was the large kitchen and breakfast room at the back that gave her a shiver of excitement. The cooking area was clean and modern with light beech units and granite surfaces, just as she would have chosen for herself. The sun streamed in through the French doors that opened onto the rear garden. Harriet looked at the children to gauge their reaction. After all, as inconceivable as it had seemed six months ago, this could be their home for a very long time. This was where Harriet would have to guide them through the nightmare of puberty and adolescence and all the ensuing dramas their combined lives would bring. Living here, she might just pull off the required miracle.

Carrie wanted to choose her bedroom, and with Joel chasing after her, she clattered up the uncarpeted stairs and crashed into the first room she came to. It was smaller than the room she had at Grandma and Granddad's, but much prettier. There was a lovely little fireplace opposite the window; it was so small it looked like something out of a dolls' house. She went and stood in front of the window. If she had a chair and desk right here, she'd be able to watch the boats going past. She couldn't think of anything nicer.

Except for having Mum and Dad back with them.

It was on a day like this, when something good was happening to her, that she really missed them. She used to love coming home from school to tell Mum about all the interesting things she'd done that day. They'd sit together and Mum would listen to everything she said and then hug and kiss her and tell her how clever and special she was.

But now Carrie kept everything to herself. It was better that way. Grandma was too tired to listen, Granddad was never around and Harriet was too busy. Although she had noticed that Harriet had asked her more questions about school this week than she normally did. She'd told Harriet that she was bored most of the time during lessons, which she was. She hadn't said anything about the letters, or how the girls had stopped writing them now. One of the girls,

Emily – the one who'd seen her coming out of the charity shop during half term – had even tried to be friendly to her in the playground the other day. At first she had been wary, expecting Emily to suddenly start laughing at her, but when she didn't say something horrible or tease her, Carrie had thought that maybe she was quite nice after all.

'Carrie! Come and see what I've found.' She turned at the sound of Joel's shrill voice and hurried into the room next door. It was bigger than the one she'd claimed for herself, but didn't have a view as nice as hers. There was no sign of her brother and she was just thinking that maybe he was in another bedroom when behind her a door flew open and Joel leapt out.

'It's a secret hiding place,' he said when he'd stopped laughing. Carrie knew that it was nothing more than a cupboard at a strangely low height, but she kept quiet; if Joel wanted this room, she'd be able to have the one with the brilliant view. 'Do you think Harriet will let me have this room?' he said.

'Let's go and ask her.'

They found her across the narrow landing in a bedroom that was much bigger than either of theirs and had the same view as the room Carrie had picked out for herself. Her aunt was talking to the man who'd come with the keys while Miles was kneeling on the wooden floor in front of a fireplace and looking up the chimney.

Joel nudged Carrie. 'Is he looking for Father Christmas?'

Miles laughed and got to his feet. 'I was trying to see if the chimney was blocked.'

'And is it?' asked Harriet, coming over to them.

'Not as far as I can see.'

'Excellent! A log fire in my bedroom; how fantastically decadent.'

Carrie noticed the happy smile on Harriet's face and thought that she should smile more often; it made her look pretty. More like Mum.

When they were saying goodbye to the man with the keys and Miles suggested they go out for lunch together, Carrie pricked up her ears. Would they be going to that Italian restaurant again? But she was disappointed when Harriet said, 'I'm sorry, Miles, but we can't. Mum's doing one of her all-singing and all-dancing Sunday roasts.'

Carrie didn't know what her aunt meant by all-singing and all-dancing, but having enjoyed herself so much looking at this lovely house, she didn't want the day to turn boring. She also hadn't forgotten her plan to try and get Harriet to spend more time with Miles. With him around, Harriet didn't seem so serious or so snappy. And hadn't she just smiled?

But Miles wasn't the only person who could make her aunt smile. Carrie had definitely seen Harriet smiling and laughing with Will the other night during the fireworks. Did that mean she liked Will as much as Miles? It was all very confusing. Were you allowed to like more than one man at a time? She didn't know the answer to that, but she decided it would be nice if Miles came home with them. 'Couldn't Miles come back with us for lunch, Harriet?' she said. 'Grandma wouldn't mind, would she?' She smiled at her aunt, willing her to say yes.

Chapter Forty-One

Harriet didn't know what had got into Carrie. For a start she'd taken it upon herself to invite Miles for lunch – much to Harriet's annoyance, he'd readily accepted – and now she was crashing around the dining room like a whirling dervish, telling them all where to sit in accordance with the place cards she'd decorated with pink and silver glitter. Perhaps it was the excitement of finding a house they all liked. She was now flinging her hands in the air in response to Joel climbing onto a chair next to Harriet. 'No,' she cried, 'that's where *Miles* has to sit. See, Joel, the card says M.I.L.E.S.' She spelled out the name pedantically. 'You have to sit on my side of the table.'

'Do get a move on, Carrie,' Harriet's father said impatiently. 'The food will get cold if we hang about any more.'

'Ssh . . . Bob, don't hurry her,' Eileen soothed. 'She's gone to a lot of trouble.'

'I don't care how much trouble she's gone to,' he muttered peevishly, 'I refuse to eat a cold roast. And Joel, do we have to have that mangy old scarf at the table?'

They eventually sat down in their allotted seats. Bob carved, with Eileen doing her usual act of supervising which bits of the joint to give everyone – something Harriet knew annoyed her father – and she offered to pour the wine for the adults and some grape juice for the children. She carried out this simple task applying all her concentration to it so that she wouldn't have to talk to Miles. Or think about him. Because whenever she did, her brain automatically assembled a slideshow of graphic images of him and Felicity in bed together – of Felicity straddling Miles, of

Miles sucking and biting her, of Felicity throwing her head back in a moment of ecstatic abandonment. It pained Harriet to admit it, but she envied her sister, for she had never felt that depth of passion for a man she'd ever been to bed with.

When everything was served and a hush had fallen on the table, Eileen said, 'Now then, tell us properly about the house, Harriet.' Her mother's voice was just a little too bright and jolly, as though she was making too great an effort for the sake of their guest.

'It was brilliant,' Carrie rushed to explain before Harriet could open her mouth. 'Completely mega brill. And the bedroom Harriet says can be mine is just *so* cool.'

'Carrie, please don't interrupt or speak with your mouth full. And whatever has happened to your vocabulary? When did everything become brill and cool?'

Another time and Harriet might have made the same reprimand as her father, but not today, not when she was only too grateful to have Carrie fully on-side. Angry that her father was in such a foul mood and had pulled up Carrie so needlessly in front of Miles, she said, 'Carrie couldn't have described the house better.' She shot her niece a quick smile and received a potato-chomping grin in return. She then turned to Miles to further diffuse the situation. 'You thought it was great too, didn't you?'

'It certainly has a great location,' he agreed. 'Stunning, in fact.'

'But it's the location that concerns me,' said Eileen. 'How safe would it be?' She inclined her head towards the children and lowered her voice. 'It's so close to the water.'

Amused that her mother thought Carrie and Joel hadn't already figured out the danger for themselves, she said, 'We could live on a busy main road and it would be just as dangerous.'

Spearing a baby carrot with his fork and waving it around in the air, Joel said, 'Harriet says we can have a boat to play in.'

Eileen looked alarmed. To allay her mother's fears,

Harriet said, 'I didn't say anything about *playing* in it, Joel. Boats have to be taken very seriously.' Privately she thought Joel's interpretation was spot on. She could already see herself mucking about on the canal when she came home from work on a warm summer's evening.

'So are you going to make an offer for it?' This was from her father.

'She already has,' chipped in Carrie. 'On her mobile in the car.'

'I hope you weren't driving at the same time.'

Harriet frowned. Just what the hell was eating her father? 'No, Dad, it was a hands-free call as always.' More to her mother than her father, she said, 'I wanted to get in quick. A property like that will get snapped up in no time. Rather than risk losing it to a higher offer, I've offered the full asking price; the agent sees no reason why the owners won't accept it. I'm going back to see it tomorrow evening after work. Do you want to come? Dad, what about you? Do you want to take a look at it?'

'Sounds to me like you've made up your mind without our approval.'

'It's not a matter of seeking your approval. I thought you'd be interested.' Her tone was sharp and it had her mother looking anxiously at her. If it weren't for Miles and the children, Harriet would have gladly pushed the matter. Her father's manner was putting a real dampener on things. Why was he behaving like a grumpy old man? Keeping quiet, she took a gulp of wine and got on with her meal. It was then that Carrie suggested they go for a walk with Toby after lunch.

'You'd like to come too, wouldn't you Miles?' she asked him across the table.

Harriet insisted that Eileen went upstairs to rest when they'd cleared the dining room and stacked the dishwater. She then told the children to get their boots and coats on, but for some reason, Carrie seemed incapable of carrying out this simple instruction without Miles's assistance.

Watching him being dragged off to the utility room to help find her coat, she wondered if her niece had developed some sort of crush on him. Maybe it ran in the family. Turning to her father, she said, 'Are you going to join us for some fresh air, Dad?'

'I'll get plenty of that in the garden,' he answered tersely.

He's worse than a sulky teenager, she thought. Why couldn't he snap out of his rotten mood and give them all a break? Just how many children had she taken on?

'You don't have to do everything bossy boots Carrie asks of you,' she said to Miles when they were crossing the road and heading for the footpath to take them on their familiar route to the canal. 'If you'd had something else in mind to do this afternoon, you only had to say.'

'That's okay; I'm used to being bossed about by the Swift women.'

She laughed uneasily and was about to ask if there was one particular Swift woman who stood out from the crowd, when he said, 'All I was going to do this afternoon was depress myself by trying to write.'

'Oh? What are you writing?' She thought of all those emails he'd written to Felicity. Perhaps this was how he was coping with his grief. Putting it all down on paper.

'I'm trying my hand at poetry. But please don't say anything to Dominic; he would only belittle what I'm doing. In his view there's only room for one poet in the family, and he's it.'

Harriet had once attempted to read one of Dominic's so-called epic poems but had soon given up; she hadn't been able to make head nor tail of it. Felicity had tried to explain what it was about and had drawn Harriet's attention to the effectiveness of his syntax, as well as the symbols and allegories he'd used, but eventually her sister had admitted defeat and told Harriet that she was a philistine. 'I refuse to believe you can't hear the beauty of his language,' she'd said. 'The man's a genius.'

'What kind of poetry do you write?' Harriet asked Miles. Part of her wanted him to come right out and just say it –

I'm writing about my love for Felicity. How much I adored her. How much I miss her. But the greater part of Harriet wasn't ready to have her hurt and disappointment further compounded by a confession. To be forced to listen to Miles opening his heart to her about Felicity was more than she could bear. She hated knowing that even in death, Felicity was always going to be the main attraction in her life. That those who had known her sister would always want to talk about Felicity in preference to her.

'Oh, you know, the usual thing,' he replied. 'Regret and lost opportunities.'

'And love? Surely that's a given. Every poet writes about that.' Stop it, she told herself. Back off before it's too late. Don't give him the chance to tell you you're nothing but a poor imitation of the woman he would have gladly ripped out his heart for.

He pushed his hands deeper into his pockets and shot her a sideways glance – a nervous, guilty glance, she noted. 'Like you say, that's a given. But as Samuel Johnson wrote, "Love is only one of many passions." It can appear in many guises. And when you least expect it.'

'I'll have to take your word on that,' she said coolly, and quickened her pace to catch up with the children.

'Can we let Toby off the lead now?' Carrie asked.

'Yes. But the usual rules apply—'

'We know,' they both chorused, 'don't go near the water!' They charged off whooping and yelling.

Miles laughed. 'They've got you totally sussed, haven't they?'

'They're much too smart for their own good. I can't think what they'll be like when they're teenagers. Completely uncontrollable knowing my luck.'

'Nonsense. They'll be great, and lots of fun. I know you won't believe me, but you really are turning out to be a great mother to them.'

'Not true. I can never be that. Felicity was their mother, and always will be. I'm merely the caretaker.'

'I think you underestimate yourself. And the children. They've become very fond of you.'

Reminded of what Dominic had said to her in Dublin – that the children relied on her and needed her – Harriet was brought up short by a bolt of self-pity. Very likely, because her situation made her as desirable as a bucket of fish eyes, the children's fondness for her would be the nearest she ever got to be being loved. Being relied upon isn't enough, she wanted to scream. Self-pity morphed into stinging bitterness and she set off at a ferocious pace, wanting to put as much distance as possible between herself and the man who had loved Felicity in a way she would never know.

But Miles was hot on her heels. He put a hand out to stop her. 'Harriet, what is it? What did I say?'

'The children,' she blurted out. 'We mustn't let them go on too far without us.' Then, hearing Toby give off a loud bark, she turned her head sharply. Further up the towpath, stooping to stroke Toby while chatting to the children, was Will Hart.

'Hi,' Will said when Harriet and her companion joined him and the children. He held out his hand to the other man, deciding on sight that if he was a rival for Harriet's affection, he'd have to shoot the good-looking young blood dead on the spot. 'I'm Will Hart, the Maple Drive neighbour from hell.'

'Hi, I'm Miles.'

'Ah, one of the McKendrick boys; I've heard about you.'

'Really? From Harriet?'

'No, from Dora Gold. I think she knows everything about everyone in the road, which makes her fascinating company.' He smiled, first at Miles and then at Harriet, and began to feel he'd walked in on something. Something between the two of them. He checked out Harriet's body-language. If it was possible, she looked more agitated than usual, kicking at the leaves on the ground and looking anywhere but at Miles. He was disappointed to see she wasn't wearing her cute beret. 'Carrie tells me that you've found the *coolest* house ever?' he said.

She looked up at him. 'Yes, it's far better than I could have hoped for. I've made an offer on it already and I've arranged to see it again tomorrow with Mum and Dad.' Her face suddenly brightened and she smiled one of her rare smiles. 'Why don't you come with us? We could make a party of it.'

Surprised at the invitation, he said, 'Thanks, I'd like that. What time?'

'Seven. It'll be dark, so you won't see the location at its best, but you'll get the general idea. We won't be able to all squeeze into the one car, so—'

'No worries. I'll follow behind. I know my place.' He wondered if Miles was also included in the party.

'Oh, and before I forget,' she said. 'That Jools Holland concert you mentioned – remind me of the date again?'

Will was thrown. He thought he'd blown it the other night when he'd deliberately asked Harriet in front of Dora in the hope that she would be too embarrassed to turn him down outright. When he'd returned home with no answer at all, he'd given up hope. But now here she was bringing the matter up of her own accord. What stupendous constellation of lucky stars had brought about this stroke of good fortune? He must remember to thank Jarvis for standing in for him so that he could have the afternoon off.

Chapter Forty-Two

Will knew from Gemma that Suzie was bored and missing her friends from university. He couldn't do anything about the latter, but to give her something to think about other than ante-natal classes, the benefits of breastfeeding and the understandable fear of giving birth, he had asked her to help out in the shop. Jarvis had said he thought it was an excellent idea. 'So long as there'll be no danger of a towels-and-hot-water situation arising,' he'd cautioned. 'I'm useless in a crisis.'

'Don't worry,' Will had said, 'she's got ages before the big day.'

'Do you think she might end up getting hooked on the business? I've a feeling you'd like that, wouldn't you? I can see the sign above the shop now: "Hart and Daughter".'

That was the thing about Jarvis; he saw the truth long before it hit most people right between the eyes. Will had never thought of it before, but the prospect of having one of his children on board was a pleasing one. It gave him a sense of pride. Was that why old man Stone had been so eager for Maxine to follow in his footsteps?

The more he thought about Suzie coming to work for him, the more ideal it seemed. Given that she would have such an understanding boss, she would be able to work the hours that would fit in around the baby. In the early phase, when the baby was sleeping like the proverbial baby, she could even bring it in. Obviously that would only be a short-term option, but it was certainly worth thinking about. However, in the long-term, to make a decent extra salary he'd have to find a way to up their turnover. She would have to accept that while she worked for him she would never be well off, but there were worse things that could happen to her.

He hadn't mentioned anything about this long-term option to Suzie – he didn't want to appear as if he was making decisions for her – but what he'd so far suggested was that she was more than welcome to help out in the shop if she wanted. He'd also offered her the chance to go round the salerooms with him. 'Any way to get out of the house would be fantastic, Dad,' she'd said.

So today, Monday morning, they were heading north on the M6 to attend an auction in Lancashire. 'You will say if you need to make a loo stop, won't you, Suzie?' he said. 'When your mother was pregnant she hated to be out of range of a loo. We once made half a dozen stops during a two-hour journey.'

'If I ask you to pull over it will be because I've got a mad desire for a Mars bar wrapped in cheese then battered and deep fried.'

'Stop the car!' Will groaned. 'I need to be sick.'

Suzie laughed. 'I heard a bloke on the radio saying it was his favourite meal, so I gave it a go. You should try it; it's bliss on a plate.'

'More like a heart attack on a plate.'

'Did Mum have any funny cravings?'

'A few. I remember stocking up on peanut butter when she was expecting Gemma. I'd made the mistake of assuming she'd repeat the craving she had when she was pregnant with you, but she'd moved onto cheese and onion crisps. She used to eat them in bed when she couldn't sleep, washed down with a bottle of Dandelion and Burdock. Hasn't she told you any of this herself?'

Suzie turned away and looked out of the side window. 'I think she's hoping it might all go away if I don't discuss it with her.'

'I'm sure that's not true, Suzie.' But sadly, it probably was.

'We took Nana Ruby out for tea on Saturday,' she said more cheerfully.

Aware that she'd abruptly changed the subject, Will said, 'I know, I spoke to her in the evening.'

'Nana told me she can't wait to be a great-grandmother.'

'Has she shown you the baby clothes she's been buying for you?'

'No, but I know about the knitted stuff.'

He laughed. 'There's more. Lots more. She's having the time of her life going round all the baby departments picking up bargains for her great-grandchild. She was the same when you were on the way.'

'Do you think she might like to help out when I need to work?'

'If she's fit and well, you'll have to fight her off not to help.' It seemed the perfect moment to tell Suzie about his idea for her. Funny how things often happened just at the right time.

The saleroom wasn't one of his favourites due to its size – large and soulless, little more than a draughty warehouse – but it was filling up fast when they arrived. Will had checked out several items he was interested in online, but with half an hour to go before kick-off, he went in search of the lots he'd come for: a George III mahogany tilt-top tripod table; a pair of silver Victorian shell-shaped salt cellars; and a round silver photograph frame with a pierced shamrock border which he wanted to buy for his mother for Christmas, for that first all-important photograph of her great-grandchild. The catalogue price had been put at an ambiguously low figure, but Will had set himself a top price of seventy pounds. After he'd inspected the lots and found them in reasonably good condition, and had exchanged a few words with the other dealers he knew who were stalking the trestle tables, he instructed Suzie to mark them off in the catalogue, just as Jarvis had once taught him. The cycle of life, he thought happily.

'Can I do the bidding for you, Dad?' Suzie asked when the auctioneer took his place on the podium.

'If you want. But you stop when I tell you to. And be sure

to hold up our card so the auctioneer's assistant can write down our number if we make the successful bid.'

'Is that it? No lecture about being careful not to rub my nose at the wrong moment?'

'That's a myth. It takes more than a nervous twitch to catch the attention of a busy auctioneer. Okay, it looks like we're off. Keep an eye on the running order. Sometimes a sale can run away like an express train.'

Later, when they were driving away with a full boot, wearing matching satisfied looks on their faces, Will said, 'You enjoyed that, didn't you?'

'It was great. Is it always that exciting?'

'It is if you come away the victor with the spoils. Unfortunately there are plenty of times when you leave empty-handed.'

'Well, I loved it. Will you bring me again?'

'If you're going to come and work for me, you'll have no choice.'

She smiled and his heart surged: it was good to see her so happy.

They were almost home, having stopped off for something to eat, when Suzie said, 'Dad, you don't have to give me an answer straight off, but is there any chance I could move in with you when the baby's born?'

Will didn't need to think about his answer. 'Of course. But only if you sort things out with your mother. She has to be happy about the arrangement.'

Suzie rolled her eyes. 'She'll be glad to see the back of me.'

'Maybe a little distance between the two of you might help,' he said. He sounded as unconvinced as the look she gave him. They both knew it would take more than this to make Maxine have a change of heart.

It wasn't until that evening, when Will was at home, checking through his post before going to see Harriet's house, that he experienced a pang of regret. If Suzie came to live with him, there would be no more seduction tricks in front of the log fire. Any future bedroom activity would have to be conducted with the volume turned down low. He was being selfish, he knew, but he couldn't help but wonder where it would leave him in his cause to get to know Harriet better. If he was going to make a move on her, he'd better do it soon, before the house was invaded by a two-man army bringing with it babygros drying on the radiators, prams and pushchairs clogging up the hall, high-chairs and bottles cluttering the kitchen, and the rest of the house given over to toys, clothes and all the messy paraphernalia the average teenage girl leaves in her wake in the belief that it will be tidied away for her. As lurve nests went, it would be a two-star romantic turn-off. He shuddered at the thought that at the age of forty-six, he might be reduced to a grappling session in the back of his car.

The cycle of life was all very well, but not if it meant he was about to catch up with his youth by having a gear stick poke him somewhere painful . . .

Carrie and Joel turned round to wave at Will every now and then as he followed behind Bob Swift's car. Will told himself that life would be a lot easier if he could put Harriet out of his mind. Why did he want to get involved with someone so complicated? Apart from the difference in their ages, there was also the two young children to add into the equation. How often would he be able to see Harriet on her own with Carrie and Joel on the scene?

When he wasn't around Harriet, Will could make himself believe that his feelings for her rated no more than a mild case of infatuation, and that her appeal lay in the challenge of stripping away her impregnable armour and discovering what soft, yielding warmth lay beneath. But the second he was in her company, he knew the attraction was more than a superficial whim to explore those hidden depths. He respected and admired her; something he hadn't felt for a woman in a long while. She had a steely tenacity he doubted he possessed. Harriet would have survived his mid-life crisis, no problem. Like Maxine, she probably had him down as a wimp for not having stuck it out.

He genuinely thought she was one of the strongest people he knew. As far as he could see, in that split-second when her sister's car had collided with another, Harriet's life had changed for ever and she had sacrificed everything she had created for herself to take on the challenge of a lifetime. She must have loved her sister an awful lot to do that. He couldn't help but wonder what it would feel like to be on the receiving end of such love.

It seemed par for the course that Harriet hardly spoke to him when they arrived at the house. If he didn't know better, he'd say she was embarrassed he was there, as though she'd regretted inviting him. But he didn't care: she was wearing that cute, sexy beret again; she could treat him any way she liked! His reaction to it had him contemplating the possibility that he was developing some kind of weird hat fetish. He mentally swapped the black beret for a bowler hat. No. Definitely nothing doing there. He then tried a cowboy hat. Still nothing.

And like the headgear, he loved the house on sight. A shame it hadn't been on the market when he'd been looking. With Harriet busy showing her parents round – she seemed to have her work cut out jollying her father along – Carrie and Joel voiced their eagerness to give him a guided tour.

'Come and see my room,' Joel said, grabbing him by the hand.

'Then you have to see mine,' Carrie said, catching hold of his other hand. 'You can see the canal from the window. And *I've* got a fireplace.'

'My room has a secret hiding place in it,' Joel added, not to be outdone.

'It's only a silly old cupboard,' whispered Carrie, dragging Will up the stairs. 'But don't tell him that, will you?'

'My lips are sealed.'

He made all the requisite noises of appreciation when he saw their bedrooms, including showing thigh-slapping astonishment at Joel's secret hiding place. They then led him back out onto the landing and into the biggest of the bedrooms. 'This is Harriet's room,' Carrie said. 'It's nice, isn't it?'

He stood in the middle of the empty room and was just taking in the proportions of it when suddenly a picture of a bed with Harriet lying invitingly on it popped unbidden into his head. He cleared his throat and went over to the window where he cupped his hands around his eyes in an effort to cut out the light so he could see the garden and view beyond. But it didn't work; it was too dark outside. When he turned round, the children had vanished but Harriet was standing behind him looking arch and remote. He started slightly.

'Sorry,' she said, 'I didn't mean to make you jump.'

'It's an age thing. When you get to be as decrepit as me, you have to watch the old ticker.'

Her eyes flickered. 'Exactly how old are you?'

'How old do you think I am?'

'Seventy-two?

'Close. I'm actually seventy-nine. Not bad going, eh?'

A half smile softened her face.

'I don't suppose I could tempt you into a drink with me when we've finished here, so I can congratulate you on finding such a great house?'

She moved away from him and went and stood by the pretty Victorian fireplace. 'Where were you thinking?' she said.

Good God! He'd got away with it. 'How does The Navigation sound? We could go straight from here if you like.'

'Okay. But I'll have to check with Mum and Dad and make sure they don't mind.'

He was about to make some quip about not keeping her out beyond her curfew for fear of getting her grounded, when he thought better of it. It couldn't be easy, having once had all the freedom of living away from home, only to be stuck there again and answerable not just to parents but to a niece and nephew.

The Navigation was busy. So busy they couldn't find a table and ended up standing around yelling into each other's ears above the swell of too many other voices and a succession of records Will neither knew nor wanted to know. Apparently it was some whippersnapper's eighteenth birthday. It was a pity his coming of age precluded meaningful conversation for anyone else.

'This is a complete disaster, isn't it?' he shouted, leaning in close to Harriet. 'Shall we give it up as a bad job?'

He could see the relief in her face. 'Yes.'

They downed their drinks and pushed their way through the scrum to the door. Once outside, they stood for a moment to settle their reeling senses. 'Not one of my finest ideas, I'll admit,' he said, enjoying the sight of her adjusting her beret. 'I'm sorry.'

'It's hardly your fault the entire population of Kings Melford had the same idea as us.'

Fishing his keys out of his jacket pocket, he led the way over to his car. Five minutes later and he was apologising again, this time for a flat battery. 'I'm so sorry,' he said, admitting defeat and slamming down the bonnet in disgust. 'This evening is going from bad to worse. I'll call us a taxi.'

'No. Let's walk along the towpath. It's a clear night, practically a full moon. Besides, I know the way like the back of my hand.'

'Boy, are you my kind of girl! Intrepid as well as forgiving. The perfect combination.'

He found a torch in the boot of the car, and once they'd taken the steps down to the path, he was tempted to risk a bit of hand-holding, but decided he wasn't brave enough. So near to the canal, she might well push him in if he stepped out of line.

Once their eyes had grown accustomed to the darkness, he found they didn't need the pathetically weak beam from

343

the torch and he shoved it inside his pocket. Along with the hand nearest to her. Better safe than sorry. He soon realised he had to alter his usually slow loping step to match her more hurried pace: he'd never known a woman walk so fast. Where did she get the energy from? 'How's your asthma?' he asked.

'It's fine. I seldom get any problems at this time of the year. It's pollen and mildew spore related.'

'And that day in my shop?'

'Ah, that was stress induced. It doesn't happen like that too often, thank goodness. How's Suzie?'

Touched that she was interested, he said, 'Oh, she's blooming.' He then told her about Suzie coming to work for him.

'Will it be a real job?'

'Are you accusing me of nepotism?'

'Yes.'

'Then guilty as charged. My only defence being that I want Suzie to be happy.'

'She must be feeling so isolated, as if she doesn't fit in anywhere any more.'

Thinking how astute this comment was, he acknowledged that Harriet's situation wasn't that dissimilar from Suzie's – they had both ended up in situations that had left them feeling marginalised and up against it. Come to that, it was more or less what had happened to him when he'd thrown in the towel as a lawyer.

'How's work going?' he asked. 'Have you settled in now?'

'Pretty well. My boss says I'm his favourite person at the moment.'

'Any particular reason why?'

'I helped to pull in a lucrative contract he'd been after.'

'The trip to Dublin you told me about?'

'Yes. He got the news today. So it was cakes all round this afternoon.'

'You should have said earlier. If we'd been able to hear one another in the pub we could have raised our glasses and made a toast to you. Another time perhaps.' When she didn't respond to his suggestion, he said, 'How's your father? I don't know him well, but he didn't seem himself when we were looking round the house.'

In the still night air, he heard her tut. 'He's being a complete pain. Nothing anyone says or does is right. I don't know what's got into him, or how Mum puts up with it. She's either a saint or a fool. I could never let anyone treat me like that.'

Will didn't doubt it for a second. 'You don't suppose he's depressed, do you?' he said. 'I only ask because when I went through my period of wanting to hack great lumps out of my colleagues, I blamed everyone else for how I felt. I didn't care a jot about anyone else's feelings. Only mine.'

Her pace slowed. 'I can't imagine you being depressed.'

'It happens to more people than you'd think. I could try talking to your father, if you like?'

'I doubt it would do any good. By the way, how's your friend you mentioned during the children's firework party? Any news yet?'

He'd forgotten he'd told Harriet about Marty. 'He has an appointment with the specialist tomorrow. I'm meeting him for a drink in the evening.' He caught her look. 'And yes, hopefully it will be somewhere quieter than tonight. Is it my age, or do they play the music louder these days?'

'Why do you keep going on about your age?'

'I don't, do I?' He knew full well that he did. He also knew that it was her youthfulness that made him more conscious of it.

'You seem determined to—' Her voice broke off as she stumbled and lurched forward. He reached out and held her tight.

'You okay?'

'I'm fine. The trees are taller here and they're blocking out the moon. You can take your hand away now.'

'Would it be very ungentlemanly to refuse the lady's request on the grounds of hanging on in case I trip as well?'

Her answer – 'Only if you promise I can fall on you if

that happens,' – gave him the courage to slip her arm through his. They walked on in silence, at his pace rather than hers, their feet kicking up the leaves and disturbing the wildlife. Something small and fast scuttled across the path in front of them.

'Was that a water rat?' he asked.

'It could have been'

A long way off an owl hooted, followed shortly by the eerie screeching bark of a fox. Pointing to the hedgerow on their right, Harriet said, 'Felicity and I used to squeeze through the brambles there to get to the far side of the field and listen to the nightingales.'

'I've never heard a nightingale sing before.' He'd also never heard Harriet refer to her sister so readily.

'People make the mistake of thinking they only sing at night,' she carried on. 'We heard them during the day quite often, but when it was dark it always seemed more magical. Once, during a particularly warm spell in early summer, we came here for a midnight picnic.'

'With Miles and his brother?'

She turned and looked at him. 'We didn't do everything with them. But yes, they were with us. Stupidly, Mum and Dad thought we'd be safer with them.'

'Are there still nightingales here?' he asked, wishing he hadn't provoked the sharpness in her voice. He was curious, too, about the 'stupidly' reference. Had something happened that night?

'I don't know if there are any here these days; it's years since I've been to listen to them. Their song period is only from April until June. It's very fleeting. Like so many things in life,' she added. Her tone had become soft and wistful now.

'You'll have to take Carrie and Joel on a midnight picnic next year. They'd love it.'

In the silence that followed, Will speculated on some of what Dora had told him the night of the fireworks about the intensely close friendship between the Swift girls and the McKendrick boys. 'Clique' was the word Dora had used to describe the foursome. 'You couldn't have got a cigarette paper between them, they were that close,' she'd confided. 'Unhealthily so, in my opinion.' According to Dora, the older brother, Dominic, whom she colourfully likened to a wily fox in a chicken coop, was the one they all followed, with Miles destined to be in his talented brother's shadow. 'Eileen and I used to feel sorry for him,' Dora had further explained. 'We blamed the parents, though. They shouldn't have treated the boys so differently. Mind you, it was Harvey who was at the bottom of it. He had some very peculiar ideas. He could also be excessively strict. Cruelly so.' Will didn't get to hear the rest of the story as that was when Eileen had announced supper was ready.

When they were just feet away from the end of his garden, Harriet slipped her arm out from his. 'Oh no you don't,' he said. 'My reputation as a gentleman will be shot to pieces if I don't see you home safely.'

'And mine too as a modern, independent young woman if I let you.'

'Fair point. In that case, let's compromise. I'll walk you as far as the footpath. There, that's my final offer.'

'There's no need.'

'I agree. But humour an old-fashioned guy.'

Minutes later they were standing at the entrance to the footpath and she had her hands pushed into her jacket pockets. He wished now that he'd suggested a nightcap or a cup of coffee when they'd been standing at the end of his garden. Behind them the canal was sleek and dark and above them the sky was immensely vast: it was a perfect night and he really didn't want it to finish.

'Well, then,' he said, playing for time and desperately thinking if there was anything else he could talk about to keep her longer. 'I'm sorry the evening was such a disaster.'

'Please don't keep apologising. I enjoyed the walk.'

'Really? I should try that old dead-battery trick more often.'

Her mouth curved into a soft smile. 'I mean it. It brought back memories.'

'Not painful ones, I hope.'

She shook her head. 'Mostly happy memories.' But as she said this, the smile melted from her face and she looked ineffably sad. He suddenly felt a tremendous surge of tenderness for her, and without thinking what he was doing, he put his arms around her and kissed her.

Chapter Forty-Three

It was a mistake. A colossal error of judgement. He knew it the second her body stiffened in his arms and her lips, cold and unresponsive, felt like stone against his. As she continued to stand rigidly impassive, klaxon bells went off inside his head. *Stop! What the hell do you think you're doing? She'll kill you, you idiot!* Then there was an excruciating moment when he lowered his arms and stepped away from her, and she simply stared back at him. There was no anger or horror in her face, just a look of such terrible blankness he felt more humiliated than if she'd slapped him.

'I'd rather you didn't ever try that again,' she said. She turned and walked away. He wanted to rush after her and say how sorry he was, or at least explain himself, but the sight of that funny little stalky bit on the top of her beret, combined with her dignified exit, rooted him to the spot. Unable to move, he watched her disappear round the corner and into the darkness of the footpath. There was no backward glance, no conciliatory gesture to say that there was a snowball's chance in hell that he'd ever be forgiven. He'd blown it. But then so what? What had he thought would come of it, anyway?

Halfway along the footpath, Harriet came to a stop. She was breathless and jangly. What the hell had happened back there? Why had he kissed her? And why had she reacted like that? Why had she experienced . . . she hesitated, hardly able to put it into words. It was all too strange. All so unexpected. The nearest she could get to describing what she'd felt was to say there had been a sudden weakening sensation deep within her, as if something sore and tender inside her chest had been touched. She had been so startled by her reaction that she had frozen in his arms and forced her brain to evaluate what was going on. When this had failed, she had decided retreat was the best course of action.

Her breath forming in the cold night air, she mentally scrolled through the evening. Had there been earlier warning signs that he wanted to kiss her? At the house? The pub? He'd certainly been keen to hold her hand once they were on the towpath, but she'd thought that had been a chivalrous thing, like the way her father insisted that he walked on the roadside edge of the pavement. 'A gentleman has to shield the lady from the splashes caused by the carriages,' he used to say.

Had there been other moments when Will had wanted to kiss her? She couldn't be sure. It wasn't in her nature to be always clocking up the attention she attracted. Spencer used to tease her that she wouldn't know a guy coming on to her if he stripped naked and threw himself at her feet. Apparently he'd been dropping hints that he fancied her from the minute he'd joined the firm, but she hadn't noticed. Over the years, Dominic had frequently accused her of living like a nun. What was it he'd said of her in Dublin? Oh, yes, that she had a frosty streak of self-denial. Even Felicity had teased her for being so restrained. She suddenly felt crushed. What was wrong with her? Why couldn't she be more like everybody else? Why wasn't she more sexually aware? More in tune with her body?

Once again she was reminded of the hurt of being rejected by Spencer. Was it possible that if she'd meant more to Spencer he wouldn't have walked away? He'd have hung in there and helped her all that he could. The word 'love' had never been mentioned between them, but then nor had lust, or passion, or desire, or any of those other words Miles and Felicity had been so fond of using in their emails. Sex with Spencer had been adequate, she now saw. Very quickly into their relationship they had slipped into the routine of making love after supper, never before, and never too late. Rarely first thing in the morning, either. Spencer had been a real sleep faddist and had to have his eight hours minimum. Looking back, there had been a predictable sameness to their relationship. At the time she had thought it suited her perfectly, that it was a part of her life she could neatly compartmentalise.

It was not an edifying discovery, but she had to face up to the truth: she wasn't a very exciting or loving person. And the net result of that, surely, had to be that she was unlovable. She would never experience the adoration her sister had experienced for the simple reason that she was incapable of giving it out herself. If Dominic was to be believed, she lacked emotion and spontaneity. As unpalatable as it was, Harriet had to admit that she was dull and unsexy. Could there be a worse crime in this sex-obsessed age?

Yet Will had wanted to kiss her. She put a hand to her lips and touched them as if recalling his mouth against hers. Why had he done it? And why, more importantly, had it provoked that weakening sensation? Try as she might, she could not recall another man kissing her eliciting such a perplexing response.

There was only one logical way to find out what had caused it. Turning back the way she'd just come, she retraced her steps, all the way to the end of Will's garden. If she was going to do this, it had to be now. Leave it until tomorrow, and she'd lose her nerve. For the second time in the last two days she was acting out of character. Yesterday she had deliberately invited Will to see the house in front of Miles to get at him, to prove some twisted kind of point: See, I don't need you, I have plenty of other friends. Friends who don't lie and cheat on people. Friends who don't treat me as second best. Within hours she was regretting freezing Miles out like that. It was no way to treat an old friend. Or a new friend, for that matter. Using Will to score a point was cheap and unworthy.

It was when they were at the house and Will had asked

her to go for a drink with him that she had undergone a moment of epiphany. She suddenly realised what it was about Will that she liked. He took her for who and what she was: Harriet Swift. He had never known her sister, therefore he hadn't and never would make a comparison. She would never be second best in his eyes. Spencer and Erin had both met Felicity and they had both independently made the same comments she had heard for most of her life – that Harriet was quieter than Felicity, that Harriet was shorter than Felicity, that Harriet was more serious than Felicity.

But that would never happen with Will.

She looked up at his house. There were lights on downstairs. Good, he hadn't gone straight to bed. She pushed open the gate, walked the length of the garden with a purposeful stride, her eyes straining in the dark to pick out anything that might trip her up, and knocked on the back door. This is a first, she told herself, a spontaneous first. This would show Dominic!

The door opened just as she was about to raise her hand and knock once more. 'Harriet?' He couldn't have sounded more surprised.

'May I come in?'

He looked confused. Alarmed, even. Is that what she did to people? 'Yes. Of course.' He stood back to let her in. 'I was just having a drink. Would you like one?'

'No thanks.'

He shut the door after her, then raked both his hands through his hair. 'Look, I'm sorry about what I did. I should never have tried it on. I don't know what I was thinking.'

'Please, I haven't come here for an apology.'

'Really? Why then? Has something happened? An accident? The children? Do you need to use the phone?'

She shook her head.

'What then?'

'I need you to do something for me.'

'Oh. Okay. What is it?'

She swallowed. 'I need you to kiss me again.'

He opened his eyes wide. 'What?'

'Please don't make this any more difficult for me than it already is. I want you to kiss me like you did before.'

'Is this some kind of crazy trick? Because if so, I ought to point out that entrapment's against the law.'

'Just kiss me, Will. And no funny business,' she added, after an agonising moment had passed while he seemed to be making up his mind whether to go along with her request.

He came towards her, slowly. Inches from her face, he tilted his head, but then pulled back and looked at her questioningly, a slight frown creasing his brow. 'You're sure about this?' he asked. He suddenly sounded as nervous as she was.

'Yes,' she murmured. And with her eyes open – she didn't want to miss anything – she braced herself for his touch: first his arms and then his lips. They felt different this time, warmer and softer. Perhaps a little more tentative. She could taste wine, too. His arms felt different. Firmer. More solid. He wasn't wearing his jacket, which meant she could feel the warmth of his body through his shirt. She could even feel his heart beating.

Her heart gave a surge and an aching tenderness filled her chest. Next a flood of warmth swept through her. It was like the sun bursting through the clouds. It was at this moment, on the towpath, that Will had pulled away. She didn't want that to happen this time and so she put her arms round him, closed her eyes and hoped he'd keep on kissing her. Except now she was kissing him, opening her mouth wide against his, wanting the warmth to go further within her, wanting him never to stop kissing her.

But he did. 'Hey there,' he said, 'you've got to breathe sometime. First rule of kissing in this house. Especially for asthmatics.'

At the sound of his voice and the touch of his hands on her face, she opened her eyes and found herself staring into his. They were the darkest shade of brown she'd ever seen.

She took a deep breath, realising that he was right: breathing was a good idea.

'I don't wish to appear nosy,' he said, while straightening her beret, 'but was there any particular reason why you wanted me to kiss you? After all, you did say I wasn't to do it again.'

'I . . . I wanted to know if I'd imagined something.'

He raised an eyebrow. 'And had you?'

'No.'

'Would you like me to do it again? Just to be sure?'

She nodded, suddenly shy.

'Presumably it's the same drill as before?' he said. 'No funny business?'

'Depends what you mean by funny business,' she murmured, lowering her gaze.

'Miss Swift, are you flirting with me?'

'I would if I knew how.'

'Now you're just fishing.' He tipped her chin up. 'But I'll carry out your bidding, if you'll come through to the other room.'

Terrified that her nerve might give out somewhere between the kitchen and sitting room, Harriet said, 'Here is fine.'

He looked amused and ran a finger over her lips. She shivered, slipped her hands round his neck and pulled him down to her. Almost immediately this time she was filled with the euphoric warmth that seemed to fill her from head to toe. She clung to this extraordinary man who could do this to her, no longer caring what she was doing, or what the consequences would be. All that was important was that Will didn't stop what he was doing. Without once ever letting go of her, he manoeuvred her out of the kitchen and along the hallway, bumping and crashing against walls and pieces of furniture. She thought he was going to take her upstairs, but instead he pushed open the sitting-room door and took her in there.

She had been undressed many times before, but never by a man as deft as Will. Or was she just too drunk on erotic desire to notice her clothes slipping away? They were on the floor. Music was playing. She leaned over to kiss Will but he resisted and, proving again how deft he was, in one easy move he tilted her onto the carpet and began kissing her. At the same time he gently parted her legs with his hand and made her gasp as he slid a finger inside her. For a split second she tensed, but as his tongue pushed further into her mouth and the palm of his hand pressed against her, she relaxed and gave in to his touch. With a swiftness she'd never experienced before, she was arching her back on the brink of climaxing. Too soon, she told herself. Much too soon. What about him? She tried to distract herself, but it was no use, the wave was getting nearer. 'Stop,' she begged.

'What, and spoil all the fun?' he whispered in her ear. He carried on, slowly, rhythmically, expertly, but now he was watching her face intently. His eyes, even darker now, had a strange look in them; an absorbed, mysterious look she couldn't fathom.

'But what about you?' she moaned as the wave came closer.

'Ssh . . . stop worrying. Concentrate on enjoying yourself.'

She did as he said and when it came, it was like nothing she had ever experienced before. It was a tsunami, the mother of all tidal waves. And just at the point when the orgasm took hold of her, he kissed her so deeply she was suddenly adrift from all her senses, swept away by something so powerful the blood pulsed in her head and she thought she was going to pass out. For minutes afterwards she lay quivering in his arms, fearing her body would never feel the same again. Finally, she broke the silence and said, 'What was that?'

'I think it's what we in the trade, Miss Swift, call a classic case of the earth moving.'

'But what did you do?'

He raised himself up onto an elbow and kissed first her

355

left breast and then her right. 'I'll show you again in a minute, if you like.'

True to his word, he did. And a lot more besides. At three in the morning, she crept across the road and fell into the soundest sleep she'd ever known.

Chapter Forty-Four

At work the following morning Harriet was having difficulty staying awake and if it hadn't been for Dangerous Dave surprising her at ten thirty with a cup of coffee and an iced doughnut, Howard may well have found her asleep at her desk. As it was, when he thumped on her door and came in she was leaning back in her chair, sucking the sticky remnants of the doughnut from her fingers and reliving with guilty shame all that had happened between her and Will. She had just told herself for the umpteenth time that it had been a night of proving that she was as spontaneous and sensual as the next person. What they'd done was nothing more than an exercise in proving a point.

'Not disturbing you, am I?' Howard said, eyeing the empty plate on her desk. 'Seeing as you're so in the zone.'

She snapped to attention in her seat and promptly knocked over a file with her elbow. She bent down to retrieve it from the floor and looked up to see Howard smiling oddly at her. 'How are you fixed for Friday?' he asked. 'Any chance you can squeeze a trip to Dublin into your hectic schedule?'

She didn't need to check her diary; she knew the day was free: it was her birthday. 'No problem.'

'Excellent. I'll fill you in on the details later. Meanwhile, I'm off to the dentist for the joy of some root canal work.'

'Ouch.'

'No doubt that's what I'll be saying when the cheeky sod bills me. See you.'

He closed the door after him, and with the greatest of effort Harriet forced her brain to apply itself to the programme she was working on. No more thoughts of

357

Will, she warned herself, adopting a much-favoured work position, that of sitting cross-legged in her chair. She soon changed her mind when she realised her body was too sore to sit that way. A picture flashed before her of her legs wrapped around Will's waist. At once desire tingled up and down her spine. The colour rose to her face, just as it had at breakfast when her mother had commented how tired she looked and had then asked what time she'd got in last night. She swallowed and put the image of her and Will on hold and got on with some work.

She didn't stop until after one, when she reached a convenient point to take a break. After making sure her door was shut, she settled in the chair again and closed her eyes. She would eat later, she decided. Her immediate priority was to catch up on some much-needed sleep. She was exhausted.

From the second the alarm clock had woken her, she had tried to remember the exact moment last night when she had relinquished her ability to think straight. In her determination to prove Dominic wrong and to prove she wasn't as dull as he and Spencer had made her feel, she had somehow lost all sense of what she was doing. One minute she was satisfied that she hadn't imagined the effect Will's kiss had had on her, and the next she was panting for more. And the trouble was, she knew that having experienced that pleasure, she wanted more of it.

But she was going to be sensible.

And firm.

What had happened last night was a one-off. She would have to make that very clear to Will.

Don't kid yourself, Harriet Swift. Don't go pretending this is just another analytical process for you to get your teeth into. You want that man to shag your brains out again, don't you?

She opened her eyes in panic. The voice – the voice of her conscience – belonged to Dominic. She could see him clearly mocking her. Sneering at her. Taunting her. '*Oh, so Miss Prissy Boots gets it now, does she? Now she knows what all the fuss is about. Well, my dear, congratulations, you've learned the all-important lesson: sex is the only thing that makes you know you're truly alive. So what are you going to do about it?'*

Knowing that she wouldn't be able to sleep now, she went and stood at the window overlooking the car park and fiddled absently with the wooden slats of the blind. But the question remained, and though her body ached in places it never had before, she knew exactly what she was going to do. Heaven help her, but she couldn't help herself. Dammit! Why was she so weak all of a sudden?

'*Oh, so you're going to use him, are you?*' taunted Dominic's voice. '*How deliciously ironic. The girl who sat in judgement of my sexual proclivities has come a long way.*'

I'm not using him, Harriet told herself, and went back to her desk for her mobile phone. No more than he's using me. We're both adults, both getting out of this what we each want. It's called fun. After what I've been through, I reckon I deserve it. What's wrong with that?

'*You know best, Hat.*'

In his office, while listening to the lunchtime news on the radio and eating a Pot Noodle – a nasty vice from his student days which he'd never grown out of – Will answered his mobile. He sat up straight when he heard Harriet's voice. He'd wondered who would ring who first. He'd spent most of the morning dithering. He wanted to speak to her for the pleasure of hearing her voice and because he knew women usually demanded a follow-up call, but he worried that she would think he was being pushy and getting above himself. This latter concern stemmed from her lukewarm response last night when they were saying goodbye. He'd handed her a business card with his mobile number and asked the dangerously loaded question of when he might see her again. 'I'll have to think about that,' she'd said.

Wrong answer! he'd wanted to shout. How about you

saying you'll show up at the shop for lunch and asking if I'd mind kissing you again? I'm sure Jarvis wouldn't mind holding the fort while we got busy in my office.

Over the years he'd been on the receiving end of some tempting come-ons, but that line of Harriet's – *I need you to kiss me again* – was without doubt the sexiest he'd heard. It had been her brisk, no-nonsense manner undercut by excruciating embarrassment that had done it for him. She had seemed so vulnerable. He suspected that she had no idea what a turn-on it had been. Prior to last night, he'd given considerable thought to what she might be like in bed, but the reality had more than lived up to his expectations. Crudely speaking, once ignited, she'd been hotter than hot and they'd had what would be termed by the pundits as 'great sex'. He got the feeling she'd been pleasantly surprised by how good they'd been together. Or was that him plumping up his ego?

'Hi there,' he said, in his best George Clooney voice.

There was a pause before she spoke. 'You okay, Will? You sound like you're coming down with a cold.'

So much for George Clooney. 'It's exhaustion,' he said. 'I hardly slept a wink last night. But when I did drop off, I dreamed this incredibly sexy woman turned up on my doorstep and demanded I made love to her for hours on end. I know it was a dream because a guy like me could never be that lucky.' He crossed his fingers, hoping he hadn't overdone it.

'That's weird, because I had the same dream too.'

'You did? You mean the woman turned up on your doorstep as well? The two-timing little minx!'

Her laughter had him relaxing back into his chair and putting his feet up on to the desk. 'So, any chance we might get together again? I know it's difficult for you, what with—'

'How about later tonight? I've got a parents' evening at school, but I should be home by eight and with you by nine.'

'Sounds perfect. Oh, but hang on, I'm seeing Marty for a drink.'

'I could come over afterwards, when you're back.'

The implication was clear, and any fears he'd had that she'd regretted last night were now gone. She was as keen to see him as he was to be with her.

Up on deck, Bob was polishing the brassware on board the *Jennifer Rose*. He'd been at it now for over an hour. One more porthole and then he'd go down below and make himself some coffee.

And then he'd ring Jennifer. He had to try to make her change her mind. She couldn't possibly have meant what she'd said during their last conversation. It must have been a reaction to her illness and the medication she was taking. She wasn't thinking straight.

When he'd phoned her at the weekend, her voice had been almost unrecognisable. Alarmed, he'd asked her if she was all right.

'According to the latest doctor who's seen me, I now have pneumonia,' she told him. 'I think they're working their way through the medical encyclopaedia.'

'I'll come down at once.'

'No. You mustn't.'

'But who's there to look after you?'

'Don't worry, my children are rallying round now.'

'Shouldn't you be in hospital? Pneumonia's serious.'

'If I was a child or an elderly old dear, then maybe. But fortunately I'm neither. I need to rest, that's all. How are you?'

'Miserable. I . . . I miss you so much.'

That's when she told him. 'Bob, you've been so sweet to me, but really, it's time to be sensible. You're married. You have a wife and a family who all need you more than I do.'

'That's not true. They're all getting on with their lives without me.'

'What you mean is that they're getting on without Felicity and you can't bear that, can you?'

When he hadn't responded, she'd said, 'I'll always be at the end of a phone to talk to you, Bob, but we can only ever be friends. I blame myself; I turned to you when I was feeling low and alone, but now I know better.'

Since then, he'd gone over and over what she'd said. Part of it was true: the bit about hating his family for being able to carry on without Felicity. It was callous and heartless of them. The worst of it was seeing Harriet so pleased about that house she was buying. How could she be pleased about anything when her sister was nothing but dust in the ground? They'd driven home with Eileen and the children all chattering on about how the rooms could be decorated and what a lovely time they'd have living there, and Harriet had selfishly waltzed off to have a drink with Will. Bob had almost aired the thought he'd vowed he never would: why couldn't it have been Harriet who had died? Why Felicity? Why his precious Felicity? He knew it was a bad thought, but he couldn't help it.

Satisfied that the brasswork was gleaming to perfection, he went down below. He was quite at home on the *Jennifer Rose* and knew where everything was kept. The boat was now safely moored at the marina, and as he'd promised Jennifer, he was keeping an eye on it for her. 'You can take it for a run, if you like,' she'd said. 'I'd appreciate those new engine parts being tested properly.'

He hadn't done that yet, but he'd got a rapport going with the older of the two men who ran the marina and they were quite happy for him to show up with Toby and potter about on the boat. He didn't have Toby with him today, because he'd known that he had to be completely alone when he spoke to Jennifer. He didn't want any distractions when he told her just how he felt about her. That he couldn't go on if he didn't think she'd be there for him.

Dora parked the car, switched off the engine and said, 'You've absolutely sure you want to do this?'

Eileen knew her friend was doubtful about what they were doing, but the time had come to think about herself.

She was tired of always making allowances for Bob. It was her daughter too who had died, but the way Bob went on, you'd think no one had loved Felicity but him. She couldn't remember the last time they'd had a proper conversation. All that passed between them these days was fragments of conversation, and now that he had become so critical, she was damned if she was going to put up with it any longer. Felicity's death didn't mean the living were condemned to a slow death as well.

'Dora,' she said, 'I'm as ready as I'll ever be.'

'Then let's go, girl.'

The office wasn't at all as Eileen had pictured it. Where was the glamour? The promise of a romance and a new life? It looked more like a dental surgery waiting room. While they waited for someone to speak to them, she whispered to Dora, 'It's a bit down at heel.'

'So was the train station where Trevor Howard met Celia Johnson in *Brief Encounter*.'

Eileen giggled. Mostly from nerves. She had never cheated on anyone but now she was about to start living a double life.

The door opened and a plump, middle-aged woman came in, bringing with her a waft of strong perfume and slick professionalism. 'Eileen, forgive me for keeping you waiting. You don't mind me calling you Eileen, do you? Here at the Soirée Club, we like to keep things informal. So much more conducive to making new friendships, don't you think?' She smiled across at Dora. 'But of course, Dora will have told you all about how we operate. Now then, I have your membership application here and I thought we might just run through it together. I think it would be advisable to pad out the section where it asks for hobbies and interests. As it stands, yours seems just a tad thin. What do you suggest we pep it up with?'

Eileen was at a loss. It was the part of the form that had worried her most. It had also made her realise just how little she did beyond the four walls of her home. She'd become as good as institutionalised.

'Do you like to travel?' the woman asked her.

'Well, yes. But I haven't actually had the chance—'

The woman put a tick in the box opposite Travel.

'And I'll bet a pound to a penny that you're a fine cook.'

'Only very ordinary, everyday—'

A tick went in the box marked Cordon Bleu Cook.

'What about trips to the theatre?'

The last time she'd been to the theatre was to take the children to a Christmas pantomine. But now that she was getting the hang of the form, she said, 'Come to think of it, I've always enjoyed live theatre.'

'Excellent.' Another tick was added. 'Music?'

'I couldn't be without it.' Well, she did have Radio Two permanently switched on.

'Excellent. Now that really has pepped things up nicely.' The woman turned the page of the application form. 'Any health problems you feel you ought to share with us? Any *mental* health problems?' she added with emphasis.

This particular question had given Eileen some cause for concern. Dora had told her to fudge it, to keep things simple. 'No mental problems,' she answered truthfully, 'but I do get very tired. For some years now I've—'

The woman shrugged and gave a light, tinkly laugh. 'Tired! Oh, tell me about it. I'm constantly frazzled down to my last energy reserves.' She put a cross in the box and turned another page. 'Ah, it says here that you're separated. May I ask what timespan we're talking?'

Without batting an eyelid, Eileen said, 'My husband and I have been separated for some time.' She had no trouble with her conscience over this; after all she and Bob had been living separate lives for months now. Maybe even longer. It was just dawning on Eileen that Felicity's tragic death had revealed the stultifying emptiness of their marriage. 'Does it matter that I'm not actually divorced?' she asked.

'So long as you're honest with the gentlemen on our books and you explain your situation, we don't mind. We're not here to judge.'

'But what about the gentlemen? Supposing they're not honest? Supposing they're happily married and playing away from home?'

'If they were really happily married, they wouldn't feel the need to be playing away, would they?' The woman gave another burst of tinkly laughter and said, 'We can only do our best. If people are intent on lying to us, what can we do? If you're at all unsure, I suggest you take the application form home with you and read the disclaimer notes on the back of it.'

Eileen looked at Dora anxiously.

'There's always a risk involved, Eileen,' her friend said. 'You could meet the most perfectly charming man through a friend of a friend and still discover he's a lying, cheating good-for-nothing.'

Or you could be married to him, Eileen thought unhappily. She took out a pen from her handbag and said, 'Where do I sign?'

The last time Harriet had attended a parents' evening she had been in the lower sixth. She'd had to listen to her form teacher telling her parents that he thought Harriet would get more out of school if she was prepared to put more into it. 'School isn't just about academic success,' he'd told them, 'it's about joining in and helping to foster a sense of community.' The day she and Felicity had received their A-level results, Harriet had mentally told Mr Forbes to go screw himself. With A grades in maths, advanced maths, physics and a B in chemistry – that B had always niggled – she was all set for Durham, where she had no intention of being bullied into anything she didn't want to do.

That was the summer she'd ended up in hospital. It was the night she and Felicity had wanted to go on a midnight picnic and listen to the nightingales singing. Their parents, not liking the idea of two young girls wandering the fields in the middle of the night on their own, had said they could only go if Dominic and Miles went with them. The night was warm and oppressively muggy, and knowing that she had to be careful, Harriet had double-checked her pocket for her inhaler before they set off. The minute Maple Drive was behind them, Dominic produced a bottle of vodka and proceeded to pass it round. By the time they'd scrabbled through the brambles and made it to the nightingale field, they were all pretty drunk. Harriet was so drunk it was some time before she realised that she was having a full-blown asthma attack, and when she couldn't find her inhaler – it must have dropped out of her pocket on the towpath – Dominic had staggered over and told her not to worry. 'I know what to do,' he'd claimed. 'I'll give you the kiss of life.' It showed the measure of how drunk and desperately ill she was that she believed it might work. But instead of kissing her, he'd been sick on her. Miles, probably the least drunk of them, had somehow got her home safely. She was so near to collapsing that he'd had to carry her for the last hundred yards. Her mother had taken one look at her and called an ambulance. Meanwhile, her father had gone in search of Felicity and Dominic. She spent two days in hospital, followed by another two in bed at home. All of them, except for Dominic, who was beyond his parents' control now, were grounded for the rest of the summer.

Sitting in front of Carrie's form teacher, Harriet had a horrible sense of déjà vu. Carrie, she was being told, was going to have to make a bigger effort to join in more. 'Carrie's a bright girl and we'd love to see her really blossom,' Mrs Kennedy explained. 'But she has to under-stand that school isn't simply about sitting in front of the blackboard or reading books all day.'

'Is that the latest government thinking on education?'

Ignoring the question, the woman ploughed on warily. 'I'll give you an example of what I mean. I'd planned a nature trail round the school field, giving the children the chance to learn about the variety of trees right here on their doorstep. We were going to collect leaves and bring them back to the classroom to make a collage. But Carrie said she'd already done that at home and couldn't she stay behind and read a book.'

Atta girl! thought Harriet proudly. 'And you have a problem with that? I'd say her request was utterly logical and shows a level of maturity a lot of other children could learn from. What book was she so keen to read?'

'I'm sorry?'

'I asked what book was she so keen to lose herself in.'

'I've no idea.'

'You didn't think to ask?'

'The point I was trying to—'

But Harriet had stopped listening. What did any of it matter? Carrie was the person she was, and no amount of squeezing round pegs into square holes was going to change the poor girl. Whether this school or any other school approved of it, Carrie was destined to be an independent thinker who would never truly conform, and Harriet would be damned if she'd sit back and let anyone try knocking it out of her.

When the teacher had finished talking, Harriet said, 'So, what you're saying is that Carrie has consistently come top in every subject, but you'd like more from her if she's to become a model pupil?' She stood up and held out her hand. 'Goodnight, Mrs Kennedy, it's been most enlightening.'

If only, she thought angrily, as she walked away. Seeing the headmistress coming towards her with a group of parents in tow, Harriet let out a sigh of irritation. What now?

'Miss Swift, let me introduce some of the other parents from Carrie's class. Rebecca's parents, Mr and Mrs Simpson, and Emily's mother and father, Mr and Mrs Woodward.'

After a round of handshaking, the headmistress excused herself and drifted away. One of the women, Harriet couldn't remember who it was, said, 'We keep hearing from Rebecca how clever Carrie is. We just wish Rebecca would show more interest in her school work.'

'Yes,' agreed the other mother, 'Emily's the same. All she wants to do is watch DVDs, or mess about with her Game Boy or her PlayStation.'

Harriet didn't know what to say. She'd never played this game before. What were the rules? Did one agree with them and say that yes, actually, my niece is brighter than your children, or did one deny all knowledge of ever seeing the child go near a book? She was saved from answering by Emily's mother saying, 'Perhaps we could get the three girls together sometime.'

'That would be lovely,' Harriet said quickly, keen to scotch any more attempts at polite chit-chat. The whole thing was too tedious for words. 'I'll let Carrie know.'

She had started to inch away from them when one of the fathers said, 'We were thinking of going for a drink when we're finished here. You're more than welcome to join us.' He turned to the others, as though checking this was okay with them. They all nodded and smiled.

Oh, my God, she thought. They're serious. They really want me to be in their gang. Her heart sank. Was this it, then? Being Carrie and Joel's guardian meant that she had a part to play herself when it came to oiling the wheels of their social lives? In fact, there was probably an inbuilt expectation that their combined social lives would fully interact. The thought appalled her. Would she have any time for herself? And was this what had driven Felicity to despair and her affair with Miles – the scary realisation that parenthood swallows you up whole?

'I'm sorry,' she said, tightening the scarf around her neck, 'but I have to get going. I promised I'd be home in time to read to Carrie and Joel before they went to sleep.'

She hurried away, not daring to look back for fear of catching a look of pure hatred in their eyes — there she goes, the perfect parent putting us to shame.

Little did they know that the real reason she wanted to get home, other than to read to the children, was to have a long soak in the bath before seeing Will.

When she'd called him at lunchtime, common sense had

very nearly asserted itself and she'd been all set to stand firm and tell him the night before had been a one-off. But the sound of his voice had dredged up the insatiable monster within and her body had ached for his touch. Before she knew what she was doing, she was arranging to see him that night.

Will had just finished changing the sheets on the bed when he heard the doorbell. Giving the room a final once over, he stuffed the dirty bedlinen into the wardrobe and hurried downstairs. His mouth was dry at the prospect of another night with Harriet. He'd spent the best part of the day anticipating her arrival, fantasising that she might turn up on his doorstep in nothing but an overcoat. Oh, and her beret, of course. He'd confided in Marty at the pub about Harriet, and his friend had looked at him enviously.

'Bloody hell, Will! How do you do it? All I get is a doctor in rubber gloves fondling me while you get a nubile thirty-two-year-old. Life just isn't fair.' The only news Marty had following his appointment with the consultant was that he was now lined up for some tests. It was progress, if nothing else.

Pausing briefly to check his appearance in the hall mirror – careful to ignore the middle-aged bloke who stared back at him – Will pulled open the front door with a flourish, then dropped his arms in disappointment when he saw it wasn't Harriet standing on the doorstep. It was Gemma and Suzie.

'Hi Dad,' they said in tuneful synchronisation. 'We thought we'd surprise you.'

'You have. Believe me.' He looked over the top of their heads, across the road to number twenty. Thank goodness there was no sign of Harriet yet.

'What's wrong, Dad? Aren't you going to let us in?'

'Yeah, get a move on; it's freezing out here.'

He ushered them in. 'What's brought this on?' he said, taking them through to the sitting room. Too late he realised it was set for an evening of seduction – a bottle of wine and two glasses on the coffee table, a few strategically placed candles and just the one lamp glowing softly in the corner.

Gemma took one look at the room and said, 'Dad! What are you *like*!' She then howled with laughter.

'Had we better go?' asked Suzie with a smile. At least one of his daughters was sensitive to his predicament.

'Had we funky-monkey!' roared Gemma. 'I want to see who she is. Anyone we know, Dad?'

'I doubt it. She's just a friend.'

Glancing meaningfully round the room, Gemma said, 'Yeah, right.'

The ring at the doorbell could not have been better timed. Marty's wished this on me, thought Will, as he went out to the hall. Either that or I'm dreaming I'm in a bedroom farce and any minute my trousers will fall down. With a further bolt of horror, he remembered his fantasy of Harriet turning up in nothing but a coat and beret. It would be just his luck . . .

He opened the door cautiously: it was Harriet, fully dressed. He explained the situation. 'Just say hello to them and then they'll be on their way.'

'I could come back later, if you want.' She was already edging away.

'No!' he said, extending a hand and pulling her inside. 'You might change your mind and not come back.' He kissed her briefly. 'God, Harriet, you look and smell gorgeous. What have you done to yourself? You're positively glowing.'

'I've just had a long hot bath.'

He groaned. 'Naked?'

'I generally am when I take a bath.'

'Come on, let's get this over with.'

There was no mistaking the look of surprise on his daughter's faces when he introduced Harriet to them. Within minutes their curiosity was satisfied and they were saying their goodbyes. 'Sorry about that, girls,' he said sheepishly as he showed them out.

'Don't worry, we'll ring next time,' Suzie said.

He kissed them both goodbye and the last comment he heard was from Gemma as she got in Suzie's car. 'I can't wait to tell Mum about this one. How old do you reckon?'

He returned to the sitting room, where Harriet was standing in front of the fire with her back to him. She was still wearing her jacket – the well-worn baseball jacket he'd seen so many times – and observing her from behind, she looked no older than his daughters. He suddenly felt unsure about what he was doing. Don't do this, his head told him. She's too young. But then she turned round and looked at him with her pale, inscrutable blue-grey eyes and he was lost. He went to her and kissed her tenderly, his mouth just grazing her parted lips, his tongue flickering against hers. Her breathing changed in an instant and her hands began loosening his shirt. 'Not so fast,' he said, tilting her head back and kissing her neck, 'let's take it slowly tonight.' He removed her jacket, dropped it to the floor and taking her by the hand, he led her upstairs.

Later, when she was lying across his chest and he was stroking her silky soft hair, he was struck how still she was. A rare moment for her, he surmised. He would have liked to ask what she was thinking, but he didn't want to disturb her; it felt good just lying here with her in his arms. He always got the feeling that she was speed-thinking, her thoughts rattling through her head at lightning speed, like a computer. She'll burn herself out if she's not careful, he mused sadly. One day he'd suggest she slowed down, but not tonight. Tonight was perfect just as it was and he wanted to enjoy it to the full, not go spoiling it by lecturing her.

There was a lot about Harriet he didn't understand, not least the reason why she was here in bed with him, but he was determined to make the most of their time together. Like the song period of the nightingale that she had told him about, he knew this pleasure would be fleeting.

December

In the midst of life we are in death.
Book of Common Prayer

Chapter Forty-Five

A fortnight had passed since Suzie and her sister had shown up unexpectedly at their father's. Before leaving The Navigation that night Suzie had told Gemma that they should phone him to make sure it was convenient, but Gemma had said, 'Give over, he's our dad; of course it'll be convenient.' The reason Gemma had been so eager to see their father was to try and get him on her side with her plan to spend Christmas in Paris with Marcel. Suzie had told her it was wrong and selfish to keep using Dad this way. With her usual bluntness Gemma had said, 'That's rich coming from the girl who wants to move in with him when the baby's born. How do you think that'll work when he wants to bring some woman home?'

Gemma had a point, Suzie could see that. Which was why she was going to tell Dad that she'd changed her mind and decided to stay at home with Mum, just until she'd got herself sorted. Whatever that meant, and however she achieved it. If she thought about the future too much it overwhelmed her and she became depressed. Nana Ruby said it was her hormones playing merry hell with her, and that every pregnant woman went through more ups and downs than a big dipper. Because her grandmother was always so positive, Suzie had taken to spending more and more time with her. It was lovely to be pampered and spoiled by Nana. She had even said that if things got difficult with Mum, there would be room for Suzie and the baby in her tiny bungalow. 'It would be a bit of a squash,' Nana had said, 'but I want you to know there'd always be a welcome for you here.' Her generosity had made Suzie cry. Burrowing her head into her grandmother's shoulder, she'd wished her mother wasn't such a heartless bitch. 'You mustn't think so badly of her,' Nana had said. 'She has a lot on her plate. And there's that husband of hers to keep happy. Relationships are fragile things, especially second-time-around ones. And talking of relationships, I hear from Gemma that your father's seeing someone. What's she like?'

'Her name's Harriet and he says she's just a friend.'

Nana had laughed. 'Same old Will. Dear me, when is he ever going to grow up? Do you like her? Gemma said she's very young.'

'I don't know how old she is for certain; we only met her for a couple of minutes, but she looks about thirty.'

'Pretty?'

'I suppose so. She's got this intense, serious look about her. I can't imagine she'd be a laugh a minute. Not really Dad's type, I wouldn't have thought.'

'Perhaps it's time your father took on someone with a bit of substance.'

'Nana! You're not suggesting he should get serious about her, are you?'

'Why not?'

'But the age difference; its—'

'No one's concern but theirs,' Nana had said firmly. 'Would you be very upset if he did marry again?'

'It would take some getting used to,' she'd said guardedly.

That their father might marry for a second time had never been a concern for Suzie or her sister. They were so used to him playing the field, it hadn't occurred to them that he might want to be with someone on a permanent basis.

'Your father would never stop loving you, Suzie,' her grandmother had said. 'He wouldn't ever let anything come between him and you. You two girls have always meant the world to him, and always will. But you have to respect his right to be happy.'

Nana's comments combined with Gemma's criticisms

meant that Suzie knew she couldn't move in with her father. It wouldn't be fair to him. But even so, she didn't want things to change. It had been all right Mum and Steve marrying, but it was different with Dad. Dad had always been there for them. He was theirs. She couldn't help it, but selfishly, she knew that she would be jealous of any woman who meant more to her father than she did.

This conversation, like so many between Suzie and her grandmother, had taken place one evening while Nana Ruby was knitting and Suzie was flicking through a baby magazine trying to picture the baby she would be holding in a matter of weeks. She couldn't believe how huge she was now or how much the baby moved around inside her. There always seemed to be an elbow, a knee, or a fist making its presence felt, usually at night when she was trying to sleep. But no matter how often she was kept awake by the baby, or how uncomfortable she felt, she didn't regret her decision. This baby was going to be the most loved child in the world.

As though to make the days pass quicker, Nana Ruby had made a special countdown calendar to go on her kitchen wall and as each day came and went, her grandmother crossed it off with a red marker pen. Suzie's due date – 15 January – was only six and a half weeks away. The midwife said she wouldn't be surprised if the baby came sooner than that.

Sinead had been in touch to see how she was getting on, but most of the phone conversation had been about her and breaking up with Richard. 'I found out he was seeing someone else behind my back,' she told Suzie. 'Can you believe it? Everyone says I'm better off without him and that they can't understand what I saw in him in the first place. I'm okay now, but I wasn't when I found out. I went a bit loopy, if I'm honest. Don't laugh, but I got very drunk and threw a brick through his car window. The girl he'd been seeing, and is still seeing, is a right stuck-up bitch. She comes from somewhere near you; Rochdale, I think.' This was a typical piece of Sinead geography – having grown up in Kent she heaped anywhere north of Birmingham into one enormous neighbourhood.

The conversation proved to Suzie that she'd been right to keep her silence about Richard. It proved there would have been no point in telling Richard that he'd got her pregnant; he was not the kind of boy who would have stood by her. That much was obvious.

Sitting in her father's office – he was out for the afternoon – Suzie looked up from the *Miller's Guide* Dad had suggested she should study, and watched a woman inspect a large jug and bowl on a pine dressing table. According to Dad and Jarvis, you had to watch every customer like a hawk; no one was above suspicion when it came to stuff being nicked. There were cameras on each floor of the Emporium, and alarms fitted to the cabinets that contained the more expensive items such as silverware and Jarvis's precious Royal Worcester china.

When the woman left empty-handed Suzie decided it was time for a packet of crisps and a Cuppa Soup. Waiting for the kettle to boil, she opened the box of Christmas decorations her father had asked her to inspect. 'Throw out anything you think is past its sell-by date and use some money from the petty-cash box to buy some replacements,' he'd said. 'But don't go mad. I don't want the place looking like a tart's boudoir.'

It was good working for Dad. She liked it that he trusted her. It gave her a sense of responsibility. Something, as her mother had told her, she was going to have to get used to.

Will was at the hospital waiting for news about Marty. His friend had been in surgery for nearly two hours now and Will had drunk so many cups of black coffee from the shop in the private wing of the hospital, his head was buzzing. Marty had told him not to be so stupid, that he didn't need anyone hanging around when he came to after the operation, but Will had told him to shut up. 'I may well be the last person on earth you want to see, but get used to the idea, because I'll be grinning from ear to ear knowing you're in such pain.'

'Bastard.'

From what Marty had told him, the operation was a relatively straightforward procedure, but nothing would convince Will that this was the case. Marty had been diagnosed as having a malignant tumour, and the only way forward, as Marty had put it, was to submit to the knife and be 'one man down'. 'Just think,' he'd said, 'I might be able to sing falsetto in the future.'

Apparently, only by resorting to surgery could testicular cancer be confirmed or discounted. It was bloody drastic stuff and Will had nothing but admiration for his friend's upbeat outlook. 'There's no other way to be,' Marty had told him.

Will didn't know what he'd do if he had to face a worse-case scenario – if Marty did have cancer and nothing could be done. To lose his oldest and closest friend would be like having both his arms ripped off. They'd been through so much together. He tried to remind himself of the statistics involved. The cure rate for early testicular cancer was ninety-five to a hundred per cent. For advanced cancer, when drugs and radiotherapy had to be thrown into the mix, the numbers were still good: eighty to ninety per cent. It could be beaten. That was the thought he had to hang on to.

Somewhere further down the corridor, he could hear some nurses singing along to 'Do They Know it's Christmas?' on the radio. How did they stay so jolly?

He took out his mobile phone, wanting to speak to someone who would take his mind off Marty. But remembering mobiles were banned, he went to find the nearest payphone and tapped in Harriet's number. Disappointingly, all he got was her endearingly prim, self-conscious recorded voice telling him to leave a message. The first time he'd got her recorded voice he'd left her an obscene message saying what he'd like to do with Miss Prim Knickers. He often teased her that she was at her

379

sexiest when she least realised it. It was the simple things that got to him; the way she wore her cuffs so long they dangled past her hands, or the way she sat on the worktop in the kitchen, her legs swinging. Then there was the way she buttoned her jacket right up to her chin and shook out her hair. When she did that, he couldn't help but undo every button and start removing the rest of her clothes to get at her slim, fluid body. She would look at him in that measured way she had and say, 'But I was just going.'

'There's been a change of plan.'

She never tried to stop him, and not once had she ever complained that all he thought about was sex – a complaint that had been levelled at him on several occasions during his marriage.

He didn't know how long this honeymoon period would go on for, but he'd come to the conclusion that it wouldn't be him who ended it. He enjoyed having her in his life. Although, to be precise, it wasn't so much his life as his bed she was in. Last night, when they were lying exhausted and slick with sweat in each other's arms, he'd propped himself up onto an elbow, and traced a finger between her small pert breasts. 'Let's go out on Friday night.'

'I'd rather be here in bed with you.'

'But I want to take you out for a special dinner, seeing as I wasn't able to help you celebrate your birthday in style.'

'You did. When I got back from Dublin you gave me a present and a . . . now what was the phrase you used? Ah, yes, a right seeing to.'

Smiling, he'd said, 'You young girls, you take all the romance out of a thing, don't you?'

'It's you men. You've taught us all you know.'

'Good, so behave yourself and let me take you somewhere romantic for dinner.'

With a movement that caught him off guard, she pushed him onto his back. 'I'll think about it. But not Friday night. I have to work late.' Then pulling the duvet up over their heads, she slowly slid down his body and the last thing on his mind was going out for dinner.

One of the things he liked most about her was that she had no inclination to change him. She wasn't interested in reorganising his kitchen or tidying up the bathroom like so many women had tried before. A woman he'd gone out with last year had kept on at him to resume his former life as a lawyer. When he'd told Harriet this, she'd said, 'People should learn to mind their own business. We are who we are.' She was refreshingly pragmatic, but at the same time very private. However, he was getting better at reading her, especially when they were in bed. He loved the way he could so easily penetrate that tough exterior of hers. 'Aha, the formidable woman melts in my hands,' he'd teased her one night. She'd given him her scariest wrath-and-brimstone look and refused to accept that she was formidable. To his surprise, she had seemed genuinely hurt by his comment and he took care never to say anything like it again.

An elderly couple walked towards him, the man's arm resting protectively on the woman's shoulder, and Will stepped back to let them pass. Long after they'd disappeared around the corner he was still standing in the same spot, lost in thought. He was thinking the inconceivable – how he wanted to be an all-out couple with Harriet. Since they'd got it together the only time they'd gone anywhere was to the Jools Holland concert in Manchester and to take another look at her house. Other than that, all they'd done was have sex. He had absolutely no complaints on that score – what man would? – but he wanted to do the whole going-out thing with her. He wanted her to meet his mother. Marty too. He wanted her fully in his life.

And that, he suspected, would be his downfall.

Marty was wheeled back to his room a short while later, still groggy from the anaesthetic, but sufficiently awake to say to Will, 'What, no flowers?'

'Don't you dare go all Barbra Streisand on me.'

Will was advised by the doctor to stay for no more than a

few minutes, and after learning that there would be no instant diagnosis, he left Marty to sleep.

He tried ringing Harriet again in the car on the way back to the shop, and this time she answered. 'Sorry I missed you,' she said. 'I was in a meeting. How's Marty?'

'Sleeping soundly.'

'Any news?'

'No. It'll be a few days before they get the results.'

'How frustrating.'

'Don't suppose you'd like to come over and cheer me up tonight?'

'I think I could manage that. How does eight-thirty sound?'

'Like music to my ears.'

Carrie listened to Harriet moving about in her bedroom. She was getting ready to go out. And Carrie knew where. She was going to see Will. She saw him nearly every night. Carrie knew because she'd watched her aunt through the gap in the curtains. One night, when it was very late and she'd got up to go to the toilet, she'd actually seen Will kiss Harriet when she was leaving his house. But the funny thing was Harriet was acting as if it was a big secret. Carrie had asked her if Will was her boyfriend and Harriet had told her not to be so silly, that he was only a friend.

'Like Miles?' Carrie had asked.

'I suppose so.'

But Carrie knew her aunt was lying. Friends didn't kiss the way she'd seen Will kissing her. He'd done it the way she'd seen people doing it on the telly; arms and bodies pushed together.

Carrie had given up wanting Harriet to marry Miles. She didn't mind because Will was just as nice and maybe Harriet would marry him. Maybe when they moved into the new house, Will would move in with them. He'd be able to help with all those jobs Harriet wouldn't have time to do and Granddad was too old and grumpy to help with. Like putting up shelves and making wardrobes. She could remember a day, a long time ago, when Mum and Dad argued about a wardrobe they had bought and were trying to make. In the end, Dad had thrown a load of screws on the floor and shouted at Mum that seeing as she was so good at screwing things, she could do it herself. He'd sworn as well and had gone outside to sit in the garden, even though it was raining.

Grown-ups were peculiar, Carrie decided. They were always telling children to tell the truth and not to use bad language, but they did it all the time. At school, Emily and Rebecca said their parents were the same. They also said they didn't like their parents, and sometimes wished they were dead. Emily had then said she was sorry for saying that, that she didn't really mean it. 'What's it like not having your parents around any more?' she'd asked. 'And did they really die in a car crash?'

It was the first time she'd talked to anyone at school about Mum and Dad. Afterwards she felt upset. But also just a little bit happy. It was good talking about them because they felt real again, not just a sad memory.

During lunchbreak Emily had asked if she'd like to go to her house after school on Friday. 'Rebecca's coming too,' Emily had said. 'You could stay the night if you're allowed. Mum said we'll get the Christmas tree down from the loft at the weekend so you could stay and help put the decorations on it. It would be so cool if you could be there too.' Emily and Rebecca were always saying things were cool or mega brill.

Carrie hadn't decided yet whether she wanted to go. If she did, it would be the first night she'd spent away from Harriet and Grandma and Granddad. She didn't know why, but the thought scared her. And what if Joel forgot she wasn't there and crept into her room and found her bed empty? Would he scream the place down like he did that time Harriet was away?

She was still wide awake when she heard Harriet go downstairs and tell Grandma and Granddad that she was going out. Carrie heard her say something about Will having problems with his computer. At the sound of the front door closing, she sat up and knelt at the window beside her bed, parted the curtains just the tiniest bit and watched her aunt through the gap. Across the road, Will's door opened and Harriet went inside. She thought how lucky Will was that Harriet was around. Harriet knew everything about computers. If anyone could sort out a computer it was her.

Chapter Forty-Six

Maxine's day was going from bad to worse. Bad enough that the police had come to the saleroom with allegations of stolen goods passing through it, but now she was stuck in traffic with the prospect of being subjected to one of Will's self-righteousness sessions when she finally got home.

He'd phoned her during the day to ask if he could call round after work. She'd agreed, albeit reluctantly, without asking him what he wanted to discuss. She didn't need to. It would be about Suzie. And probably Gemma and her crazy plan to spend Christmas in Paris. She had absolutely no desire to see Will this evening, or any other evening for that matter. She was sickened by his behaviour. What kind of example did he set for Suzie and Gemma with all his carryings on? Why couldn't he just remarry and have done with it? Why all the women, one after another? And now this latest itch to his groin, a girl not much older than his own daughters, according to Gemma. What was he trying to prove, other than draw attention to what a pathetic, middle-aged laughing stock he'd become?

The house was empty when she let herself in – Steve was down in London attending some conference or other, and the girls had gone to see Nana Ruby. Dumping her bag and briefcase on the Victorian church pew in the hall, she went straight to the kitchen and made herself a gin and tonic. She gulped half of it down straight off, then added more gin and a token splash of tonic. At least with Steve away there was no one to mutter about how much she was drinking. His pious comments were beginning to get on her nerves. Sure she enjoyed a drink; who didn't after a hard day's work? She took the glass upstairs to the bedroom, switched on the lamps, kicked off her shoes and sat down on the bed, not caring that she was crumpling her suit. She was knackered. How good it would be to flop back against the pillows and sleep for the next two hours. She took another gulp of her drink and pushed herself to her feet. A shower was what she needed. She checked her watch. Will wouldn't be here for another thirty-minutes. She just had time.

She stripped off her clothes, for once not caring whether she hung them up or folded them carefully to put away later, and took the remains of her drink with her to the en-suite bathroom. While she waited for the hot water to come through the shower, she looked at herself in the mirror. Nana Ruby was right; she did look tired. Though perhaps wrecked was a more apt description. She sighed, and raising the glass to her reflection, she knocked back the remains of the gin and tonic.

Tying her hair up so it wouldn't get wet – drying and restyling it would be too much bother – she stepped into the shower and stood beneath the scalding jets. Ruby was always telling her she worked too hard and for the first time in her life, Maxine was prepared to admit that this might indeed be true. 'Hard work never killed anyone,' her father used to say. 'It's idleness that finishes people off.' It was this work ethic that had kept him working for as long as he did, and as if to prove his theory, exactly two years after retiring he dropped down dead of a heart attack while reading the newpaper at his golf club. At the rate she was going, Maxine reckoned she'd go the same way, probably before she retired. She consoled herself with the thought that it would be better to go quickly than suffer the humiliation of a gradual decline into incontinence and senility.

Her father's death had been a terrible blow. It had affected her much more deeply than her mother's death eighteen months earlier. Christopher Stone had been a formidable and powerful presence in her life, a force that she admired and respected. He represented everything she thought a man should be: intelligent, ambitious, highly motivated and above all, hardworking. Will used to say that no man could ever live up to the image she had of her father. 'He has chinks in his armour the same as everyone else,' he once said. If he had, Maxine had never seen them. And that was the point. He'd been strong enough to cope with whatever problems he'd encountered. Unlike Will, who had almost gone out of his way to tell the world he couldn't cope. Weakness wasn't a trait she could tolerate in a person and she saw no reason to apologise or justify herself for thinking this.

She poured a dollop of the expensive shower gel Steve had bought for her onto the palms of her hands and massaged it into her shoulders. It was a shame he wasn't here to do it for her, she thought. But then when was the last time he'd taken a shower with her? Weeks ago? Or months? Probably as long as it was since they'd had sex. She was neglecting him, she knew, but it was only while she was getting the new saleroom knocked into shape and fully under the umbrella of Stone's. Once that was done, she would make amends. She would clear a space in her diary so they could go away. With a newborn baby in the house, they would certainly need to make some time and space for themselves. Steve was being remarkably good about the forthcoming upheaval to the household and their lives. He'd even joked in bed one night that it wasn't too late for them to have a baby of their own. At least, she certainly hoped he'd been joking!

Out of the shower she wrapped a towel around her and looked again at her reflection in the mirror. She pulled at the skin beneath her eyes, imagining a fresher, perkier face. She'd considered cosmetic surgery before, in a desultory, off-hand way over a drink with friends, but now she was beginning to view it as an inevitable necessity rather than an extravagant indulgence. What wouldn't she give to be young like Suzie and Gemma? And how little they appreciated what they had. Not just their youth, but everything she'd ever given them. She'd worked damned hard to give them the kind of lifestyle they had and what thanks did she get? Bugger all! She slapped her hand down sharply on the surface, but cursed aloud when she saw her empty gin and tonic tumbler go flying. It slipped off the surface and dropped to the tiled marble floor with a crash, scattering glass. Instinctively she stepped back but it was the wrong thing to do. She let out a yelp of pain and bent down to see a piece of glass protruding from the heel of her foot. Her stomach turned at the grizzly sight and, steeling herself, she pulled out the shard of glass just as the doorbell rang.

Will. Damn him for being early. This was not how she wanted him to see her.

Grabbing some toilet paper, she wrapped it around her foot, but by the time she'd limped downstairs, the blood had seeped through and the pain had started.

'Don't even think about making a wisecrack,' she told him when she opened the door. 'Do that and I'll grind up the glass that I broke and feed it to you.'

'Anything I can do?'

'Yes. You can make me another gin and tonic while I get dressed.'

He looked at her foot doubtfully. 'You shouldn't be doing anything until we've put a proper dressing on that. Here, lean on me. Let's go into the kitchen so I can take a good look at it. From the amount of blood there, I reckon you might need stitches.'

'Rubbish.' Even so, she allowed him to help her into the kitchen. She sat in the nearest chair and watched him take off his leather jacket then kneel at her feet and inspect the damage: blood immediately began to drip onto the floor. She knew he'd never had a strong stomach, and said 'You're not going to be a wimp and faint on me, are you?'

'I wouldn't dare. Where do you keep the first-aid box?'

'Upstairs in the airing cupboard. Third door on the left on the landing.'

He was back within seconds. The pain had started to build now and she winced when he took her foot in his hands and mopped up the blood with a wad of cotton wool. 'I really think you need stitches,' he said, reaching for another wad.

'Since when did you become a doctor?'

He looked up. 'Maxine, I'm trying to help. Okay? Where's Steve? Do you want me to ring him so that he can take you to the hospital?'

She shook her head. 'He's down in London.'

'And the girls?'

'At your mother's.'

'So all you've got is me. What's it to be? Are you going to let me help you? Or would you rather bleed to death?'

'Couldn't we just bandage it up and see how it goes?'

He sighed. 'You always did get your own way, didn't you?'

Relieved he wasn't going to make her sit for hours in an overcrowded casualty department, she smiled and said, 'My father's daughter, you used to say.'

He didn't say anything else until he'd put a dressing on the wound and had bandaged it carefully, his hands gentle yet sure. 'How does that feel?' he asked.

'You've made a good job of it, Will. Quite the craftsman. I'll go and get some clothes on while you make me that drink.'

'Are you sure you can manage the stairs?'

Holding the towel firmly around her body, she stood up to prove she was capable of climbing Everest, never mind the stairs, but flinched when she put just the slightest amount of weight on the bandaged foot.

'Why don't I find you something to wear and you change down here?' he said.

She gave in. 'My bathrobe's hanging on the back of the bedroom door. First on the right at the top of the landing.'

Once she was wrapped in her bathrobe and Will had made her a drink, she allowed him to help her through to the sitting room. While she made herself comfortable on the sofa, he drew the curtains and switched on the lamps. She felt both annoyed and grateful that he was here, and knew she should make more of thanking him, but she couldn't bring herself to do it. Something about him rankled more than usual. The confident ease with which he was moving about her home irritated her, as did his appearance. He looked too damned well. Younger too. There didn't seem to be an ounce of tiredness in his body, which was just as slim as it had always been. It pained her to admit it, but he looked good. Bloody good, in fact. Was that what sex with a young girl did to a man? Rejuvenated him? There again, he didn't have the kind of responsibilities she had. Bitterness darkened her mood. Will had only ever played at life, opting out of anything that got too challenging.

He sat in the chair nearest her and she raised her glass to him. 'Sure you won't join me?' she asked.

'Better not. I'm driving. How's the foot doing?'

'It'll be fine. Why don't we get on with why you're here? I'm surprised you can spare the time,' she added tartly.

'Meaning?'

She shrugged. 'Meaning I don't want to keep you unnecessarily.'

'Don't start, Maxine. You know perfectly well I've always got time when it comes to the girls.'

She sniggered. 'That's what I hear. It used to be women, but apparently now it's young girls you're chasing.'

He pushed a hand through his hair and leaned forward. She could see he was angry; could see it in his mouth, the way it hardened. She suddenly remembered how it used to feel to be kissed by him, and looked away.

'My private life is exactly that,' he said coolly. 'Private.'

'Then perhaps you shouldn't flaunt your young girlfriend so blatantly in front of our children.'

'I resent that. I have never flaunted any relationship I've had in front of Gemma and Suzie.'

'Well, you did this time! Have you any idea how much enjoyment Gemma gets out of rubbing my nose in it?'

'She can only do that if it's something you're bothered about. Who I go out with should have nothing to do with you. Do I need to remind you that you're married to Steve, not me?'

'Oh, please, I couldn't give a damn who you're sleeping with, but what I am bothered about is Gemma's need to ram it down my throat.'

He took a moment before saying, 'I'm sorry, but that's between you and Gemma. Have you tried talking to her about it?'

Maxine took a long swallow of gin, annoyed at the way her words had come out. She hadn't meant for that to happen. She didn't want Will to know that she resented growing older, or that she hated the evidence before her eyes that Will was clearly still on top of his game, while she was sliding rapidly into middle age. Pulling herself back to his question, she said, 'What do you think? She only ever speaks to me when she wants something. As with this proposed trip to Paris. Presumably she's wrapped you round her little finger and you've said she can go.'

'Wrong. I told her you and I would have to discuss it, which is why I'm here. What do you really think about her going?'

'She's not going,' Maxine said with finality. 'For the simple reason I'm not having another daughter coming home pregnant.'

Will let out his breath and shook his head. 'You don't think that's being too simplistic? It's not a just-add-water-and-stir situation. She could be here in Maywood and get pregnant just as easily.'

'Not under my roof, she won't.'

'She's eighteen next year; you can't treat her as a child. Or as a prisoner.'

'Don't you dare lecture me, Will. I know exactly how old my children are and what's best for them.'

'*Our* children, Maxine. They're our combined responsi-bility. And for the record, I'm not happy about her going either. It'll be the first Christmas without both of the children around and it feels like a milestone too far and too soon. Mum would be disappointed not to see her, too. Why don't we compromise and say she can go for New Year?' Smiling, he added, 'We could even give her a joint pep talk about the birds and bees, especially those French ones. Just for the fun of making her squirm, of course.'

Maxine drained her glass and looked at Will. How did he do it? How did he always manage to make her feel so shitty? 'Maybe,' she demurred. 'But she'd better get her act together meanwhile. She has mock exams in January.'

'She's on the ball with everything as far as I can see. A bit of fun will be just what she needs.' He relaxed into his chair and stretched his legs out in front of him. 'So how are things between you and Suzie?'

Determined not to lose any more ground to him, Maxine said, 'We're getting there. I'm organising for a decorator to turn the spare room into a nursery. I haven't told her yet.'

Will smiled. 'That's great. She'll be delighted, and if she's not too tired, she could help with some of it. I remember you being a whirlwind of activity in the last month of pregnancy. Do you remember when you were expecting Gemma and I woke up in the middle of the night and found you downstairs stripping the wood-chip off the walls in the hall?'

Maxine cast her mind back and recalled her heavily pregnant self with a scraper in one hand and a cup of hot chocolate in the other. 'I'd forgotten about that,' she said faintly. 'How do you remember so much?'

'You used to say I had a typical nitpicking lawyer's brain. That I absorbed and stored away every useless detail I came across.'

She swallowed the last mouthful of gin and stared into the bottom of the glass as though searching it for more memories from the past. I'm drunk, she thought. When she looked up, Will was on his feet. He was going. She suddenly didn't want to be alone. Even through the haze of alcohol, she could feel the pain throbbing in her foot. She was also hungry. She had missed lunch because she'd had to talk to those two wretched police officers. She thought how convenient it would be if Will was to stay and make her something to eat. But the thought of asking him for help was out of the question. However, in her experience there was a sure-fire way to get a man to do what you wanted: you just tapped into their basic urges and they were putty in your hands. She loosened the belt on her bathrobe and reached forward to put her empty glass on the table, knowing that the action would reveal her shoulder and a generous amount of cleavage. Will had always liked her breasts. She used to like it when he'd come up behind her and gently take them in his hands while kissing the nape of her neck. Her head swam at the memory, remembering how explosive they'd been in bed together. By comparison, Steve was good . . . but only good.

'It's okay,' she heard Will saying. 'You stay there, I'll see myself out.'

'Do you have to go so soon?' she asked, sinking back into the cushions and smiling up at him; the bathrobe had parted yet more. She caught his glance skating over her body and congratulated herself on not having lost her old seductive powers. How pathetically simple men were! She could see the hesitancy in him. Another push and she'd have him just where she wanted.

'I'm . . . I'm afraid I can't stay,' he said.

'Really? Are you sure I can't tempt you?'

'Err . . . no, I'm . . . I'm meeting someone.'

'Can't you ring and put them off? I thought we could have something to eat. Or maybe we could . . .' She lowered her gaze coyly, letting the suggestion hang in the air.

'Sorry, he said more firmly, edging away. 'I can't. I'm taking Harriet out for dinner.'

His words slapped her hard. Of course! His latest girlfriend. The latest groin itch. It was only then that she registered he was better dressed than usual. In place of the regulation faded denim was a properly ironed shirt, black and white striped, open-necked, and worn casually over smart black jeans. He smelled good as well. Why hadn't she noticed that before? Not knowing who was the bigger fool,

Will for deluding himself that he could still behave like a twenty-year-old, or the fool of a girl he was bonking, she said, 'Well, then, don't let me keep you.'

When he'd shut the door behind him, she realised it was she who was the biggest fool of all. How could she have even thought of coming on to him like that?

She blamed it on the gin. Steve was right; she really ought to cut down.

Chapter Forty-Seven

Will drove out of Maywood in a near state of shock. He didn't know what was scarier: a furious Maxine venting her spleen, or a tipsy Maxine coming on to him. What had got into her? Okay, she'd obviously had a bit to drink and was in a degree of pain, but to try that old number on him . . . why? What had she thought he would do? Climb into bed with her for old times' sake? No offence, but he'd sooner chew his leg off! One thing was for sure, he didn't fancy being around when she sobered up and realised what she'd done.

To his surprise, though, he felt sorry for her. Was she lonely? Was that it? Was marriage to PC Plod turning out to be a disappointment? Or had she just been playing with him? Seeing if he'd be tempted, only then to humiliate him if he did react.

But whatever had got into Maxine, it wasn't his business. What was his business this evening was Harriet. He'd finally pinned her down – quite literally while in bed – and got her to agree to him taking her out for dinner. 'Most women would be cross if they didn't get taken out,' he'd said.

'Nice try, but I'm not most women,' she'd replied.

'Funnily enough, I sussed that the first time I met you.'

'Yeah right, that was when you thought I was a boy.'

'Crikey! You mean you're not?'

'If it makes you feel better I do have a reputation for being an honorary bloke.'

He'd placed a hand on her breast and ribcage and once more marvelled at the fragility of her body: there seemed so little of it. It was only without her clothes on that he appreciated just how insubstantial she was. Except Harriet was one of the most substantial women he knew.

'You don't eat enough,' he'd said that same night in bed, taking hold of one of her slender wrists and easily wrapping his fingers around it.

'I'll have you know I eat four times my own bodyweight every day. I just burn it off faster than anyone else.'

'That's because you're usually vibrating at the speed of light.'

'I find it difficult to relax, that's all.'

'That's not good.'

'It's just my make-up; my metabolism.'

'It's still not good.'

'Well, you can't talk. You're hardly beefcake material.' She'd prodded his stomach, which even the middle-aged bloke in the mirror had to admit was in pretty good shape. No love handles for him!

'Hey, are you calling me weedy?'

Laughing, she'd said, 'You can dish it out but you can't take it yourself, can you?'

Comparing Harriet's elfin proportions to those of the previous women he'd been attracted to, Will wondered whether he'd undergone some kind of conversion. Perhaps he had, without knowing it, grown out of the stereotyped Hollywood version of glorified womanhood – the woman who didn't exist, in other words.

Did it also mean that he was looking for a relationship that was more real and more lasting than anything he had previously experienced?

But with Harriet? Surely not. How could that ever work?

Joel hovered anxiously outside Harriet's bedroom door, peering in at her as she got ready to go out. Everyone was going out. Except for him. Oh, and Granddad, he was staying in. Grandma was going out with her friend Dora, Harriet was going out with Will, and Carrie had already gone to Emily's. Last night Carrie had told him to be good while she was away, and not to have any bad dreams. 'You mustn't spoil it for everyone,' she'd said. She made it sound like he did it deliberately. He didn't. And anyway, he hadn't had any nightmares for ages. But maybe tonight he would. He wished Harriet wasn't going out. He always felt better in bed knowing she was downstairs watching the telly or in her bedroom working on her computer. She was different from Mummy, but reminded him of her. If he couldn't find his reading book to take into school, or his PE bag, she always seemed to know where to look. That's what Mummy had been like.

Carrie said that she thought Harriet and Will would get married. But then she'd said that about Harriet and Miles. It was difficult to keep up with Carrie; she was always changing her mind. Now she thought school was great and that they would stay there for ever, even when they moved to their new house. He liked the idea of living in that nice little cottage, but what he wasn't sure about was what would happen after school. Carrie and Harriet had explained it to him, but he'd forgotten. Would Grandma and Granddad come for them and take them to their new home, or would they bring them back here? Where would they have their tea? And something else he wasn't sure about, all those boxes he'd have to put his things into when they moved – what if he forgot something? What if the boxes got lost? What if—

'Joel, is that you?'

Hearing Harriet's voice, he nudged open the door and went inside. He'd ask her about the boxes. She'd know if his toys and books would be safe.

'What were you doing out there, Joel? Were you spying on me?'

She was smiling as she said this, but feeling silly, he blushed and looked down at his slippers – they were too small for him and his toes were pushing through the ends. He needed new ones, but Carrie had told him he shouldn't make a fuss about them, because Harriet would need all her money to buy their new house. 'Are we very poor?' he'd asked Carrie.

'Yes,' she'd said. 'Orphans are always poor.'

He went and sat on Harriet's bed and watched her as she brushed her hair. She had nice hair. Long and straight like Mummy's. He wondered if she would let him touch it.

'You're very quiet, Joel. You okay?'

She was staring at him in the reflection of the mirror above her desk. He nodded, kicked off his slippers and wriggled his toes. 'Harriet?'

'Yes?'

'You know when we move?'

'Yes?'

'Do you think everything will be safe?'

She turned round to look at him. 'Safe from what exactly?'

'From being lost.'

She put the brush down and came and knelt on the floor in front of him. 'Joel, I promise you, nothing will get lost in the move. I'll mark all the packing boxes with what's inside and you can watch every single one of them being loaded onto the van. Then at the other end, you can help me put them into your bedroom. How does that sound?'

He instantly felt better. He put his arms around her neck and hugged her tight. She smelled lovely. Sort of clean and like a big bunch of flowers. Once more he was reminded of his mother. When he let go of her, he plucked up the courage to ask if he could brush her hair.

For a moment she looked as if she didn't understand him, and he felt silly again. But then she smiled. 'What a strange thing to ask,' she said. 'But if you really want to, go ahead.'

He bounced off the bed and fetched the brush. 'I used to do this for Mummy.'

'Really?'

'Yes. She wouldn't let anyone else do it. Only me. Not Daddy. Not Carrie. Only me. Sometimes when she was upset, she asked me to brush her hair because it made her feel happy.'

'Was she often upset?'

'Just sometimes. Am I doing it right?'
'You're doing it brilliantly.'

Harriet opened the door to Will with mixed feelings. His calling for her made the evening seem too much like a date. When she saw how smartly dressed he was, the feeling was reinforced. 'Don't leave the poor man hanging about on the doorstep,' her mother said, coming down the stairs in a calf-length dress and high heels, a tiny evening bag swinging from her wrist. Since Harriet had arrived home from work, her mother's behaviour had struck her as being nothing short of frisky girlishness. But there again, it was a long time since Eileen had enjoyed a night out – especially a dinner dance – so maybe that explained the excitement. Apparently there had been a cancellation on Dora's carefully arranged table of guests and she'd asked Eileen to make up the numbers. Harriet hoped her mother wouldn't overdo it.

Will said, 'Wow, Eileen! Where are you off to, looking like a million dollars?'

Harriet bit back a smile as Eileen blushed and laughed, clearly enjoying the flattery. 'Just out with Dora. You don't think this dress is pushing the bounds of credibility? I treated myself to something new, and now I'm beginning to regret the colour.'

'It suits you perfectly. You look terrific.'

Harriet listened to the pair of them in amusement. Was this really her mother talking to a man, other than Dad, about her appearance? Mind you, when was the last time Dad paid Mum such a generous compliment? Half listening to Eileen asking how Marty was – he was now at home resting – she looked round the door of the sitting room and saw her father slumped morosely in front of the television, a corny Christmas advert playing. Perhaps Will was right and Dad *was* depressed. If so, he needed help. But it was difficult at times to feel like helping him, or to feel sympathetic when he didn't seem to want to help himself. Occasionally he'd look at Harriet with such an expression of indifference that it was all she could do not to shout at him to bloody well pull himself together.

Joel, on the other hand, had all Harriet's sympathy. Whereas Carrie had turned a corner, was making friends at school and bringing home a daily update on her expanding social horizons, Joel seemed ever more isolated and anxious. He was permanently digging around looking for something new to worry about. Harriet wished she could do more to put his mind at rest. There was so much going on inside that young head of his. Worryingly, she suspected that the anxieties he actually expressed represented only the tip of the iceberg. Often she found herself wanting to scoop him up and make everything better for him. She'd known right from the start that he would be the one to get to her but what she hadn't bargained on was the extent of his vulnerability and the ferocious protective streak it brought out in her; a protectiveness she didn't know she was capable of feeling.

His earlier remarks about his mother had been an encouraging sign that he was now prepared to talk more openly about his parents, and Harriet had been pleased by this step in the right direction, but at the same time she'd been saddened by his account of brushing his mother's hair. As a consequence, Harriet now had a disturbing mental picture of Felicity looking in the mirror and holding back the tears while her precious son tried to make her feel better. Was this before or during the affair with Miles?

It was some time since Harriet had seen Miles. The last occasion was when he'd come for lunch and they'd gone for a walk afterwards and she'd been scared he might own up about Felicity. With hindsight it might have been better to have encouraged him to tell her, because at least then it would be over and done with. As it was, the unspoken confession was forcing them apart. Was that what Felicity would have wanted? She didn't think so.

Harriet had insisted she would drive, and after she'd dispensed with Will's attempts to argue with her and was driving away from Maple Drive, he leaned over to kiss her. 'By the way, did I mention you're looking gorgeous?'

'No, you didn't. You were too busy schmoozing my mother. But thank you anyway. You've scrubbed up well yourself.'

He patted the front of his shirt. 'Like your mother's dress, it's new.' He rested a hand on her thigh and gave it a gentle squeeze. 'I had hoped you might wear a skirt. Didn't you know that it's the law when a chap takes his girl out for dinner that she has to show her legs. It's a sexist thing.'

'Yes, and it's the kind of thing that will get you a bloody nose.' Her words were spoken with humour, yet she felt a tightening of anxiety in her stomach. What did Will mean by *when a chap takes his girl out*?

But she knew exactly what he meant and that was what frightened her. Without realising it, she had become hooked on this man. He was generous, amusing and endlessly diverting – he gave her something to think about other than how daunting the future looked when she and the children moved into their new house. And, of course, there was always the sex. The intensity of it was mind-blowing. Not just the act itself, but the anticipation of it – the bittersweet pleasure of waiting for him to get in touch, the constant longing – they were all part of the attraction. Being with him invoked in her a heady desire to lose control. The moment she stepped over his threshold and he took her in his arms, she became another person. A happier and more alive person. She was both appalled and delighted that he could arouse in her such all-consuming passion. As a consequence she had made a frightening discovery; just how powerfully transformative sex could be.

Ironically, she now knew what had driven Felicity to become obsessed with Miles. She was just as obsessed with Will, always thinking of the next time they could be together in bed.

But common sense hadn't abandoned her completely. She knew she wasn't playing fair with Will and that the decent thing to do was to end it. If he was beginning to see her as *his girl* – something she hadn't planned on – she had to act sooner rather than later. He was too nice to use for her own selfish needs. She was extremely fond of him and felt horribly guilty. He was the first man she had truly opened herself to, and yet logic told her they weren't right together. The basis of their relationship was skewed. For a start there was the age gap, but more importantly she despised her motives for wanting to sleep with him in the first place.

Chapter Forty-Eight

All during dinner Harriet kept looking across the table at Will and thinking how much she was going to miss him. He was quite the best thing to have happened to her in a long while, but she mustn't weaken. She couldn't go on using him. She may well have proved Dominic wrong, and metaphorically stuck her fingers up at Spencer, but knowing that she had achieved it at the expense of another person upset her. Each time she resolved to say something, she just couldn't do it. As if to torture herself, she kept recalling some aspect of their lovemaking – the way Will taught her to relax and take things more slowly, to feel the delicious intensity of what they were doing; or the way he could keep her on the edge of climaxing for what felt like an eternity.

She knew also that he was concerned about his friend Marty. What he hadn't told Eileen earlier, probably in deference to her good mood, was that the tumour that had been removed had turned out to be cancerous and Marty was now set on a course of radiotherapy. Could Harriet really add to his problems? Or perhaps she was being arrogant and assuming too much of his feelings for her.

'Hello, anyone at home on planet earth?'

She roused herself from her thoughts. 'I'm sorry; I'm being boring, aren't I?'

He put down his glass of wine and reached across the table, the palm of his hand face up. She looked at the scar that she knew caused him pain every so often and placed her own hand on top of his. His fingers wrapped around hers. 'You okay?' he asked. 'You seem quiet tonight.'

Very slowly she withdrew her hand. It was time for her

reason to rule over her heart. Meeting his concerned gaze, she said: 'Will, I think we need to talk.'

She knew that he was smart enough to recognise that contained within those few words was an unequivocal message. In the hubbub of the busy restaurant he stared back at her, and she saw that he understood.

He surprised her by saying, 'Give me your hand.'

She did as he said and he raised it to his lips and kissed it softly. It was such a tender gesture. 'Please don't say anything else,' he said. 'I was always on borrowed time with you, so let's not have any grim words or grim faces.'

'But Will—'

He pressed her hand to his lips again. 'It's okay. I pride myself on knowing when to bow out gracefully. I guess it was the age difference, wasn't it?'

She nodded. It wasn't the whole truth, but it was kinder to let him think it was.

Shortly after, when he'd paid their bill and they were outside in the car park, he put his arm round her. 'Don't look so glum, Harriet. I had it coming. I should never have tried my luck with such a class act.'

For an aching moment she wished she could turn back the clock. 'I'm not a class act,' she said miserably. 'I'm shallow and—'

He stopped walking abruptly and made her face him by placing his hands on her shoulders. 'Hey,' he said, 'you're about as shallow as the Atlantic. And if I catch you beating yourself up again, I'll have to take steps to put a stop to it.' He then kissed her lightly on the mouth. It was a poignant farewell kiss that made her heart feel heavy. She closed her eyes and kissed him back. *I must be mad,* she thought wretchedly as her body instantly responded to his. *How can I give him up?*

When they drew apart, she made a play of fishing around in her bag for her keys so that he wouldn't see how upset she was. She had just found them when the sound of a mobile rang out in the cold night air. It was Will's.

'Oh, hi, Mum,' he said, shrugging apologetically at

Harriet. She opened the car so they could get in. 'I hear you've got the girls with you this evening. I hope they're behaving themselves and not . . . *What* . . .' There was a long silence while Will didn't speak, just listened. His eyes grew wide and Harriet became concerned. 'I'll be right there,' he said. 'No, second thoughts, I'll go straight to the hospital.'

'What's happened?' Harriet whispered, going round to his side of the car, where he was leaning against the door.

He ignored her and carried on talking to his mother. 'Look, you've done the right thing. Have you tried ringing Maxine? Okay, don't worry about it. I'll try in a minute . . . you just keep everyone as calm as you can. And thanks, Mum you're a star.'

He hung up and let out his breath. 'It's Suzie. She's collapsed. It doesn't sound good.'

'Is it the baby? Is it on its way?'

'I don't know; it's not due until the middle of next month. They've called an ambulance. Any chance you can rush me home so that I can get my car and go to the hospital?'

Opening the car door and pushing him inside, Harriet said, 'No way. You're over the limit. I'll drive you there instead.'

In between trying to reach Maxine – she wasn't responding to her mobile and the answering machine was switched on – and cursing every driver who got in front of them, Will kept replaying what his mother had told him: 'We were just tidying away the supper things when she bent to pick up a fork I'd dropped,' Ruby had said. 'She crumpled, Will. Just like that. She fell to the floor, gave us all a real fright. When she came round, she was obviously in pain. She says she feels like she's been hit on the head with a metal bar. She keeps moaning and clutching her head and she says she can't move. She's been sick, too. Gemma's called an ambulance. I think you'd better get here, Will. I don't like the look of this.'

Will didn't like the sound of it either, but he hadn't said that to his mother. He needed her to be calm to take care of his daughter.

'She must have hit her head when she fainted,' Harriet said when he explained what Ruby had told him. 'It sounds like concussion.'

'But what made her faint in the first place?'

'Perhaps her blood pressure's too high. Or too low. I seem to remember Felicity having problems when she was expecting Joel.'

Thankful for Harriet's clear-headedness, Will relaxed a little. It seemed the obvious answer.

When they arrived at the hospital, she dropped him off at the entrance to the A & E department and went to find somewhere to park. 'I'll catch up with you in a minute,' she said.

It was a while before Will could find someone to talk to inside. It was bedlam; medical staff rushing about the place, rows of seats occupied by people in varying degrees of injury and drunkenness, and somewhere a child crying loudly.

'Has my daughter, Suzie Hart, been admitted?' he asked a harassed woman behind the desk.

After an interminable wait, she shook her head. 'Sorry, there's no one of that name.' A telephone rang and as she picked up the receiver, she gestured for him to take a seat. Frustrated, he moved away; he'd get no more help from her. Not knowing what else he could do, he went back outside and called Gemma's number on his mobile to find out what was going on, assuming that she would be in the ambulance with Suzie.

She answered immediately. 'Dad, it's a bloody nightmare here. The ambulance hasn't sodding well come and Suzie's completely crashed out. We can't wake her. What the hell do we do? Shall we get a neighbour to drive us to the hospital?'

'I'll ring for another ambulance,' he said, hearing the panic in Gemma's voice. 'Hang in there, Gem. It'll be fine.'

But he knew as he put a call through to the emergency services, his hands shaking and his heart pounding, that things were far from fine. He was just putting his phone back in his jacket pocket when Harriet appeared.

'What's the news?' she asked.

'It's a total cock-up! The ambulance hasn't arrived. I've just called for another.' He swallowed. 'Gemma says Suzie's unconscious. They can't wake her. I should have gone there. We could have got her here by now.'

'Let's go inside,' she said. 'You find us a vending machine for some coffee and I'll have a word with someone on the desk.'

'It's no good, I've tried already. They're all so busy.'

'Just find the coffee, Will.'

Harriet explained the situation to the woman on the desk as clearly as she could, describing Suzie's condition, that she was eight months pregnant, that she'd collapsed for no apparent reason, and that it sounded as though she was now in a coma. At no stage had Will mentioned the word coma, but Harriet feared the worst.

Satisfied that she'd done everything she could to prepare for Suzie's arrival, she found Will pushing money into a vending machine. 'They'll be ready for Suzie when she comes,' she told him. 'We just have to wait now.'

He handed her a cup of something that smelled more like chicken soup than coffee. 'But for how long?' he muttered.

Each time there was a new arrival through the main entrance – a disorientated half-awake child carried by a parent, an elderly man in a wheelchair, a young lad in biker gear on a trolley with his neck in a brace – Will's hopes would rise. But it was twenty minutes later, almost midnight, when they heard and saw a rush of movement that had both him and Harriet on their feet. It was the sight of Gemma coming in behind the paramedics that confirmed for Will that it was Suzie on the trolley – her face was partially hidden beneath an oxygen mask. He rushed over but was immediately pushed aside by a whirlwind of activity. Forced to stand back helplessly while Suzie was wheeled away and the paramedics briefed the medical staff, he caught snatches of what was said: 'Coma . . . preceded by vomiting and drifting in and out of consciousness . . . foetal heart beat dropping . . .'

Paralysed with shock, he stared after his daughter. How could this be happening? How could his beloved Suzie be in a coma?

'Dad? She'll be okay, won't she?'

He turned. Gemma was standing next to him and the sight of her pale and dazed face brought him up short. He put his arm round her. 'She'll be fine, love. Once they've got her on the right medication or whatever it is they have to do, she'll be as right as rain.'

'Do you think she's going to lose the baby?'

'Let's hope not. I'm no expert, but it's probably strong enough to be born this early without coming to too much harm.' He led her away from the main entrance to a quieter area beside an artificial Christmas tree, and suddenly remembered his mother. 'Where's Nana Ruby? Didn't she come in the ambulance with you?'

'She's gone to Mum's. I got her a taxi and gave her my key. Mum should be here, Dad.'

Proud of his youngest daughter for her foresight, he gave her another hug. 'Good thinking, Gem.'

'I don't understand why she isn't answering her mobile or phone. What's she doing?'

'I saw her earlier in the evening,' Will explained. 'Before I went out for dinner.' He then told Gemma about Maxine cutting her foot. He didn't go into details about the odd mood her mother had been in when he'd left her. 'She probably decided to have an early night,' he said.

Gemma sighed. 'I just wish I'd learned to drive. If I had, I could have got her here quicker. Nana was upset too that she couldn't do it. Oh, Dad, we both felt so helpless. What if she—?'

Will cut her short. 'Don't even say it. Do you want a drink?'

No sooner had he spoken than he saw Harriet coming over with a plastic cup in her hand. 'I thought you might like this,' she said to Gemma. 'Hot chocolate. With sugar. I can get you one without, if you'd prefer.'

Gemma took the cup. 'No, this'll be fine. Thanks.'

For the next few minutes they stood in a huddle of awkward silence, watching the clock and waiting for news. When a young doctor in a white coat approached them, Will tensed. He could see straight away from the man's face that the news was bad. Suzie must have lost the baby. His heart went out to her.

Chapter Forty-Nine

After a brief round of introductions, the doctor ushered Will through to a room that was as cramped as it was uninviting. There were blinds pulled down over the windows blocking out any views – or perhaps it was to stop anyone looking in. There was a stark central light, chairs lined against the walls and Christmas decorations hanging wearily on a pathetically small tree in the corner. The doctor suggested they sit. He looked tired and much too young to do the job he did. Poor devil, thought Will. He probably hasn't slept in the last forty-eight hours.

'Mr Hart,' the doctor began gently, 'I'm so very sorry to have to tell you this, but you daughter suffered what we think, at this stage, was a ruptured aneurysm, specifically a subarachnoid haemorrhage. We won't know for sure, not until—'

Will's mouth went dry. He tried to swallow but couldn't. 'I'm sorry, could you explain what that is? In simple layman's terms.'

'Of course. It's a type of brain haemorrhage, in which blood from a ruptured blood vessel spreads over the surface of the brain. In your daughter's case it was a severe haemorrhage, which sent her into a coma. We did our best to carry out an emergency caesarean to save the baby, but I'm afraid—'

Will took in the deepening expression of sympathy in the young doctor's face. 'The baby didn't survive, did it?' he said helpfully. 'Does Suzie know?'

A shadow of what looked like awkward confusion passed across the man's face. It made Will's blood turn to ice. 'Mr Hart, I'm afraid that neither the baby nor your daughter survived. Suzie never regained consciousness. I'm so very sorry.'

Will heard the words but it was as if his brain wouldn't compute the information. He blinked hard. 'I . . . I don't understand. Dead? Are you telling me Suzie's *dead*?' Suddenly he was finding it hard to breathe. A convulsive trembling had seized him.

'Would you like someone to sit with you for a while, Mr Hart?'

While his body was caving in, his brain forged on trying to prove the doctor wrong. 'But she can't be dead. There must be some mistake. You're mixing my daughter up with someone else.'

'I'm sorry, Mr Hart—'

Whatever else the doctor had to say, Will was deaf to it. A crashing noise had filled the space between his ears. He slumped forward, his head in his hands. His whole body seemed to have turned inside out and disintegrated. A terrible animal-like sound escaped him and he thought he might pass out. The next thing he knew, Harriet and Gemma were in the room with him. Harriet was trying to hold him, but he was shaking her off. He didn't want anyone to touch him. He looked around for the doctor and saw him standing in the corner talking to Gemma. Tears were streaming down Gemma's face. The doctor's hand was on her shoulder. He knew he should go to her, but he couldn't do it. All he could think of was Suzie. His beloved Suzie.

'Can I see her?' he said to the doctor. 'My daughter. Can I see her? Please.'

'Of course.'

'I want to see her too, Dad.'

'No.' Will's voice was flat. 'I want to do this alone.'

Harriet stood at the door and watched Will walk hesitantly beside the doctor. At one point he almost stumbled and the doctor put a hand to his elbow to support him. As they disappeared beyond the double doors at the far end of the corridor, it was a painful reminder for Harriet of the night Felicity and Jeff had died, when she had accompanied her father to identify the bodies. No parent should ever have to go through this, she thought. Poor Will. He was utterly devoted to his children. How would he ever come to terms with this?

Remembering Gemma, Harriet turned round to see if there was anything she could do to comfort the girl. She sat next to her, but sensed that Gemma wasn't even aware that she was in the room with her. Minutes later, when the sound of raised voices broke the unearthly hush, Gemma's head jerked up and she was instantly on her feet. 'It's Mum,' she said. 'She won't know what's happened. I'll have to tell her.'

Feeling nauseous with impotent shock, Harriet once more found herself standing helplessly in the background. Gemma and her mother embraced, while an older woman, presumably Will's mother, hovered to one side. With a burst of fresh tears, the young girl broke the devastating news.

With tears in her own eyes, and unsure now what part she could play in this horrific drama, Harriet decided to leave. She wouldn't be wanted here.

Chapter Fifty

Eileen and Dora were taking it in turns to cook for Will. Each evening they would leave a plastic food container in his porch with instructions on how to reheat whatever was inside. Harriet kept telling Eileen that he probably wasn't eating any of it, and that there was every chance he would feel patronised by their Meals on Wheels approach. 'It doesn't matter,' Eileen told her, 'at least he knows we care, that we're here for him if he needs us.'

A week had passed since Will's eldest daughter had died and Eileen wished she had the courage to knock on their neighbour's door and tell him just how well she understood the pain of his grief. But Will had made it very clear that he didn't want to talk when Eileen had called over with the first of the food parcels. Most days the curtains stayed shut; his car had moved only once from the drive and that was the day of the funeral. She had arranged for some flowers to be sent to the church in Maywood where the service had been held and had hoped that Harriet, on behalf of the family, would attend. But she hadn't. When Eileen had asked her why not, Harriet's reply had taken her aback. 'I think I'm the last person he'd want there,' she said.

'But you'd been such good friends,' Eileen pressed, keeping to herself that she and Dora had long since suspected that there was more than friendship between Harriet and Will. This suspicion had been backed up by Freda telling Dora that Miles had said much the same thing. She would have liked to probe further, but Eileen knew of old that Harriet wouldn't welcome any intrusion into her private life. Especially as these days, living back at home, she had so little of it. All Eileen could imagine was that there had been a disagreement between them. Probably the night Will's daughter had died.

That was the night Eileen had deliberately gone all-out to deceive her husband. Determined to push Bob as far from her thoughts as possible, she had gone with Dora and Derek to the pre-Christmas dinner dance put on by the Soirée Club, all set to have some fun. Disappointingly, she had been put on a different table from her friend and had found herself sitting between two very different men. The one on her left was about ten years younger than her and totally full of himself – if he was to be believed, he was hardly ever in the country because he was so busy playing golf in the Algarve or Palm Springs. The other man was possibly the dullest person she'd ever met. His only redeeming feature, which kept her entertained for most of the evening, was his hair. She'd heard about hair transplants and she supposed this was what the pasty-faced man had had done. All over the top of his head she could see where the 'seeds had been sown' so to speak; tufty shoots of fine black hair looked as if they had sprouted in neat rows. Halfway through dinner she had suddenly got a fit of giggles as she pictured herself with a watering can poised over his head.

During the course of the evening, even when she was asked to dance by a variety of men, she knew that the night was not proving to be the success she had thought it would be. Yes, she was flattered by the attention, and yes, it was lovely to be wearing a new dress and feeling happily light-hearted as they pulled crackers, wore party hats and danced till midnight – one man even asked her for her phone number – but there was only one man she wanted to enjoy the evening with and that was Bob. But not the Bob he'd become. She wanted her old Bob back: the man she'd always loved and still did.

Driving home with Dora afterwards – Derek had driven home separately – Eileen had realised that cheating on Bob to teach him a lesson would solve nothing. A tit-for-tat affair wasn't the answer.

'I could have told you that,' Dora had said when Eileen confided in her.

'Yes, but I had to see for myself.'

'So what are you going to do next?'

'I'm going to get Christmas over with and then I shall talk to Bob. Really talk. I'll tell him I knew about the affairs all those years ago, that I forgave him then, as I will this time round. I'll also tell him that I know why he's done it, that I understand.'

'You're more forgiving than I could ever be.'

'Please don't make the mistake of thinking I'm being terribly righteous. I'm not. It's just that I believe in my marriage and want to keep what's left of my family intact.'

'Will you tell Bob about tonight? How you were tempted to do the same because you were so angry and hurt, and that it was him who made you feel that way?'

'Yes.'

'And have you thought about the consequences if it backfires on you – if bringing everything out into the open gives him the courage to walk away?'

'Oh, Dora, I've thought of little else. But I have to risk it.'

When Dora dropped her off, the house was in darkness and there was no sign of Harriet's car on the drive. With Toby sniffing at her heels, Eileen had tiptoed upstairs, her shoes dangling from her hand. Bob was already asleep, but it was a restless sleep, his breathing ragged, his body twitching. Popping her head round Joel's bedroom door she saw that his bed was empty. She found him sleeping peacefully in Carrie's bed, his silky wrapped around his hand. She pulled the duvet over his shoulders and kissed him fondly on the cheek. He didn't stir.

Back downstairs, with Toby curled up again in his basket, she made a pot of tea. She was exhausted and knew that she would pay for her night of duplicitous excess the next day. However, right now, she wasn't sleepy; her mind was too active. She kept thinking how Felicity's death seemed to be a catalyst for change between her and Bob. She was still dwelling on this when she heard Harriet's key in the front door. As soon as she saw Harriet's face, she knew something awful had happened. Despite what Harriet had always thought, that she could compose her face to make it unreadable, Eileen knew how to read it perfectly.

'What's happened?' she asked.

'I've just come from the hospital. Will's eldest daughter died this evening. She had some kind of aneurysm and died, just like that.' She clicked her fingers.

Eileen had only ever seen Will's daughters from a distance as they came and went from his house, but she knew, as any parent would, what they meant to him. She put a hand to her mouth. 'Oh, the poor man. What about the baby?'

'Dead too.' Harriet pulled out a chair and sat down heavily. She lowered her head and rested it on her arms on the table.

Without asking her if she wanted one, Eileen poured a cup of tea for Harriet and joined her at the table. 'How is Will taking it?'

Harriet slowly raised her head. 'At a rough guess, I'd say it's damn near killing him. Oh, Mum, why do we have to go through so much shit? What's the point of it all?'

'I've no idea. I gave up wondering why and how a long time ago. Have some tea.'

Harriet obediently reached for the mug, but before she put it to her lips, she said, 'Will doesn't deserve this. He really doesn't. He's one of the nicest people I know. I wish I could turn back the clock for him.'

'None of us deserve it. But it happens, and somehow, don't ask me how, we find the strength to survive. Look at us. Look how we've coped, particularly you.'

Harriet shook her head vehemently. 'I'm barely coping, Mum. Believe me.'

'Rubbish. You've shown amazing strength. Without you, your father and I wouldn't have managed at all. And the children, who have lost the most, really look up to you.'

'Only because I'm taller than them.'

They both smiled, but then suddenly they weren't

smiling, they were both crying and hanging on to each other, just as they did the night Jeff and Felicity died.

Since that conversation, Eileen had felt as if a barrier had lifted between her and Harriet, although until that moment she hadn't been aware of its existence. But it was obvious to her now that while they'd all been thrown higgledy-piggledy together, they'd each been living their separate lives with the barriers firmly in place. The children had school, Harriet had work, she had Dora, and Bob, well Bob had had to go in search of something to distract him – first Toby and then this woman who was consoling him.

Even aside from her animosity, Eileen didn't think much of this other woman because from what she could see, Bob was anything but consoled.

Dusting a plate of mince pies with caster sugar, Eileen covered the dish in foil and placed it carefully alongside an individual portion of shepherd's pie in a large plastic box for Will.

It was Saturday morning, exactly a week before Christmas; Bob was out with Toby (allegedly), the children were upstairs playing – she could hear them thrashing around in Joel's bedroom and shaking the floorboards – and Harriet was sitting at the table, a foot tapping the floor while she read a letter from her conveyancing solicitor, a colleague of Will's friend, Marty, who was still covering for him while he was off work. One way or another it had been an eventful week. School had finished for the Christmas holidays and there had been the carol concert to attend, several parties Carrie had been invited to and the school nativity play to prepare for. Harriet had made Joel's day by managing to get the afternoon off work to see him perform as one of the innkeepers. He'd been so excited about his part that he'd refused to wash off the moustache he'd had painted onto his top lip until two days later. By then he resembled a miniature Hitler and Harriet had insisted on scrubbing him clean.

Watching Harriet slide the letter back inside the envelope, Eileen said, 'Everything still on track? No problems with the house?'

'It looks like we might be able to bring the completion date forward by a week,' Harriet answered without looking at her.

'Is that good?'

'It doesn't really make any difference. I'll be ready for either date.'

A sudden extra-loud thump from upstairs had them both glancing anxiously at the ceiling and listening for a subsequent scream. No scream came and Eileen said, 'I'll get them to simmer down in a minute when I go up for my nap.'

'Don't worry, I'll take them out with me. I need to do some Christmas shopping. Anything I can get you?'

'I don't think so, but are you sure you want to go anywhere near the shops? They'll be horrendously busy.'

'I'll cope. Besides, if I don't do it today, I never will.'

It was good to hear Harriet sounding more positive and upbeat. Nothing had been said, but Eileen knew that the death of Will's daughter had affected Harriet deeply; a whole raft of painful memories and emotions that had just begun to settle must have been stirred up by it. 'I don't suppose you'd take this box across to Will before you go out, would you?' Eileen asked. She had decided that whatever had caused the rift between Harriet and Will, it had gone on for long enough.

'I will, but only if I can leave it in his porch.'

Eileen recognised the scratchy warning look Harriet was giving her but, undaunted, she said, 'Don't you think it would be better to give it to him in person? Who knows, he might be ready to talk to someone now.'

'If he is, I guarantee it won't be me.'

In the spirit of openness between them, and determined that people were going to open up to one another whether they wanted to or not, Eileen said, 'Look, Harriet, I know there was something a lot more than just friendship going on between the two of you, but whatever went wrong, I don't think now is the time to—'

'*Mum!*'

'Oh, please, after everything we've been through, don't be shocked that I know what you've been up to. I'm concerned about you. And Will. Something was obviously working well between you, and now when he most needs someone close to him, you're not there.'

Her face a picture of forbidding censure, Harriet muttered, 'How did you know?'

'It wasn't difficult. You were spending nearly every evening together, often coming home with a glow that no amount of computer fixing could have put there.'

To Eileen's relief, Harriet's hitherto unyielding expression softened and she smiled faintly. 'I don't know whether to be embarrassed or outraged,' she said.

'Neither. So what happened?'

'I ended it with him. It wasn't right between us.'

'Was it the age gap?'

Harriet frowned. 'It was more complicated than that, but that was the excuse I used.'

'That would have hurt him.'

'I think he's got more to worry about than me right now, Mum. I doubt I even figure on his radar any more.'

'But you're upset about it, aren't you?'

'Yes. I behaved badly. I turned into the kind of person I've always despised. And please don't expect me to explain what I mean by that.'

Knowing she'd gone as far as she could with her taciturn daughter, Eileen said, 'I'd still like you to take this food over to him. It would be an olive branch of sorts.'

'You realise, don't you, that you're as subtle as Carrie when it comes to matchmaking?'

Eileen smiled. 'You think so? I didn't think you'd noticed Carrie's crafty hints. Mind you, she seemed quite keen on the idea of you and Miles for a while.'

'Well, she got that completely wrong. And if it's allowed, I'd appreciate a change of subject. Tell me what's going on with Dad. I think he's depressed, and I don't mean a bit down in the dumps, I mean clinically depressed. In my opinion, he needs help. Will thought so too.'

Surprised at the turnaround in the conversation, Eileen reminded herself that openness was her new watchword. 'I agree with you. But it's not as straightforward as you think.' She took a deep breath. 'Your father's having an affair. It's not the first time it's happened. He did it years ago before Felicity was born, when I had all those miscarriages. It seems to be his way of handling grief.'

Harriet's jaw dropped.

Half an hour later, Harriet went upstairs to tell the children they were going out. Leaving them to tidy the war-zone they'd created in Joel's bedroom, she went into her room and stood at the window that overlooked the garden. She had only brought up the subject of Dad to stop her mother interrogating her, but after listening to Mum's revelations, she suddenly felt displaced. Her family was falling apart around her. Her father wasn't the man she'd believed him to be. In fact, he was a virtual stranger. How dare he treat her mother so shabbily! Just let any man treat *her* that way! No wonder Mum had decided to play him at his own game. It was difficult to say why exactly, but Harriet was glad Mum had thought better of it. There were some people in the world who had to be beyond reproach.

Perhaps as shocking as what her mother had shared with her was the fact that so much had been going on right under Harriet's nose. Could their lives become any more complicated? And how likely was it, given Felicity's affair with Miles, that adultery was hereditary?

But that was ridiculous. There was no such thing as an adultery gene. She was on the road to madness if she started buying into irrational nonsense like that. Stick to plain old logic, she told herself. However, there was something that her mother had said that struck a chord with her; something she couldn't dispute. Felicity's death had set off a chain reaction of events that would leave none of them the same.

Her mother's last words on the subject had been to make Harriet promise that she wouldn't say anything to her father, or treat him differently. 'I want to get Christmas behind us, then I'm going to talk to him,' Eileen had said. While her mother had been telling her all this, it would have been the ideal opportunity to confide in her about Felicity's secret affair, but she hadn't. Her mother had enough to worry about as it was. Coincidentally, Harriet had decided the previous night that she wanted to clear the air with Miles. She wanted to tell him that she knew about him and Felicity. As brief as her relationship with Will had been, it had taught her something vitally important: to be less judgemental of what Miles and her sister had done.

But this new-found tolerance did not extend to her father. What he had done, and was continuing to do, was unforgivable. At a time when Mum needed him most, he'd betrayed her in the worst way possible.

Harriet's change of heart towards Miles was the reason she wanted to go shopping. She planned to go to Novel Ways in Maywood, to buy her parents Christmas presents and at the same time ask Miles out for a drink.

But before then she had to perform a far more difficult task.

Leaving the children with one final mind-boggling challenge – to find their coats and put on their shoes – she took the plastic box of food across the road. It was a gloomy, cold day with a sky the colour of pewter. It looked as if it might snow. A lamp was glowing softly in the room at the front of Will's house and that, with the presence of his car on the drive, led Harriet to think he was in. But whether or not he would open the door to her was another matter. She rang the doorbell; just one short ring. Anything too loud or strident would have seemed offensively inappropriate. In the immediate weeks after Felicity's death, Harriet had frequently thought that in times of mourning doorbells and door knockers should be muffled. For all she knew, the

Victorians probably had come up with such a rule of etiquette.

Having got no response, and reluctant to press the doorbell again, she bent down to leave the food parcel on the floor of the porch. To her surprise, just then the door opened and Will stood before her. His face was gaunt and unshaven, his hair unwashed, his clothes crumpled. But it was the pain in his ravaged eyes that shocked her most. Feeling stupid and inadequate, she held out the box like a gauche child delivering Harvest Festival boxes to the needy. 'Please just say if you'd rather my mother and Dora didn't keep on doing this,' she said.

He looked straight through her, his expression blank. The blankness hurt her almost as much as when she'd tried to comfort him at the hospital and he'd shrugged her off. He took the box from her. 'Tell them no more after this. I'm okay.'

No you're not! she wanted to shout. I know how you feel. I've been there. Whatever you're feeling, I felt the same when Felicity died. But all she said was, 'My mother wants you to know that if there's anything we can do, just give us a call.'

Without another word, he closed the door.

Carrie was in one of her investigative journalist moods during the drive to Maywood. 'Why does Grandma keep cooking for Will? And why don't you go to see him any more? Don't you like him now? I heard Dora saying he—'

'Which of those questions would you like me to answer first?' Harriet cut in.

'Um . . . the first one.'

'He's not feeling very well at the moment and we're all trying to help him.'

'Has he got flu?'

'Yes,' Harriet lied. She and her mother thought the children had been touched by enough death in their young lives and had decided to say nothing about Suzie dying.

422

They would cross that bridge of truth as and when it was necessary.

'Is that why you're staying away from him?'

'Yes.'

'So you still like him?'

'Yes.'

'When he's better will you help him with his computer again?'

Maywood was crowded with Christmas shoppers intent on getting themselves so far into the red that it would make the Third World debt look like a quid had been pinched from the petty-cash box. 'With each Christmas that passes, I'm becoming more and more cynical,' Harriet thought disconsolately. But this festive period was going to be particularly difficult, especially for Carrie and Joel, and she knew she had to make an effort for their sake. Carrie no longer believed in the strange spectre of a white-bearded man coming down the chimney bearing gifts, but Joel did and there would have to be an element of subterfuge to satisfy him.

After depositing the children in the children's section at Novel Ways, with the promise of a milkshake and a chocolate-chip cookie from the coffee shop to follow, Harriet went to find the latest Alan Titchmarsh gardening book for her father and the new Delia for her mother.

When she'd found the books and queued for ten minutes to pay for them, she asked the teenage girl behind the counter if Miles was around. She was told he was upstairs with a customer in the Mind, Body and Spirit section. How apt, she thought as she went to find him.

'Got anything to improve my mind?' she said when the customer he'd been helping went to pay for a copy of *Men Are from Mars, Women Are from Venus*.

'Harriet!' he said. 'How . . . how are you?' There was no disguising his awkwardness. Which made her feel even guiltier. There he'd been, silently grieving for the woman he loved, and she'd come along and metaphorically kicked him in the teeth. How could she have been so insensitive? Again she was reminded that she never seemed to be quite in step with everyone else. Perhaps Dominic was right and she really was incapable of genuine affection. And hadn't she proved that already by using Will? Realising that Miles was waiting for her to speak, she said, 'I think I must be suffering from a severe case of jingle-bells madness to be out shopping on the last Saturday before Christmas. How are you? The shop seems manically busy.'

'It's been like it for days. As if that wasn't enough, I'm organising an event here for the writing group I belong to.'

Thinking that this was something else he'd kept quiet about, she said, 'Is that a recent thing? The writing group?'

'Not really. It's just a case of lights and bushels.'

She smiled, wanting him to relax. It pained her that he was so ill at ease in her company. 'What kind of event are you putting on?'

'Poetry and short story readings. It's on Monday evening. I . . .' His voice broke off and he fiddled with the pen behind his ear. 'I don't suppose I can interest you in a ticket?'

She smiled again, filled with relief that a bridge was forming between them. 'Why not? And how about a drink afterwards? Or will you be luvving it up with your fellow writers?'

He viewed her sceptically for a brief moment, his expression tense and unsure.

'I'd really appreciate talking with you, Miles,' she said, pressing the point. 'There's something we need to discuss, isn't there? And I think we'll both feel a lot better once we've got it over and done with.'

The tension disappeared from his face. 'A drink would be great. But you'll have to hang around after the event while I tidy the shop and lock up.'

'No problem. I can give you a hand if you like. What time does it start?'

'Kick off's at eight o'clock and tickets are available on the door.'

424

A sudden burst of schmaltzy Christmas music had Miles cursing. 'I've told them no boy bands or Americanised crap with sleigh bells, only traditional carols. But will they listen? You'll have to excuse me while I commit some festive genocide amongst the Saturday staff.' He put a hand on her arm, kissed her cheek – sealing an end to their estrangement – and hurried away. 'Oh, by the way,' he called over his shoulder, 'Dominic's coming home for Christmas. Latest estimated time of arrival is some time on Monday. But who knows with my brother? He might grace us with his presence on Boxing Day, or with any luck, not bother to show up at all.'

Harriet went downstairs to round up the children for their promised milkshake, hoping that Dominic's impending visit wouldn't cast a shadow over Christmas.

She knew of one person, though, who would be delighted at the news: Carrie.

Chapter Fifty-One

Will opened the plastic box Harriet had delivered earlier that morning, and without looking at the foil packages he put them straight in the bin. As he'd done with all the others. He wished he could feel more grateful for what his neighbours were doing, but he couldn't. Gratitude was beyond him. His feelings were centred on the one agonising and inescapable truth that would haunt him for the rest of his life: he'd failed Suzie. He knew in every fibre of his being that if he'd only acted differently that night, his daughter would still be alive.

Every day, over and over, he replayed the sequences of that dreadful night in his mind.

If only he hadn't insisted on taking Harriet out for dinner.

If only he and Harriet hadn't thought it would be better to go directly to the hospital.

If only he had gone straight to his mother's.

Jarvis, Marty and his mother kept telling him on the phone that it was futile to think this way, that Suzie's death had occurred after events that no one could have foreseen. As though it would make him feel better, his mother had pointed out that Maxine's guilt was far worse than his. Apparently, when Ruby had let herself in with Gemma's key, she had found Maxine lying comatose on the sofa.

But he didn't care a damn that Maxine had to live with the knowledge that she'd been so drunk she'd been oblivious to the constant ringing of the phone. That was her problem. She'd have to find her own way of dealing with it.

The post-mortem had revealed, as the medical staff at the hospital had suspected it would, that the cause of Suzie's death had been a ruptured aneurysm – a subarachnoid haemorrhage – on the right side of her brain. There had been a fatal loss of blood and severe damage. Time, they had been told, was of the essence if there had been any chance of saving Suzie. The wheels of an official enquiry had been put into motion, and while Maxine was determined to fight tooth and nail to sue the ambulance service, Will knew it wouldn't make any difference. Suzie was dead. No amount of legal wrangling would bring her back. Somehow he would have to learn to live with the incalculable weight of his grief. A grief that went far deeper than mere tears and words. His heart and soul had been crushed. He was regularly consumed by the need to lay waste to anything that got in his way. To tear out his own insides. To roar and howl. The gut-wrenching anguish he felt at times left him in a state of catatonic numbness when he could think of nothing but the futility of carrying on.

He raked his hands through his unwashed hair and, feeling sick to his stomach, filled the kettle to make some coffee. But when he plugged in the kettle, he remembered he'd run out of coffee. It was just about all he was surviving on. That and toast. After checking the breadbin and finding just a pair of crusts left in the bag, he knew he had to summon the energy to go to the shops. He couldn't face going into town – all those cheery-faced shoppers preparing to celebrate Christmas with their loved ones – but thought he could manage the short walk to Edna Gannet's. He searched the mess on the work surface for his wallet and keys, pulled on his coat in the hall and locked the door after him.

It was a while before he noticed how cold it was and that a heavy stillness had settled on the day. The light was fading, drawing the afternoon to an early close. Snow had begun to fall. A delicate flake landed on his nose: it melted instantly, prompting a memory that made his eyes sting with tears. Suzie had been two years old when she'd first seen snow. She'd stood at the open kitchen door, a red-booted foot hovering cautiously on the brink of exploring the magical whiteness, but only when she'd taken his hand had she plucked up the courage to venture forth. Before long she'd been giddy with excited wonder and had helped him make a snowman, patting the snow with her tiny gloved hands and refusing to go inside even though her nose was turning as red as her boots.

Edna Gannet's was empty when he pushed open the door, and completely quiet. He felt a wave of gratitude towards Edna for not filling the shop with piped carols or the meaningless chunterings of a local radio station. From where she was restocking a shelf of Christmas cards and wrapping paper, her infamous steely gaze fell on him as he ducked behind a shelf to find some coffee. He picked up two of the largest jars so that there was no danger of him running out and having to make another trek to the shops, and went to look for some bread. Then, picking up a packet of butter, half a dozen eggs and bacon – who knows, he might get around to eating it – he put his purchases on the counter, behind which Edna was now standing. He knew that she would know about Suzie; it had been front-page news in local paper: '*Young Girl Dies Because of Ambulance Blunder.*'

Avoiding any eye-contact with Edna, he opened his wallet while she rang up his bill. To his annoyance, he found that it was empty, save for a twenty-pence piece and a petrol receipt. He couldn't remember the last time he'd been to the bank or the cash machine. 'I'm sorry,' he mumbled, 'I don't seem to have any money with me. Will you take a credit card?' Without meaning to, his eyes had found hers and he flinched when he felt the full force of her scrutiny.

'I'll have to add on a charge if you pay that way.'

'So be it.'

'Cheaper_not to. Why don't you pay me another day?'

Will had lived in Maple Drive long enough to know that this was an unheard-of proposition: Edna Gannet never put anything on a tab. 'No, really, I'd rather pay now.'

'It's a one per cent charge.'

'I don't care.'

'Any time you're passing.'

'I don't plan to be passing for some time,' he said, his voice rising. 'Please, just take my card and charge me whatever you want.' He pushed it across the counter. If he didn't get out soon, he'd end up doing or saying something he'd regret.

'Suit yourself.'

Back out on the street, it had stopped snowing; it was almost as if he'd imagined it. If only the last week could vanish as easily, he thought as he walked home, his head down so as not to attract any more eye-contact with passers-by. He'd had enough of that from Edna. He recalled Harriet telling him how Edna had once tried to be nice to her and the children because of her sister's death. 'It's too much of a shock to the system if people you rely upon to behave brutally suddenly act out of character,' Harriet had said. 'Unexpected acts of kindness should be outlawed.'

She was right. Just as she'd been right to end things between them. He didn't know what he'd been thinking of to get involved with her. Perhaps he'd been trying to prove something to himself. He wasn't sure what, but it no longer mattered. Harriet was in the past. As was any semblance of a normal life. His mother and Jarvis had been on at him since the funeral that he should get back to work. 'Laddie, you need something else to think about,' Jarvis had said during one of his many phone calls. 'Just do a few half days to begin with.'

'I'll give it some thought,' Will had said, instantly putting it far from his mind. How could anyone expect him to work when it was as much as he could do to get up of a morning? Sometimes it was hard to breathe for the pain. This trip to Edna's had been a major expedition. It was also his first step beyond his front door since the day of the funeral. If it hadn't been for Jarvis and Marty he didn't know how he'd have got through the service; they'd sat either side of him in church, literally propping him up.

Outwardly he'd looked calm enough, so Marty had said, but inwardly as he'd stared at his daughter's coffin and at the pitifully small one next to it – containing the grandson he would never know – he'd been howling like a madman. He had no recollection of anyone else at the funeral. Not until afterwards, when everybody had assembled at Maxine and Steve's. By this stage Maxine had disappeared. Later he was told she'd gone to bed, too traumatised to talk to anyone. It had been down to Steve and Ruby to dole out drink and food. To Will's eternal shame, Steve had been the one who'd taken charge of organising the funeral. Despite the cold, Will had wanted to spend most of the time outside in the garden. But Marty, still not a hundred per cent from his operation and now embarking on a course of radiotherapy, had forced him to come inside for a drink. It was a mistake, because once he'd started to drink he couldn't stop and he began bludgeoning himself with snapshot memories of Suzie, in particular the day he'd driven her to the abortion clinic and she'd asked him to sing 'Scarlet Ribbons' to her. He didn't think he'd ever forget that day.

He'd been drinking solidly for some time when he'd caught sight of a group of youngsters – friends of Suzie's from school and university, Gemma had said.

'Who's the lad all done up in the suit and tie?' he'd asked, curious. He stood out, being the only boy in the group of girls.

'His name's Richard,' Gemma had said. 'He used to go out with Sinead, Suzie's closest friend at university.'

Through the blur of whisky and grief, something nagged at him, but it wasn't until people started drifting away – Suzie's friends had been the first to leave – that he realised what it was. Seized with a fury he didn't know he possessed, he had wanted to chase after the lad and beat the shit out of him. 'You're the reason my daughter's dead!' he wanted to scream. 'If you'd kept your hands off her, she wouldn't have got pregnant and she'd still be alive!'

But he didn't. He let the murderous sense of outrage

pass. Blaming his daugther's death on anyone but himself wouldn't wash. She'd been his responsibility, no one else's.

When he let himself in there was a message on the answer phone from his mother. She phoned him every day. He wished she wouldn't. Her need to care for him, to make sure he was eating and sleeping properly, only added to his self-pitying guilt.

Now that he'd been out, the house was making Will feel claustrophobic, and after drinking a mug of coffee and managing half a slice of toast, he put on his walking boots and warmest fleece and went down to the end of the garden to walk along the canal. Perhaps it would have a restorative effect. Nothing else did.

He'd been walking for no more than a few minutes when he saw Harriet's father coming towards him with Toby lagging behind. If it had been possible, Will would have turned round and gone back home, but Bob had seen him and so an exchange was unavoidable. So long as it was mercifully brief, Will thought he'd survive. So long as there were no cloying words of sympathy, he'd be okay.

'How's it going, Will?' Bob asked when they were face to face.

'Oh, you know, each day as it comes.' It was a stupid thing to say and Will regretted it at once.

Bob looked at him hard. 'I used to lie as glibly as that,' he said. 'What you really mean is that you wish you were dead yourself. Don't let anyone tell you it gets better. Take it from me, it doesn't.'

His words were so vociferous and tangibly bitter, as though Bob was glad someone else was suffering as he was, they were like a knife thrust between Will's ribs. Wanting to get away from him, Will took a step back. He suddenly realised that he needed to believe what Marty, Jarvis and his mother had told him: that, given time, the pain would lessen. Whatever else, he didn't want his grief to consume him like an incurable disease and turn him into an embittered, malevolent old man like Bob. Or worse, like his father.

He made his excuses and walked away, ignoring Toby as he briefly danced around him.

Bob watched him go, disappointed. He'd thought Will would appreciate some honesty. Some straight talking. But apparently not. He sighed and called Toby to heel. There was no helping some people.

Jennifer was another person who was refusing his help. Whenever he phoned her to see if there was anything he could do for her, she would say he wasn't to keep ringing. For heaven's sake, she made him sound like a stalker! All he wanted to do was speak to the one person who had taken the trouble to listen to him. 'I can't just forget about you,' he'd said.

'But you must. You're a married man and I should never have encouraged you.'

'But it was so natural between us.'

'No, Bob, it was very unreal. When people are away from home they act differently. Looking back on it, I behaved like a silly twenty-year-old looking for a holiday romance.'

'Please don't say that. Let me believe that it meant something. Leave me that much, if nothing else.'

He'd been reduced to begging and it had got him nowhere. In the end she had agreed that he could call her occasionally, especially if there was anything to report about the *Jennifer Rose*, which would be staying at the marina until the warmer weather in the spring, when she planned to come up and travel home on it.

It was this thought that kept his hopes alive. In the spring, when she was fully recovered from the pneumonia, he would see her again. Then he'd have the opportunity to make her understand just how real and natural it had been between them.

Chapter Fifty-Two

So far Miles hadn't shown so much as a flicker of annoyance, but Harriet felt it on his behalf. The last person in the world that he would have wanted to be in the audience was sitting on Harriet's left: Dominic. While Miles was managing successfully to ignore Dominic's presence, others were not. People – mostly women – were openly staring, some craning or twisting their necks to get a better look at this dark, saturnine and elegant figure in their midst. Just as Dominic would want it, of course. He was dressed in black, apart from a white shirt which was open at the neck and revealed a small ebony crucifix on a leather thong, and still wore his long, flowing overcoat as well as a wide-brimmed hat, despite the warmth of the shop. Lolling back in his seat, his head tilted as though examining the ceiling, he looked even more arresting than he normally did. If his plan had been to upstage his brother and other members of the writing group, who were taking it in turns to stand at the lectern and read, it had worked. He was without doubt the entire focus of attention.

He'd arrived in Maple Drive that afternoon, so Eileen had told Harriet when she got home from work. 'Have you been twitching the net curtains again, Mum?' Harriet had teased her.

'Certainly not. I was dusting Carrie's window sill and saw Harvey's car pull onto their drive. He must have just collected Dominic from the station. I've never understood why that boy hasn't learned to drive.'

'Because it would be so culturally at odds with the way he sees himself,' Harriet had replied. 'He'd much rather be driving a horse-drawn carriage with a whip in his hand.

And let's not forget his ego. How could he be expected to take instruction from so lowly a person as a driving instructor?'

After a hurried supper, and while Harriet was upstairs reading to the children, the doorbell had rung. Her mother was on the phone and her father was goodness knows where, so Harriet went to the door.

It was Dominic. 'Hello, Hat. Like Christ himself, I bring you salvation and good news. Can I come in?'

She shut the door after him, conscious of the patter of curiosity above their heads.

'I've just heard of the literary extravaganza my brother's putting on tonight,' he said, brushing her cheek with a careless kiss, 'and I've decided I would be letting him down if I wasn't there to offer him my inimitable support. Also, I feel I'm honour-bound to save you from such a tedious horror show without some kind of succour. Aha! And who do I spy peeping round the banister?'

Rendered uncharacteristically shy, Carrie hovered coyly at the top of the stairs, her dressing-gown cord trailing on the floor, the bedtime book Harriet had been reading to them held close to her chest. From behind her Joel poked his head out to see who was there.

'Hello, you two,' Dominic called up. 'What's that you're reading?'

'*The Lion, the Witch and the Wardrobe*,' Carrie said, stepping forward. 'I've read it already, but Joel doesn't know the story. Do you know it?'

'It was one of my favourite books when I was your age. I loved the Queen of Narnia; such a gorgeous trollop. As for Edmund, he was a snivelling little wimp who should have been buried up to his neck in the snow. Now, scat you two while I finish talking to your wicked aunt Harriet.'

Having dismissed them with all the ease of a magician waving a wand, he said, 'I'll be back in half an hour. You will be ready then, won't you?' He cast a disapproving eye over her baggy trousers and hooded top.

'What about your father? Isn't he going?'

Dominic laughed. 'Good God, no. It's not his kind of evening at all.'

Thinking it might have been nice for Miles to have his father's support, just once, Harriet closed the door after Dominic and went upstairs to finish reading to the children. Sitting on Joel's bed and answering Carrie's excited questions about Dominic – how long was he going to be around and how often would they get to see him? – she had hoped he would behave himself at Novel Ways, and wouldn't flex those pumped-up egotistical muscles of his too much in front of Miles.

The wiry-haired woman who had been reading out a lengthy poem about growing old – lots of clumsy, clichéd references to withered breasts and limbs that were knotted and gnarled – finally sat down and the audience clapped enthusiastically. Perhaps because the poem had at last come to an end.

Next to Harriet, Dominic took out a pen. She watched him scribble something on the ticket he'd bought at the door when they'd arrived. Where it had once said, '*For One Night Only, Hidden Talents Writing Group Presents an Evening of Wit and Thought-Provoking Prose*' he changed it to read '. . . *an evening of relentless dreich shite*'. And because he knew she was watching him, he then wrote, '*Save me from this freak show, Hat!*'

She tried to keep herself from smiling but failed miserably. She covered her mouth with her hand and tried to disguise her laughter by clearing her throat. She did it too loudly, though, and the row of people in front of them turned and stared.

After the next speaker, Dominic leaned into her and said, 'Just as well it's for one night only; another evening of this interminable drivel and I'd be mixing myself a palliative cocktail of hemlock and prussic acid.'

When Miles took his place behind the lectern, Harriet shot Dominic a warning look. 'Behave,' she whispered, 'or I'll stamp on your hat when we get out of here.'

He blew her a kiss. 'I'll be as good as gold. I promise.'

Even to Harriet's unappreciative ears, there was no mistaking the beauty of what Miles was reading out. It was a strikingly tender and poignant poem of love and longing, and knowing that he must have written it for Felicity, it moved Harriet almost to tears. Her sister, she decided, had been lucky to have been loved so consummately.

When Miles read the last line of his poem and signalled to the audience by a barely perceptible nod that he had finished, Dominic snorted loudly and a spontaneous burst of applause rang out. Hoping that Miles hadn't heard his brother, Harriet dug her elbow into Dominic's ribs. 'You pig!' she hissed. 'Don't say I didn't warn you.' She snatched his hat from his head, threw it onto the floor and stamped on it hard. His reaction was to slap her thigh, causing her to yelp loudly. This Miles did hear, along with the ensuing scuffle as Dominic tried to retrieve his hat and at the same time pinch Harriet's ankle. As he remained at the lectern to invite people to stay and enjoy a mince pie and a glass of wine, Miles glared at his brother. He didn't look too happy with Harriet either and she sank down into her seat feeling like a naughty child.

The conversation Harriet had planned to have with Miles had been put on hold the second Dominic had muscled his way into the evening, and she was now resigned to the three of them going for a drink instead. Miles had greeted Dominic's announcement that he would join them with lukewarm agreement, and having said goodnight to the members of staff who'd stayed on, he locked up and led the way along the main street of Maywood. The wine bar they were going to, which had opened only last month, was opposite Turner's, the town's old-fashioned department store.

'So what did you think?' Miles asked when they were settled with their drinks and Chris Rea was singing that he'd be home in time for Christmas – their table was slap bang beneath a speaker. The question was directed at Harriet, but before she could answer, Dominic – prodding and poking at his hat to get it back into shape – said, 'It was a glorious example of why the written word should be kept out of the reach of those who would cause it such harm. In short, it was nothing short of rape. A violation of the English language.'

'Dominic, can't you ever stop living up to your reputation as an insufferable bastard?'

'It's okay, Harriet,' Miles said matter-of-factly, 'a great scholar like my brother is welcome to his erudite opinion. How else would he view a homespun writers' group? Even if one of our members has probably outsold anything he's ever had published. Sales of your last literary offering were what, Dominic? Two thousand? Or am I being generous? Whereas our novice little scribbler has made it onto the bestseller lists in no less than seven different countries. Not bad for a violator of the English language, wouldn't you say?'

'Don't make it so easy for me, Miles. You of all people should know that it's rarely the well-written novels that make it onto those disreputable lists.'

'Yes, but it's those books that subsidise most of the unreadable stuff you'd have everyone reading.'

Harriet had heard enough. She wasn't prepared to sit here a minute longer listening to them batting insults across the table. 'Shut up and be nice, you two!' she said. 'Or I shall walk away right now.'

Miles looked shamefaced but Dominic raised his eyebrows sardonically. 'You're beginning to annoy me, Harriet. First you massacre my hat, now you tell me how to talk to my own brother. Motherhood clearly doesn't suit you; you're far too bossy these days.'

Miles rolled his eyes. 'Not funny, Dominic.' Then addressing Harriet: 'How's your friend Will? I read about his daughter in the paper. It must have been awful for him.'

Momentarily wrongfooted, Harriet took a sip of her wine before saying, 'It was the suddenness of it that made it so devastating. I was there at the hospital when it happened.'

'That must have been a comfort for him, at least.'

437

'Not really.'

Dominic, who was sitting opposite Harriet, clicked his fingers in front of her nose. '*Hello*. Remember me? Who's Will?' he demanded. 'And what happened to his daughter?'

'Will is Harriet's boyfriend,' Miles explained patiently, 'and his daughter died recently. Okay? Does that bring you back into the loop to your satisfaction?'

Harriet felt her face redden and she squirmed in her seat at Miles's assumption, but Dominic sat up straight. 'Boyfriend?' he said, with what she knew was prurient interest. 'You never said, Hat. How long has that been going on for?'

'It hasn't.'

'But Miles just said—'

'He's wrong! So just leave it.' More gently, she said, 'Sorry, Miles, it wasn't really anything as heavy as a girlfriend–boyfriend situation.'

Miles looked confused. 'But I thought that was why you—'

'Hey,' interrupted Dominic, his face petulant, 'stop doing that, you two – leaving me out of the conversation. Who the hell is this Will character? Where's he popped up from?'

'He lives in Maple Drive, in the house opposite Harriet and her parents.'

Getting tired of Miles speaking for her, Harriet said, 'He's just a friend, Dominic. No one with whom you need to bother yourself.'

A calculating look in his eyes, Dominic said, 'Come to think of it, Mum and Dad have mentioned something about a new neighbour. The daughter who died was nineteen, wasn't she?'

'Yes,' Harriet said.

There was a brief pause and then Dominic said, 'Which must mean this Will, the father, is . . .' He pursed his lips and sucked in his breath as though thinking hard. 'Gosh, Hat, exactly how *old* is he?'

'Forty-six,' she said, staring fixedly at Dominic's hateful, smug face and wondering if anyone in the wine bar would notice her strangling him with her bare hands. 'Do you have a problem with that?'

He shrugged. 'No problem at all.'

'I'd advise you leave it right there, Dominic,' Miles said in a low voice. 'Harriet's had enough to deal with without you stirring things up.'

Dominic leaned back in his chair and ran a finger round the rim of his glass. 'But just to satisfy my curiosity,' he said, 'why did it not turn into a boyfriend–girlfriend situation as my brother clearly thought it was?'

'I warned you, Dominic—'

'It's okay, Miles, I'm quite capable of answering for myself.' She leaned across the table. 'What exactly do you want to know, Dominic? Did I sleep with him? Is that it? Did I have a fling with the man? Is that what you want to know? Well, yes, I did. Put a tick in all of the above boxes. There! Satisfied?'

He smiled. 'How disagreeably suburban you make it sound. Miles? You've gone awfully quiet. Don't you have anything to say on the matter?'

Ripping a bar mat in two, Miles said, 'I'd say it's none of our business.'

'Really? I'd have thought it would have been very much *your* business. After all, the last time I was home you were practically falling over yourself for a bit of action in the sack with our frigid little Harriet.'

Seeing the look of horror on Miles's face, Harriet did the only thing she could have done. She picked up her wine glass and threw its contents in Dominic's face. 'You vicious bastard! Why couldn't it have been you who died and not Felicity?'

She was outside, slinging her bag over her shoulder and doing up her coat, when Miles came after her.

'I'm sorry, Harriet. I don't know what's got into him. He seems to be getting worse. Let me walk you to your car.'

'Please,' she said, 'I think I'd rather be alone.'

439

Chapter Fifty-Three

The Office Christmas Party had never been one of Harriet's favourite pastimes. In years gone by she had devised all manner of excuses why she couldn't attend – a doctor's appointment, a crucial telephone call she had to make, a new washing machine being delivered – but Howard had warned her yesterday that he'd make her life a living hell if she so much as thought of not joining in. 'You'll wear a paper hat and laugh at my jokes whether you want to or not,' he'd told her.

'And if I don't?'

'I'll start a rumour that we're having an affair.'

'I could have you for harassment.'

'With your fierce reputation no one would believe you, Hat. I'd tell them that the boot was on the other foot; that you forced yourself upon me and made unnatural demands of a happily married man. I'll say I asked you to be gentle with me, but that you had me on the desk, up against the wall, then tied to my chair. It would make a sensational court case, don't you think? I can see the headlines: "Insatiable nymphomaniac employee harasses boss for New Year pay rise."'

'And just how long have you been living in La-La Land, Howard?'

'Cheeky bint! Now get your sassy arse into gear and dig out your best party frock for tomorrow. I ought to warn you, anyone who doesn't laugh at my jokes will be dismissed on the spot. Message received?'

'Loud and clear, oh great leader.'

When it came to organising a Christmas lunch, Harriet had to hand it to Howard; he spared no expense. He'd not only organised a bus to ferry everyone into Manchester, but was treating them to a meal at his favourite Chinese restaurant, the Yang Sing. Despite her natural inclination to opt for pushing needles through her eyeballs rather than sit through such an ordeal, Harriet had to admit that she was very nearly enjoying herself. With Dangerous Dave on her left and Tina, a lively fifty-year-old from accounts getting more raucous by the minute on her right, Harriet had somehow found herself entering into the spirit of the occasion. She was one of the few sober people, having had no more than a glass of wine because she would be driving home once the bus dropped them off back at the office, unlike the others who at Howard's expense were all sharing taxis. And because she was sober, she was probably the only person who would remember Howard's appalling jokes in the morning. But God love 'em, she thought with surprising affection, he knows how to instil a sense of loyalty in his employees. Devotion was perhaps putting it too strongly, but looking round the tables of red-faced men and women, their party hats askew, their eyes glazed and bloodshot and their voices raised, she knew they were as tight-knit a bunch of workers as she'd come across, who would more than go the extra mile for Howard. As he doubtless knew. Harriet had come to realise that nothing happened by chance at ACT. Howard was a formidable player; he made things happen through the sheer force of his personality, and she counted herself lucky to work for him. She watched him working his way round the room, bestowing his outrageous brand of bonhomie on the tables of work colleagues. There was a lot of matey back-slapping going on, as well as a good deal of amorous charm being dispensed by the bucketload.

'He's one in a million, isn't he?' Tina said, following Harriet's gaze and leaning drunkenly against her shoulder. 'Did you know he paid for me to go private when I was told there was a ten-month waiting list to have my varicose veins done? He said to me, "Tina, the sooner you get them done, the sooner you can chase me round the office."' She raised her glass to him. 'He's the best boss I've ever worked for.'

Later, she felt a hand clamping down on her shoulder. 'There you are, Hat! Having fun?'

'This might surprise you, but yes I am.'

Howard laughed. 'Excellent. Now come and sit with me.' He grabbed her by the arm and pushed her towards his table. Most of the chairs were empty, people having got up to wander about and chat. Howard pulled out the one next to his. 'Drink?' he offered.

'No thanks, I'm driving home later.'

'You mean you're sober and still enjoying yourself? You'll be telling me next that the world is round. So tell me how the kiddies are. Looking forward to Christmas, I'll bet. When mine were little they would write wish lists to Santa that were as long as my arm.'

'They're pretty much on the case,' Harriet said lightly. This was a huge understatement. On an hourly basis Carrie was changing her mind about what she wanted. Her requests included a pair of purple rollerskates that lit up with flashing lights, a bike with at least ten gears, a CD player, some kind of disco-babe game (like Emily has), bright-pink nail varnish (again like Emily has), a sticker collection, a bumper pack of felt-tip pens, and a hamster (like Rebecca's). In contrast, Joel's list was heartbreakingly thin on the ground; he'd asked for a new pair of slippers.

'But I guess their excitement must be tempered by knowing this will be their first Christmas without their parents,' Howard said. 'The same must be true for you; you'll miss your sister, won't you?'

Touched by his solicitude, she said, 'We'll cope.'

'Of course you will. But it won't be easy. How's the house move going?'

'All set for the fourth of January. I've booked a day off, by the way.'

'Only the one? Take two, at least.'

'There's no need.'

He shook his head. 'You're a stubborn little thing, aren't

442

you?' He filled his wine glass and took a mouthful. 'So how's your love life? Any men on the scene?'

She laughed out loud. 'Do I have to answer that?'

'Yep! It's a new office rule. Come on, tell Uncle Howard about all the blokes who must be interested in you. I know for a fact that Dangerous Dave would give up his real-ale fetish for a night of bliss with the delectable Miss Swift.'

'What rubbish!'

'It's true. I've seen the way he hovers round your office, his ears pricked up and his tongue hanging out like a randy dog. How about that bloke in Dublin? Is he still keen?'

Alarmed, she said, 'Dominic's an old friend. Nothing more. As I recall telling you at the time.'

'No other blokes then? I find that hard to believe. A great-looking girl like you.'

'For all you know I could be gay.'

'And I'm a Dutchman's uncle! Believe me, I'd know if you were, Hat. Besides, my sources tell me that you were heard talking to a guy called Will on the phone. Who's he? Another *friend*?'

Was there nothing this man didn't know? 'Have you been tapping the phones?'

'No, just listening to office gossip. It's the best reason to employ women: through them I can keep up to date with everything that's going on. Yeah, I know, it's shocking, isn't it?'

'You must be the most non-PC boss in business.'

'And I get away with it because I'm a world-class sweetheart. Come on, talk to Uncle Howard. Tell me all. You know you want to. I've noticed a few changes in you recently; one minute you're fizzing away like a nun who's just been snogged, and next you're looking like the mother superior who wasn't so lucky.'

Harriet shook her head in bewilderment. How did he do it? But the extraordinary thing was, she was actually tempted to open up to Howard. It made her wonder if she really was sober. Was it possible to be a passive drinker, inhaling everyone else's alcohol fumes? But to talk to

Howard about Will – about how much she missed him, how she wished she could spend an evening with him just to make sure he was all right, how she felt so screwed up by dumping him when she did – was she mad? Apparently yes, because before she could stop herself the words were leaping from her mouth and she was unburdening herself.

When she'd finished, he said, 'The poor devil. I don't know what I'd do if anything happened to either of my children. They're both in their early twenties and living away from home, but I still worry like hell about them. So why didn't it work out between you two?' he asked. 'Was it the age gap?'

'Yes,' Harriet lied. No way was she going to tell Howard the whole truth – that a moment of madness had caused her to become hooked on the thrill of being with Will.

'Do you want to know what my advice is?' Howard asked.

This she had to hear. 'Go on,' she said warily.

'It sounds to me like you still fancy the bloke, with or without the extra years he's carrying, but I'd advise you to put him out of your mind. After what's just happened to him, he's seriously damaged goods. Best keep away from him altogether. Start offering your shoulder for him to cry on, as you girls love to do, and you'll end up in big trouble.'

'You really think so?' Harriet was surprised at Howard's take on the situation. She had expected him to say something crass like, 'Get stuck in; you know you want him!'

'Trust me, he's in no fit state to get involved with anyone right now. Why? Were you thinking of getting back with him to ease your conscience, given the timing of your dumping of him?'

'No!'

'Good, because the man will be vulnerable and if you come along and toy with his affections again, he'll very likely tip over the edge. Leave well alone is Uncle Howard's top tip for the day.'

*

Harriet drove home with Howard's words echoing in her ears. The thought of rekindling her relationship with Will hadn't crossed her mind, but it had certainly gone through her mind to provide him with a shoulder on which to lean, if not to cry on. If Howard was right and Will was vulnerable, her being there for him could well make matters worse.

She had to admit to being impressed with Howard's advice; it struck her as being both shrewd and prudent. All the same, she felt disappointed. She missed Will and hated the thought of him suffering. Naively, she had imagined that if they couldn't be lovers, they could at least be friends. But it looked as if it was not to be.

As for her so-called friend, Dominic, after his foul behaviour the other night he could go to hell as far as she was concerned. His interest in Will had been nothing more than a malicious desire to make Harriet look stupid, to rub her nose in whatever sick joke he was playing with her. And why had he tried to make out that Miles had been interested in her, when it was Felicity who had been the love of his life? Okay, Dominic didn't know it for sure – Harriet hadn't told him about the email that had given Miles away – but what kind of twisted mind continually made him want to provoke and embarrass people? Had he got a kick out of pushing her until she flipped, just to see if he could make her lose control? It was possible. Frankly, she wouldn't put anything past him. She had never thrown a drink in anyone's face before, but she'd do it again without a second's thought or regret if Dominic played any more games like that with her and Miles. Miles was right to say that he thought his brother was getting worse. He was. It had struck Harriet in bed that night that maybe Dominic, given that he suspected Miles had had an affair with his perfect Felicity, was jealous, just as she'd suggested to him in Dublin. Perhaps he hated himself for being gay, knowing he couldn't have Felicity in the way that Miles could, and had lashed out at the easiest targets to hand.

The following morning Miles had phoned her on her

mobile and apologised again for Dominic's behaviour. 'That comment he made about you and me, it . . . it was totally out of order. I hope you didn't—'

This constant apologising from Miles was getting on her nerves and Harriet had cut him short by saying, 'Dominic isn't your responsibility, so don't keep saying sorry on his behalf.'

'You're right, I know. I'm sorry. Oh . . . there I go again. I don't suppose there's any chance we can get together for that chat, just the two of us, is there?'

Knowing that while Dominic was around it would be impossible to do anything without him wanting to get in on the act, Harriet said, 'Not for a while. Let's do it in the New Year when Dominic's gone back to Cambridge.'

'But I'll see you over Christmas, won't I?'

'Sure. I'm counting the days until your parents' New Year's Day sherry fest.'

He groaned. 'Promise me you'll be there. I don't think I could hack it without you. And if you change your mind and want to get together before then, you know where to find me.'

She'd ended the call feeling happier that her friendship with Miles seemed to be back on track.

Gemma was in town, wandering aimlessly. She had thought a look round the shops in Maywood would cheer her up, but it wasn't working. She'd been stupid to think that anything would make her feel happy or normal again. Every morning she woke feeling the same intense loneliness. She'd open her eyes and for a split second it would feel like any ordinary day, but then she'd remember: Suzie was dead. Suzie and her baby, both dead. Dead in the ground. Their bodies side by side; one normal-sized coffin, one obscenely small coffin. But as bad as the mornings were, they were nothing compared to the nights when just as she was nodding off she would relive the terrifying journey to the hospital in the ambulance. With the siren wailing and the paramedic bent over Suzie's inert body, she had tried to convince herself that Suzie was going to be okay, that any minute her sister would wake up and wonder what all the fuss was about. Then there were all the questions the paramedic kept firing at her – how long had Suzie been unconscious? Had she vomited? Had Gemma noticed anything peculiar about her eyes? Had Suzie complained of a headache earlier? Was there a history of migraine attacks? On and on the questions went and with each one that was asked, Gemma dreaded getting something wrong. Something vital that might save her sister. It had been a relief when they finally arrived at the hospital and Gemma had been left alone. Later, when Dad had been taken away on his own, she'd thought the same as him, that the doctor was going to break the news that Suzie was okay but the baby had died. Had it been wishful thinking on their part – let the baby die so that Suzie might live? And had it been so wrong of them to hope for such a compromise? Even if it was wrong, Gemma didn't care. If it happened all over again, she'd wish for exactly the same, for her sister to be alive and looking forward to Christmas.

There would be no Christmas this year. And certainly no going to Paris to see Marcel. Mum had made Steve put the decorations back into the attic. She'd also thrown away all the cards they'd received; any new ones that arrived got the same treatment. Gemma had found Steve fishing them out of the bin one night and asked him what he was doing. 'These people don't know about Suzie,' he'd said. 'Someone has to write and tell them.'

She'd always despised Steve for being unimaginative and interfering but now Gemma was grateful for his rock-steady help. She didn't know what any of them would have done if he hadn't been around. He was endlessly patient and kind with Mum and Gemma could see that it wasn't always easy. Sometimes Mum would shout at him as if she was taking it out on him that Suzie had died. She had gone back to work the day after the funeral, which Gemma had thought was a mistake. Steve had thought so too and Mum had told him she didn't have any choice; she had a business to run. Steve did too, but he'd said a few days off wouldn't hurt anyone, that she ought to take a leaf out of Will's book and stay at home for a while. His advice had sent Mum into one of her screaming fits. 'Don't you dare tell me what to do!' she'd yelled. 'And don't ever compare me to that man.' She was being scarily irrational.

Dad's behaviour was equally scary. Since school had finished, Gemma had tried many times to go and see him but whenever she phoned to invite herself over, he'd say, 'Not today, love. I'm not very good company just now.'

The only person Gemma was able to talk to was Nana Ruby. Out of them all she was the one who seemed to be coping best. 'Don't worry about your father,' she told Gemma. He has to sort this out himself. He'll get there. Just be patient with him.'

But Gemma didn't want to be patient; she wanted her father *now*. She'd never been deprived of him and she saw no reason to go without him when she needed him most.

It was with this thought in mind that she decided to get the bus to Kings Melford. She wouldn't ring Dad; she'd just turn up on his doorstep.

Twenty-five minutes later, she was getting off the bus and heading for Maple Drive. It was dark and the houses along the main road had their lights switched on and some hadn't drawn the curtains. Through the windows she could see Christmas trees decorated with lights and baubles, cards strung up between pictures. One house had an illuminated snowman in the front porch. She didn't know why, but the sight of it made her want to cross the road and kick its cheery, smug face in. Again, not knowing why, she began to cry. Dragging her hands across her eyes, she turned at the sound of a car behind her. Dad? But it wasn't her father's tatty old estate; it was a smart Mini Cooper, like the one Yasmin's parents were buying her for Christmas. As it drew level, she recognised the driver; it was her father's girlfriend. Except Gemma had the feeling she wasn't his girlfriend any more. He hadn't invited her to the funeral or even mentioned her since the night Suzie died.

Harriet stopped the car when she realised who she'd just driven past. She had no idea what she was going to say, but knew it was something she had to do. With no traffic behind her, she reversed the short distance and lowered the passenger window. 'If you're going to see your father, would you like a lift?'

'It's okay, I can walk.'

'It's freezing out there. Go on, hop in. It's no trouble.'

When the girl had strapped herself in, Harriet drove on in silence. She badly wanted to find the right words of sympathy and support for Will's daughter, but could think of nothing helpful to say. Nothing that wasn't unspeakably trite. She suddenly felt sorry for all those people who had tried to be nice to her in the aftermath of her sister's death. In the end she said nothing until she had pulled onto her parents' drive.

'I know how it feels to lose a sister you're really close to,' she said quietly. 'My sister died earlier this year . . . She was my best friend, too.'

Her words were received with a crashing silence. Gemma released her seatbelt, and as she fumbled in the darkness for the door handle, Harriet quickly reached for her bag and dug out a business card. 'Look, any time you think a chat might help, just give me a ring.'

The girl stared at the card and for a moment Harriet didn't think she was going to take it. But then she put it into her jacket pocket. 'Thanks,' she said. 'But I'm okay. Really I am. It's my parents who are going to pieces.'

Harriet watched her cross the road to her father's house, where the lights were on and smoke was coming out of the chimney. Poor kid, she thought. She was far from okay. And Harriet should know; she'd been there herself. Every step of the way.

Chapter Fifty-Four

It was Christmas Day and Maxine felt sick. The sight and smell of the food on the table made her want to flee from the room. If only Ruby hadn't gone to so much trouble. And if only she'd held firm and not agreed to spend the day this way. 'We have to do something for Christmas,' Ruby had said with her customary reasonableness, 'so let's do it differently. I want you all to come to me. Will too. There won't be much room but it will do you both good.'

'I don't think it will work,' Maxine had said. She could see a mile off what Ruby was up to, but her ex mother-in-law was deluding herself if she believed she and Will could be united by a bond of grief. She hadn't bargained on Ruby's no-nonsense determination, though.

'I'm doing this for Suzie,' the older woman had said firmly. 'For one day you and my son will sit round my dinner table and put your differences aside. You'll do it for Gemma's sake as well. She needs her family to act with a degree of solidarity and normality if she's going to come through this.'

So here she was reluctantly sitting in Ruby's cramped dining room, watching Will stare vacantly into mid air while Steve carved the turkey and showered praise upon their host for providing them with such a spectacular meal. Will didn't look well. But then nor did she. She'd lost weight and was only managing to sleep for a couple of hours each night. Steve had suggested they go away for Christmas and New Year, but Maxine hadn't been able to bear the thought of being parted from everything that reminded her of her firstborn child – the room Suzie had slept in, the clothes she'd worn, the chair she'd sat in.

Maxine hadn't told anyone, but she'd hidden some of Suzie's unwashed clothes; they still smelt of her and when she was alone she would take out a piece of clothing and bury her face in it. Sometimes she cried, but more often she sobbed dry-eyed, the pain of her grief wedged in her throat, her breath difficult to catch, her head aching with every scrap of memory connected with Suzie.

There was regret too. All those times she hadn't been able to make it to a play or concert Suzie had been in. The sports days she'd missed. Even a birthday party one year. She'd been a lousy mother. She hadn't deserved a daughter like Suzie. But it was too late now to put it right. Suzie was dead and Maxine would never be able to say how sorry she was.

'Red or white wine, dear?'

Maxine looked up from her plate which, without her noticing, had been filled with food she wouldn't touch. 'None for me, Ruby,' she murmured. 'I'll stick with water.' She hadn't touched a drop of alcohol since Suzie had died. The shameful memory of Ruby rousing her from her drunken stupor was still palpable. As was the memory of her disgusting behaviour with Will that night. That was something she had no intention of every referring to again.

When lunch was over, Will insisted on doing the washing up. He didn't want to watch the Queen crow about the nation's achievements for that year. Nor did he want to join in with the board game Steve and Gemma were suggesting they all play. He poured his mother a glass of Baileys, settled her in front of the telly and disappeared to the kitchen. Closing the door behind him, and glad to be alone at last, he unbuttoned his shirtsleeves and took stock of the mess. He had just cleared a space around the sink, stacking the plates, pots and pans to one side, when the door opened and Maxine came in. 'Your mother suggested you might like some help.'

'It's okay. I've got it covered. You go and relax with the others.'

'She said you'd say that. Don't ask me why, but I'm under orders to stay.'

Annoyed that he was to be deprived of some much-needed time alone, he turned on the hot tap. 'It's not like you to do something against your will,' he said irritably. At once he realised how petty he sounded. 'I'm sorry,' he said, meaning it. 'It's just that I wanted to be on my own. I find it's easier that way.'

'Me too.'

He looked at her over his shoulder and saw that her face – so often resolutely proud and hostile – was clouded with tiredness and misery. 'I'll wash, you dry,' he said.

They worked in silence until Maxine handed a plate back to him. 'You've missed a bit,' she murmured. He took it from her and gave it another scrub. When he'd rinsed it under the tap and passed it to her again, she said, 'How's Marty coping with the radiotherapy?'

'You know Marty; it would take more than a bit of cancer to get to him. How about you? How are you coping with everything?'

'People at work say I'm doing brilliantly.'

'And what does Steve think?'

'He thinks I'm burying myself in my work.'

'And are you?'

'Probably.'

Tipping the dirty water out of the washing-up bowl and refilling it with clean hot water, Will said, 'I never thought I'd say this, Maxine, but Steve's not a bad bloke. I'm not sure how either of us would have got through this if he hadn't been around.'

'That's very magnanimous of you.'

'I have my moments.' Out of the corner of his eye, he watched her putting the cutlery in the drawer. He'd forgotten that Maxine didn't put cutlery away like most normal people did; she lined everything up neatly, the spoons and forks all layered with precision, the knives blade-side down. 'By the way, how's your foot?' he asked.

She looked at him sharply. 'Please let's not go scraping the bottom of the barrel for something to talk about.'

'Are you saying you'd rather talk about something more important?'

'No,' she said hurriedly. Her hand jolted, sending the forks askew that she'd just lined up. 'Damn!'

He looked away, disconcerted at seeing her so flustered. This wasn't the Maxine he knew of old. But what else could he expect? They were both changed. Everything they ever experienced from now on would be affected by Suzie's dying. Her death would find its way into every thought they ever had. Suzie would be there in every piece of music they heard, every conversation they had, every meal they ate, every journey they undertook, every sleepless night they suffered. It would always be Suzie. For the rest of their lives there would be a bottomless pit of memories to refer to: that was the way Suzie liked her toast . . . Oh, Suzie used to love that film . . . Do you remember the doll Suzie used to take everywhere she went?

He knew that had Suzie lived, she might well have been severely brain damaged as a result of the aneurysm; she would have been completely reliant upon others for her every need. Sometimes Will thought even that would be preferable to her being dead. At least then he would have been able to devote the rest of his life to taking care of her.

He didn't know whether it was a relief or a comfort, but already Suzie's presence seemed to be greater in death than when she was alive. It was as if he'd been made raw from grief and his mind, body and soul were sensitive to everything he'd ever known about her. Memories he'd forgotten he had had been brought vividly and painfully alive.

The most painful memory was of him kneeling by the side of her bed on her third birthday. She was still overexcited from an afternoon of too much sugar and a houseful of squealing friends from nursery school. Her tiny party frock was hanging from the handle on the wardrobe door, her brand-new black patent shoes had been left out to wear again to Nana Ruby's the next day, and he had soothed her by stroking her back and singing to her. His heart thumped as he pictured her small, restless body gradually relaxing, her eyelids fluttering, her lips gently parting as she slept. But without warning, the picture changed and it was a grown-up Suzie he was looking at – Suzie dead in the hospital, the lights bright, the ground rising up to meet him as he pitched forward, hands reaching out for him, voices asking if he needed to sit down, did he want a drink? No, he silently screamed, I want my daughter back. Give me back my daughter!

He lowered his head, squeezing his eyes shut against the burning tears that threatened to destroy what few defences he could still rely on. He plunged his hands into the washing-up bowl, clenched his fists and tried to take a gulp of air.

'Will?'

Fighting hard to regain his composure, he forced himself to swallow. He didn't want Maxine to see him like this. It was too reminiscent of a lifetime ago, when she had despised and scorned him for his weakness.

'Will, are you okay?'

Ignoring her, he went over to the drawer where his mother kept the clean hand-towels. He pulled one out and dried his hands roughly, and still with his back to Maxine, hunted through his pockets for something to blow his nose on.

'Here, try this.'

He turned round; Maxine was holding out some kitchen roll towards him. He took it but was careful not to look at her. 'Thanks,' he muttered. 'Sorry to let the side down. You never did like seeing me when I was upset, did you? In your eyes men should behave like real men. As your father did.' His tone was bitter.

'As usual, your biting cynicism isn't far from the truth.'

'And?'

She shrugged wearily, and once again he realised how

454

changed she was. There was little evidence of the determined and ambitious Maxine in her face. She looked haggard, thoroughly defeated.

'I'm sorry,' he said, 'old habits die hard. I keep having a go at you, and I shouldn't. Not now when we're going through—'

She raised her hands. 'No, please, don't say any more.' She looked terrified that he might offer her sympathy.

It upset him to think how divided and entrenched they'd become. How could they have created a beautiful child like Suzie, only to end up hating each other? Surely, for Suzie's sake, they could learn to be kinder to one another. Couldn't they? Emboldened, he decided to test the water. 'Maxine,' he said softly, 'do you think it's possible that we—?'

But once again, she cut him off. 'If you're tired of washing, I'll take over and you can dry.'

Taking his cue, he thought better of what he'd nearly said. Perhaps it was hopeless anyway. They'd probably left it too late.

Chapter Fifty-Five

It had rained steadily over Christmas, but the day after Boxing Day, the sky suddenly brightened, and seeing as she was off work until January, Harriet phoned the estate agent to ask if she could borrow the key to number one Lock Cottage to do some measuring. She wanted to make sure there wouldn't be any last-minute surprises, such as discovering her bed wouldn't fit up the stairs.

The biggest surprise of the move so far was how much Carrie was looking forward to it. To Harriet's amazement her niece spoke of little else and was constantly on at Harriet about when she could invite her new friends to see the cottage and when they could have their first sleepover. Harriet viewed this enthusiasm with a mixture of relief and horror; it was good that Carrie had now made friends at school, but the thought of having to entertain them on a regular basis scared her rigid.

As was to be expected, Joel was more reticent about the move. Harriet had lost count how many times he had asked her how he would get home from school. It was as if he had a mental block on the subject. His anxiety was contagious and whenever Harriet found herself beginning to worry too much about her nephew, she reminded herself of something Will had once told her; that as soon as Joel had made a special friend at school, everything would come together for him and he'd feel more settled and secure. Will had been right on so many other matters when it came to the children, she hoped he was right on this one. It really mattered to her that Joel was happy. He wasn't a strong, resilient child the way Carrie was; he was quiet and sensitive and too prone to introversion. He was entirely his father's child, Harriet had come to realise.

Harriet had seen Will only twice during the Christmas period, and that was when he came and went from his house. Mum had wanted to invite him over for a drink, but Harriet had begged her not to. Seeing Will floundering over a glass of wine and a flaky cheese straw in their sitting room would have been too much. 'It's far too soon to expect him to be sociable,' she'd told Eileen.

'I'm not expecting him to be sociable,' her mother had said, 'but it seems wrong to leave him out in the cold, as though we don't care.'

'He knows we care, Mum. Just leave him be until New Year.'

Their own Christmas had, of course, been over-shadowed by Felicity and Jeff's absence, and Harriet knew that at times her parents had struggled to keep a brave face on the proceedings. It was particularly palpable when it came to the children opening their presents. Felicity had had a rule with Carrie and Joel that they could have their stockings as soon as they were awake, but the rest of the presents had to be kept until after lunch. Eileen had decided to stick with this tradition, but when the children were sitting expectantly round the tree, their hands itching to root out something with their name on it, Harriet's father had left the room abruptly.

'It was their faces,' he told Harriet later, when he was helping her to make some ham sandwiches for tea. 'There was such joy and excitement in their expressions. And poor Felicity not here to see it. It's so bloody unfair. It's like they've forgotten her already, as though she never mattered to them.'

'They'll never forget their mother,' Harriet had said, quick to defend her niece and nephew. 'They're just adapting faster than us. Perhaps we should take a leaf out of their book.'

These had been almost the only words exchanged between Harriet and her father since she had learned of his double life, and she could muster up little sympathy for him. Mum had said she mustn't judge him too harshly, that his behaviour was a reflection of the depth of his grief, but it simply wasn't in her to offer him any consolation. The rest of them were coping; why couldn't he?

The children had wanted to come and help her measure up at the house, and just as they were climbing into the back of her car, a voice had Harriet turning round. She hadn't seen either Miles or Dominic since the evening at Novel Ways, but here was Dominic coming towards her. 'Just the person I wanted to see,' he said. 'Are you on your way out or coming back?'

'Going out.'

'Anywhere interesting?'

'Yes, my new house.'

'Excellent. I'll come with you.'

She moved away from the car so that the children couldn't hear her. 'Firstly,' she said, 'you're not coming anywhere with me until you've apologised. Secondly, who says I want you to see my new house?'

He raised his eyebrows. 'Good God, Harriet, you're quite magnificent when you're angry. It's enough to make a gay man straight! Here, let me kiss you to see if you're the answer every fundamentalist Christian out there has been praying for.'

He put his gloved hands on her shoulders but she pushed him away roughly. 'Don't even think about it.'

'Ah, not even a little kiss? It is the season of good will, after all. Besides, I'm told my technique is something to behold.'

'Well hold onto it yourself; I'm not interested. So how about that apology?'

'It would help if I knew what it was I'm supposed to be sorry about. Remind me what heinous crime I've committed. Don't tell me your stultifying priggishness didn't appreciate the card I pushed through your letterbox. Is that what I've done wrong?'

Staggered at his glibness, she tightened her scarf around her throat. She was also blushing at the thought of the card he'd sent – a picture of two naked men having sex in the snow. Definitely not one for the mantelpiece! But only Dominic could pretend that scene in the wine bar had never happened. 'I suggest you cast your mind back to last week when I threw my drink in your face,' she said, 'and in particular, the reason why I did it.'

'Surely you're not still cross about that? A silly off-the-cuff remark about my little bro fancying you?'

She looked at him hard. 'You called me frigid.'

'Did I?'

'You did.'

'And is that what you want me to apologise for? For you having an underdeveloped sexuality? Not for my teasing you about Miles swapping his affections from one sister to another? Which was, I admit, rather cruel of me, but I wanted to see the look on his face. By the way, presumably you've now proved me right; that it *was* Miles with whom Felicity was having an affair?'

Having no intention of letting him off by being side-tracked, Harriet said, 'Dominic, I'm warning you. You apologise to me, right now. Or I'll—'

'Or what?' he interrupted her. 'What will you do, Harriet?' He suddenly flung his arms out wide. 'What can anyone do to me?' To her horror and amazement, he started to cry, and lurching towards her, he wept uninhibitedly, his sobs catching in his throat.

Stunned, and wondering if he'd been drinking, Harriet stood in his arms not knowing what to do. She tried to slip out of his grasp. 'Dominic,' she said. 'Please stop. The children. You'll upset them.'

To her relief he let go of her abruptly, almost flinging her away. But with his head back, his face open to the sky and tears streaming down his cheeks, he said, 'I don't give a damn about anyone else. Don't you understand I'm beyond that? . . . Please let me come and see your new house.' He was pleading with her.

What could she do but give in? She bundled him into the passenger seat of her Mini, hoping that he'd stop crying so that the children wouldn't ask what was wrong with him.

But he didn't stop crying, and they did ask what was wrong with him.

'Dominic's not feeling well,' she explained as they hurtled down Maple Drive and he leaned against the passenger window, his face partially hidden behind a handkerchief.

'Has he got flu like Will?' asked Joel.

'Would he like a sweet?' asked Carrie, leaning forward and offering a paper bag of Edna's pick'n'mix.

By the time they'd picked up the key from the estate agent and had driven on to the house, Dominic had calmed down. 'I'm sorry,' he murmured, when at Harriet's instruction the children had taken the keys and gone round to the back of the cottage. 'I warned you in Dublin that I was losing it.'

'Dominic, have you thought seriously about seeing someone? A doctor? Or maybe a therapist?'

'No!' He slammed the car door shut. 'Come on, I'm bored with this conversation. Show me your house. Show me where I'll come and visit you, where we'll sit by the fire eating crumpets on a cold winter's afternoon.'

His mood swings were so difficult to keep up with. Not for the first time, Harriet wondered if drugs were responsible. She knew from Felicity that years ago he went through a phrase of using amphetamines and coke. It was the reason Jeff had said he wouldn't ever allow Dominic to stay with them; he didn't want his children coming within a mile of someone with a drug habit. But whatever the reason behind Dominic's current erratic behaviour, Harriet knew she couldn't stay cross with him for long. She never had been able to. That was the trouble with him; he was his own constellation. You couldn't judge him by normal standards.

The house was freezing cold inside and Harriet quickly got on with the job of measuring up. Leaving the children to give Dominic the guided tour, she worked out where all the larger pieces of furniture would go. When the solicitor had given them the all-clear, she and her parents had sold most of Jeff and Felicity's things. Forever practical, though, she had kept most of the kitchen appliances as well as the more useful pieces of furniture, such as the kitchen table and chairs, a range of book cases, and of course, everything the children had had in their old bedrooms. It was all stored in her parents' garage, along with her stuff from the flat in Oxford. While she was looking forward to having her own belongings around her again, she wasn't so sure about resurrecting such tangible reminders of her sister. Her original thinking had been that their presence would be a comfort for Carrie and Joel, but supposing she'd got that wrong? Supposing it just chafed at the wound that was slowly healing?

Dominic made no comment on the house until they were locking up and the children were dragging him by the arm to come and look at the garden and canal. 'Felicity would approve,' was his only comment as he rested his elbows on the wall and watched a pair of swans gliding past. From nowhere, a smile appeared on his face. 'Let's go for lunch,' he said. 'A pub lunch. We should celebrate this day.'

'Why this day in particular?' she asked.

'Because I've decided I'm going to apologise to you.'

'Really? Why?'

'I'm not sure, to be honest. Now this pub you're taking me to, I'm assuming it's one of those dreadful family pubs where they pander to the whims of diminutive savages? Any chance of there being some kind of quicksand pit in which these two can be thrown, thereby allowing us to have a quiet conversation?'

There was no quicksand, but there was the next best thing; a pit of brightly coloured plastic balls and an enormous obstacle course above it. The children's eyes lit up when they saw it.

It was a surreal experience having lunch in such an environment with Dominic: only the Queen could have looked more out of place. 'Felicity told me these places existed,' he said, tossing his paper napkin onto his half-eaten plate of beef and ale pie and casting a disdainful glance around the Muzak-pumped pub, 'but I had no idea they were as ghastly as this. Whoever came up with the idea for this one obviously couldn't decide whether it was to be a crèche or an S and M dungeon.'

'Trust you to make that comparison.'

'What's an S and M dungeon?'

Harriet jumped in smartly. 'Nothing you need ever think about, Carrie. Have you chosen what you want to eat for pudding? The ice-cream sounds good.'

Carrie puffed out her cheeks. 'I'm too full to eat anything else,' she said.

'Me too,' agreed Joel. 'Can we go and play?'

'If you like. Carrie, keep an eye on your brother for me, please. And make sure you don't forget where you've left your shoes.'

Joel immediately looked uncertain. He came round to Harriet's side of the table. 'Why don't you come and watch us?'

'I'm sure you'll be all right, Joel.'

He leaned against her, his small body heavy against her side. '*Pleease*.'

'Okay, just until you're settled in.'

His face instantly brightened and he slipped his hand in hers and pulled her to her feet. 'You can either stay here on your own,' she told Dominic, 'or you can come and watch as well.'

'I wouldn't miss it for the world. What do you think, kids, shall we throw Harriet in too? She's no bigger than a child, so no one would notice, would they?'

Carrie and Joel laughed, but Harriet scowled back at him. 'Don't even think about it.'

He ruffled her hair and laughed. 'I'll think exactly what I want to.'

Fifteen minutes later, she and Dominic were still standing next to the ball pit where a swarming army of small children had the place under siege. Each time Harriet tried to move away, Joel would come over to make sure they were staying. 'I'm sorry,' she said to Dominic, 'but it looks like we're stuck here.'

He shrugged. 'I can think of worse places to be.'

'You can?'

'Lunch with my parents in Maple Drive would be a hundred times worse, I assure you. And for the record, I'm sorrier than I can say for what I said to you that night with Miles. I deserved what you did to me. Am I forgiven?'

'I'll think about it.'

He smiled. 'So now we've got that behind us, why don't you fill me in on what you've found out about Felicity and her not so mysterious lover. You must have come across some proof by now.'

Harriet hesitated. If she told Dominic what she'd discovered, and he then knew for sure that Miles had had a passionate affair with Felicity, how would he react? In his current state of mind, would he think that Miles had defiled his dearest friend in some way?

But it had been a mistake to hesitate. He leapt on it. 'You've found something, haven't you? What a clever sleuth you've become! Come on, don't hold back.'

It was pointless even to think about lying to Dominic. Any prevarication on her part would have him turning up the pressure until she caved in. So she told him about the last email she'd read.

'I knew it. I knew it from the moment you told me in Dublin. Well, well, well. And isn't it always the quiet ones you have to watch? What did Miles say when you confronted him?'

'I haven't spoken to Miles about it and I'm not sure it's a matter of confronting him.'

'Really? And yet, if I'm not mistaken, there was a moment not so long ago when you had hopes for Miles, didn't you? Oh, don't insult me by feigning shock and denial. Is that why you had a fling with this Will character? To get back at Miles?'

The accuracy of his guesswork was breathtaking. But it was only guesswork, she told herself. He had no way of knowing what had been in her mind when she'd asked Will to kiss her that night. 'Stop fishing, Dominic,' she said firmly. 'What passed between Will and me was private, and it will remain that way.'

'Don't be absurd, Hat. Old friends like us don't have secrets from each other. You realise, don't you, now that Felicity's dead, you're my oldest and closest friend?'

Unsure whether to be flattered or even more on her guard, she said, 'That's as maybe, but I'm not going to tell you anything; it wouldn't be fair to Will. He deserves that much respect from me, if nothing else.'

'How very honourable. I wish I could be more like you. But the sad truth is; there isn't an honourable bone in my body. My father saw to that.'

His voice echoed faintly with something that, coming from him, didn't add up. It was regret. Harriet studied his face closely.

'Don't look so surprised,' he said. 'I was always going to blame my father for my behaviour at some time or other. After all, he's made me the man I am.'

'That's a cop out.'

'Perhaps so in your eyes. However, it's the truth. I knew a long time ago that I had to distance myself from him and to do that I had to recreate who I was. I would have happily killed myself rather than turn out like Dr Harvey McKendrick, local do-gooding General Practitioner but healer of no one and nothing. Ironically, he destroys people rather than heals them. He used to make me look at porn magazines when I was a boy. Oh, nothing too vile, just the run-of-the-mill stuff that he secretly enjoyed. You see, he suspected then that I wasn't normal. He once caught me brushing my mother's hair and he beat me senseless afterwards. That's when he decided I had to go away to school. Stupid old fool thought an all-male environment would cure me of my tendencies and I'd have it knocked out of me. I was raped three times in my first week by the head boy and his cohorts. I was eleven. Not much older than Carrie.'

Harriet was appalled. She and Felicity had known that Harvey McKendrick was a fierce disciplinarian, and they had always been a bit scared of him, but this was awful. How could any parent victimise their child so cruelly? And what would he have done with a sensitive boy like Joel . . . who also liked to brush his mother's hair? She shuddered. Let anyone lay a hand on that boy and she'd kill them. Which begged the question what Freda McKendrick had been doing to protect her eldest son. 'But we all thought you were sent away because you were so bright,' she said.

He let out a short, bitter laugh. 'A convenient enough cover. And it had the added bonus of making me even more of an outsider. My father was and still is an overbearing, sadistic bully. It suits him perfectly that he has an agoraphobic wife; it means he can control her completely. These things don't happen by accident.'

'Did Felicity know all this?'

He nodded. 'Felicity knew everything about me. It's why I miss her so much. As Victor Hugo put it so well, the supreme happiness of life is the conviction of being loved for yourself, or more correctly, of being loved *of* yourself.' He put an arm around Harriet and drew her to him. 'But now I have you.' He kissed her forehead. 'Oh, Hat, it feels good being able to talk to you. Hey, you know what we should do, we should get married. We could bring up Carrie and Joel together. We wouldn't be the best or the most orthodox of parents, but we'd be better than the majority of idiots who attempt it.'

She laughed nervously. It was difficult to know when he was joking sometimes. 'I think you need to go outside and get some fresh air. You're talking crazy now.'

He tilted his head back and looked deep into her eyes. At once his close proximity aroused in Harriet a dangerous mix of emotions – love, hate, admiration, affection, fear, but most of all confusion. She tried to keep her face from

465

betraying her; she couldn't stand for him to know the effect he had on her.

'Actually, I'm being serious,' he said. 'You could come and live in Cambridge. You'd easily get work there.'

'And what kind of marriage would we have?'

'An unconventional one. They're usually the best sort.'

'Mm . . . so while you were off having sex with the entire male population of Cambridge, I'd be doing what exactly?'

He grinned. 'I'd leave that to your imagination. You do have one of those, don't you?'

He was mocking her now, and knowing they were back on safer and more familiar ground, she said, 'Believe me, Dominic, there's nothing wrong with my imagination.'

January

'The Mermaid'

A mermaid found a swimming lad,
Picked him for her own,
Pressed her body to his body,
Laughed; and plunging down
Forgot in cruel happiness
That even lovers drown.

W.B. Yeats

Chapter Fifty-Six

It was New Year's Day, the day of the McKendricks' drinks party. Upstairs the children, having minutes earlier pulled back the curtains, were going crazy with excitement. Overnight, a heavy fall of snow had covered the garden, and as Bob stared out of the kitchen window he could see that not a breath of wind stirred. The sky was leaden with the threat of further snow showers. The weather forecasters had said they were in for a big freeze. Bob filled the kettle and plugged it in, hoping the weather wouldn't delay Harriet's move. Her moving out with the children heralded the start of their lives getting back to normal. Or rather, a life that resembled some kind of unreal normality, for he knew that nothing would ever feel truly normal again. Jennifer had told him that his life had been changed irrevocably and that he had to accept that. But how? How did one go about that? Accepting it seemed a wounding insult to Felicity's memory, as brutal as it had been to witness Carrie and Joel enjoying Christmas without their mother. He could not bring himself to do it. Never. Others were all too willing to consign Felicity to the past – and how he hated them for it – but he would not betray her.

After Harriet had fulfilled her promise to help the children build a snowman and they were thawing out in the kitchen drinking mugs of hot chocolate, she told her father – her mother was resting in bed after a sleepless night – she wanted to sort through some of Felicity's things in the garage. He looked up sharply from polishing his shoes ready for the McKendricks' party. Knowing that he couldn't handle the idea of any of Felicity's things being thrown away, she said, 'I don't want to move with anything that will just lie around in the attic or garage. I won't have the luxury of space you have here,' she added reasonably.

'You haven't got much time,' he muttered, glancing at the clock above the fridge. 'We're expected at Harvey and Freda's in two hours.'

'The sooner I get started, the sooner I'll be finished,' she said, and before he could invent another reason why she shouldn't touch Felicity's things, she slipped out of the kitchen.

There was a gas heater in the garage, which her father used on cold days when he was tinkering at his workbench, but given the densely packed state of the place, Harriet thought better of using it. Quite apart from the worry of reducing Felicity's furniture and possessions to a heap of ash, there was her asthma to take into account. The combination of the damp cold, a dusty environment and gas fumes could very likely bring on an attack. Her last attack had been with Will, in his shop; it felt like a long time ago. Reminded of Will and the kindness he'd shown her that afternoon, she then recalled the illogical feeling she'd had during the drive to Kings Melford, when she'd imagined Felicity in the car with her and had a chilling sense that she'd failed her sister.

That day when she and the children had had lunch with Dominic, she'd tried to share this feeling with him, but he hadn't shown the slightest interest. Instead he'd wanted to know more about her and Will. 'You really like him, don't you?' he'd said.

'Yes,' she'd answered, without a second's hesitation. 'Will's a hundred times the man you are, or will ever be.'

'My, but you have it bad for him. Isn't he the lucky one?'

'Lucky is not the word I'd use. His eldest daughter is dead and his world's just ground to a halt.'

He'd looked at her with a bemused expression. 'You're angry. Why?'

'Perhaps I'm tired of the perverse games you play. Like

suggesting you and I should get married. It's practically the sickest thing I've ever heard.'

'I think you expect too much of me. But as I've said before, your stubborn one-track brain allows you to see things only in black and white. One day you'll realise there are myriad shades of grey in between.'

Putting Dominic and Will from her thoughts, Harriet got on with the job she'd come out here to do. She regretted not doing it sooner; there was so little time left before the move. She cleared a space in front of her father's workbench, deciding to create a pile there of anything she didn't want to keep. Her father could then go through it for anything he thought he couldn't live without.

An hour later, knowing she ought to go and change, she opened one last box. It was one she remembered packing herself and it contained a selection of photograph albums as well as several bundles of snaps clumsily held together with rubber bands. At the time, she hadn't had the courage to look at any of the photographs; she had simply boxed them up as quickly as she could to get the job done. One of the albums had a discoloured photograph stuck on the front of it. Harriet recognised herself in the picture, along with Felicity and Dominic. Why was Miles absent? Then she remembered; he had been behind the camera, taking the photo. They had been walking by the river in Durham. It was a freezing cold day and Miles and his brother had come to stay with them. It was before Jeff had arrived on the scene. Dominic was threatening to pull his trousers down if Miles didn't get a move on and take the picture. How young they looked, Harriet thought as she opened the album to revisit those days. Arrogant too, she thought with a wry smile as she turned the pages. We thought we knew it all. How wrong we were.

She turned another page and out fluttered a single photograph; it landed on the dusty floor at her feet. She stooped to pick it up and flipped it over to see the picture, then did a double take. Her initial reaction was to turn it over again, to pretend she'd never seen it. But her eye was drawn to it. Holding her breath, she took in the naked bodies, the absorbed intimacy of the act. It must have been taken using the camera's timer device and it was graphically explicit, yet at the same time wholly erotic. The two people in the photograph were doing nothing she hadn't recently done with Will, yet Harriet could hardly bring herself to look at it. It wasn't what they were doing that chilled her, it was the knowledge that this represented so much more than just an affair. Putting the photograph face down in the palm of her trembling hand, she saw that Felicity had written on the back of it – '*Soul and body have no bounds.*' Underneath was a date; it was February of this year.

Harriet felt sick. How could she have been so stupid?

From his sitting-room window, Will watched another carload of guests arriving for the McKendricks' drinks party. An invitation had been slipped through his letterbox, but he'd thrown it in the bin. They couldn't honestly think he'd show up.

He stayed by the window, absently watching the road until a car he recognised appeared and turned cautiously into his drive, which he'd cleared earlier. He'd half expected – half hoped – the snow would have put Maxine off and that she would have phoned to cancel. But she hadn't. She was here. It was too late now for him to wimp out.

He had no idea how his words would be received, but he owed it to Suzie to give it his best shot. He'd decided that if he and Maxine could put the past behind them, the future might not seem so pointless.

He opened the door to Maxine and surprised her with a kiss. She looked startled, as if he'd pinched her. 'What's that for?' she asked.

'Happy New Year,' he said, ignoring her question and offering to take her coat. It was fur. Real fur; the colour of butterscotch.

'I'll keep it on for now,' she said with an exaggerated shiver. 'It's freezing.'

Suspecting that the real reason she didn't want to part with her coat was because she had no intention of stopping for long, he said, 'I'll make us some coffee. Fresh coffee,' he added before she refused it on the grounds of never drinking instant.

'I'm not really thirsty,' she said, prowling uneasily round the small kitchen.

'I'll make some anyway.'

He was just filling the cafetiere when Maxine cleared her throat and said, 'Okay, Will, let's make this easier on each other. What was it you wanted to say?'

He stopped what he was doing, took a deep breath, and turned to face her. Courage, he told himself. Besides, what did he have to lose? 'Maxine, I know this is going to be hard for you to believe but I want us to be friends.' His words came out in a nervous rush. Then more slowly, he said, 'I want to feel comfortable around you and I want you to be comfortable around me.' He forced himself to meet her gaze. 'At the very least I want you to feel that you can take your coat off when you're in my house.'

'Why? Why should any of that be important to you?'

'Because the love we once had for each other should still mean something.'

'What if it doesn't?

'Then I'm buggered.' He leaned back against the work-top and dragged his hands over his face. 'It might sound crazy, but by being emotionally close to you again I think I'll feel closer to Suzie. To put it bluntly, I'm terrified I won't survive this mess unless you help me.'

'Nothing will bring her back, Will. Don't delude yourself.'

'I'm not. I just know that she was a part of you and me and that by bringing the two of us together—' But his nerve failed him and he hung his head. Moments passed and then: 'Look, Maxine, I'll admit it, I'm desperate, I can't do this alone.'

'You are only talking about being *friends*, aren't you?'

she said more gently. 'You're not suggesting we get back together again?'

He looked up. 'I think that would be a challenge too far, don't you?'

For the first time since she'd arrived, her expression softened. 'You're right. And Steve might have something to say on the matter too.'

'I know I'm repeating myself, but he really is one of the good guys. I envy you having such a supportive partner right now.'

'What about the girl you were seeing? What happened to her?'

'She reached the conclusion that an older man wasn't appropriate.'

'What was the age gap? Gemma implied she wasn't much older than . . . Suzie.'

'I think that was Gemma wanting to stir things up. Harriet's thirty-three.'

He watched her mentally do the sums. 'That's not so bad,' she said. 'It's not much more than the gap between Steve and me.' She then shrugged off her coat and put it over the back of a chair. 'Is that offer of coffee still on?'

He swallowed his relief that his plea for help hadn't been met with an outright rejection. 'I've lit a fire in the sitting room; why don't you go and sit down in the warm?'

She did as he said and minutes later, he joined her with the tray of coffee things. He found her standing by the desk where he kept his collection of framed photographs. She was holding one up to the light: it was of Suzie and Gemma as toddlers; all blonde hair and best party frocks. He put the tray down and went and stood next to her. 'I never meant to be such a bad mother,' she murmured.

He put a hand on her shoulder. 'You haven't been a bad mother, Maxine. Don't ever say that about yourself.'

She put the photograph back with the others. 'What I regret most is that she never knew how much I loved her. I never took the time to tell her. I never once showed her what she really meant to me. I . . . I was always too busy.

Too busy trying to be the person I thought my father wanted me to be.' Her voice caught in her throat and she put a hand to her mouth.

'Come and sit down,' he said.

'I idolised him, Will,' she said, making no attempt to move. 'But then you always knew that, didn't you?' Her voice was tight with emotion.

He nodded.

'As a child I thought he was better than Superman. I was utterly devoted to him. I wanted to be just like he was; all-powerful and utterly invincible.' Tears filled her eyes. 'I sacrificed everything for him. The silly teenage dreams I'd had for myself. You. And now Suzie. If I hadn't been so obsessed with following in his footsteps, to prove myself to him, Suzie would still be alive. It's all my fault. I know it is.' The tears really flowed now and Will took her gently in his arms. He tried to soothe her but she wouldn't listen, just went on berating herself. With tears filling his own eyes, he let her cry it out.

He'd only ever seen her cry once before, and that was when her father died.

Half an hour into its stride, the McKendricks' sherry fest had looked as though it would be as tedious as it always was. The usual suspects had been circling the buffet table and Harriet had been doing her usual act of trying to appear sociable while totally ignoring everyone.

She'd had no intention of causing such an almighty scene, but when it happened – when Dora and Derek offered to find the children some orange juice in the kitchen, and she found herself alone with Miles and Dominic – the red mist came down and she gave in to it all too readily. By now she'd had sufficient time to figure things out, and was more than ready for a confrontation.

'There's something I want to discuss with you two,' she said. 'Let's go outside where no one will hear us.'

'Harriet, are you quite mad? It's about minus six out there!'

'Dominic, trust me, I'm in no mood to argue with you. Now get outside. You too, Miles. Unless you'd both prefer for your parents to hear what I've got to say.' Her voice had risen and people were staring, but she didn't care. She took hold of Dominic's elbow. 'Move it,' she snapped. 'Now!'

She slammed the front door shut after them. 'Right,' she said. 'I'll start with you, Miles. How long had you been having an affair with my sister before she died? To the nearest month will do.'

Chapter Fifty-Seven

Miles stared back at her in horror, just as Harriet had expected him to. 'Don't be shy, Miles,' she said. 'After all, it's not the big secret you think it is. Your brother had it all worked out ages ago. Isn't that right, Dominic?'

Dominic looked at her warily, his eyes slightly narrowed, his composure jolted imperceptibly out of line. He didn't answer her, though.

'Lost for words, are you?' she said nastily. 'Wow, that must be a first.'

'Look, will somebody tell me what the hell's going on here?' Miles said.

Switching her gaze between the two brothers, Harriet said, 'Now that's what I call a seriously good question. Dominic? Do you have an answer for your brother? You usually have an answer for most things.'

Still Dominic said nothing.

'Well, Miles, in view of your brother's refusal to speak, allow me to fill in the gaps. Several months ago I discovered Felicity had been having an affair, and when I mentioned it to Dominic, guess who he suggested as being the most likely candidate to be her lover. Yes, that's right. You.'

Miles's jaw dropped. He turned to his brother. 'Why? Why in hell's name would you say that?'

'Oh, I think that's obvious,' Harriet said. 'Don't forget he's the master manipulator. What better way could there be to prevent me from viewing you as anything more than a friend, than to put the idea into my head that you'd been screwing my sister on the quiet?'

If it was possible, Miles looked even more horrified. 'But

that's sick. Dominic, surely not even you would sink to that!'

'Believe it, Miles,' Harriet said, without giving Dominic a chance to respond, 'because it gets a whole lot worse. He couldn't handle the thought that anyone else might find happiness when he couldn't. I blame myself for being so gullible. It never occurred to me that he could be bisexual. I made the fatal mistake of taking him at face value, just as you probably did. We thought he was only interested in men. And why wouldn't we, because he made such a big thing about it, didn't he?' Reaching into her trouser pocket, she pulled out the incriminating photograph she'd found amongst Felicity's things. She pushed it under Dominic's nose. 'See anyone you recognise?'

Before he could reply, Miles snatched the photograph out of Harriet's hand. He stared at it, first in disbelief, then in understanding. '*You!* You and Felicity. Oh, you bastard! You complete and utter bastard.'

The first punch was a direct hit on Dominic's cheekbone. It was so direct and unexpected it knocked him backwards and he lost his footing. As he scrambled to stay on his feet, Miles came at him again, this time throwing all his weight against him; the powdery snow softened their fall. His fists smashed into Dominic's face, and spots of blood began to splatter the snow. It was then that Harriet realised Dominic was making no attempt to defend himself – he was just lying there submitting himself to his brother's vengeful anger.

Behind them the front door suddenly flew open and Harvey McKendrick's voice demanded to know what was going on. 'Have you taken leave of your senses?' he shouted at his sons. 'Stop it at once!'

Knowing there would never be a better opportunity, Harriet said, 'Congratulations, Dr McKendrick. You turned your eldest son into a monster. Because of you, he has no sense of right or wrong. He uses people. Abuses them too, just like you do.'

Miles was getting to his feet now and straightening his

clothes, but Dominic continued to lie in the snow, his arms outstretched, blood trickling from his mouth and nose. A crowd had gathered at the door behind their host, gasping when they saw Dominic. Harriet felt a prickle of regret when she caught sight of her mother and Freda looking out from the sitting room window, but she tapped into her anger – there was still plenty of it – and delivered one final blow. 'For once, Dr McKendrick,' she said, 'I've actually enjoyed one of your miserable drinks parties.' She then walked away from the house, along Maple Drive.

Bob helped Harvey get his eldest son to his feet. He'd never been particularly fond of Dominic and suspected that whatever the fight had been about, Dominic had probably deserved what Miles had done to him. Although what Harriet had to do with it, he couldn't think. He was just gathering up the loose change that must have fallen out of the brothers' pockets when something caught his attention: it looked like a photograph half-buried in the snow. He bent down to pick it up.

'I wouldn't, if I were you. Really, it's not something you want to see.' Miles was standing next to him and something in his tone made Bob turn the photograph over at once. He froze. It was a while before he could speak. 'When was this picture taken?' he said.

'I don't know exactly.'

'It looks recent to me,' Bob murmured. He turned the photograph over again and looked at the date on the back.

'Perhaps it would be better if you gave it to me.'

Miles's bloodied hand reached out for the picture, but Bob stepped away from him. It was just the two of them in the McKendricks' front garden now; the show over, everyone else had gone back inside. In the silence of the snow-muffled day, Bob could feel an enormous bubble of anger rising within him. The pressure of it was filling his body, forcing the air out of his lungs. 'Is this what you were fighting about?' he said breathlessly. His chest felt so tight he wondered if he was about to suffer a heart attack.

479

'It's part of it,' Miles said.

'Felicity would never have an affair,' he whispered. 'She wasn't . . . she wasn't that sort of a girl. She was so good . . . She was a loving and devoted mother. Your brother must have forced her. It's the only explanation. Yes, that's it, he must have forced her.' But the thought of Dominic making his darling girl do something she didn't want to do was too much for Bob and the bubble of anger suddenly burst. He looked wildly around him. 'Where's that filthy bastard? I'm going to finish off what you started!'

'No, don't! He's not worth it.'

But Bob wasn't listening. Shaking Miles's hand from his shoulder, he marched back inside the house to the sitting room. 'Where is he?' he roared. 'Where's that conniving bastard?' Everyone looked at him, startled. Pushing his way through the guests, he went into the kitchen. Dora was there with the children, but there was no sign of any of the McKendricks. He then crashed his way up the stairs and that was where he found Eileen and Freda in the front bedroom with Dominic. They were tending to the cuts to his face.

'I want to speak to you, Dominic McKendrick,' Bob said, working hard to catch his breath.

'Can it wait, Bob?' asked Eileen, breaking off from dabbing at Dominic's mouth and exchanging a worried look with Freda. On the verge of tears, the stupid woman looked as useless as she always did.

'No. It's got to be said now.'

'What's got to be said now?' It was Harvey and he looked furious. He must have followed Bob up the stairs. 'Isn't it bad enough that your daughter has embarrassed my wife and me by provoking my sons to brawl in front of our guests?'

Bob realised then just how much he'd never liked his neighbour. Now he knew he despised him. 'Your son,' he inclined his head towards Dominic, who was still sitting on the bed between his mother and Eileen, 'has behaved far worse than Harriet ever could. He's nothing but a marriage wrecker. See for yourself.' He held out the photograph. 'There! What do you say to that?' He immediately wished he hadn't. Parading Felicity's naked body like this was an obscene slur on her virtue; as her father, he couldn't have failed her more.

A stunned silence fell on the room. Freda began to cry and Harvey looked with disgust at his son.

'I knew all along that you weren't gay,' he said. 'It was just an act to annoy and disappoint me.'

At this, Dominic suddenly sprang to his feet. He pushed his mother away. 'You, you, *YOU!* It's always about bloody you, isn't it, Dad? And for the record, I'm bisexual. I fuck women as well as men.' He towered over his father and prodded him in the chest. 'Tell me, is that more acceptable for you? Or is that equally shaming and disappointing?' He came towards Bob now and before Bob could stop him, he had snatched the photograph out of his hands. 'And if it's any concern of yours, I loved Felicity. I always did and I always will. She was the only person on this Godforsaken earth who made my life worth living. I can't function without her. She was my life. My dearest friend *and* my lover. Now I have nothing. But then I wouldn't expect any of you to understand that when all you're capable of doing is flimflamming your way through the shoddiness of your dull, suburban, unimaginative lives. You're devoid of any real emotion, the whole damn lot of you.' He took a last look at the photograph, stuffed it into his pocket and stalked out of the room, slamming the door after him.

Will had witnessed the extraordinary commotion in the McKendricks' front garden; it had taken place only minutes after Maxine had left. He'd also seen Harriet leave and make her way home. With nothing else to do, he remained at the window, watching the road for any further action. He didn't have long to wait. First an angry-looking, dark-haired man marched past, his coat tails flying – quite a feat, given the treacherous state of the pavements – and just as a flurry of fresh snowflakes began to fall, Harriet reappeared. This time she was wrapped in a purple duffel coat along with a scarf, gloves, boots and a hat – the famous black beret. His heart, so heavy these days, gave a small surge. Surprised that he was able to feel anything, he continued to watch Harriet. Picking her way carefully through the snow, she crossed the road in the direction of the footpath. In an instant, he made a decision he hoped he wouldn't regret.

Eileen asked Dora to take the children back to her house for the rest of the afternoon, and hurried after Bob. She'd never seen him so angry. He was cursing out loud to himself and she was worried he might go after Dominic again and do something silly. But there was no sign of Dominic anywhere. Eileen didn't know what to make of Bob's accusation; she hadn't managed to see the photograph but she could guess what it showed. In a way, it didn't surprise her. Felicity and Dominic had always been as thick as thieves. She used to worry that they had an unhealthy relationship, and maybe her instinct had been right. She could remember thinking how relieved she was when Felicity had told her that Dominic was gay; she'd naively thought that his obsession with Felicity would magically stop. But it looked like she'd been wrong. Instead it had grown and grown. And what about Jeff in all of this? Had the poor man known what was going on? Did the children know too? Had they had an inkling that something was wrong between their parents?

She called out, 'Bob, please, slow down. I can't keep up with you.' But her cries went unheeded and she slipped on the snow and nearly went over.

Bob went round to the back of the house. He knew exactly what he was going to do. He'd spent far too long covering up his feelings, pretending to the world that he was okay.

The snow was falling harder now and brushing it away from his eyes, mouth and nose, he felt the cold wetness of it seeping through his shoes as he trudged across the lawn.

The door at the back of the garage was open and going inside he found what he was looking for: his old spade. As soon as it was in his hands and his fingers were gripping the familiar, well-worn smoothness of the handle, he felt a detonating current of energy flow through him. How dare that foul-mouthed devil incarnate accuse him of not being capable of feeling any emotion! He'd show him!

His first act of destruction was to obliterate the snowman Harriet and the children had made that morning. Like an executioner, he took off the head in one clean, satisfying swing. The carrot nose flew past him and as the head came to rest at his feet, two round stones stared reproachfully back at him. He kicked it away, then hacked at the body. From there he went over to the wooden bird table and took a hefty two-handed swipe at it. Pain ripped through his shoulders as he made contact, but it toppled to the ground with a thud. He brought the spade down heavily on it and gritted his teeth as the sound of splintering wood filled the air.

In his mind he was smashing Harvey McKendrick's skull to a pulp.

Dominic McKendrick's head too.

And that joy-riding bastard who'd killed his beloved Felicity.

The bird table dealt with, he moved onto the rose bed. It was hidden deep beneath a drift of snow, but he knew the lie of the land like the back of his hand and in no time he was flattening the area.

The first blow was for all those unborn babies he'd never know.

The subsequent strikes were for cheating on his wife. For not being a better husband.

Next he attacked the pergola he'd made three summers ago after watching Monty Don build one on *Gardener's World*. That was for making a fool of himself over Jennifer. For being so pathetically weak.

Petrified by cold and fear, the snow settling on and around her, Eileen stood shivering on the patio, watching Bob systematically decimate the garden to which he'd devoted so much of his life. She was glad she'd had the sense to leave the children in Dora's care. He was oblivious to her presence – and to Toby barking frantically the other side of the patio doors – but she would stay watching over him until he'd unleashed every last demon of grief-fuelled anger and frustration from his body.

That moment came when the light began to fade and at last, spent, Bob fell to his knees and covered his head with his arms. His cries were terrible to hear. It was a sound Eileen hoped never to hear again. She prayed that it signalled the end of her husband's nightmare. 'Please let him be at peace now,' she murmured as she walked stiffly to where Bob was crouched like a wounded animal dying in the snow.

Chapter Fifty-Eight

'Harriet?'

'Yes, Joel.'

'When will Granddad be feeling better?'

'I don't know. He's very poorly at the moment. He needs a lot of rest.'

'Carrie says he's got flu and that she saw him crying yesterday. Was he crying, Harriet?'

'I don't know; I wasn't there.'

'Why do you think he was crying?'

'Because he's not feeling very well.'

While he continued to help Harriet put his toys and books into a box, Joel thought that talking with grown-ups could be a bit like going round in circles. It didn't usually happen with Harriet, but maybe, because they were moving tomorrow, she didn't have time to talk to him properly.

Mummy used to say that she couldn't talk properly when she was busy. 'I'll answer your questions in a minute, Joel,' she'd say. 'Just let me finish what I'm doing.' She was always busy on her computer. Every morning when they came home after taking Carrie to school she'd go into the spare room and switch on the computer. 'Go and play while I send an email to your auntie Harriet,' she would say. Mummy used to say that Harriet wasn't just her sister, she was her best friend, too. Carrie was his sister but he didn't think she thought he was her best friend. She had all her friends from school to play with now. She was always talking about them. He had no one. Only Harriet and Grandma and Granddad. And they were all too busy to talk to him. He suddenly felt sad. And a bit frightened. Things kept changing. He blamed it on that boring party the day it snowed. Ever since that day things had been different. First he'd overheard Dora talking to someone about Will and what a shame it was about his daughter dying and how upset he must be. Hoping it wasn't that nice girl they'd met ages ago in that funny old shop that smelled, he'd asked Grandma about it. He could tell she didn't really want to talk to him, because she'd hugged him and said he wasn't to worry about anything. But he was worried. *Everyone* was dying. Who would be next?

Granddad?

Carrie said that Granddad had caught his flu germs at the party and that was what had made him go mad and wreck the garden. But Joel didn't believe Carrie. He'd never heard of anyone wrecking a garden because they weren't feeling well. He knew what had really happened. Granddad must have drunk too much wine at the party, like Dad did that time when he got cross with Mummy and threw all her books out of the window. It was raining, but Mummy went out in her slippers to get them. But they'd fallen into a puddle and she cried because they were ruined. She said they were her favourite books of poems. But they weren't like the poems she read to them at bedtime, the funny ones with the nice rhymes. They were serious ones without any pictures. He hadn't liked seeing Daddy like that, all angry and using bad words.

Harriet didn't approve of lying to the children. When it came to important matters, she'd always believed in being straight and honest with them, but out of respect for her parents she had agreed, for the time being, to keep quiet about Dad's breakdown. Just as she'd done with Suzie's death. Perhaps, when she and the children had moved, and she didn't have her mother's wishes to tiptoe around, she would talk more openly with them.

Meanwhile, she had the move to deal with. 'Come on, Joel,' she said, brightly, 'a little faster with those toys or we'll still be here when the removal men arrive in the morning.'

'What time are they coming?'

'About nine o'clock, so we need to be ready nice and early.'

They worked together for another twenty minutes, until finally every last cuddly toy, book and game had been sealed up in a packing box. 'There,' she said, 'all done.' Noting that Joel was looking uncertainly at his now-empty room – all that was left was his silky lying on top of his folded pyjamas on the bed, along with his new slippers – she added, 'You've done a fantastic job, Joel. I don't know how I would have managed without you.'

He gave her one of his notoriously wobbly smiles, the one that he knew was expected of him, but he didn't really mean. 'Can I have my bath now?'

'You'll have to see if Carrie's finished in there.'

It was bound to happen sooner or later, but Carrie had decided that she was too old now to share a bath with her little brother. Harriet knew that Joel didn't like this new arrangement, which made him feel excluded. She listened to him talking to his sister through the closed bathroom door and yawned hugely, stretching her arms above her head. She was exhausted. She had spent most of the day getting ready for the move. A blessing really, because it had taken her mind off the events of the last forty-eight hours.

No one had come right out and said it, but it was officially all Harriet's fault. If she hadn't taken it upon herself to confront Dominic so dramatically, and to make Miles stand up to him once and for all, her father wouldn't have gone berserk and smashed up the garden. Nor would Harriet's mother been forced to witness him go through such a harrowing ordeal.

The first she'd known about Dad's breakdown – and that he knew all about Felicity's affair with Dominic – was when she'd come home later that evening and found Miles in the kitchen drinking tea with her mother. Mum had told her she'd had to call out the doctor for Dad. 'He's fast asleep,' Eileen had explained. The doctor gave him something.' Her mother had then taken her outside to show her the garden and even in the dark, Harriet could see the extent of the damage. What hurt most was the sight of the Wendy house – it was the only thing her father had left standing. It stood there bleakly in the snow and shadows, like a lone, traumatised survivor of a massacre.

At no stage did Eileen ask where Harriet had been for the last three hours, for which she was grateful. Perhaps her mother had guessed where she'd been and was saving Miles's feelings. Harriet could see that Miles was desperate to talk to her but Harriet had done enough talking, so she offered to go back out into the cold and fetch the children, who were still with Dora. Across the road, the curtains were drawn at Will's and she pictured him sitting by the fire where she'd left him earlier.

Immediately after telling Harvey McKendrick what she'd thought of him, she had decided that only a walk in the punishing cold would make her feel better. She had come across Will clearing the snow from the bench at the end of his garden. It had seemed an odd thing to be doing, seeing as a fresh fall of snow was now coming down. When he saw her, he'd stopped what he was doing and, without a word, had started walking beside her in unnerving silence. She could feel his sadness reach out to her. Several minutes passed before she asked him how he was.

'I've been better,' he replied. 'How about you? I saw punches being thrown over at the McKendricks'. Was there a problem with the sherry? Not dry enough, perhaps?'

She stopped walking and looked at him. 'I've missed you, Will.'

'I've missed you too.' The snow was falling faster and heavier now; swollen flakes of it were forming a thick layer on their clothes. He glanced up at the sky and catching sight of the vulnerable paleness of his skin above his scarf she felt an urge to kiss his neck. 'We need to make a decision,' he said, stamping his feet in the cold. 'We either brave this snowstorm or we turn for home.'

'I don't want to go home. Not yet.'

'Then come back to my place. I could do with the company.'

'Even my company?'

He wiped away a snowflake that had settled on her eyelashes. 'I told you, I've missed you.'

They hurried back the way they'd just come, kicked off their boots at the kitchen door and shook the snow from their clothes. He offered her a glass of wine, but she declined, not trusting herself to drink any alcohol and stay in control of her emotions.

While Will threw some logs onto the fire and she knelt in front of it gratefully she saw that there wasn't a trace of Christmas in the sitting room: no tree, no cards, not a single festive knick-knack. Exactly as she would have predicted.

'How's Gemma?' she asked when he was settled in the armchair nearest her.

'Difficult to say.'

'Did she tell you I spoke to her before Christmas?'

'No.'

'I gave her my mobile number, in case she wanted to talk to someone, other than family.'

'That was kind of you.'

'I know how it feels to be the surviving daughter – the daughter who gets overlooked in favour of the one who's died.'

He visibly bristled. 'She isn't being overlooked. I'd never do that to Gemma.'

'Good. Because it's the worst thing that can happen to her.'

'I'll keep your advice in mind,' he replied coolly. He stretched his legs out in front of him and rested his feet on the hearth. She could see from his expression as he stared into the fire that she'd rattled him, and he'd taken her comment as a criticism. She was just about to apologise when he said, 'Tell me about the fisticuffs. What was that all about?'

She sighed. 'It's complicated.'

'Life is.'

'Mine especially.' She turned slightly so that she was sideways on to the fire and facing him, her chin resting on her drawn-up knees. 'I realised this morning that I've been deliberately played with. For months I've been fed a pack of lies. I've been manipulated in a way you wouldn't believe. And I hate myself for having been so naïve, for not being astute enough to realise what was going on. I seem to have a singular lack of talent for reading between the lines.'

'Would I be right in thinking that your old friend Dominic, the one on the receiving end of the punches being swung, is at the bottom of this?'

She nodded. And then she told him the whole unedifying story, the lies, the secrets, the betrayals. She poured everything out: how she'd grown up with a love–hate relationship towards Dominic, how she'd worshipped him yet despised him. Finally she told Will about Miles and how their friendship had begun to change when she moved back home. 'I suddenly saw him in a different light,' she explained.

'No longer as a friend but as a potential boyfriend? A lover?'

'Yes. It suddenly seemed the perfect answer. Almost as though this was what Felicity might have wanted for us; you know, two people who had been really close to her coming together to bring up her children.'

'But Dominic had other ideas?'

'It looks as if he couldn't bear for anyone else to find happiness if he couldn't. So he deliberately set out to scotch whatever feelings Miles and I were beginning to have for each other.'

'But all you had to do was confront Miles about his alleged affair with your sister. Why didn't you?'

'With hindsight it seems madness that I didn't, but I couldn't bring myself to do it. I felt angry with him for a while, and . . . you probably won't understand this, because you don't know our history, but believing him to be in love with Felicity made me feel second best. And of course I believed Dominic when he said that unless I had proof, his brother would probably deny the affair.'

'So instead of questioning Miles, you went on the hunt for evidence?'

She nodded. 'I kept going through Felicity's emails looking for something that would give Miles away, while all the time keeping him at arm's length.'

'Meanwhile I came along. I might be jumping to conclusions, but did I become part of what you were going through?'

Ashamed, she turned and looked into the flickering flames. 'On top of being ditched by my last boyfriend because I now came with two non-negotiable complications, and feeling second best, I felt horribly rejected. Pathetically, I needed to prove to myself that I was attractive, a person in my own right. Does any of that make sense to you?'

'Yes,' he said.

She could see the hurt in his eyes, though, and it pained her. 'I'm sorry. I soon realised I'd got myself into a situation that was all wrong. I was getting too fond of you and I hated myself for having used you to bolster my stupid ego. You deserved better. You're the nicest, kindest, funniest, most generous and straightforward man I've ever met and I shall always regret the way I treated you.'

'I'd have made do with just being the sexiest man you've ever met.'

She gave him a tentative smile. 'That's a given. And before you ask, there was no faking on my part. Every moment we spent in bed together was genuine.'

He briefly closed his eyes. 'What more could a guy ask for?' He suddenly looked and sounded extremely tired.

Bored of talking about her own troubles, she said, 'So how have you been? And no glossing over anything. The truth.'

'Bloody awful is the truth. I feel detached from the

outside world, as though it's not really happening.' He let out his breath. 'I don't think I'm handling this at all well, if I'm honest.'

'There's a lot of rubbish spoken about being stoically resilient and hanging in there. We're all different and have to handle things at our own pace. For what it's worth, I reckon you're not doing too badly. Have you been into work much?'

'Once or twice. To prove I can still do it, and to please Jarvis. Some mornings I wake up feeling like I'm made of glass; one bump and I'll fracture into a thousand pieces. When does it start to get better?'

'I can't answer that. But some day soon you'll catch yourself thinking about something else, and then you'll feel as guilty as hell because you'll think it's wrong to be happy. Or even distracted.'

She'd left him a short while later, sensing that he'd had enough company and wanted to be alone. 'No need to see me out,' she'd said. 'I know the way.' She'd squeezed his hand and closed the front door quietly after her.

She may have escaped the immediate aftermath of her public confrontation with Dominic for those few hours she'd been with Will, but it was waiting for her when she got home. As indeed it had been ever since. Two days on and her father was in bed suffering from mental exhaustion, as the doctor had described his condition; she and her parents would never be welcome at the McKendricks' again – Eileen said this might well turn out to be a blessing – and there was still Miles to talk to.

There was also Dominic to deal with. She hadn't finished with him yet. Not by a long way. Which was why she'd hurried Joel with his packing; she'd arranged to meet Dominic later that evening. Unbelievably he hadn't got the first train back to Cambridge, and even more unbelievably, he was staying with Miles in Maywood. He'd phoned her that morning to say that he wanted to talk to her. She'd told him he had lousy timing, but she'd agreed anyway to meet him at the wine bar in Maywood.

He was waiting for her at the same table they had used the night she'd thrown her drink in his face. He looked dreadful. Bruised and battered, his nose was swollen, his right eye blackened, his top lip sporting a couple of stitches. She felt moved by the sight of him but reminded herself that he deserved every bit of the pain he was experiencing.

'I can't even say you should see the other guy,' he quipped when she sat down and he indicated the glass of wine he'd already bought her. 'I risked a glass of Pinot Grigio for you,' he added.

'Thanks.' She took off her jacket, but kept her scarf on. Odds on she'd lose her temper with him before long and would want to leave in a hurry. 'You look awful,' she said matter-of-factly.

'But perhaps not as bad as I'd have turned out if you'd got your hands on me.'

'You're right; you could have wound up dead with Felicity.'

He took a mouthful of wine. 'I'm impressed; you said that without a hint of remorse.'

'What can I say? I've learned at the feet of the master.'

'Okay,' he said in a bored voice, 'it's official, I'm a monster. Can we move on?'

'Yes, but on my terms. For starters, I want to know exactly what was going on inside that twisted mind of yours when you made me suspect Miles was Felicity's lover. Did it give you some kind of sick pleasure knowing that you were playing God with our lives?'

'You know me; I get my pleasure any which way I can.'

She drummed her fingers on the table impatiently. 'Look, I get the whole sexually ambiguous thing, that you're capable of shagging your own shadow if the wind is blowing in the right direction, but why the double-bluff games? Why pretend you were gay when you're clearly not?'

'Why, do you fancy your chances with me now? Now that you know I could find you attractive after all? That I could be as equally aroused by your body as I could with that guy over there?' He tipped his head towards an attractive, dark-haired man at the bar.

'Just tell me what I want to know.'

He smiled. 'I'm unnerving you, aren't I? That's the great thing about a strong sexuality; it delivers such a powerful punch. You see, Hat, I've always known I could have had you in bed any time I wanted.'

His arrogance made her want to get up and leave right away, but she had to stay, to know everything that had gone through his mind and brought them to this moment. 'So why didn't you *have* me,' she asked, 'as you so delicately put it?'

'I don't know. It's a mystery that's puzzled me for some time. Perhaps I was leaving the best till last.'

She snorted. 'Rubbish! It's because your so-called prowess never really worked on me. I'm the one person who could see through you.'

'But not entirely.'

'True,' she conceded, knowing that would always annoy her. 'But answer my question. Why pretend you were gay?'

'Queer. Straight. Gay. Bi. They're all just words. I'm me. This is the way I am.'

'You're not answering my question.'

'Okay. It was part of the subterfuge. A game Felicity liked to play. I could openly kiss her in front of Jeff and there wasn't a damn thing he could do about it. Gay men are notorious for flirting with women; it's practically *de rigueur*.'

'But you professed to be gay before Jeff came into Felicity's life.'

'True. I guess I hadn't made up my mind just where I stood until she got serious about another man. I was shattered when she told me she was going to marry Jeff. I could have killed them both. I asked her to marry me instead but she said no, that like Maude, the only woman Yeats ever really loved, she wanted to have my love for the rest of her life. She believed that marriage would kill what we had.' He paused to take another mouthful of wine. 'If you were more literate, you'd know exactly what I'm talking about.'

'Pardon me for being such an ignorant oik.'

'You're forgiven.'

'So why all the secrecy in your emails? You went to extraordinary lengths.'

'Again it was what Felicity wanted. She got a thrill out of creating a special world in which only the two of us existed. She loved secrets. She particularly enjoyed the idea of us pretending to everyone else that it was only men I was into; it heightened the bond between us, you could say. She knew I was devoted to her and would do anything for her. For her part, she loved the power she had over me. So long as she was in the world I could only ever be truly happy when I was with her. There was a wildness about her that only I saw.'

'You make her sound like that crazy piece from *Wuthering Heights*.'

'That crazy piece was Cathy; please don't overplay the dumb card.'

Ignoring the put-down, she said, 'So when did the affair start?'

'Do you mean when we first made love?'

'I'm assuming you did that before we all went away to college. No, I'm talking about when the pair of you started sneaking around behind Jeff's back.'

'That was the day they returned from their honeymoon.'

Having just taken a sip of her wine, Harriet nearly choked on it. 'You're joking!'

'No. I was there waiting for her. Jeff had to go away on a course and I made love to her in their bed. It was what she wanted, in case you're thinking I forced her to do it. You see, what you never realised about your sister was that she was a lot like me. She had an intensely strong sexual nature. So strong that it emasculated dull old Jeff. He just wasn't man enough for her.'

'But you were?'

'In every way.'

'Were you faithful to her?'

'In mind, yes.'

'Meaning that when she wasn't available you carried on with other men or women in Cambridge?'

'You probably won't understand this, but in recent years I only slept with men. To sleep with another woman would have seemed unfaithful.'

A sudden burst of laughter from a nearby table had them both looking over. 'You're right,' she said, when the laughter had died down, 'I don't understand. You're beyond the realms of my comprehension. But I'm intrigued: how did you feel knowing that Felicity was betraying you by having sex with Jeff?'

'I hated it.'

'And the children. When they came along, how did that make you feel? After all, they were a special bond between Felicity and Jeff that you couldn't deny or take away from them.'

'You think so?'

His voice was so sure, his face so composed, Harriet stopped in her tracks. It's another of his twisted games, she told herself. Don't let him get away with it. 'Please don't insult my intelligence by hinting that Jeff wasn't Carrie and Joel's father.'

He shrugged and picked up his wine glass. 'Okay then, I won't.'

But the damage was done. She had to know. 'Go on. Tell me, and make it the truth or you'll wish you'd never asked to meet me here tonight.'

'It's possible Carrie is my daughter.'

'And?'

'And what? What do you want of me? A paternity blood test right here?' He pushed back his sleeve to expose the underside of his forearm and pressed a finger to a prominent vein. 'There, cut me open and watch me bleed some more.'

'Oh, stop being so melodramatic. Just give me a straight answer to a straight question.'

'I can't. And if you think it's that easy then you're living in cloud cuckoo land. This is real life: ends don't always get neatly tied up with a silk ribbon of convenience. Some things we just have to live with as unknowns.'

'Bullshit! Who did Felicity think was Carrie's father?'

'Because she couldn't be sure, she decided to keep it that way. She once said she thought I'd make a terrifyingly inconsistent father. That was something Jeff was good at, apparently.'

'Was it why she stayed with him?'

'One of the reasons. She thought the children would have more stability that way.'

'How disappointing that must have been for you, to know that love doesn't conquer all.'

'Please don't make fun of me.'

'What about Joel? Why don't you think you could be his father?'

'Basic biology. We didn't see one another during the time he was conceived.' He drained his glass in one long swig. 'I need another drink. How about you?'

'No thanks, I'm driving.'

The moment he was back in his seat, she started interrogating him again. 'How often did you get to see each other? And where?'

'It varied. Once a month. Sometimes twice a month. I always went to her. For obvious reasons it was easier for me to get away than it was for her.' He suddenly laughed. 'We had our lovers' trysts in some hellish places, I can tell you. I can never pass a Travel Inn or cheap motel without thinking of Felicity.' But as quickly as his face had brightened, it darkened. 'Oh, shit, Hat, I miss her so much. I used to believe that no one could understand a person fully. But Felicity knew me inside and out. She shared every emotion I ever experienced.'

'Do you think she would have approved of you lying and manipulating me? How you deliberately set out to destroy a potential relationship between Miles and me?' It was only now that Harriet trusted herself to acknowledge that her original instinct about Miles wanting more than friendship with her had been correct. That she hadn't imagined the intimacy of that moment in the park with him.

'If you'd been serious about Miles,' Dominic said, 'it wouldn't have mattered what I said or did.'

'That's absurd. You nipped it in the bud before either of us really knew what was possible. You still haven't told me why you did it. Do you really hate your brother so much?'

'It's got nothing to do with hate. It's about love and happiness and being deprived of it. Why should you and Miles have what I couldn't?'

'You admit it, then? That it was purely a selfish motive? As soon as you suspected Miles might be interested in me, you put a stop to it.'

'But of course. What else could it have been? If you're dying from a disease, why would you wish others good health? You want that good health for yourself.'

'Destroying my chance of happiness would have made you feel better?'

'Do you feel better for punishing me here this evening? Does making me explain my feelings for Felicity make *you* feel any better? Yes, it does, doesn't it? Inflicting pain on others is really quite pleasurable when you get down to it.'

'That's the most depraved thing I've heard you say.'

'On the contrary, it's merely a matter of understanding and coming to terms with the innate treachery of the life we're given. One thing is for sure: I shall never again allow myself to become emotionally dependent on another person. From now on I shall be a confirmed tart. I shall be as promiscuous as I want and, as Byron said, I shall spend the rest of my life trying to save myself from myself.'

'I don't believe you. You're covering up the fact that the driest of souls got scorched by love. You've discovered the hard way that there's something more powerful in the world than your ego.'

'How exceedingly poetic of you. Are you talking from experience?'

'That's none of your business.'

'So be it.'

They sat in silence for some minutes while a group of people at a nearby table gathered up their coats and bags and made a noisy exit. It was getting late, the wine bar was thinning out, and by rights Harriet should be making a move herself, but she still had a list of questions she needed answering. 'How long did you think you could keep the lie going for?' she asked.

He smiled, even though it must have hurt his mouth to do so. 'Which lie? I've told so many.'

She didn't return the smile. 'The one about Miles being Felicity's lover. The game would have been up the moment I confronted him.'

'Ah, but the damage would have been done. Would you have believed his denial? Every time he kissed you, you'd have wondered if his lips had kissed your sister's before yours. I know how you hated the thought of being second best to Felicity.'

Determined not to rise to the bait, she said, 'But the photograph put an end to it all, didn't it? Did you know I would find it eventually?'

'No. I didn't know she'd kept it. We had an agreement that only I would keep pictures of the two of us together. It was a good one, wasn't it? Caught me at my best, I like to think.'

Again she refused to be reeled in. 'It was clear from the last few emails you and Felicity exchanged that she was going to leave Jeff for you. But according to what you said earlier, she'd stayed with him to give the children the stability you couldn't provide. Why the U-turn?'

'What you have to understand is that the really important things in life often happen to us through a snap decision. A decision made by instinct. You don't decide to fall in love; it just happens. When it's the real thing, there's no shilly-shallying involved. You suddenly know for sure that you have to be with that person or life has no meaning.'

'What provoked the snap decision in Felicity's case, then?'

'She'd had enough. Plus Jeff had started to suspect that she was having an affair. He was becoming irrational. He got drunk once and threw some of Felicity's things out of the window. He was also accusing her of being unfaithful in front of the children.'

'Did he suspect you?'

'Why would he? He thought I was gay.'

'You really think—?'

He suddenly held up a hand. 'Enough! More than enough of you playing the grand inquisitor. Now it's my turn to ask a question. It's the reason I wanted to talk to you in the first place. I've kept it to myself all this time, but I don't want to carry my suspicions alone any more. Have you ever wondered about the accident that killed Felicity and Jeff?'

'What kind of a question is that? I think about it practically every day.'

'But have you wondered if it was an accident that could have been avoided?'

'You're not suggesting—'

He leaned forward, placed his elbows squarely on the table, his battered face inches from hers. 'I'm convinced Jeff deliberately made no effort to avoid that car. I think he was mad at Felicity because she'd finally told him she wanted to leave him, and he took matters into his own hands.'

A tremor of fear ran through Harriet. She swallowed. 'You have no proof of that.' Her voice was little more than a whisper.

'I have the memory of the last conversation I ever had with Felicity. She said she'd just told Jeff that she wanted to leave him.'

The tremor grew and Harriet feared she might be sick. The thought of Felicity knowing, in the last seconds of her life, that she had driven her husband to kill them both was too horrifying to take in. 'Then you must accept your part in their deaths,' she said, fighting hard to keep her composure. 'If you hadn't been so obsessed with Felicity they'd both be alive today.'

'You think I don't wake up every morning reminding myself of that?'

She shook her head wearily. 'Oh, Dominic, how do you live with yourself?'

'I exist, Hat. Nothing more. I'm the swimming lad the mermaid took for her own, and now I'm drowning.'

'Have you told anyone else about this?'

'I just told you, I've kept it to myself all this time.'

'Good. I don't want the children ever doubting their parents. I want them to grow up feeling proud of their mother and father. You must swear on whatever is most precious to you that you will never utter to another living soul a word of what you've just said. Because if my father hears about it, he will kill you. I'm serious; he will tear you apart, slit your throat, rip out your insides. He'll do just about anything to exact his revenge on you for depriving him of his favourite daughter.'

'Who knows, maybe I'll spare him the trouble.'

They left the wine bar at chucking-out time. Harriet offered to give Dominic a lift to Miles's flat down by the river, but he refused. 'I need some fresh air,' he said. 'Unless that was a subtle attempt on your part to see Miles. He'd probably appreciate seeing you.'

'No. I'll talk to him another time. I'm too tired now. I need to get to bed; I have a busy day tomorrow. When are you going back to Cambridge?'

'I think I'll slip away quietly in the morning. I shouldn't take advantage of my brother's hospitality any longer than necessary.'

'I'm amazed he's let you stay at all.'

'That's because he's one of life's incorrigible optimists. A shame he never got into religion; he'd have made a wonderful evangelist, always hoping for a quick conversion. He'd love nothing better than to prove to me his way is better than mine.'

'His way is infinitely better than yours, Dominic.'

'But it hasn't got him what he wanted, has it?'

'I don't know. What is it he wants?'

'Oh, Hat, haven't you figured that out? He wants you, of course.'

She frowned. 'Is that one last try to stir things up?'

'You really are hopeless when it comes to matters of the heart, aren't you? Why do you suppose Miles did this to me?' He raised a hand to his face. 'Think also of the poem he read that night at Novel Ways. It was written for you, when you were shagging Will and he thought he'd lost you. Now give me a gentle hug goodbye so that I know we're friends again.'

In spite of everything that he'd said and done, Harriet put her arms round him and kissed his cheek. He was such an integral part of her life – and her sister's – she couldn't say goodbye without making her peace with him. A car went slowly past in the slushy snow, illuminating them with its headlamps. A voice shouted out, 'Phwoar! Give her one mate!'

They both smiled. 'Take care you horribly sick, perverted man,' she said.

He kissed her again. 'Take care yourself, you hard-hearted bitch. I shall await an invitation from you to eat crumpets by your cosy fireside one day. Maybe Miles will be there too. Oh, and just so that I can be sure of having the last word, remember that in a really dark night of the soul it is always three in the morning, day after day. Also, the big, crucial questions are unanswerable. Goodbye, sweet thing.'

Harriet watched him buttoning his coat as he walked away. A sadness came over her as she wondered what would become of him. And what had he meant by that reference to the mermaid?

February

'Imitation of Life'

This sugarcane
this lemonade
this hurricane, I'm not afraid
C'mon c'mon no one can see me cry.
This lightning storm
this tidal wave
this avalanche, I'm not afraid.
C'mon c'mon no one can see me cry.

R.E.M.

Chapter Fifty-Nine

At weekends, and when the children's social engagements permitted, Harriet liked to sit up in bed and look at the view from her bedroom window. If she was really lucky, Carrie and Joel would bring her a cup of tea and a slice of marmalade toast. Her luck was in this particular bright and sunny Saturday morning and she was munching on a piece of toast while enjoying the sight of the canal and the field beyond where a light frost was melting in the sun. There were drifts of snowdrops along the towpath and their delicate flowers were swaying in the breeze. It was a perfect morning, Harriet decided.

A month had passed since she and the children had moved into number one Lock Cottage; a month too, since she had last seen Dominic and he had made those comments about never knowing all the answers, that life's loose ends weren't always tied up. His words still had an irritating resonance for her. At work she was so used to resolving, reasoning, evaluating, analysing, processing – thinking her way through problems – that she found it particularly galling she couldn't do the same in her private life. She could approach Dominic's revelations with all the logic in the world but it would resolve nothing. She had to accept she would never know what had really happened that night when Jeff and Felicity died. If Jeff really had been so out of his mind with jealousy that he had decided, in a split second of madness, to kill them both, he had taken the truth to his grave.

She knew, though, that she had to let go of the thoughts Dominic had planted in her brain. If she allowed them to grow she might well go mad. But what he'd said went a long way to explaining his episodes of inexplicable behaviour; the unpredictable mood swings, the volatile outpourings. Of them all, Dominic had the most to live with. As long as she'd known him, he'd given the impression that he didn't have a conscience, but it turned out he did. How he would learn to live with the knowledge that he may well have been instrumental in killing the woman he'd loved, Harriet didn't know. He needed help, but she doubted he'd ever seek it. It wasn't in his nature. She felt enormous pity for him.

As to him being Carrie's father, whether he was or not was immaterial for now. It was one of those loose ends that had the potential to come together when the time was right. She had tried pushing Dominic that night in the wine bar, about there being a responsibility on his part if he was Carrie's father, and had asked him if he wasn't curious to know the truth. 'What's the point?' he'd replied.

'The point is, it could be important to Carrie.'

'I'd be a hopeless father, Hat. I'd only screw her up. She's better off always thinking Jeff was her dad.'

Despite the apparent indifference, he appeared, in his own way, to be adopting the role of avuncular uncle to Carrie and Joel. He'd sent them both cameras and photograph albums with instructions to fill them with pictures of things they thought he'd approve of. He'd also sent Harriet a book of Yeats' poems. The accompanying card read: *Time to educate yourself! Best wishes from your oldest friend, Dominic.*

'What does he mean?' Joel had asked. 'Pictures that he would approve of?'

'He wants us to think before we stick any old picture in our albums,' Carrie had said, perceptively.

'Well, I'm going to put a picture in of Tom and me in the garden.'

Tom was Joel's new best friend. He was two months older than Joel and lived in the house three doors down the terrace of cottages. He'd made his first appearance the day they'd moved in, bringing with him a confident, breezy disposition and a bunch of flowers, along with his mother, who invited Harriet and the children to join them for a cup of tea and a slice of cake when they fancied a break from unpacking. It turned out Tom's father, Stewart, was a programmer like herself and his wife, Diana, was a freelance graphic designer. Harriet took to them straight away; they were friendly and welcoming without being at all pushy. The perfect neighbours, in fact. Especially as their son Tom, who, although he attended a different school, was doing wonders for Joel's self-confidence. These days Harriet nicknamed her nephew Motor Mouth. There was no ignoring him, either. He was suddenly an unstoppable cruise missile of self-discovery. How did the remote control for the television work? Why did the microwave hum? Why was there always fluff between his toes? Where did goosebumps come from?

But for all his questions, Harriet was only too delighted with the change in him. He still worried over the slightest thing, but she was getting better at winkling out his concerns and anxieties and dispelling them for him.

All in all, the move to number one Lock Cottage was proving to be the refuge she'd hoped for. It was as if, from the day they moved in, it had cast an aura of calm over their lives. Perhaps it was because it gave them all something new to think about.

Miles had been a godsend, too. Despite being so busy himself, he was always offering to help with any odd jobs that needed doing, and while she was quite capable of wielding a paintbrush or a hammer and a screwdriver, it was good having him around. The children enjoyed his company as well and he often had supper with them. He was joining them this evening for a Chinese takeaway after he'd finished work.

There had been a lot of cautious side-stepping around each other in the days after New Year's Day, particularly on Harriet's part. She kept thinking what Dominic had said about Miles and his feelings for her. Wanting to be sure just how she felt, she was determined to take things slowly.

Having rushed into things with Will, she didn't want to make a similar mistake. Being with Miles made perfect sense, though. They had a shared history, were the same age, and best of all, she didn't need to be anything other than herself with him. They'd even wandered the aisles of B & Q together!

Once they'd opened up to each other and had put the misunderstandings and embarrassing memories of New Year's Day behind them, they were again able to talk more freely, just as they used to. She had showed him the decoded email that she had thought proved he had been Felicity's lover. 'Like the fool I am, I read it the way I'd been primed to. It never occurred to me that it could have been Dominic referring to that sweltering hot day in the cornfield. Your guilt had been so firmly planted in my head, I simply leapt to the conclusion I wanted to. I've been very stupid,' she'd admitted.

'No you haven't. Given what Dominic had said, you interpreted the email in the only way you could. Anyone would have made the same mistake. And for the record, I got over my crush on Felicity a long time ago.'

'I always suspected that you had a thing for her. What changed?'

'I grew up.' He then shyly confessed to having had a soft spot for Harriet for some years.

'Why did you never say anything?' she'd asked.

'Don't laugh, but I was also a bit scared of you. You were so fearless. There was always Dominic to consider too. I was convinced you preferred him to me. He was, and still is, the more dynamic and interesting of the two of us.'

'Now that's just the kind of talk I don't want to hear from you ever again.'

She'd told him the reasons she'd got involved with Will, and in turn he said he regretted not being more forcible in making his feelings known to her before, particularly that day on the canal. 'I'd been trying to pluck up the courage for weeks to tell you how I felt,' he'd said, 'and when you started asking me about what I wrote in my poetry, whether I wrote about love, I thought perhaps you were hinting that you knew how I felt. But then for no reason at all you went rushing off and the next thing, you and Will were organising a cosy evening out together. You couldn't have made your feelings clearer, as far as I was concerned. I was crushed.'

'I'm sorry,' she'd apologised. 'I was scared that you might tell me about your affair with my sister. I just couldn't stand the idea of hearing you open your heart to me about her. I grabbed at the easiest and nearest thing to shut you up.'

The first time Miles kissed Harriet, Carrie walked in on them in the kitchen. 'This isn't going to be easy, is it?' he'd said with a half smile as Carrie turned bright red, giggled loudly and thumped her way back upstairs to share the big joke with Joel.

He was right. Carrying out any kind of romantic manoeuvre was proving impractical. This didn't worry Harriet too much, as the last thing she wanted was to rush into anything. She suspected Miles might see it differently because he had hinted several times that maybe she could arrange a babysitter – her parents, perhaps – and come to his place where they could be alone. But her parents had their own problems and she was reluctant to ask them to babysit just so that she could have sex with Miles. The juxtaposition was too weird for words.

As was the strained relationship between their respective parents. Eileen had extended the olive branch by speaking to Freda, but Bob and Harvey were definitely not in the mood for a reconciliation.

Not surprisingly, Harriet and Miles had spoken a lot about Dominic and how they were both worried about him. Without Felicity in his life, he seemed dangerously adrift.

Thinking of Felicity now, as Harriet watched a colourful barge chug steadily by her bedroom window, she recalled Dominic saying that Felicity had known him inside and out.

For her part, Harriet no longer felt as though she knew her sister. She'd become a stranger. It saddened her, but Harriet wasn't even sure she liked the person her sister had turned into. She hadn't been fair to Jeff, and her treatment of Dominic – a man who was obsessed with her – wasn't much better; she'd kept him dangling by his heart strings for far too long.

Although Harriet didn't really believe in heaven, she sent up a silent message to her sister. 'It's time to let Dominic go, Felicity. You couldn't do it in life, but you must do it now or he'll never know peace of mind.'

It was a while before Bob could look at his garden without being consumed by a humiliating sense of shame and sorrow. He couldn't believe he'd destroyed something from which he'd derived such pleasure. The grief counsellor he was seeing said it was quite common to lash out at that which meant most to you when the chips were down, and he saw now that the therapist wasn't only referring to the terrible madness that had overtaken him on New Year's Day. The affairs he'd had – including the one he'd tried to have with Jennifer – had been a way of punishing poor Eileen. Subconsciously, he'd never properly grieved for those babies he and Eileen had lost, and he had blamed her for the miscarriages. Perhaps, more disturbingly, he'd also blamed her for not being able to keep Felicity alive.

The worst counselling session he'd had to sit through had been the one with Eileen present. The therapist had suggested she should be there and it was during this two-hour gruelling stint that they had openly discussed his affairs. He'd been devasted to learn that Eileen had always known about them and that she had suspected he'd met someone more recently. Humbled and broken-spirited he'd wept in her arms that night in bed – how could she be so forgiving? 'I don't deserve you,' he'd said to her.

'Don't ever say that.'

'But I don't understand how you've stood by me all these years.'

'It's called love, Bob. No matter what, I'll always love you.'

'I'm a lucky man.'

I'm a lucky man . . . The words echoed in his head as he continued to stare at the garden, which he was now trying to put right. Only a matter of weeks ago he would never have thought he'd be able to describe himself as lucky, but he knew now that he was. His physical breakdown had been a blessing in disguise. He was now able to put his grief into context. It was still there, and would never go away entirely, but it was no longer the constant focus of his thoughts.

It pained him to know that Felicity had been so unhappy in her marriage, but nothing could help him to understand the relationship she'd had with Dominic McKendrick. How could she have been attracted to such a freak of nature? The therapist had suggested this was a typical father's reaction to an unsuitable suitor. 'But I accepted Jeff,' he'd told her. 'Jeff got my vote right from the start.'

'That was possibly because he was entirely suitable,' the quietly spoken woman had said, 'a safer bet than the wild and dangerous man who had the potential to be a genuine threat to your love for Felicity. From what you say, Jeff was a quiet, thoughtful man; a malleable man perhaps. Very likely, you saw him as someone who would never outshine you in your daughter's eyes.'

They had scarcely touched on his relationship with Harriet, but Bob knew there was a lot to be said on the matter. He knew also that he would be further shamed. It was rapidly becoming clear to him that he hadn't been altogether fair to Harriet. He hoped that one day she would forgive him.

He was also glad that he'd never gone ahead and had a full-blown affair with Jennifer. With Eileen's full knowledge he had written to Jennifer and apologised for his behaviour, to draw a line under the episode. By return of post he received a card wishing him all the best for the future. The therapist had suggested that his attraction to

Jennifer had been more to do with the sense of freedom and independence she represented than the need for a sexual relationship.

It was with this new understanding in mind that he had a surprise in store for Eileen. He'd been planning it for the last few days and he hoped Eileen would take to it as much as the therapist seemed to think she would.

It was Saturday evening at Bellagio's.

Gemma didn't know whose idea it had been to go out for dinner, but she was glad they were here. It was good seeing her parents together like this. She wished Suzie was here to see it. Sometimes, late at night, when she couldn't sleep, she imagined herself writing a letter to her sister, as though she was away on a long holiday rather than dead. In the imaginary letters she would tell Suzie everything that was going on: how school was going, how Marcel had stopped writing to her because he'd got a girlfriend, how Nana Ruby was having a hip replacement next week and that Mum was paying for her to go privately, *and* that Dad had actually kissed Mum when she'd told him what she was doing. It was quite something to see Mum and Dad getting on better than they had in years. Nana Ruby said it was a shame they couldn't have done this ages ago, but that it was better late than never.

Hearing her name mentioned, Gemma tuned in to what her parents were saying. They were both looking at her expectantly, their glasses raised. 'What?' she said, realising that they were no longer talking about Mum and Steve's long weekend away in a few weeks' time.

'Here's to you,' her father said. 'Congratulations on the offer from Durham.'

Gemma frowned, embarrassed. 'It's only an offer; I've got to get the grades yet.' She felt uncomfortable that she could think about going to university when Suzie was dead. it didn't seem right.

'You'll do fine,' her mother said.

'I might not, though.'

'And if you don't,' her father said after glancing quickly at her mother, 'that'll be fine too. Whatever happens in the summer with your exams, we'll be right behind you, won't we, Maxine?'

Gemma could see what they were up to and cringed. *Dear Suzie*, she imagined writing, *Mum and Dad are driving me mad with their consideration and support. Help! Who will crack first; them or me?*

After dropping Maxine and Gemma off, Will drove on to see his mother. She never went to bed early so when he rang the doorbell at half past ten he did so confident that she would still be up. 'I was just making myself a cup of tea,' she said when she opened the door. 'Would you like one?'

'No thanks, I'm buzzing full tilt on Maywood's finest Italian triple-strength espresso.'

'Been dining out, have you?'

'With Maxine and Gemma.'

He caught the twinkling smile in his mother's eyes as she poured herself a mug of tea. 'And yes, before you ask, Maxine and I really are making an effort these days,' he said.

'Good. How is she? I haven't seen her for a couple of weeks.'

'She still looks tired, but then that's probably because she's working too hard on top of everything else.'

'Does she know about Steve's surprise for her?'

'No, she doesn't have a clue. She thinks he's taking her to London and then on to a health spa for a few days.'

Ruby smiled. 'Oh, I'd love to see her face when he tells her they're going to Rome and Florence. She'll be thoroughly made up. All those art galleries and museums to lose herself in. It'll be just the ticket. Now come and sit down.' She pulled out a kitchen chair for him. 'I want to get a good look at you. You still look like you're not eating enough. How are you sleeping?'

'Mum, I'm forty-six years old; can you drop the parent

routine for a bit and let me ask how you are? How's the hip?'

She sat down with a wince and a sigh. 'Sore.'

'Are you taking the painkillers and anti-inflammatories the doctor prescribed?'

'Yes.'

'Are they working?'

'Some days are better than others.'

'I know the feeling.'

Their eyes met. 'It'll get easier,' she said. 'Trust me.'

He watched her sip her tea and mentally thanked Maxine for what she was doing for his mother. It was only in the New Year that they had realised just how much pain Ruby was in. As was so typical of her, she'd kept it from them for several months because she didn't want to make a fuss.

'So how's business at the shop?' she said.

'Quiet. It's that time of the year.'

'And Jarvis? How's he?'

'Nagging me to get out and about more. You know, visiting the salerooms.'

'It makes sense. It you haven't got the stock you won't get the customers.'

'I know. I'm gradually getting back into the swing of it.'

'And your love life? How's that?'

'That's the last thing on my mind.'

'Then you're making a big mistake. A kiss and a cuddle would go a long way to making you feel better right now. What was that girl's name you were seeing before ... before Suzie died?'

'Harriet.'

'I liked her.'

'Don't be ridiculous! You never even met her.'

'I heard about her from Gemma and I did see her at the hospital that night. She looked a sweet little thing.'

'She wouldn't thank you for that description.'

Ruby tutted. 'These modern girls are all the same: toughened exteriors with silky soft centres. Gemma's the same. You'll need to keep a careful eye on her this year.

She's got a lot on her plate, what with grieving for her sister and the pressure of exams in the summer. I've told Maxine to go gently with her, to give her plenty of space.'

'You're a wise woman, Mum.'

'I know. I'm also tired. I think I'd like to go to bed now.'

'Why don't you go on up and I'll sort everything out down here?'

'There's no need. You look more worn out than me. Better you push off home and get some sleep.'

Tired as he was, Will didn't go straight to bed when he got home. There was a message from Marty on his answering machine. It was almost midnight but he returned the call anyway. They had an agreement; it didn't matter what time of day or night it was – if either of them needed to talk, the other would be at the other end of a phone. Marty had finished the course of radiotherapy but Will still feared that the all-clear his friend had been given would turn out to be a hospital error.

'Did I wake you?' he asked Marty when he eventually picked up.

'No, I was in the shower.'

'Everything okay?'

'Everything's fine. More than fine, actually. That's why I rang. I wanted to . . . well, the thing is . . . Oh, hell, now I feel silly, as if I'm bragging.'

'Get on with it, Marty. If it's good news, I could do with hearing it.'

'I've met someone. She's the specialist who's been treating me.'

'Is that ethical?'

'It is now I've finished the treatment.'

'That's brilliant! When do I get to meet her? What's her name and what's the protocol when I shake hands with her? Will it be rubber gloves and a discreet cough?'

'Her name's Jill and you can meet her if you promise not to try out any of those awful jokes. Hers are far better and I guarantee they'll make your eyes water into the bargain.'

It was good to hear Marty sounding more like his old self; Will was genuinely pleased for his friend.

Lying in bed later, he thought about what his mother had said about Harriet – in particular Ruby's description of her being a sweet little thing. At this he imagined Harriet giving him one of her looks that could split the atom. He then pictured her in the snow on New Year's Day. He closed his eyes and a whole series of memories came to him: the night he'd mistaken her for a boy; the day she'd had an asthma attack in the shop; the first life-threatening time he'd kissed her; the first time they made love. But the best memory of all was the one of her sitting by the fire with him after their New Year's Day walk had been snowed off. Her company that afternoon had meant more to him than she would ever know. It didn't matter that she had confessed to using him – people used one another all the time and he could live with that. Bizarrely, he admired her for having the guts to be so honest with him. But that was her all over. She didn't believe in taking hostages. After she'd gone, he'd poured himself another glass of wine and put on R.E.M.'s CD *Reveal*. When he heard the lyrics for 'Imitation of Life' and listened to Stipe singing about not being afraid and no one seeing you cry, he suddenly found himself weeping uncontrollably. Sorry Stipe, he'd thought, but I *am* afraid. I'm terrified, if you really want to know.

One of the things he hated most about mourning the loss of Suzie was that he had to do it alone. Was there anything more pitiful than crying alone? Despite the improved relations between him and Maxine, he was still very much isolated in his grief.

His mother was right; a bit of affection would be nice. More than that, it would be bloody fantastic.

He turned onto his back, resigned to it being one of those nights when all that was on offer was restless torment. He wondered what Harriet was doing right now. Whatever it was, it had to be better than him lying here in the dark realising just how much he missed her.

*

'Come on, Harriet, the kids are fast asleep; they'll never hear us.'

'But what if they do?'

Miles raised himself up onto an elbow and smiled. 'I'm prepared to risk it if you are.' He went back to unbuttoning her shirt and kissing her. She closed her eyes and tried to relax. But she couldn't; she was trying to think if it was better to do it down here in the sitting room or upstairs in her bedroom. If they were in bed at least they'd have the duvet to hide under if they were interrupted. But if they were upstairs, they were more likely to wake the children; the bed would probably make more noise than an orchestra tuning up. Never mind waking the children, they'd probably wake the neighbours!

'Harriet, are you okay?'

She opened her eyes and realised that Miles was staring down at her hands, which were balled into fists either side of her. 'I'm sorry,' she said, 'I'm just finding it hard to concentrate. You know, with the children upstairs.'

He frowned. 'Married couples manage it all the time.'

'I know; that's what makes me feel so silly. I'm sorry.'

The frown disappeared and he smiled again, kissing her once on each eyelid and then on the lips. 'Let's try it on the floor. The sofa's a bit confining.'

It'll be fine, she told herself as she allowed Miles to take off her top. The children went to bed hours ago. They'll never hear us. She kissed him on the mouth and began undoing his trousers. He gave a groan of pleasure as her hands touched him. 'Now yours,' he said. Unzipping her jeans and kicking them off, she suddenly felt shy. The last time he'd seen her in her knickers was when they were children. He lay on his side and ran his hand the length of her thigh, then put it between her legs. She almost jumped at his touch. He then parted her legs and lay on top of her. 'I love you, Harriet,' he whispered into her ear. 'I always have.' He was breathing heavily now.

Oh, God, she suddenly thought, squeezing her eyes shut. He loves me. But I don't love him. Why don't I love him?

What's the matter with me? I've known him nearly all my life; he knows me better than anyone. So why do I keep thinking this is so wrong?

She opened her eyes, and as if looking down at herself she realised it felt as if she were having sex with a brother. She felt enormous affection towards Miles, but no desire; she was about as aroused as the ceiling she was staring up at. She began to panic. What should she do? If she backed out now, she would hurt Miles's pride. She couldn't do that to him. In that case, she had no choice but to grit her teeth and let him get on with it. Oh, why couldn't it be like when she'd been in bed with Will?

Her heart gave a small leap. Was that the answer? Could she imagine it was Will making love to her? She closed her eyes and pictured him. At once her body relaxed and she felt his smooth, firm hands caressing her, his tongue working deep into her mouth, his body pressing against hers. She put her arms around his neck and moved her body against his. 'Oh, Will,' she murmured, 'I've missed you so much.'

She suddenly heard what she'd said. Will. *Will!* His name reverberated off the walls.

Miles heard it too. He rolled away from her and sat bolt upright. For a while neither of them spoke. She reached for her clothes. 'I'm sorry, Miles. It just came out. I don't know what to say.'

'Sorry might be appropriate.'

'I just said I was sorry.'

'Is that what the problem's been all these weeks?'

'I don't know what you mean.' But she did. It was all too clear to her now. The prevaricating had had little to do with the children and everything to do with Will: her feelings for him had never gone away.

'You've been putting off sex with me because you've still got a thing for Will, haven't you?'

'I didn't know it until just now,' she said. 'You must believe me, Miles. I would never consciously do anything to hurt you.'

518

He sighed and his eyes met hers with a sad candour. 'Either way, it's obvious to me we're not going anywhere, are we? What was I? A shoulder to cry on?'

All she could do was repeat how sorry she was.

Chapter Sixty

While Eileen was in the shower, Bob got the fire going and made a start on cooking breakfast: Toby looked on expectantly. There was nothing like the smell of bacon on a crisp, bright morning to make a man feel glad to be alive. And Bob did feel glad to be alive. His plan had worked and already he was feeling a lightness of spirit he could never have hoped for. When he'd been planning to spring his surprise on Eileen, he'd been scared that she would turn him down, that she would think he was still suffering from the madness that had consumed him these long, terrifying months. If she'd refused to go along with him, he didn't know what he would have done. But the risk had paid off and yesterday afternoon, after giving Eileen no more than an hour to pack a bag, he had driven them, plus Toby, to the marina and introduced her to their home for the next week. 'You're sure you want to do this?' he'd asked her. 'It could turn out to be a disaster.'

She'd kissed his cheek and said, 'We won't know until we've tried it, will we?'

The man from whom Bob had hired the narrowboat had instructed them on how it worked and explained how to operate a lock, and they were soon unpacked and off. They didn't have much daylight time left and before long they were mooring up for the night. It didn't matter that they'd only travelled a couple of miles north of Kings Melford; just to be away from the claustrophobic atmosphere of Maple Drive was enough to make Bob feel free. There were no other boats moored around them and it felt as if they had the entire canal to themselves. Eileen had heated up a steak pie he'd bought from Edna Gannet, along with some peas and carrots, and they'd had tinned peaches and cream for pudding. Accompanied by a bottle of wine, it had tasted like the best meal he'd had in ages. Things had then taken an amusing turn when they'd made a pot of coffee and were opening a box of chocolates he'd also bought from Edna. When he'd got the lid off the box, they'd found that the chocolates had turned a mottled white colour. 'That woman is priceless,' Eileen had laughed. 'We should keep them to see what excuse she comes up with to avoid giving us our money back. She'll probably eat one just to prove there's nothing wrong with them.'

They'd sat with their cups of coffee in the soft light cast from the lamps, listening to the sounds of the night – water gently lapping, an owl hooting, the wind gently rustling the nearby undergrowth. They'd talked too, as they did all the time now.

He still felt he didn't deserve Eileen's forgiveness and occasionally he doubted that he could ever make amends. She kept reassuring him that he had to stop thinking this way. 'What we should do is pretend we've just met for the first time,' she'd said in bed last night. 'That we know nothing about each other and have to learn to get to know one another.'

'That would make us pretty fast and loose seeing as we're already in bed together,' he'd said with a smile.

She'd smiled shyly back at him and said, 'Maybe that's how I want to feel.'

He was still thinking about her remark and his response to it when Eileen appeared in the saloon. 'Mm . . . that smells wonderful,' she said. 'Anything I can do?'

'Yes, you can sit down and pour yourself some coffee. The cafetiere's on the table. How was the shower? Hot enough?'

'Plenty hot enough. I tried not to use too much water. I hate the thought of running out.'

'Don't worry, we'll top it up later today if need be. Toby, don't be a pest! Get out of my way or you'll end up with an egg on your head.'

*

Eileen watched her husband spooning hot oil over the eggs in the frying pan. The transformation was incredible. Bob was looking and sounding just like the man he used to be. If one night away from home could bring about such a miracle, maybe they should consider spending the rest of their lives on board this boat and just float away. It was a joy to see him so happy, something she never thought she'd see again. He'd been so tender with her in bed last night. Cocooned in the compact little sleeping area at the front of the boat, she had lain awake long after he'd fallen asleep, listening to his breathing, just loving the thought of being so close to him again. Even the dull ache in her back and the heavy tiredness she felt this morning couldn't take away her happiness.

When they had tidied breakfast away, Bob got the boat ready to move on: they were doubling back on themselves today and heading south. Eileen's job – the only job he would allow her to do – was to catch and coil the ropes neatly after he had untied and thrown them to her, leaving the one at the front of the boat till last so that he could get back on board before the boat slipped away from the bank.

She felt a twinge of sadness at leaving their tranquil overnight spot as Bob opened up the engine and they pushed through the water, disturbing the glassy surface and the peace and quiet. Although the sun was out and there was little wind, they were both dressed for near-arctic conditions, with numerous layers beneath their fleeces, windproofs over the top, and thermal-lined hats and gloves. They stood side by side, Bob's arm resting on the tiller as he steered their course, his expression one of contented purposefulness. Down in the galley, Toby lay curled up in front of the fire. He might be warmer, thought Eileen, but she knew where she'd rather be. She had no idea how far she and Bob would travel in the week ahead, but she didn't care so long as they were together and as happy as this.

Harriet wasn't a gambler by nature, and she'd spent all of

the last week agonising over the risk Miles had urged her to take.

After he had recovered his composure and they were both dressed, he'd sat with her at the kitchen table with a mug of coffee, and as was so typical of him, had given her the opportunity not just to apologise but to talk about Will.

'I don't seem to be able to get him out of my mind,' she confessed.

'What do you think the attraction is?' Miles had asked.

'I don't know.' But she did. It was everything. The shape of his eyes, the way they crinkled at the corners when he smiled, the way he wore his hair – just a bit too long – the way he tried not to wear his glasses in front of her because he was vain and thought they aged him. And then there was the way he held her, the way his hands could skilfully undress her – 'Did I mention that these hands are licensed to undress?' he'd once joked. The way he kissed her, the way he could make her weak with longing, and the way he could make her climax for ever and for ever.

'Do you want to get back together with him?' Miles had asked.

'I don't think it's possible,' she'd said. 'Or even a good idea.' She was thinking of Howard's advice to leave well alone, that Will was damaged goods and too vulnerable to get involved in a relationship.

'You can tell me to mind my own business,' Miles had said, 'but if I were you, I'd talk to him. Tell him how you feel. If he agrees with you that it's not a good idea, and there's every chance he might, then so be it.'

'But what if—?'

'There are always going to be what-ifs, Harriet,' he interrupted. 'But for once in your life, stop analysing the situation and just go for it. If it all comes to nothing, so what? What will you have lost? And on that final piece of advice, I'm going home.'

She hugged him at the door. 'You're such a good friend, Miles. I'm sorry it worked out this way.'

'So am I. But perhaps we were only ever destined to be

friends. Give me a ring next week to let me know how things have panned out.'

It was only now, a week on, that she had convinced herself to do as Miles had suggested. She would go and see Will and tell him how she felt about him. He might well throw her words back in her face, but at least she would have tried. She would call him later and see if he wanted to meet her for a drink.

Meanwhile, she had promised the children a walk.

They'd just stepped onto the towpath when Joel said, 'Look, there's a boat coming.' Sure enough, coming from the Kings Melford direction was a traditional narrowboat, its green, red and black paintwork cheerfully bright in the morning sunlight.

'They've got a dog on board,' Carrie said. 'He looks just like Toby.'

'It's Grandma and Granddad!' squealed Joel. 'Look, it *is* them! They're waving at us.'

Within minutes, her father was steering the boat in alongside them, and after Eileen had thrown Harriet a rope and they had the boat securely fastened, the children were helped on board. 'We can't stop for long,' Bob said. 'We're off who knows where.'

'Can we come?' asked Joel, down on the floor cuddling Toby.

'Another time, perhaps. Come and see the rest of the boat. We've even got a fire in the saloon.'

'Is it a real fire?' asked Carrie.

Leaving her father to show off the boat to the children, Harriet held her mother back and said, 'What's going on, Mum? Dad looks and sounds like a different man.'

'Not different. How he used to be.'

'Where's the boat come from? Have you hired it for the day?'

'We've got it for a week. Your father planned it as a surprise. It's so we can get away from everything and spend some time alone. We've only travelled a couple of miles from home, but in so many other ways we've covered more ground than you could ever imagine.' She gave Harriet a hug. 'Come on, let's go down and join the others in the warm.'

It was six o'clock when Will let himself in that evening. It had been a busy afternoon in the shop. Which was a good thing, he had decided. Having too much free time on his hands was to be avoided. Now that he could face people, including regular customers with their sympathy, the shop seemed a better option than being at home on his own. It was progress, he acknowledged, shrugging off his jacket and hanging it up. He checked to see if there were any messages on his answering machine. There was only one, from Jarvis, saying he wouldn't be in until after lunch the next day – 'Just in case you were thinking of having a lie in, Laddie.' Will felt like ringing Jarvis back and telling him to stop worrying; he could be trusted to make it in to work these days. Even so, he was touched that the old man was still looking out for him, quietly working in the background to make sure his protégé was functioning as he should be.

He went upstairs for a shower and after he'd changed into some clean jeans and a shirt, he went back downstairs to throw some supper together. He'd just opened the fridge to consider his options when the doorbell rang.

His first thought when he opened the door and saw Harriet was that he was glad he'd cleaned himself up. His second thought was to tell himself not to be so stupid and vain. She wasn't interested in him. Trouble was, just one look at her and he knew he'd never lost his desire for her.

Harriet's first thought when she saw Will was to forget the carefully prepared speech she'd practised in the car. Her decision to phone him and invite him out for a drink had also gone by the wayside, because she'd decided to let fate intervene. If he'd been out when she called in, she'd have taken it as a sign to leave well alone.

'Hello Will,' she said. 'Is it a bad time to drop by?'

He stepped back to let her in. 'It's perfect timing. You

can help me choose what to cook for supper. Better still, how about I open a bottle of wine and defer such a difficult decision?'

'That would be nice. But make mine a small glass – I'm driving.'

'Whatever you say. Here, let me take your coat.'

Their hands brushed as he took it from her and she knew she hadn't imagined what she still felt for Will.

'Where are the children, by the way?' he asked. 'You've not left them on the doorstep with a bottle of pop and a bag of crisps, have you?'

'No, they're with some neighbours.'

'Nice neighbours?'

'Horrible neighbours. They worship the devil and carry out satanic rites on the under-tens.'

He smiled. 'Sorry, that was a silly question. Come on through to the kitchen. You've settled in okay, then?'

'Yes, it feels like we've always been there. You must come and see us. Carrie and Joel would love to see you again.'

'I'd like that. Chardonnay okay for you?'

'Thank you.' While she watched him take out the cork and pour the wine, she wondered if she could go through with what she'd come to say. The fear of being rejected, of being rebuffed, was making her nervous. And she'd never been nervous in Will's company before.

'There you go,' he said. 'Cheers. Good to see you.'

They clinked glasses and she took an enormous swig of Dutch courage.

'How are your parents?' he said, leaning back against the worktop and crossing his legs at the ankles. 'Your father in particular.'

'They're well.' She told him about them going off in the boat Dad had hired and how much good it was doing them already.

'That's fantastic. I almost wish I could do the same.'

'Yes, it certainly has its appeal,' she said absently. She chewed on her lip. As happy as she was for her parents, their unexpected holiday was the last thing she'd come here to talk about. She fiddled with the metal links of her watch strap. What if Will wasn't strong enough yet to consider his own happiness? What if, just like her after Felicity had died, he thought it indecently inappropriate? She knew all too well that grief could behave like a demanding and possessive lover. From nowhere it could jealously strike you down with a guilt-laden blow, reminding you that you didn't deserve to be happy or move on.

'You okay?' he asked. 'You look on edge. Something bothering you?'

Tell him. Go on, just say the words. 'Oh, you know me, always something on my mind. What was it you said once? That I vibrated at the speed of light?'

He smiled. 'Let's go and sit down and see if that will have the required calming effect. I'm afraid I haven't lit a fire yet. It's all ready to go, though; I just need to throw a match at it.'

In the sitting room, she watched him light the fire and after he'd put the box of matches on the mantelpiece, the phone rang.

Will made his excuses and disappeared out to the kitchen to answer the telephone. Within seconds he had returned the receiver – it was one of those wretched overseas cold calls – and was wondering what to do about Harriet. It was obvious that she'd come here to tell him something, but at the rate she was going, she'd still be here at midnight trying to get the words out. He decided to give her a helping hand. If he'd got it wrong, then so be it.

Back in the sitting room, he said, 'Sorry about that. It was one of those polite but annoyingly persistent women from a call centre somewhere along the banks of the Ganges.' He sat on the sofa next to Harriet, just inches from her, but kept his gaze on the fire straight in front of them. 'I told her to call later when I'd finished entertaining an ex girlfriend of mine. She was most intrigued and asked why you were an ex. I said it was complicated. She asked if there was any way of starting afresh and I said I didn't know, that I'd have to look into it. She suggested I get right back in here and ask you straight out if there was any chance of us getting it together again. I told her, "Hey, this is no pushover currently sitting on my sofa. She's one sassy girl who isn't going to be rushed into anything."' He tutted and shook his head. 'I don't know, these call centres, they have some nerve, don't they? Poking and prying into other people's lives. Where will it all end, I wonder?'

There was a slight pause before Harriet said, 'Did the woman offer any other words of advice?'

Picking up his glass of wine from the coffee table and turning to face her, he said, 'Well, she did finish off by saying that she thought you sounded like you were too good for me.'

'I'm sure she didn't and if she did, she was wrong. It's the other way round if you ask me. Did she say anything about you being particularly vulnerable at the moment and maybe a relationship would be unwise?'

'Actually, she said it would be the best possible answer. That having someone special in my life would stop me from feeling sorry for myself.'

'She sounds like she knows what she's talking about.'

'Yeah, I thought so too.'

'So what do you think we should do?'

'I think that rather depends on you, doesn't it?'

Harriet took his glass from him and put it back on the table. She then touched his face with her fingers, tracing the outline of his jaw. He briefly closed his eyes. When he opened them, she kissed him softly on the mouth. 'The thing is, Will, I can't stop thinking about you. I tried to, but you wouldn't go away.'

'Are you saying I'm like a bad smell?'

She smiled. 'No. You're the kindest, funniest—'

He put a finger to her lips. 'I told you before; I'd make do with being the sexiest.'

'Care to prove it?'

*

'I'm nothing but a sex toy to you, aren't I?' he said later, in bed.

'You mean far more to me than that, Will.'

Hearing how serious she sounded, he said, 'I was joking.'

'For once I'd like you not to.'

He leaned over, suddenly needing to hear the words. 'Tell me what I mean to you, then.'

She swallowed. 'You mean more to me than anyone has before.'

'Does that scare you?'

'Yes.'

'Imagine how I feel. Definitely the wrong side of forty and totally blown away by you.'

'It's not the age thing that bothers me.'

'What, then?'

'It's . . . it's the logistics of being together. I can only be here now because my neighbours have helped me out.' She looked at her watch. 'And I really ought to get going soon. I mustn't take advantage of Stewart and Diana.'

He shushed her with a kiss. 'Stop worrying. We'll sort it. There's always a way to do these things.'

'It doesn't sound like a lot of fun for you, though. Seeing someone in my position.'

He raised an eyebrow and took in her naked body. 'Frankly, Miss Swift, I can see nothing remotely off-putting in your current position. It seems perfect to me. And I think you should know that you can give up trying to talk me out of being a part of your life. Easy relationships are for wimps. Real men pick women with a bit of challenge to them, and you have that in abundance. So tell me, what is it about me that got you hooked?'

She slapped his chest playfully. 'No way am I going to play that game!'

'Spoilsport. But I'll tell you what did it for me. First off it was the wrath and brimstone looks you gave me— Oh no you don't,' he laughed as she opened her mouth to protest. 'No interrupting or denying; that's not how the game works. And then it was your fierce love for your sister and her children that touched me.'

'No, you've got it all wrong. Every decision I made was done out of a sense of duty and the fact that I didn't have a choice.'

'That may have been true in the beginning, but what about now? Those kids really mean something to you, don't they? They're a part of your life and there's not a damn thing you wouldn't do for them. I'm right, aren't I?' When she didn't reply, he became aware that they were a stone's throw from getting too serious. 'And on a lighter note, I'd like it to be known that regarding my attraction for you, there was one more thing that clinched matters for me.'

'What was that, then? My razor-sharp wit? My scintillating intellect?'

'Um . . . actually, it was the sight of you in your beret. Any chance you could wear it in bed for me some time?'

When Harriet had gone, Will remembered he hadn't had anything to eat. He rustled up an omelette, ate it hungrily, put his plate in the dishwasher and checked what time it was. Another twenty minutes, he reckoned, and then he'd ring her.

On the stroke of eleven he was back in bed and phoned Harriet. 'Hi,' he said. 'Are we on for some phone sex now?'

She laughed. 'Is this how it's going to be?'

'Yes, every night when we're not together, this is what we'll do.'

'What about in the morning?'

'Mornings are good for me too.'

'Lunchtime?'

'That might be pushing it a bit. Jarvis is a stickler for observing old-fashioned decencies in the shop. Right then, fire away. Say something smutty.'

'You're insane.'

'And you're blushing, aren't you?'

'Certainly not. I was just putting on my beret.'

He groaned exaggeratedly.

'Goodnight, Will. I'll speak to you tomorrow.'

Smiling, he switched off his mobile and put it on the bedside table. Harriet was right about her current situation being complicated. A serious relationship with her would not be straightforward. Could he really picture himself with two young children along with Gemma and the grieving process he still had to get through? He didn't know for sure, but what he could picture was being with Harriet. He could imagine that all too clearly.

He turned out the light and within minutes he'd nodded off. For once he'd fallen asleep without torturing himself by reliving the last conscious moments of Suzie's life.

At work the next day, shortly after Harriet had taken a call from Will, Howard came into her office. She was still smirking at the thought of something Will had suggested he would like to do to her when Howard pressed his considerable backside against her desk. 'You've got that look on your face again, Hat.'

'What look?' she said.

'The nun who's just been snogged.'

'I'm going to treat that remark with the contempt it deserves. What can I do for you, Howard? I'm a busy woman.'

He regarded her closely. 'You're seeing that bloke again, aren't you?'

She turned back towards her computer and pretended to be concentrating on the code she was compiling. 'And which bloke would that be?'

'The one I said you should leave well alone.'

'Perhaps you were wrong. Let's face it, it can't be a first.'

'Hah! I knew it. I knew I could rely on feminine logic.'

She swivelled her chair so she was facing Howard again. 'What do you mean, feminine logic?'

'I knew if I told you not to do something, you'd do it. I haven't worked with women and computers as long as I have to know that unlike a computer, a woman doesn't function to the accepted rules of logic. You've got to employ cunning and reverse psychology to make them do what you want. Well done, Hat. I knew I'd get you and that bloke back together. I reckon you'll be good for each other.'

'Get out! Out of my office, you conceited, horrible man!'

He ducked the file she threw at him.

That evening, while Harriet was getting the tea ready and Carrie and Joel were setting the table with their usual propensity to clatter the cutlery and crash the crockery, she asked them how they'd got on with Dora doing the afternoon school run. With Eileen and Bob away, Dora had stepped into the breach and Harriet was concerned about Joel's reaction to the change in their normal routine.

'Auntie Dora took us to Maywood,' Joel answered.

'She never said anything when I picked you up.'

'We saw Miles in his bookshop,' joined in Carrie.

'Oh, yes? How was he?'

'I asked him if he was coming to help you with any jobs this week and he said if there was anything you needed doing, you knew where he was.'

Later, during their bedtime story, Joel said, 'Carrie thinks you're going to marry Miles. Is that true?'

Carrie rolled her eyes and kicked his foot. 'I told you not to say anything.'

'It's okay,' Harriet said. She decided to be completely honest with them. 'Miles and I have always been very close; after all, we've known one another nearly all our lives. But friends is all we'll ever be.'

'But I saw you kissing him.'

'Yes, Carrie, you did. But—'

'You don't want to shag him, is that it?'

Harriet's eyes opened wide. 'Carrie! Where did you get that from?'

Her niece didn't even blush. 'Is shag a very bad word?' she asked.

'Put it this way: it's not the kind of word you should repeat in front of Grandma and Granddad.'

'What does it mean?' asked Joel

'It means to be sexy with someone,' Carrie informed him importantly.

The definition was near enough for Harriet to let it go. She was about to suggest they get back to their book when Joel said, 'Auntie Dora says she thinks you're more likely to marry Will than Miles. Are you sexy with Will?'

Harriet felt the colour cover her from top to toe.

'Is he your boyfriend?' asked Carrie.

Thinking that she must stick to her policy of being honest with the children, she said, 'Sort of.'

Her niece looked at her doubtfully. 'What does *sort of* mean?'

'I suppose it means yes. Will is my boyfriend. Is that okay with you two?'

Both of the children smiled.

'I'll take that as a yes, then. Now how about this story? Shall we get back to it?'

'Do you kiss him?'

'Yes, Carrie, I do.' Harriet tapped the book on her lap. 'The story?'

'What about being sexy? Are you sexy together?'

'Carrie!'

When Harriet was lying in bed, her mobile went off. It was Will.

'Hi,' he said. 'How was your day?'

'It kicked off with an obscene caller, followed by an interrogation by my boss on my love life and then this evening the children gave me a thorough grilling.'

'What did they want to know?'

'It appears that Carrie has picked up the word "shag" from somewhere and wanted to know if that's what we get up to.'

'She knows about me?'

'Apparently she had her information from Dora. I thought it best to be honest with them. Is that okay?'

'Hey, does the ambassador like chocolates? So am I officially your boyfriend now?'

'I thought that was a given.'

'Excellent. It makes me sound at least ten years younger. So when do I get the chance to show off my girl round town?'

'That'll have to keep for a few days, but you can come for supper tomorrow evening if you like.'

'Count me in. What time do you want me there?'

'I've got to fetch the children from Dora's after work at six thirty, so any time after seven.'

'I could pick them up if you want.'

'Really?'

'Sure. I can do it when I've finished at the shop; that way they can cross-examine me without you around. And I shall tell them we do much more than shag.'

Laughing, she said, 'Will?'

'Yes?'

'I'm so glad that woman from the call centre phoned you last night and you had such a good chat with her.'

'So am I. If I'd left things to you, you'd still be fiddling with your watch strap and wondering how to tell me you fancied the pants off me.'

'You knew?'

'Of course I did. I've always known.'

'Liar.'

'Well, okay then. When you turned up out of the blue, my pathetic male ego kicked in and I hoped my luck was in too.'

'Am I that obvious to read?'

'Nah. It's my stunning intuitive powers of deduction.'

When they'd said goodnight and Harriet had switched off her mobile, she thought she heard a noise coming from Carrie's bedroom. She got out of bed and crossed the landing, her feet sinking into the new carpet. 'Are you all right, Carrie?' she said softly at her open door.

Carrie raised her head from the pillow. 'I heard you talking to someone. Who was it?'

Harriet went and knelt by the side of her bed. 'It was Will. He's coming to see us tomorrow evening. Is that okay with you?'

Carrie nodded sleepily. 'Mm . . . that'll be nice. Will's fun.'

'Yes, he is.' Bending down to kiss her niece goodnight, Harriet thought that the word 'fun' summed up Will best. Despite everything he was going through, he still managed to be wonderful company. He made such a difference to her life. She just hoped she did the same for him.

'Harriet?' Her niece didn't sound so sleepy now.

'Yes, Carrie?'

'You won't . . . you won't ever leave us, will you?'

'Hey there kiddo, what kind of a question is that?'

'You might if you got bored with us. Or if we did something really bad.'

'And have you done something really bad?'

'No. But what if we did?'

Harriet sat down on the edge of the bed and mentally rolled up her sleeves to get to the bottom of what was on her niece's mind. 'Are you worrying about something, Carrie? Has something happened at school?'

Carrie shook her head.

'Come on, you can tell me. No matter what you've done, I promise I won't be cross.'

'It's nothing to do with school. It's just that everything feels . . .' She hesitated and gave a little shrug. 'Everything feels so nice since we moved here . . . and it makes me feel happy.'

A flutter of understanding made Harriet say, 'And that worries you, doesn't it?'

'Yes, because what if it stops being nice?' Raising herself onto her elbow, Carrie sat up. 'What if it all turns nasty and horrible again?'

The flutter of understanding became a surge of heartfelt love for this young girl who had so bravely learned to live through the pain of losing her parents, but who was afraid to trust the happiness she was now experiencing. Swallowing back the lump in her throat, Harriet put her arms round her niece and hugged her tight. She kissed the top of her head. 'I'll make you another promise,' she said, leaning back so that Carrie could see her face in the half-light. 'I'll do my absolute best to make sure nothing ever turns nasty and horrible for you again. Now come on; it's way past your bedtime. And mine too, for that matter.'

Will was right about the children, Harriet thought as she looked in on Joel a few minutes later. They did mean the world to her. She couldn't imagine her life without them now. With the back of her hand, she stroked her nephew's cheek gently and felt a jolt of tender love for him, just as she had with Carrie. She still experienced moments of paralysing fear when she remembered that she was totally responsible for these two children, but she was learning to accept and maybe even enjoy it a little by rising to the challenge. She was also learning that while the buck stopped with her, she wasn't as alone as she'd initially felt. No longer did she feel as though she was fighting a one-woman war against an unfair lot. It seemed an impossible turnaround in her attitude, but from where she was now standing, her lot didn't look so bad.

But it was the awesome trust Carrie and Joel put in her that frequently knocked her sideways. Could she really live up to their hopes, needs and expectations?

Only time would tell.

Love & Devotion

~

Reading Group Notes

In Brief

On the cold, starry winter's night, Harriet had agreed so easily. It's the sort of thing you say: 'Yes, I'll look after your children if anything happens to you.' Then the years pass, the promise is forgotten, and everyone gets on with their lives – well, for four years anyway.

Naturally, when the car crash killed Harriet's sister Felicity and her husband, all thoughts turned to their children, Carrie and Joel – their world ripped apart in an instant. Harriet and her parents would cope; they were the type to best foot forward their way through the worst of times. How true this was, Harriet was beginning to wonder.

In Detail

T̲he family were living in a stop-gap world, and
had been for three months. Carrie and Joel were
living with Harriet's parents, who were looking after
them during the week, while Harriet was at work in
Oxford, battling up the M6 every Friday to spend the
weekend with them in Cheshire. Harriet's mother,
Eileen, was obsessively worried that the two children
weren't eating properly and Harriet knew that this
up-in-the-air life can't have been helping – she
certainly knew that the constant nausea she felt didn't
encourage a proper diet.

Harriet had to face some uncomfortable truths,
including a growing knowledge that she was possibly
the most unsuitable person in the world to look after
children. She was entirely unprepared and most
certainly not what you would call a natural. Harriet
knew she would have to rely on her parents. The
children couldn't come to live with her in Oxford –
even if she sold her flat, the childcare during the week
would be unsustainable. She would have to leave
behind both her career and social life, find work near
her parents' house, living there until she could buy a
home for herself, Carrie and Joel. Not the way her
life had been planned, but she loved her sister, and a
promise was a promise.

Harriet's father, Bob, was all at sea. He couldn't pin down when the change in his life had happened. Theirs had been a normal family, with him at the head of it. But, even before the death of his daughter, he'd felt a subtle shift. Felicity had started ending phone calls by telling him to take care. What had prompted that? Suddenly he was no longer the parent. And now, though he'd be ever grateful to Harriet for discarding her life in an instant, it was she who seemed to be making all the decisions. He felt somehow disenfranchised – he'd have to pull himself together – and soon.

Harriet saw the white van with its tailgate down as she left the house. She momentarily wondered who was moving in over the road, but didn't spare much of her overburdened mind to wonder for long. As she hurried away, Will Hart was behind the sofa in his new house plugging in the CD player. When he'd set out on his adult life, a vision of the future would not have been like this. He'd begun as a lawyer, married and on the way up. Now what was he? A divorced antiques dealer – and so much happier for it. Life might not have turned out as he'd expected, but with his two beautiful daughters and a new career, he had no complaints.

Will soon finds himself becoming ever more closely involved with his new neighbours as they try to cope with their radically reshaped world, and Harriet and he are to be drawn together. Until an unimaginable twist in his own life threatens to unravel his world and his mind, leaving Harriet helpless.

About the Author

E rica James grew up on Hayling Island in
Hampshire, and has since lived in Oxford,
Yorkshire and Belgium. She is the author of eleven
bestselling books, and says her main qualification for
writing is that she's 'a nosy devil and loves watching
and eavesdropping on other people's conversations'.
She now lives in Cheshire.

For Discussion

- 'Constant activity, she'd come to know, was the only answer.' Is it?

- 'Do you suppose there's a chance that this is my fault? You know, the whole dysfunctional family bit.' How far do you think Will is to blame, if blame is the right word?

- How important is the theme of sibling rivalry in the narrative?

- Why is Dominic as he is? Is it nature or nurture do you think?

- 'It was another reason why she often preferred computers to people. You knew exactly where you stood with them.' What does this tell us about Harriet? Does she really think this?

- 'Why did people do that? Hide their real self behind another?' Do people in Harriet's life do this? Or does she fail to see the depths that other people see?

- 'Your stubborn one-track brain allows you to see things only in black and white. One day you'll realise there are myriad shades of grey in between.' Does Harriet ever see the grey? If she does begin to, what changes her?

- How does the author deal with the theme of identity in *Love and Devotion*?

- 'This is real life: ends don't always get neatly tied up with a silk ribbon of convenience. Some things we just have to live with as unknowns.' How real did the novel feel to you? How did the author make it seem real?

- How do the different characters deal with the guilt they feel?

- Did the author surprise you with the events in the novel, or did she give you clues?

- Did you like Harriet?

Suggested Further Reading

Tell it to the Skies

• • •

As children, Lydia and her sister were sent to live
with grandparents they'd never even met. It was a
cruel and loveless new world for them, and it
forced Lydia to grow up fast. She learned to keep
secrets and to trust sparingly, and through it all
she was shadowed by guilt and grief.

Then, as an adult, the beautiful city of Venice
gave Lydia peace, fulfilment and even love. But
in a single moment, a stranger's face forces her
to revisit the past she has been hiding from for
the last twenty-eight years . . .

• • •

'It is a captivating read: beautifully written and
heartrendingly sad' *Sunday Telegraph*

£6.99
ISBN 978-0-7528-9336-5

A Breath of Fresh Air

• • •

Charlotte Lawrence is consumed by guilt – after months of agonising she finally asked her workaholic husband for a divorce. The very same day, Peter was killed in a tragic accident. Charlotte's only wish is to return home to the idyllic Cheshire village of her childhood.

Ivy Cottage and Hulme Welford are all Charlotte remembered – lunch in the shade of the fig tree and fork suppers. And her interfering sister Hilary hasn't changed either, organising everything from milk on the doorstep to Alex, the sitting tenant. Hilary is determined that Charlotte, far too young for a widow's weeds, should find love anew. And what better place to start than with the eligible bachelor next door?

• • •

'Erica James's sensitive story of a woman coming to terms with guilt and grief is as sparklingly fresh as dew on the village's surrounding meadows' *Sunday Express*

£6.99
ISBN 978-0-7528-4339-1

A Sense of Belonging

• • •

Set deep in the Cheshire countryside, Cholmford
Hall Mews, a converted 18th-century barn, offers
more than an exclusive place to live. For Jessica,
it is the perfect bolthole for recovering from a
love affair long past its sell-by date; for Kate,
it represents a fresh start where her love for
recently divorced Alec can flourish; for
Amanda, whose marriage is one of
straightforward convenience, it is a chance to get
the most out of her situation; and for Josh, his
new home offers a place of sanctuary to help him
come to terms with his uncertain future.

In their different ways, everyone at Cholmford
Hall Mews is searching for something –
love, peace of mind, a sense of belonging – but
will they find more than they bargained for?

• • •

'As their colourful stories unfold, you feel as if
you've moved in next door and are eavesdropping
from behind the nets. A brilliant read you'll find
impossible to put down' *Best*

£6.99
ISBN 978-0-7528-4342-1

Act of Faith

• • •

Ali Anderson is determined to stand on her own
two feet – even if it means spending Christmas
alone. Because for Ali, Christmas is not the
season of good cheer but a poignant reminder of
the tragedy that tore her life apart and destroyed
her once-happy marriage to Elliot.

In a defiant gesture of independence she turns
down Elliot's unexpected invitation to spend
Christmas with him and his father, but gives in to
her friend Sarah's cajoling to share the festive
period with her. The problem is, it means having
to be nice to Sarah's awful husband Trevor. Sarah
may be a saint for putting up with him, but Ali is
no such thing. As Trevor's cranky behaviour
escalates, Ali takes it on herself to play God with
her friend's incomprehensible marriage . . .

• • •

'A poignant story, written with
humour and emotion' *Daily Mail*

£6.99
ISBN 978-0-7528-4341-4

Precious Time

• • •

In order to spend more time with her four-year-old son, Clara Costello trades in her secure, well-paid job and two-seater sports car for a camper-van called Winnie, and sets off with Ned in search of adventure. Of course, her friends and family think she's gone mad.

But when they arrive in Deaconsbridge in the Peak District, Clara and Ned become drawn into the lives of the locals. Then Clara finds herself having to confront a dilemma much closer to home, and one she had hoped she would never have to face . . .

• • •

'Erica James spins a genuinely heartwarming yet unsentimental tale – a perfect recipe for restoring . . . our . . . trust in humanity' *Sunday Express*

£6.99
ISBN 978-0-7528-4795-5